D0839164

MY CRUEL
SALVATION

NEW YORK TIMES BESTSELLING AUTHOR

J. KENNER

PRAISE FOR THE FALLEN SAINT SERIES

PRAISE FOR THE FALLEN SAINT SERIES

"MY BEAUTIFUL SIN was another mysterious and sexy book in this beautiful new romantic suspense series! ... I can't wait to see where this story will take us in the final book. And can someone please get Netflix on the phone for this already!!!????" *BJ's Book Blog*

"J. Kenner knows how to deliver a tortured alpha that everyone will fall for hard. Saint is exactly the sinner I want in my bed." *Laurelin Paige, NYT bestselling author*

"J. Kenner has done it again! Fans of her Damien Stark series are going to totally fall for Devlin Saint in this sexy, compelling page-turner." *NYT Bestselling author Carly Phillips*

"This story ticked all my boxes, I swooned, I sighed, and at times I held my breath as Devlin and Ellie push trust and love to the limits, the chemistry is sizzling, the characters loveable and I can't wait to see where we go with book 2 in this series." *Thelma and Louise Book Blog*

"Devlin Saint rocked my world. And he definitely ain't no saint. He's the best kind of bad...sigh. I have to say, this new series, Fallen Saint is so damn good I want to read it again, and I just turned the last page." *iScream Books Blog*

"Move over Damien Stark. A new king is here. Something unimaginable and extraordinary has happened in My Fallen Saint. Devlin Saint just captured my heart's number one spot as a broken, dominating and delicious alpha man from J. Kenner. This story was explosive and enticing. It was such a powerful mix of passion, suspense and angst. I have no words. No words." *PP's Bookshelf*

"MY FALLEN SAINT was a very exciting & mysterious & sparky & sexy & heartbreaking first book in a brand new epic romantic suspense series!" *BJ's Book Blog*

ALSO BY J. KENNER

cherish me
embrace me
enchant me

STARK SECURITY
shattered with you
broken with you
ruined with you
wrecked with you
destroyed with you

SEE MORE TITLES AT WWW.JKENNER.COM

MY CRUEL
SALVATION

NEW YORK TIMES BESTSELLING AUTHOR
J. KENNER

M&O

My Cruel Salvation Copyright © 2021 by Julie Kenner

Cover design by Michele Catalano, Catalano Creative
Cover images from Deposit Photos: Red Roses with Candles on Black by YAY images & Red Rose with Rose Petals by alarm.marina.yandex.ru)

Print: 978-1-949925-98-2

Published by Martini & Olive Books

CHAPTER ONE

B*efore...*
  Alejandro Lopez held the gunmetal black Glock in his hand as he stood on the range beside his father, the desert sun beating down on them. He was ten years old and tall for his age, lanky and thin. He came up almost to his father's shoulder. Soon, he'd probably be taller than the man. Stronger, too.

That would be good. Maybe then he could stop being scared. Maybe then he could tell his father that he wanted to be called Alex again, just like his mom had called him when they were alone. Back when they were safe. Back before she'd died.

He could barely remember her now, but every night he made himself think about her hugs and bedtime stories. The ones where he was Alex, and he was brave, and he was fighting the bad guys.

She never told him who the bad guys were, but he knew the answer now. They were these men he lived with. All of the men, but his father most of all. *The Wolf.*

He swallowed the lump in his throat, forcing his shoulders

not to shake and his face to stay expressionless. Showing emotion wasn't allowed around The Wolf. No exceptions and no excuses.

Alex had the bruises to prove that rule.

He needed to work hard. To get better. To bury everything he felt deep inside so that his father would never, ever see the hate. Or, worse, the fear.

He had to make a life here. Had to figure out a way to belong even while honing that deep and secret hate. Even while planning his revenge.

He had to, because that was the only way that Alex knew he'd be safe. The only way he could be certain that his father wouldn't decide to get rid of him, too, the same way he'd gotten rid of his mother.

Not that The Wolf had ever admitted that to him, but Alex learned a long time ago that it was better to listen than talk. He'd heard things over the years. And even though he'd only been a little kid when his father had dragged him back here to the desert, he remembered things. Things he made sure The Wolf never knew about.

The Wolf.

That's what his father liked to call himself. It's what he made everyone at the compound call him when they talked about him.

The Wolf called a meeting; you need to report to the office.

The Wolf is angry today. The Phoenix operation went tits up. Steer clear.

The Wolf has his eye on Frank. Poor bastard.

And then Frank wasn't ever seen again. It sucked, because Alex had always liked Frank. The gray-haired man used to sneak him butterscotch candies wrapped in yellow cellophane. But Frank talked to someone he wasn't supposed to, and The Wolf found out. And that was the end of Frank.

Beside him, The Wolf shifted, his own weapon held casually at his side. "You have been practicing, Alejandro?"

Alex nodded.

"Yes, Father." His father made everyone call him The Wolf; everyone except Alex. The Wolf wanted Alex to know who he belonged to. Alex was careful to call the man Father when he spoke. But in his head, he mostly thought of his father as The Wolf. Because that man wasn't a father. Not really. Not like the men he remembered from Los Angeles. The kind and loving fathers that his friends called Pop or Daddy, and who they'd run to with outstretched arms to receive hugs and praise.

Alex had wanted that, too. But as he felt the weight of the gun in his hand, he knew he'd never have it.

"Let's see it then." The Wolf nodded across the stretch of parched Nevada desert. In the distance, several bushels of hay had been set up, white paper targets attached to them with outlines of men in solid black. On each face, someone had painted two red eyes.

"That man is your enemy. He has wronged you. He thinks that you are less than him because of what you are and what you do. Is that man right?"

"No, Father." Alex worked to make his voice not tremble. His father scared him when he was in this mood. Alex once saw him crack the skull of a man who didn't answer a question exactly the way The Wolf wanted. The man had been named Michael, and he used to tell Alex funny stories about the time that he had visited Paris. Now, Michael couldn't remember that time.

Most days, he couldn't even remember his name.

"What do we do with men who have wronged us?" The Wolf asked.

"We teach them a lesson, Father." Alex's voice sounded

dull to his own ears. He hoped his father couldn't hear the fear that he was trying so hard to bury. Fear and loathing. He hated this man. But he knew that he couldn't let it show.

"Yes. *Yes.*" Alex could hear the pride. It made him feel sick. "That's my son. Now you show me how to teach that lesson. The man who wronged you is right there, looking at you across this field. Are you going to let him diminish you?"

"No, sir."

"Then lift your weapon and show me what you can do."

Alex did as he was told. He lifted the handgun, working hard to keep his arm from shaking. He aimed the way he had been taught. His father wanted him to hit the target's red eye.

Precision and accuracy, Alejandro. That is what I require of the men who stand at my right hand. You are my son, but you must earn your spot. Precision, accuracy, and the utmost loyalty.

Alex had been working for weeks to be able to hit the target from this distance. It was far for such a small target—twenty yards—and his father expected him to work his way up to at least forty, then move on to practicing with a rifle. He drew a breath, gave himself a moment to study the wind, then gently pulled the trigger.

He felt the blast in his arms, and his ears rang despite the plugs his father allowed him to wear while training.

And then he went completely cold.

He had missed.

Those two red eyes were both still intact. But there was a hole between them, a black splotch against the white paper.

The target would be dead for sure. But that wouldn't be enough for his father.

"I thought you said you had practiced." Disappointment colored The Wolf's voice. Disappointment laced with fury.

"I did, Father." He heard the shake in his voice and

wanted to cry. Tears pricked his eyes, and he knew he was the biggest baby in the world.

"You did not practice enough. Look at me, boy."

Alex turned slowly, then tilted his head up. His father scowled at him, his hard gaze taking in his face and then skimming down his skinny body. The disappointment wasn't just in his voice now. Alex saw it all over the man.

"You must be better," The Wolf said. "Tell me, boy. Who is your father?"

Alex swallowed. "You are."

"And did you make me proud?"

He forced himself not to wince; he knew what was coming. "No, Father."

Slowly, The Wolf nodded. "It is good you know this. Now," he added as he lashed out, the cold steel of his pistol connecting with Alex's jaw and knocking his head back, "now you will remember."

Alex staggered, his knees like spaghetti. But he didn't fall. Falling would only make it worse. "Yes, Father."

"Good."

He held his eyes wide, his chin steady, and he repeated the words in his head. *It didn't hurt. It didn't hurt. It wasn't his face that felt shattered and on fire. It was someone else's. He was fine. Fine. Fine.*

He bit back a whimper because the mantra that his stepmother, Aurelia, had taught him wasn't helping at all. He wanted to press his hand to his face.

He wanted to cry.

Instead, he stood like a statue. He had to. If he didn't it would be worse. Much, much worse.

Years passed in the next few seconds and still he stood frozen.

Finally—*finally*—his father put his hands on Alex's shoulders. "Look at me, boy."

Alex tilted his head back and once again met his father's eyes, their dark cruelness softened now with something that The Wolf might actually believe was love. "I do this to make you a man," his father said. "I do this so that when you grow up to take what is yours, you will be respected. Feared. Your lieutenants will fight for you because they will know that you are strong. That you will lead them. And that if they betray you, you will hunt them down like the dogs they are. Do you understand, boy? Do you understand that all that is mine will one day be yours?"

"Yes, Father."

"And can you run our empire if your men do not respect you?"

"No, Father."

"How will you earn their respect?"

"I will excel, Father. I will be the best at everything I do."

"Including striking down your enemies?"

"Yes, Father."

"If you cannot aim your skill with razor-sharp precision at your target, you will fail, boy. Not just at the eye of a target, but at any goal that you set. You learn that, and you will deserve to inherit what I have built, and you will make it even greater than I have. Do you understand how much I love you? How much I have built for you?"

Bile rose in Alex's throat as he nodded. "Yes, Father."

"Go to your mother. Tell her you failed. But because you will do better tomorrow, you may have a cookie with your lunch."

"Yes, Father." Once again, his knees were rubbery. This time, with relief.

"Go. I must speak to Eric, then I will see you at home."

"I—" He shut his mouth. He knew better than to question or argue. He only hoped that Eric—the man who trained him daily at the range—would still be alive tomorrow. "Yes, Father," he said. And then, before his father could say another word, Alex Lopez took off running.

CHAPTER TWO

"I hate him," Alex said as his stepmother, Aurelia, stiffened beside him.

"Hush." Her voice was soft but stern, full of love and also tinged with fear. "If he hears you..."

She trailed off, the sound of her voice making Alex shudder. She was right. He'd been stupid saying that.

Even so, he couldn't help himself when he said, "He's not a wolf. Wolves are nice. They protect each other. I looked it up in my encyclopedia. He should call himself The Hyena."

Beside him, Aurelia giggled, then shushed him again. "You're gonna get us both in trouble."

She was his father's wife, but she wasn't that much older than him. Only eighteen, and she seemed a lot younger. His last stepmother had been twenty-four. She was gone now. One day she just disappeared. The Wolf had called her a bad name—the C-word that Aurelia said was really, really bad—and he'd told Alex that she'd gone away and wouldn't be back.

That was two years ago, and back then Alex had thought she'd gone on a trip. She used to tell him that one day they'd drive to California and go to Disneyland, and he'd been mad at her for going without him. But he'd been a stupid kid, then. Now he knew the truth. Now he knew she was dead.

He was ashamed that he'd kept talking even when Aurelia told him to hush.

He didn't want to get her dead, too.

"I'm sorry," he said, snuggling closer as she put her arm around him. He whispered the words, not even sure that she could hear him over *Friends* playing on the television. "I don't want him to hurt you like he hurt my momma."

He felt her body go tense again.

"What do you know about that? You can't possibly remember her. I mean, *I* barely remember her. I was thirteen when she—I mean, when you came to live here."

"I remember she cried a lot. And I remember the police coming to the house that night. They said she drove her car off the road, but she didn't, did she?" He turned and looked at her defiantly. "*He* did it. He killed my momma. And then he brought me here."

He saw the answer on her face, but all she said was, "You can't say things like that. You can't even think them."

He started to reply, but he saw the boy in the doorway and heard Aurelia's soft sigh. "Manny, you get your little bottom to bed. Do you hear me?"

"*He* gets to stay up." The boy had a mop of black hair, a nose with a tilted tip, and dark eyes that he focused on Alex.

"He's ten. You're seven."

"I want to show you the game I made."

She cocked her head. "I told you to go to bed an hour ago. You're supposed to sleep, not play on that computer. Now mind me and go to bed. You can show me your game in the morning."

"You're not my Momma. You can't tell me what to do."

"I'm your sister, and our Momma's dead, and I can tell you what to do. *He* said so."

Nobody in the room needed to be reminded who *he* was.

With a final scowl towards Alex, Manuel Espinoza turned back into the hall.

"He misses her," she said. "Now all he does is play on that computer. I'd let him stay up with us, but if your father came in, he'd beat all three of us."

Alex nodded. "I know. It's okay. I miss my mother, too."

"I know you do."

He frowned. "Did you know her?"

She nodded, her lips pressed tight together.

"Tell me something about her."

She blinked, her eyes filled with tears. "She was nice. When you were a baby, she used to pay me to help her. I liked her. She told me to call her Cat. And she was so pretty." She stroked his hair. "You look like her, you know."

He scowled, even though he liked hearing that. "I'm not *pretty*."

She laughed. "You're going to be a fine man. Inside and out. You promise me that, okay? For her. You have to be good for her. To make her proud. She loved you so much."

"My dad doesn't."

Her brow furrowed, her eyes darting toward the opening to the kitchen on the far side of the room. No one was in the house then, and they'd see if someone came in through the front door. But if someone came in from the back, they wouldn't see.

He felt suddenly cold. His father could be in there right now—he could have come in silently through the door from the yard into the kitchen—and Alex had said that out loud. What if his father heard and—

"He does," Aurelia said. "He ... he loves you in his own

way." She nodded, like she was trying to make herself believe it. "But—but you don't want to make him mad, okay? Promise me you won't make him mad. He stops—"

She bit her lower lip, then let go of him so that she could hug herself.

"He stops loving you when you make him mad," Alex said defiantly. Why shouldn't he say it? It was true.

She blinked, then nodded. "Yes." The word was a whisper. "But don't ever say that to anyone but me."

He felt small then, and alone. He wanted her arm back around him. "I know. I won't."

"Good."

He heard the relief in her voice. He hesitated, but he couldn't stop himself from asking the question. "It's not really love, is it?"

Her throat moved as she swallowed. "No. It's not. And you're too smart for your own good."

He smiled because he knew that's what she wanted. But he didn't feel smart. If he were smart, he would know how to make her not be scared. He'd know how to not be scared himself. He sat up straighter as an idea occurred to him. "Don't tell me anything else about my momma," he said.

"Why not?"

"Because it might make him mad. And people get dead when he gets mad."

"Alex ... you should know about her."

He nodded slowly. "Okay. But if he finds out, I'll protect you. I was too little to protect her, but I can protect you. I will. I promise."

He saw fresh tears in her eyes as she smiled. "You're a good boy, and you're going to grow into a good man." Her voice caught as she continued. "You're going to be just like your daddy. Strong and powerful and—"

"*You fucking bitch.*"

Alex froze. He hadn't seen his father step in through the kitchen doorway. Aurelia must have, though. That was why she'd said that. But it didn't help. With his father, nothing ever helped.

"You telling that boy about the kind of man he's going to be? You think because you spread your legs for me that gives you the right to talk to my son like you know who he is?"

"I—no, Daniel. We were just—"

"Fucking little whore. That's all you're good for. That's all any woman is good for, Alejandro. You remember that. You remember the day this worthless bitch sat her cunt self beside you and tried to tell you what kind of man you would be. You'll be the man *I* tell you to be. The kind of man you should be. Not some pussy with a woman's ways. You hear me, boy?"

He lifted his chin, forcing himself not to look at Aurelia, because if he did, he might cry. "Yes, sir."

"Simpering little bitch is sitting here telling you you're special, isn't that right?"

"I—" He swallowed, unsure what to say.

"You," The Wolf said to Aurelia. "Get out of here."

She nodded, shot a quick glance toward Alex, then bolted toward the kitchen.

"Special." His father's lip curled into a snarl. "You aren't special, boy. You could be, but you have to work for it. Grow into it. You're nothing until you do that. You have to make something of yourself. You have to grow your legacy like I did. Grow it bigger than mine. Prove yourself, just like I did with what your grandfather left me, and his father before him. Your great-grandfather started out running alcohol over the border during Prohibition. One of the Tequila People they called him. But he was more than that, and so was his son, my father."

Alex swallowed and nodded.

"Now I have surpassed them both. I've grown those tiny seeds of a business into an empire."

"Yes, Father."

"You must do even better, Alejandro. You must make me proud. Until you do that—until you make your own way—you are nothing. Un-molded clay. And in case you didn't know, wet clay looks a whole hell of a lot like shit."

CHAPTER THREE

The present...

"I've never seen you nervous before," Ellie said, stepping up beside Devlin as he straightened his bowtie for the fourth time that night. She met his eyes in the free-standing mirror that took up one corner of the penthouse suite's bedroom, her smile laced with a hint of a tease. "The great Devlin Saint with tummy butterflies. It's kind of adorable."

"It's not nerves," he said. "It's—"

"What?"

He exhaled. "Okay. Maybe it's nerves." They shared a smile. Him and his El, the woman he loved. The only person he could truly be himself with. The only person to whom he was willing to admit how much tonight meant to him.

Beautiful inside and out, she'd enchanted him the first time he'd first seen her on her sixteenth birthday. She'd smiled shyly at him—just one glance before her eyes had darted away from his—but he'd felt that glance ricochet all through him. He'd been eighteen, and he'd known in that moment that she was his. Even if nothing ever happened between them—and how the hell could it?—he had claimed her completely.

Then, by some miracle, what he knew in his heart came true. It had been a long and harrowing road, but despite everything, they were finally, truly together. She was a treasure. His miracle. And now here she was standing in front of him, her eyes shining with love despite who he was and everything he'd done.

"You deserve this," she said, clearly reading his mind. She put her hands on his shoulders to smooth the line of his tuxedo jacket, her head tilted up so that she could look into his eyes. "You're an incredible man. You've come a long way from being Alejandro Lopez, the Wolf's son. Or even from being Alex Leto, my first boyfriend. You're Devlin Saint now. Influential. Powerful. Incredibly sexy," she added with enough of a leer to make him smile. "You're the man I love. The most incredible man I've ever known. And you've built something amazing."

She stepped back, looking him up and down. Then her eyes met his again, and the pride he saw reflected back at him nearly made his heart stop. "The World Council Award for Humanitarian Services. It's amazing. An acknowledgement of everything you've worked for. Recognition of everything the Devlin Saint Foundation has accomplished. Aren't you proud?"

He drew in a breath. "I am," he admitted. "This was the one thing my father got right."

Confusion flickered in her eyes, and he smiled. "He used to tell me that I was nothing unless I built something of my own. Made something of myself. Well, I did. And what I built is a hell of a lot more valuable than anything that sonofabitch ever accomplished."

"Yes," she said simply, the word filled with so much love

and pride he thought his heart might burst. At the same time, though, he knew that this conversation was only about the Devlin Saint Foundation, the philanthropic entity he'd established about five years ago. An organization involved in the rescue and rehabilitation of human trafficking victims, education, and so much more.

But how would she answer if he asked her about the other organization that he'd founded? One that he held just as dear. Saint's Angels did incredible work, but it operated below the radar. It had organized the rescue of hostages and kidnapping victims, true, but no humanitarian organization would hand over a plaque. In part because no one knew Saint's Angels existed. More importantly because no one gave awards to vigilante groups who fired bullets through the heads of the kidnappers, ensuring they never tortured children again. Least of all Ellie, with her cop heritage and strong moral code.

Still, she knew the truth now, and she was standing at his side. He wanted her full blessing, but for now at least, he was going to have to be satisfied with the absence of condemnation.

"Devlin?" She was looking at him, her brow furrowing as her mouth turned down into a frown. "Did I lose you?"

"Sorry. My mind was wandering." He forced the thought of the lingering breach between them away, focusing instead on what he was most grateful for—*her*.

"Do you know what else I'm proud of?" he asked.

She studied him, then slowly shook her head.

"To be seen with you on my arm. Believe me, El. I couldn't be prouder than to be the man you love."

He watched as her cheeks flushed with pleasure.

He grinned, then mimicked the way her eyes had roamed over him earlier. "Of course, it doesn't hurt that you look so damn gorgeous."

She laughed, delighted. "I take it you like the outfit?"

"You know I do."

They were in Manhattan for the award ceremony, and she'd told him yesterday that she was going to go shop for the perfect gown while he was shuffled through his various PR appointments as this year's award recipient. "I've lived here for years," she'd said, "but I've never had a reason to do any serious shopping. Fifth Avenue, here I come."

Now, he made a spinning motion as she twirled for him, showing off the slinky, bronze gown that glimmered in the light, seeming to reflect fire with every tiny movement. She wore strappy sandals that perfectly matched the dress's color, and the four-inch heels not only gave her the height to almost look him in the eye, but added a delicious curve to her calf, revealed by the thigh-high slit.

He took it all in. The way the material clung to her ass in a way that his palm envied. The curve of her waist. The swell of her breasts against the low-cut, draped bodice, and the smoky topaz set in bronze that accentuated her cleavage and brought out the red highlights in her brown hair that hung in loose curls around her face.

She was stunning, and the more he looked at her, the more awed he was that she belonged to him. This woman, the greatest miracle of his life.

"How much did that necklace set you back?" he teased. "For that matter, the outfit?"

She waved her hand. "On my reporter's salary? Let's just say I'll be paying it off for the rest of my life." She slid into his arms. "Fortunately, my boyfriend is worth it."

"Hmm," he said, making a note to replenish her bank account first chance he had. "Well, you can't put a price on perfection."

Her smile widened, making her caramel-colored eyes

gleam. "I love you," she said, and miraculously, his heart swelled even more.

"Careful, or we won't get out of here on time." The front desk had called up a few minutes ago to say the limo would arrive in fifteen. They needed to start heading down.

"I'm not worried," she said, moving closer and easing her arms around his waist. "You're the guest of honor. Nothing starts without you."

She rose up on her toes to kiss him, and though his entire body tightened with the need to throw her back on the bed, strip her bare, and work out every one of his roiling emotions in hot, wild, demanding sex, all he did was shake his head and push her gently but firmly away.

"No."

Her brow rose. "No?"

"Not that you aren't temptation personified," he told her. He meant it, too. Was there ever a time he didn't want her? Under normal circumstances, he craved her. Right now, things were definitely not normal, and that only worked to increase his need. He felt off, as if he should be shying from this award. As if he should believe himself undeserving or hypocritical because of the secrets he held.

But he didn't.

He knew the good he did. He'd worked all of his adult life to try and make the world a better place. To ease suffering, fight crime, provide education. Whatever could be done, was done, and the foundation he'd built brick by brick and day by day had acted as the solid base for so many lives that were now back on track. So many victims who'd been rescued. So many of the lost who'd been found.

He thought of all the children he'd hugged, the parents he'd consoled, the abuse victims he'd sheltered. And, yes, the many villains he'd personally killed, their life taken in payment for their crimes, and without a shred of remorse on his part other than that he hadn't found and destroyed the bastards before they'd had the chance to inflict even one more moment of pain.

Ellie's smile was gentle as she reached up, then slowly traced the line of his scar, moving over his brow, his eye, along his cheekbone. A battle scar he wore with pride, because it represented the downfall of one more bad guy. Another pawn in a never-ending game of chess.

"I hate that you were hurt," she said. "But you do look damn sexy with your warrior scar and your tuxedo and those tortoise shell glasses."

"I'm very glad you think so."

"You know what else I think?"

"Tell me," he said as he cupped her ass and pulled her close enough that he knew she could feel his hard cock against her belly.

"Exactly what you're thinking," she teased, wiggling just enough to drive him a little crazy. "But like you said, right now we have a limo waiting downstairs, and we need to go so you can be the man of the hour."

"We do," he said, releasing her ass so that he could take her hand. He paused at the door. "I'd give it up, you know." He looked at her hard, wanting to make sure she understood the heart of what he was saying. "I'd give everything up if that's what it took to keep you by my side."

He watched her face, assuring himself that she understood fully what he meant. What he was willing to walk away from in order to keep El in his life.

"I believe you," she said, taking her hand in his. "But if you did, you wouldn't be you. Now come on before we're late."

CHAPTER FOUR

She tempted him in the limo, of course. That dress with the slit that revealed way too much thigh. How delicious would it be to burn off some of this pent-up energy? To take her here in the back, with the privacy shield up? To fuck her hard as the sights of Manhattan flew past them? To have the taste and scent of her on him when he stood at that podium and made his speech?

She made him strong, his Ellie. And God knew, she'd been his talisman throughout the long journey of his life. The beacon that had shined along his path to becoming the man that he was. Good. Bad. However you took it, he was that man because of her. Hell, he *was* hers.

And she was his as well.

As if he had to prove it, he pressed his hand lightly on her thigh, then started to slide it up her bare, silky skin. He heard her soft intake of breath and noted the way her nipples tightened under the thin material that covered her breasts. Her legs parted, and her soft moan did a number on his cock before she gently pressed her hand over his, halting his upward trajectory.

"There is no way you're getting me mussed up before you accept this award."

He heard the heat in her voice, and his pulse kicked up in response, his cock twitching in anticipation. He smiled. How many times had he told her how much he got off on anticipation?

"And after?" he asked.

Her hand remained on his, but she spread her legs wider. He was watching her, the gloss on her parted lips, the promise in her eyes. "After's a no-brainer. How many girls get to say they fucked the Humanitarian of the Year in the back of a limo?"

"Would hate for you to miss out on that." He brushed his thumb back and forth on her thigh, his whole body tightening as he watched her body tremble in response to that minuscule touch.

"Good. Because I don't intend to. Still..." She trailed off with a smile, then laid her hand back on top of his again. For a moment, she just held it there. Then she slowly—so wickedly slowly—started to slide his hand higher until his thumb brushed her bare pussy. "Just a preview..."

He moaned aloud.

"Baby, how the hell do you expect me to make a speech knowing what you have on under this dress?"

She squeezed her legs together, trapping him in place. Practically insisting that he slide his eager fingers inside her slick folds. "I have faith in you," she said. "Think of this as inspiration," she added on a sigh as the tip of his finger found that sensitive spot that made her arch back and then gasp in pleasure.

"Oh, no," she said, her words belied by the breathiness of her voice as she tugged his hand away. "That's for later. We'll take the long way back to the hotel."

"Yes," he said, his mind on the return trip and not the speech he was about to give. "We will."

She grinned at him as she settled back in the seat, her head on his shoulder as he slipped an arm around her. They still had a few more minutes before they arrived, and silence lingered as the limo traversed the city blocks.

After a moment, though, she reached for his hand again. "Are you okay?"

He understood why she was asking the question. After all, the last few weeks had been significantly out of the ordinary. Anna Lindstrom, one of his oldest friends and his executive assistant at the foundation, had proven herself to be a traitor to him and the organization.

As if that weren't enough, an old enemy had appeared on the horizon. And he'd almost lost Ellie herself, only fate, timing, and the deep roots of an ancient tree had kept her from falling to her death before he'd arrived in time to save her.

As much as it pained him to lose Anna, her death and betrayal had been almost nothing compared to the knowledge of how close he'd come to almost losing Ellie.

And the biggest miracle of all? That even though she'd been reeling after finally learning his deepest and darkest secrets, that night when her car had gone over the cliff, she'd been on her way to tell him that she still loved him. That she still needed him.

She was his goddamn universe. And Anna had almost stolen her from him.

"Devlin?"

"I'm fine," he assured her. He caught her eyes and saw the worry that lingered there. "I only—"

"What?"

He frowned, not sure how to put voice to his fears. She'd

come back to him even after learning the truth about the Myers assassination. More than that, after learning that he was the brains and funding behind Saint's Angels, a super-secret, off-the-books vigilante organization that, as far as Devlin was concerned, did at least as much good in the world as the very above-board and internationally lauded Devlin Saint Foundation.

That, however wasn't common knowledge. And with her background in law enforcement, it hadn't been something he'd expected Ellie to understand. It had been his biggest secret ... and his biggest fear.

And yet here she was, right at his side. Their love stronger than even the most potent of obstacles, including her own hesitations about what he did.

"Devlin?" She was studying him, her forehead creased with concern.

He stroked her cheek. "I'm fine. I only—"

"What?"

He swallowed, the doubts he'd pushed away rising back to the surface. "This award," he said. "What do you think of it?" Was she proud of him for what the foundation had accomplished, or did she think that the existence of Saint's Angels and its methods made a humanitarian honor hypocritical?

She hesitated before answering. Only enough to draw breath, but his fears bubbled during that infinitesimal delay. Then he saw pride flicker in her eyes, and even before she spoke, he knew what her answer would be, and his heart swelled as she told him that she thought he deserved not just the award, but more. And, she added, that he shouldn't doubt himself.

At that, he laughed. "I rarely do." With El, however, he knew he didn't have to be strong all the time. He could show his doubts, his fears. And no matter what, she would love him.

It was a simple truth, but it still awed him, and he let the glow of that reality fill him through the rest of their conversation until the limo finally pulled up in front of the Dorset Theater, a recently restored theater in Manhattan's theater district that was serving as the ceremony's venue. "We're here," he said, then pulled her in for one last kiss before the valet opened the door and they stepped out onto the red carpet.

He paused, taking in the crowd, the noise, the cameras, and then Ellie's face, which was positively glowing with pride. He soaked it in, letting her happiness for him seep into his bones as they began to walk toward the door. Then she turned to him, and he saw the confusion flicker in her eyes. He started to ask what was wrong, but realized he didn't need to.

He'd tuned out the cacophony, but now voices were getting through. Shouts from the reporters, raised voices with harsh questions. At first, it was all a blur. And then he heard those two horrible words—*The Wolf.*

No.

His blood turned to ice as he searched for the source, but as he did, he realized the question could have come from anyone, and he tightened his grip on Ellie's hand as an anonymous reporter shouted the question—*Is your name really Alejandro Lopez?*

He picked up his pace, his shoulders stiff and his expression impassive as he moved toward the doors with Ellie keeping pace beside him. He knew he should answer. Should stop and speak, and maybe he even would have if one question hadn't burst through, louder and bolder than all the rest—

Mr. Saint, did you kill your father?

No.

No, no, no.

Whatever strength he had faded in that moment. He felt

ten years old again, back at the compound, his father demanding that Alejandro make him proud, because one day the boy would inherit his father's legacy.

He'd never wanted it. He'd worked his whole life to avoid it. To shed it.

And here it was, thrust upon him under the fire of questions and cameras.

Goddammit.

The curse rang through him, but he kept his expression calm. He was stone. He was ice. He'd learned a long time ago how to not show emotion. He had his father to thank for that. And right now, the lessons he'd learned at that bastard's hand were going to get him and Ellie safely inside that building.

"I'm sorry, Mr. Saint." A tall woman with flaming red hair rushed to usher them inside. She signaled to the doormen to hurry and get the door closed, and only when they were completely shut did Devlin let his guard down the tiniest bit. Just enough to look down at Ellie.

She looked back at him, her expression as lost as his. "Devlin," she whispered. "You're hurting me."

That's when he realized that he'd almost crushed her hand. He let go immediately, opening his mouth to apologize. For the pain, for the crowd. For being the man he was—a man whose very existence had made her endure a spectacle like that.

But the words didn't come. Instead, they were joined by a lanky man in a tuxedo. He had salt-and-pepper hair, a friendly face, and sad eyes. "I'm Arthur Packard," he said, extending his hand. "The committee chair. Do you think we could have a word?"

Devlin's heart flipped. He wasn't a fool. He knew what that meant, and he kept his fingers twined with Ellie's as

Packard led them to a back room before excusing himself for a moment.

"They're going to withdraw the award." He knew he was talking, but he could barely hear the words. He was numb. Completely numb.

Beside him, Ellie nodded. "Yes."

"*Goddammit*." He slammed his fist into his thigh, wanting to feel. He wanted fury. Wanted indignation. He wanted something other than this haze of numbness. And the horrible, pressing fear that no matter how far he ran—no matter what he accomplished—he would forever be tainted with the sins of his father.

CHAPTER FIVE

"Devlin."

Her voice was soft, almost tentative. And just like that, he knew that he could get through this. Because no matter what else the universe threw at him, he still had El beside him.

Slowly, he reached for her, closing his hand gently around hers. She squeezed, as if offering her strength, and he pulled her close, then held her tight before bending his head to press a soft kiss on her sweet-scented hair.

"Are you okay?"

He pulled back, and she tilted her head to meet his eyes. "I'm fine," he said, wanting only to erase the worry in her eyes.

"No, you're not."

"No," he agreed. "I'm not. But so long as you're with me, I'll get through this."

"I'm not going anywhere."

He wanted to pull her close. To bury his anger in passion. But that wasn't possible now. Hell, with the door opening and Packard walking back in, even a kiss wasn't in the offing.

Instead, he held her hand as he turned to face Packard and the second man who'd joined him.

Devlin saw the truth etched in the lines of their faces and spoke first. "You're pulling the award."

"I'm very sorry," Packard said, looking both frustrated and embarrassed. "It wasn't my decision."

"It was mine," the other man said, his chin lifted as he stepped forward. "I'm Blair Livingston. I'm in charge of all of the council's operations. And under the circumstances, I'm afraid we can't risk our reputation."

"You think your reputation will be served by denying a humanitarian award to my foundation simply because of who my father is?"

"I think it's a public relations risk we aren't willing to take. You've kept your parentage a secret." Livingston shrugged. "Who knows what other secrets you've been keeping."

Devlin tensed, a violent fury rising in him. This wasn't something he could fix with money or power or a sniper's rifle. This was the shadow of his father all over again, and right then all he wanted was to release this pent-up fury by pounding his fists against the leather of a punching bag. Or, better yet, flesh.

The pulling of this award was only the beginning, he knew. For years, he'd built a name and a reputation. *Devlin Saint.*

And now all of that was tumbling down. Packard and Livingston weren't the cause of his fury—they were just a symptom.

Devlin had bigger worries now. Much bigger.

So instead of arguing or pleading his case, Devlin simply drew in a breath and slowly released it. "I understand your position," he said. "I assume you'll understand that Ms.

Holmes and I won't be staying for the banquet. In fact, if there's a back exit, I think we'll slip out now."

"Yes," Mr. Packard said, looking slightly embarrassed. "Please, follow me."

Livingston stayed behind as Packard led them down the corridors to the alley. As they walked, Devlin tapped out a text to the driver, instructing him where to meet them.

"Here," Packard said, stopping in front of a solid metal door. "I could step out with—"

"That won't be necessary." Devlin gave the bar a push, and the door swung open. He gestured for El to go first, nodded to Packard, who looked utterly miserable, then stepped into the alley himself.

The limo wasn't there.

That wasn't too surprising; the driver had probably parked blocks away, intending to pass the hours reading or listening to music.

What *was* surprising was the man he saw leaning against a rusty fire-escape ladder. A dark-haired, lean man with the kind of face that could make an actor's career and a confidence that he wore like a familiar coat. A man Devlin had never met, but who he recognized instantly—former tennis pro turned tech billionaire, Damien Stark.

"Mr. Stark," Devlin said, his brows rising in surprise. "I'm going to assume you're not out here because you wanted some fresh air."

"I wish it were something that innocuous. No, I wanted to let you know that committee's decision to pull your award wasn't unanimous." He shrugged as he pushed away from the ladder and held out his hand to shake, his dual-colored eyes meeting Devlin's. "I also wanted to introduce myself, something I'd intended to do after your speech. But I think this is the best I can manage."

"I'm afraid so," Devlin said, taking the other man's hand. "But it means a lot that you came out here. Thank you." He turned to El. "Elsa Holmes, I'd like you to meet Damien Stark."

"I recognize you, of course," she said. "And call me Ellie."

"The pleasure is mine, Ellie," Stark said. He turned his attention back to Devlin. "It's good to finally meet you. I'm sorry about the circumstances. By all rights, we should have met about five years ago."

For a moment, Devlin didn't understand. Then it clicked. "The foundation. Our offices in Laguna Cortez." He turned to Ellie, answering her questioning look. "The architect who designed the offices—Jackson Steele—he's Damien's brother."

"It's a small world," Ellie said.

"That it is." Stark glanced down the alley toward the approaching limo. "Looks like your ride is here. I won't keep you. I just wanted to offer my condolences. And my congratulations."

Devlin's brows rose. "Congratulations?"

"You don't need an award, Saint. The work your foundation does speaks for itself."

Devlin nodded, letting those words sink in. "Thank you," he said. "That means a lot."

"I know a thing or two about being scrutinized by the press. Even more about what it's like to be encumbered by the reputation of a father I neither like nor respect. You'll do fine. It won't be easy, but you'll overcome all this bullshit."

"I will," Devlin said, because Stark was right. Devlin had no choice but to overcome it.

But what he didn't say was that while it might be easy enough to shake off the controversy of being The Wolf's son and prove to the world at large that his philanthropic efforts were legitimate, that wasn't the real issue.

No, what neither Stark nor the committee nor the press realized was that by outing Devlin's parentage, those eager reporters may have just plastered a target on Devlin's back, one at which both his father's former allies and enemies would be taking aim.

What was worse, though, was that their real goal would be to punish him. To *hurt* him.

And that meant that the very press Ellie worked for had painted that same fucking target on her back as well.

CHAPTER SIX

My heart aches for Devlin, and not just because that asshat Livingston maneuvered the committee into withdrawing the award. No, what Mr. Stark said was true— award or not, the Devlin Saint Foundation does amazing work, and the world damn well knows it. An award won't change that.

What makes me shake with rage is that those fucking reporters have now painted him with the same brush as The Wolf. And Devlin isn't anything like the murderous, drug-pushing, human-trafficking prick who fathered him.

We're in the back of the limo, heading toward the hotel, and Devlin hasn't said a word in the last five minutes. I reach over and take his hand, giving it a gentle squeeze. "Are you okay?"

There's a pause before he answers, and when he turns to me, I see the pain in his eyes. "I think I always knew the truth would get out someday, no matter how much I hoped I could bury it. I would never have chosen to associate with that man, and the fact that I managed to break from him was one of the primary joys of my life. To now have—"

He cuts himself off, his hand tightening painfully around mine as if he's trying to funnel the pain of his parentage out of his body.

"I know," I say. "But you're nothing like him. The world knows that. This is just so much smoke, and once it blows over, the world will only see the good that you've done. The sins of your father aren't your sins."

He turns to face me, and I see the shadows on his face along with the doubt in his eyes. "Aren't they?"

Fury stabs through me. "Don't you dare say that. You don't believe it, and neither do I."

"Don't you?"

I feel my shoulders sag in frustration. Not at him, but at myself. "You know I don't," I say. "I wouldn't be with you if I did. Devlin, I—"

I cut myself off as I take a breath. "I love you no matter what. And Saint's Angels is nothing—*nothing*—like what your father was."

"He killed. We kill."

"Are you trying to piss me off?" I snap. "Or are you just in a pissy mood and you're trying to punish yourself. You *know* that's not true. Your father killed for revenge. Because people annoyed him. Saint's Angels rescues people. It balances the playing field. It renders justice."

The words are out of my mouth before I have time to consider them, and I see the way his eyes widen as he tilts his head to the side. His brow furrows as he studies me, and right then I want to call back the words. Not because they aren't true, but because I don't know what to do with that truth.

"Justice," he repeats softly. "I wasn't sure that was how you felt."

I shrug, hoping I look more casual than I feel. "It is what it is."

Saint's Angels is a vigilante group that Devlin founded even before he started the Devlin Saint Foundation. They're entirely different entities—no money flows from the legitimate charitable organization to the not-so-legal secret vigilante operation. But there are players who overlap, Devlin and his best friend Ronan Thorne being the primary two.

I'd been knocked sideways when my journalistic investigation into the assassination of a serial murderer and child abuser had revealed that Devlin was the shooter. That kind of vigilante justice goes against everything I'd been brought up to believe. There's a reason that law enforcement and courts exist. A reason why the rules of the Wild West have faded away.

But that's about the rules and who is meting out the punishment. Not about whether the outcome looks like justice. Maybe that's a fuzzy line, but it *is* a line. For a while, it was even a chasm. But it's one that I crossed to be at Devlin's side, and I don't regret it. And I am damn sure not going to let him latch on to my personal mores to fuel his pity party about being aligned with his father.

"Your father murdered and cheated and manipulated. He put people in danger. He exploited them. And he killed on a whim. You so much as whisper that you are like him again, and I swear I'll slap your face."

For a moment, he's silent. Then he pulls me roughly to him and kisses my forehead. "God, I love you."

"Good. Stop talking shit about the man I love. You're in the business of justice, Devlin. Don't forget it."

His gaze remains steady, then he nods and looks away, his hand tightening around mine. I don't know if he truly feels better about what he does versus what his father did, but for now the conversation is tabled because we've reached the hotel. The driver foregoes the regular entrance and heads around back like Devlin had instructed once we were away from the theater. He'd also called ahead and asked the manager to gather our luggage and bring it to the limo.

Originally, we'd planned to spend one more night at the hotel on the Council's dime, drinking champagne and making love in the well-appointed suite to celebrate his award.

Now, we don't want to linger. Not when the press knows perfectly well where the Council had put him up.

Instead, we're going to my apartment near Columbia University and Morningside Park. It's small, but I like to think of it as cozy. And since we'd planned all along to go there tomorrow, I'd already asked Roger, my friend and editor at *The Spall Monthly* where I work as a staff writer, to stop in and stock it with food.

In a way, Roger's the reason I'm with Devlin. I'd been assigned to write a profile on the Devlin Saint Foundation, located in my hometown of Laguna Cortez, California. I'd accepted the assignment eagerly, especially since I'd also intended to use my time there to investigate my uncle's murder back when I was a teenager.

At the time, I'd had no clue that Devlin was also Alex Leto, the only boy I'd ever loved. Let alone all the rest of the secrets and drama that came with that revelation.

Now, of course, I'm planning to stay in California. And part of the purpose of this trip is to pack my things, find someone to sublet my place, and enjoy a bit of time in New York with Devlin before I become a full-time West Coaster.

As we wait, the driver opens the trunk for the valet and secures our luggage. Then we're back on the road. "I like this better," Devlin says. "The hotel was nice, but your apartment is a home." He squeezes my hand. "And right now, the idea of being home with you is very, very appealing."

"It is," I agree, snuggling close as he puts his arm around

me. I close my eyes, wishing that I had magical powers so that I could wave a wand and make it all better for him. Instead, I simply let myself be soothed by the rhythm of the limo and the feel of Devlin's arm around me.

Traffic is light, and before I know it, we've pulled to a stop in front of my building. The area isn't exactly one of the best neighborhoods in Manhattan, but it's close to Columbia, which was great for me. And because I have rental income from the house I inherited when my dad died, with the studio's cheap-for-Manhattan rent, I was able to cover all my personal and school expenses without having to hold down a job while I was working on my Masters.

I stayed after I graduated because even though I have a job now, I'm not exactly pulling in the big bucks. Plus, despite the dicey neighborhood, I really do love the place, and my unit is darling. Or it is now, since I spent my first few weeks in New York painting walls and sanding floors.

It's small, but well-appointed, and there's more than enough space for me. Even the terrible plumbing has become something I think of as character rather than an irritation. The place has improved considerably over the years, too. A new owner came in about six months after I signed the lease, and now there's a full-time security guard in the expanded lobby, shiny new paint throughout, and rumors that an elevator may be in the works. Even the plumbing that had given me fits those first months is better, though the pipes still make a strange howling noise that I've come to think of as the ghosts of residents past.

Under normal circumstances, I'd be sad to leave it behind. But since I'm moving back to Laguna Cortez and Devlin, all I really care about is finding someone to take over the lease who will love the place as much as I do.

"This is it," I say, taking Devlin's hand. It's dark, so it's not as if we can see the architectural details, but the new owner added decent exterior lighting and a freshened up look for the entryway.

"Ms. Holmes, so good to have you back." William, the night guard, smiles at me as we step inside, following the driver who's already taken in our bags. "Want me to send your luggage up?"

That was the best thing the new owner did—installed a dumbwaiter at the same time the plumbing was revamped. Not big enough for people, but it's great for luggage and groceries.

"You're the best," I tell him.

"The bags will meet you upstairs." His smile broadens. "We've certainly missed you around here. And Mr. Saint." He gives a quick nod toward Devlin. "Sir, we weren't expecting to see you today. I read about your award, though. Congratulations."

"Thank you, William," he says, not bothering to explain that William clearly doesn't have the full story yet. I frown, hoping William doesn't feel awkward in the morning the next time he sees Devlin and realizes that the congratulations were misplaced. After all—

My thoughts come to a screeching halt. *I'd never said William's name aloud.*

So how did Devlin know it? For that matter, why was William so familiar with Devlin Saint? I've known William for years, and he's never seemed to be the type to keep up with celebrity gossip.

I'd been heading for the stairs, but now I come to a stop.

"Ellie?"

I look up at him, then flash a smile at both him and William. "Nothing. Just tired. We should head up. I'm on the sixth floor," I add, though at this point I'm certain that Devlin knows exactly where I live. Not to mention how long I've lived here, my credit score, and how much I pay in rent.

By the time we reach the landing, the dumbwaiter has brought our bags up. We grab them, and as soon as I open the door, Devlin takes them inside.

"This is it," I say, sweeping my arm to encompass the studio. After I graduated, I'd splurged and hired a handyman to come install a sliding bookcase, both because I wanted a place for my books and so that it could act as a wall to form a DIY bedroom in the studio apartment. Right now, the two components of the bookcase are together, so that the bedroom area is visible. But if I have guests, I can slide one set of bookcases over, to form a solid wall.

"It's nice," he says, with what sounds a bit like pride.

I smirk. "Well, I hope you'd think so. You own this building, after all."

He chuckles. "Busted." Then he points to the bookcases. "I think that might be in violation of your lease."

"Ha ha. Seriously, Devlin. You freaking own this building. What the hell?"

He shrugs. "It was a good investment. Plus, I wanted to make sure you were safe and comfortable."

"You bought this place so that you could fix up the building I live in?" It's not really a question since I already know the answer.

His smile broadens, and I shake my head, not sure if I'm awed, annoyed, or amused. "But how did you—" I pause. I know perfectly well how he managed it. He'd watched me in the years after he'd killed Peter and fled from Laguna Cortez … and from me. And all the while, he'd carefully ensured that I didn't know he was there.

Because he was watching me, he would have learned when I applied for grad school, not to mention when I was accepted. And then all he had to do was make a too-good-to-be-true offer to the building's owner once I'd signed the lease.

"At least I know who to go to when the plumbing goes wonky."

"Baby," he says, "you know I'll always take care of your plumbing."

He says it with such a ridiculous leer that I can't help but laugh as I pull him toward the couch with me. I push him down, then straddle him. "We lost so much time," I say. "Especially when you consider how close we were during those years when I thought we were so far apart."

"You know why."

I nod. I understand why he left, and why he became Devlin Saint, and even why he never intended to seek me out and tell me the truth. "I do," I admit. "But I still mourn the past we could have had."

"The past always comes back to you," he says, his voice turning harsh.

I tense, hating that we've circled back to the award and his father, even though I know that in reality it was always hiding there beneath the surface of our banter. We'd put it away in front of the driver and William. But now that we're alone, things are different. Now, he's free to feel the pain, and I'm here to help him get through it.

I press my hand to his cheek. "You have every right to be pissed," I say. "At your father, at the committee. Hell, even at Damien Stark. He obviously didn't manage to convince Livingston to not pull the plug."

He half-grins at that, then his expression turns serious. "I'm pissed," he says. "I can admit it. Angry and hurt and —*goddammit*."

He pushes me aside as he rises off the couch and starts pacing as if talking about it has flipped a switch. I see the anger bubbling inside him, but there's something else, too. Something bigger. Darker. Something I'm not sure I understand yet.

For that matter, something I'm not sure I want to.

"Devlin?" His name feels tentative on my lips. "Devlin, are you okay?"

He stalks back to me, the air around him practically vibrating with an unfamiliar wildness as he tugs me to my feet. He reaches out, twining his fingers in my hair then tilting my head back as his mouth claims mine in a wild assault of teeth and tongue filled with so much passion and need that my knees go week. I reach up, gripping his shoulders for balance.

His other hand goes to the zipper on my dress, and he tugs it all the way down so that my back is bare to the curve of my rear. He slides his fingers down, parting my butt cheeks, and I tremble as he strokes the sensitive muscles of my ass. I hear a low growl in his throat. His thumb stays in place, making me long for something I've never had before as his other fingers move lower, finally thrusting roughly inside me.

"Yes," I murmur, writhing against him, wanting him deeper. Wilder. Wanting him to throw me down and fuck me hard because all I really want at this moment is to be connected to him. To be one with him.

I start to lift a hand, intending to slip out of the dress's spaghetti straps.

"No." That's all he says, and before I have a chance to question, his fingers are no longer twined in my hair. Instead, he's ripping the damn straps free so that the shimmery material now falls down around my feet, leaving me in nothing except the strappy Louis Vuitton heels I've yet to take off.

"I liked that dress," I murmur, not remotely upset.

"I like you better naked."

I try to answer, but his fingers thrust deeper, stealing my words. And then, before I even realize what's happening, he's no longer inside me. I barely have time to draw a breath before I'm pushed up against the wall. He grabs my thigh, lifting it up and hooking it around his hip. Then I hear the metallic scrape of his zipper and the next thing I know, he's inside me, fucking me hard as my back scrapes against the wall with each powerful, demanding thrust.

I start to cry out, but his hand clamps over my mouth, silencing me as he slams into me over and over with a wild brutality that has my nipples tightening and an orgasm rushing like an out of control train toward an explosion so intense I think I just might rip apart from the tremors that tear through my body.

All too soon, Devlin explodes inside me, our eyes locked on each other as my body clenches tight around his cock, and though my back feels raw, I can't remember ever feeling this wonderfully, deliciously used.

"El," he says, his voice so soft I can barely hear it. He pulls me down to the floor, and we land hard.

"Holy fuck," I say, not even caring about the hard wood floor beneath me. My heart is pounding and every inch of my skin feels alive. "That was—"

"Did you mean it?" His voice is low. Steady. But there's something in his tone that worries me.

I roll onto my side and prop myself up, my brow furrowed as I try to figure out what he means.

"You once told me I could use you," he explains his hands going to my hips and urging me to straddle him. "Rough, sweet, whatever I needed." He's still semi-hard, and he guides my hips so that I'm stroking my pussy against him, and the friction on my sensitive clit sends tremors of ecstasy ricocheting through me. "Did you mean it?" he repeats.

"About using me?" My voice is breathy. "I think you just did."

His expression darkens, and I frown, regretting my teasing tone. "Devlin, oh, God, yes. Of course, I meant it. Whatever you need. However you want. And you don't have to ask." I bend forward, my bare breasts brushing the smooth silk blend of his tuxedo jacket as I brush my lips over his ear. "It's better when you don't ask."

I feel, but don't hear, his laughter. "I love you, El. I love you, and I'm so damn sorry."

"Sorry?" I pull back to study his face. "What on earth for?"

"I lied, El. I'm a goddamn coward, and I lied."

CHAPTER SEVEN

I stare at him, fear cutting through me as I push myself up and off of him so that I'm on the floor beside him, my knees hugged to my chest. "What are you talking about?"

He sits up, too, then slowly takes off the jacket and lays it on the floor, the silk lining exposed. "I once told you that I'd leave if that's what it takes to protect you, but that was bullshit. Even if me walking away right this minute could take that target off your back, I wouldn't go. You're mine," he says fiercely. "Dammit, El, tell me you're mine."

I study his face. His expression that is both determined and vulnerable. "Devlin. Oh, Devlin, my love. You know I am."

I don't realize I'm crying until I feel the warm tears trickle down my cheeks. I move closer to him, then start to unbutton his shirt. "I'm yours," I repeat. "Spank me, fuck me. Use me however you want. Just never, ever leave me."

"I won't. I can't. And dammit, El, I hate myself for it."

"No." I can feel my heart breaking. "Devlin, no."

"Do you realize the danger tonight put you in?" There's fury in his voice. At whoever leaked his identity and at himself. "If I'd just pushed you away when you came back to Laguna Cortez. If I'd never let you see under my goddamn mask—"

"What?" I snap. "Then I might not be in danger? I *was* in danger, and you know it. I was a fucking danger to myself." It's true. I'd taken so many risks. Stupid things like fucking dangerous men to really stupid things like taking mountain curves too fast. I'd been reckless, tempting that bitch Fate because she'd stolen everyone I love from me.

"You're not putting me in danger," I tell him. "God, Devlin, after everything we've been through, don't you get it? You're the one who keeps me safe. You keep me centered. It's not *me* flipping the bird at Fate anymore. It's you and me together, telling whoever's trying to harm us that they better run far and fast. Because you—*we*—won't let them get away with it."

I squeeze his hands. "Please, please hear what I'm saying. I'm safe with you. I'm alive with you. In here." I take his hand and press it over my heart. "Whoever is out there that wants to hurt us? Fuck them. We're stronger together."

For a moment, silence lingers. I feel my pulse pounding in my throat—and also between my legs. My words were true, but they also turned me on. My nipples are tight, and I can't deny that I want him to take me again. No, to *use* me again. Wild. Rough. Dangerous. I want it all. I want to *feel*. Flying down a canyon road in Shelby at a hundred-plus? That's nothing compared to where I want Devlin to take me right now.

And yet he's not saying anything, just looking at me with the kind of heat that hints at danger. That suggests he wants to devour me. So help me, I want to be devoured.

I almost whimper, and I want so desperately to reach between my legs and get myself off. This is so fucked up, and right now I don't even know if it's only me or if he feels it too. But oh, please God, I hope he does.

There must be a potency to my desire, because I see a corresponding need building in his eyes. "Tell me," he says. The room's dim light barely illuminates the scar that bisects his eye and cuts over that perfectly chiseled cheek. The effect is heat and danger, and oh, dear Lord, I am so turned on I'm practically vibrating. "You get nothing until you tell me what you want."

My pulse pounds in response to the demand in both his words and his tone. "Use me," I say.

That sexy brow rises. "I thought you told me that I already did that."

I lick my lips. "I want more."

"You want my mouth. My cock."

"Yes."

He traces a finger over my bare breast. "Rough?"

My pussy clenches and my mouth is dry. "Yes."

He rolls my nipple between with two fingers, then tightens it to a hard pinch that I feel all the way to my clit. "Intense?"

I nod, my body arched and my breath ragged. "God, yes."

"Greedy little thing, aren't you?"

"With you, always." Where Devlin is concerned I'm the greediest woman on the planet.

Without warning, he uses his grip on my nipple to pull me toward him. I cry out in surprise and from the hint of pain that only heightens the pleasure. My body is throbbing, my skin sizzling with electricity. I'm so turned on that I'm certain I'll explode from even the slightest touch, then break apart all over again and again and again, tossed around on this sea of pleasure that the intense demand of his touch is pounding through me.

He bends forward, then teases my ear with the tip of his tongue. "You tell me rough. You tell me intense. But who says you get to ask for anything?"

I almost explode right then, even more when he senses my reaction and reaches down to cup my pussy. "No," he says. "Your orgasm belongs to me, baby. You have to earn it."

I swallow, then nod, lightheaded from this game we're playing. Or maybe it's not a game. Maybe it's just us. I only know that Devlin rarely denies me, and the fact that he's doing exactly that is so fucking erotic that I'm practically melting. There's an unfamiliar edge to him. An intensity that seems reflected in those green eyes that that never belonged to Alex and in the scar that defines the powerful, dangerous man my teenage love grew into.

Dangerous.

The word bursts into my head, coloring my emotions. He's the danger I've been courting all my life. The knife-edge I've sought on every fast turn, every random fuck. I've always known it, but I'm seeing it so clearly now. I've been chasing danger my whole life, not just because of my guilt for being alive, but because, dammit, I've been chasing him.

"Tell me," he says. "Tell me what you're thinking."

"I want you," I tell him, my voice raw. "I want what you are."

"And what am I?"

I swallow. "A dangerous man."

He barely reacts. Just the slightest widening of his eyes. I might not have noticed if I didn't know him so well. But what I don't know is if he expected that answer, or if I took him by surprise. All I know is the way my heart races when he wraps his large hand around both my wrists and pulls me close, the angle of my body odd enough to be painful.

I wince a bit, but he doesn't release me. Instead, he whispers, "I'm incredibly dangerous. Does that turn you on?" His fingers slip between my thighs and he makes a low noise in his throat. "Oh, yeah, baby. It damn sure does."

He shifts us, pushing me forward so that I have to work to untangle my arms in time to keep myself from falling forward. "On your elbows," he says, and I put my arms down on the silk lining of his jacket as he kneels behind me, his hands cupping my ass. He bends over me, the material of his shirt and slacks brushing sensually over my bare skin.

He sweeps my hair aside, and his lips tease the back of my neck. He trails kisses down my spine, stopping at the indentation above my ass. He pulls back, then gently spreads my butt cheeks, and I whimper as he teases me with a fingertip pressed against that tight knot of muscles. "I'm going to fuck you here someday," he says, the words sending sweet tremors through me simply from the promise. "Have you ever been?"

I shake my head. "No men."

"No men?" he repeats, his voice rising with the question.

Ridiculously, I blush. "You know. Toys."

He makes a rough noise in the back of his throat, then bends over me, the pressure of his finger against my ass increasing as he whispers, "Why?"

I repeat the word, not understanding the question.

"You must like it if you used toys. So why not men, when you and I both know there must have been scores who were willing? Most likely wanting."

I wince a little at the reference to those years when I fucked for the thrill of walking that ledge, of surviving for another day despite all my bad choices, so that I could wake in the morning and tell Fate to go fuck herself.

"Tell me," he demands his finger pressing harder so that I gasp with longing. "Tell me why."

I actually blush, and I'm *so* not a blushing girl. "I told them no."

He eases back, his lips tracing a path down my spine. "Will you tell me no?"

"Never."

"Why not?"

"I want everything from you, Devlin. And I—don't you know that with every man I fantasized about it being you?"

"Tell me."

I frown, shaking my head a bit.

"Tell me one of your fantasies."

I bite my lower lip, thinking of one in particular after a night in New York when both Alex and Devlin Saint had been on my mind. "You remember when I told you about the time you were in New York, and I was so angry because some fucking billionaire named Devlin Saint was building a foundation in my hometown right in the spot that Alex and I considered our own?"

"How could I forget?"

He eases me up, then leads me to the bedroom area, shutting the bookcase behind us. I expect him to strip, but he doesn't. He just stretches out on the bed, his back against the headboard. He's entirely dressed, and he urges me forward, then tells me to straddle him, so that I'm kneeling over him. He puts his hands on my hips and gently rocks my body, sending tremors through me as he continues to speak casually, as if completely unaware of the effect he's having on me.

"You went out that night," he says. "You wanted to burn off your anger and your memories by picking up some asshole and fucking him."

"I picked the wrong guy," I say, moaning a little at the way his rock-hard cock presses against his slacks and teases my clit. "And a white knight came to my rescue."

"I was so furious with you." He practically growls with the memory. "Furious and frustrated, because I wanted to toss you down in that alley and fuck you myself. God, El, I wanted to slam you against the wall of that alley and fuck you so hard your screams would rock the city. I wanted to take you to the edge, to make you truly afraid. *I* wanted to be the one who fought your demons with you, and yet I couldn't tell you a damn thing."

"I never had any idea it was you in that alley," I admit. "Not consciously, anyway. But I think part of me knew, because I had this fantasy. I played it in my head so many times after that night, over and over, alone in the dark."

"Tell me." His eyes are hard on mine, their intensity matching the sensual edge in his voice.

I put my hands on his shoulders, my eyes locking on his as I grind myself against him. His hands go to my breasts now, teasing my nipples as I try to speak despite the rising climax threatening to overtake me like a tsunami. "He followed me home," I say. "That man in the alley. He'd told me to leave so he could take care of the guy who'd wanted to hurt me."

I tremble with the memory, knowing full well I could have died that night. I draw a breath, moaning as he tweaks a nipple, then force myself to continue, my voice rough and halting. "He, he broke into the apartment. The stranger who saved me, I mean. I don't know how. But in the fantasy, I'm changing for bed, still shaken, freaked from what had happened. I'm naked and I hear a noise behind me, and I turn. And he's there. Standing right there behind me."

I'm breathing hard now, the memory of the fantasy coming back fast. "He got close, and I could smell him. It was your scent—Alex's, I mean—and I was so confused. Then he looked in my eyes and said, 'if it's danger you want.'"

"What then?" He's unfastening his slacks, tugging the

zipper down. I rise up, then moan when I look down and see that he's freed his cock. He's so hard, and my body clenches, desperate for him. I meet his eyes, and he nods—one short, quick movement. I'm so wet that it's easy, and we both gasp as I lower myself, taking all of him in, then rocking slowly as he strokes my clit, both of us breathing hard, our eyes never leaving each other.

"He pushed me back against the wall," I say, remembering the way Devlin did that very thing. "He—he was angry. He told me I could have died." I swallow. "And he asked if it was danger I needed."

"And you told him it was."

"Yes."

I draw in another shaky breath, then meet his eyes as I ride him. "It is," I say. "Or it was. Danger, I mean. I needed it desperately, because I needed to feel alive." I lick my lips, thinking about all the times I'd stretched out naked on this very bed, touching myself as this fantasy played like a movie in my head.

"And what did he do? This benevolent stranger?" He reaches up with one hand for my breast as the other teases my clit. "Go on," he says. "Tell me."

"As if I could talk," I grumble. "I can barely think."

"Tell me." This time, the words aren't a request. They're an order, and my body clenches tight around him in response to that commanding tone.

"He ... he gave it to me," I confess, closing my eyes as I draw out the memory. "Danger, I mean. It was rough. Wild. Hard." With each word, I rock against him, my eyes closed as I let the memory of that night crash over me again. "I knew it wasn't real, that it was just a fantasy, but I still got lost in it."

Devlin's hands cup my hips, helping me ride him, hot and hard. "Go on," he says. "Tell me the rest."

"I was on him, like this, but he flipped us over, and his hand cupped my throat. He was inside me, pounding into me, and I couldn't breathe, and I was trapped." I feel my pulse quicken in both fear and excitement as the memory rakes over me. "It wasn't real, but at the same time it was, and I came so hard I thought I'd explode right there."

I swallow, then open my eyes. "He looked at me the way you're looking at me now. And he whispered, 'there's no pleasure without pain.'"

"He was right."

My lips twitch. "He was. And he told me..." I draw in a shuttering breath, surprised by how hard my heart is pounding. "He told me that if I wanted that—if I needed it—I could come to him."

"And did you?" he asks, as if we're talking about a real man and not a figment of my imagination.

"No," I say, my voice low. I hold his gaze hard. "I said I didn't want him. That I only want you."

For a moment, he doesn't move. Hell, he doesn't even breathe. Then he lifts a hand and brushes my cheek, and it's only then that I realize I've begun to cry. "I knew, Devlin. Not consciously, but somehow, deep inside, I knew that my savior in that alley was you. And I—I brought you back here. In my mind, at least."

He brushes a tear away. "That wasn't how it had been between us."

Our one night together had been sweet. Wonderful, yes. But sweet. So I understand what he's asking. That shift from sweet too rough. From gentle to punishing.

"No," I say. "But what else could it be?"

He studies me, and I know he understands, because he's seen the way I flirted with danger. The way I'd pushed the envelope in order to cling to that thrill of surviving. Of flipping off Fate who had ripped everyone I loved away from me. But, dammit, she hadn't grabbed me yet. It's addictive, that rush. Even now that Alex is back in my life as Devlin, pulled out of the void into which Fate had thrown him, I can still taste the thrill. I don't push in the same way that I had before, when the way I drove could have sent me off a cliff. I'm careful now because of him. Because I can't bear the thought of rolling my car and losing him. But do I still crave that rush?

Yeah. So help me, I do.

He's studying me, and I know perfectly well he sees that need in me. How could he not? Devlin has always been the one who saw me clearly. And then, before I can even wrap my mind around what's happening, he lunges forward so that I land on my back with him on top of me, still inside me.

"What—"

But I don't get the question out, because his hand is at my throat, and his eyes are hard on mine, full of the question. With anyone else, I would never say yes, but with Devlin, it's different. I trust him completely. I know that he understands my limits, and that he would never play this game if he didn't know how. "Yes," I whisper, then close my eyes as he takes full control, his cock thrusting deep inside me as my body tingles and a wild euphoria takes over me, painting my rising orgasm in bright colors and vibrant sensations.

I feel him inside me. I hear his groans mixed with his low words telling me to come with him. But I'm not me anymore. Instead, I'm sensation and experience, passion and pain, I'm at that place we all try to reach and so rarely get there. And as I burst apart—as I explode completely in his arms—all I know is that I actually reached the stars.

He eases off me, and I draw a deep breath, snuggling close as his arms go around me. "I love you," he whispers, the words bringing me even more pleasure than the orgasm and filling me up all over again.

"I know," I say. "I love you, too."

I'm not entirely sure how he managed it, but he's shifted us around. We're both on our sides, spooning, and he's behind me with one hand reaching over, lightly stroking my pussy. "Keep that up, and we'll need a round two," I tell him.

"I'd be okay with that." He pauses, then adds, "You liked it." As he speaks, his hand snakes between my thighs, as if how wet I am is proof of that truism.

"God, yes."

"Tell me why."

"You know why. I've gone from flirting with danger to flirting with you."

He chuckles. "If that was flirting, I'm very interested in your definition of actual sex."

I have to laugh. "Good point."

"But you haven't answered the question."

"You know why," I say. "Because I flirt with danger."

"It's more than that," he says, and there's a rawness in his voice that compels me to shift in his arms so that I'm facing him. "Pain, pleasure," he continues. "They're intimate."

I nod, his words cutting straight to my core.

"You're at your most vulnerable when you experience pain or joy. But joy can be ripped away, and pain can go beyond what's safe. But trust ... Trust is the most intimate thing of all."

"Yes," I say, my eyes pricking with tears. "I trust you completely. I know you'll always take care of me. And, Devlin," I add, reaching up to stroke his cheek, "I'll always take care of you, too."

CHAPTER EIGHT

Devlin dozed, but he never managed to sleep, and when he finally decided to give it up and pry himself out of bed at three in the morning, her words still filled his head. *I'll always take care of you, too.*

It was truer than she realized. She'd always taken care of him, always been that compass that kept him at true north. His version of true north, anyway. He and Ellie differed on the details, sure, but they'd never wavered in the truth of what they saw at the core of each other.

The only real question was how he'd survived so long without El in his life.

And the only real answer was that he hadn't. Not really, because how the hell could he have been alive all those years with a piece of his heart missing?

He pulled on a pair of pajama bottoms, then paused by the bed, looking down at her. At his woman who had pulled his focus from the first moment he'd laid eyes on her. And why? It was a question he'd asked himself on and off for years. It wasn't as if her beauty had claimed him in that first moment. She was pretty, no doubt about that, but Ellie had never had the kind of cover model looks that would have turned the head of an eighteen-year-old boy.

On the contrary, at sixteen, she'd been a bit awkward, as if she hadn't yet become comfortable in her woman's body. There'd been a shyness about her, too, and that wasn't something that usually compelled him, not even back then. And yet compelled him she had, and with such force and power that she'd left his head spinning.

He'd had the same effect on her; he knew that. But why?

He'd never found the answer, and maybe it didn't matter. But what he believed in his heart was that they were two halves of a whole. Proof that soulmates truly existed. Which was, of course, why he was only truly alive when he was with her.

He bent over and pulled the thin sheet over her bare shoulder. She smiled in her sleep, and his heart twisted a little. She was content. Despite everything that had happened last night and all the ramifications the press leak brought with it, she was sleeping peacefully, secure in the belief that no matter what, they would be just fine in the end.

He smiled, because he believed it, too. He only wished that they didn't have to clamber over the rocks and barbed wire to get to that glorious place called Fine.

He stretched and yawned, deciding that coffee was very much on the agenda. He pushed the bookcase aside, opening up the room, then started toward the small kitchen area, only to freeze at the sight of the figure on the sofa.

It was only a split-second of terror—a flash of frustration that he had no weapon—then his body went slack, and he cursed his friend. "What the fuck, Ronan? You ever heard of knocking?"

Ronan aimed intense blue eyes at him, his golden hair gleaming in the dim lamplight. Ellie once told Devlin that

Ronan looked like a Nordic god, and right then, that assessment seemed spot on. An amused god, apparently, as Ronan's mouth curved into an almost mocking grin. "Yeah, well, I tried that, buddy. Rang the bell, called your phone. Wouldn't have barged in, but under the circumstances I thought a wellness check was in order."

Now his mouth outright twitched. "Almost burst into the bedroom, too, until I realized those weren't screams of torture. Or, at least not the bad kind of torture."

"You're an ass," Devlin said mildly. "And if you know what's good for you, you won't tell Ellie that. She'll fry your balls for breakfast." In all honestly, knowing that someone was listening probably ranked high on El's turn-on list. But that wasn't something Ronan needed to know.

"You've been working the leak," he said, changing the subject as he moved into the kitchen and put a pod into the coffee maker. They hadn't talked since the fiasco, but even so, it wasn't a question. He knew his team, and he knew his friend, and Ronan would have taken point immediately.

"Been analyzing the video footage to identify the reporters who had early knowledge—the ones asking the question on the red carpet. Over a dozen shouted out, and we managed to track down five of them already. We should catch up with the rest of them today. Most weren't answering calls or texts last night."

"And?"

"Anonymous gmail from NYCnewsFairy@gmail.com."

"That's it. No one tried to get confirmation first?"

Ronan scowled. "The one guy I talked to said he was willing to take the risk and go on faith. There'd be value in being the first one out of the gate, and for all he knew, he was. Toss it at you out of the blue, and if you flinch, then it's true. But if you react with confusion and denial, he'd back off, tell you where the info came from, and everyone would publicly investigate." He shrugged. "Wasn't like they were stating a fact and facing a defamation claim. They were shouting questions, right?"

"For the most part, yeah," Devlin said. "As for defamation, maybe, maybe not. But I'd hardly want more light shining on the allegation, so it's a moot point."

"Which they'd also know."

"True enough," Devlin said, then passed the first cup of coffee to Ronan before making another for himself. "You came over in the middle of the night to tell me that?"

"And to let you know I've put a team on you. Charlie and Grace. They've got eyes on the building now."

Devlin nodded. His pride wanted to protest, but he agreed with the necessity. More than that, he was onboard with anything that helped create a shield around Ellie. "Let them know she's the priority, not me," Devlin said, knowing Ronan would understand he meant Ellie.

His friend frowned.

"I mean it. Their instinct will be to protect their boss. The public figure who's supposedly their mission objective. I'm altering that objective."

"Dev—"

"I know you don't understand it," Devlin said. He didn't know why Ronan had protected his heart all these years, only that his friend had done exactly that, holding his emotions close and working out any pent-up sexual frustration through vetted call girls, one-night Tinder hookups, and the kind of clubs that aren't advertised and required a membership. "But you're going to have to take me on faith." His voice cracked. "I can't lose her, Ronan. I always knew it. But after she went over that cliff and almost—"

He couldn't even say the word, so all he said was, "I can't lose her."

"I do understand," Ronan said gently. "And I envy you for it."

Devlin waited for Ronan to say more; it was the first time his friend had even hinted at opening up.

But in the end, all Ronan said was, "They'll keep her safe. They'll keep you both safe."

CHAPTER NINE

A shaft of sunlight coming in from the east-facing window wakes me, and I open my eyes to a new day. Hopefully a better day, though I have no complaints about the night I just spent in Devlin's arms. He'd used me so deliciously, and now my body is stiff and sore in a way that I relish. Not because the sex was so incredible—though God knows it was—but because he'd needed it. Needed *me*.

And I'd needed him, too. The intensity. The passion.

Mostly, I'd needed to hear the promise he'd made to me. No secrets. Not ever again.

And I'd needed to hear him speak the reality I already knew. That Devlin had stayed hidden all these years for a reason, and now the wolves are circling. He'd told me they want to hurt him. To punish him.

And the best way to punish Devlin is to hurt me.

I sit up slowly, letting that unpleasant reality fill my head. A year ago, that truth would have invigorated me. It would have lit a fire inside me. A passion. A need.

A yearning to go out and face whatever sonofabitch intended to come after me. I'd go into the fight intending to win. And, hell, I probably would. It's easy to fight when you don't fear the outcome. Because when had I ever feared death? On the contrary, I'd welcomed it. Expected it.

Death was like an old friend, opening a locked door and inviting me into the party.

Not anymore.

Now, there was fear. Not of death—after so many years of living and breathing nihilism, I've banished that particular fear. Instead, my fear is of not being alive. Not being *here*.

My fear is of not being with Devlin.

Death isn't to be feared because of what it is. If death is to be feared at all, it's because of what it can do—take the man I love from me. Or take me from the man I love.

They're going to try. They're probably coming right now.

The words fill my head, like the mantra of a Texas Marshall warning his deputy in one of the old westerns my dad liked to watch after a long day's work.

I stand up, shaking myself like a dog ridding itself of fleas, only I'm trying to get rid of these dark thoughts.

I glance back at Devlin, still asleep, his face turned away from the window and the beam of light that had awakened me. He's wearing pajama bottoms, and I frown, wondering when he'd gotten up during the night.

Not that it matters, I think, and I go close the blinds, then move quietly into the bathroom.

I freshen up, then splash cold water on my face and clean away the smear of mascara beneath my eyes. Then I slip on the short silk robe I keep hanging behind the door, and pad quietly out, careful not to wake Devlin as I leave the bedroom area and head into the main room.

As soon as I'm past the wall of bookcase, I turn back, confused as I realize it's open. But I'm sure that Devlin closed it completely last night, enclosing us completely in the passion that had gripped both of us.

At first, I think he must have gotten up for a snack, but it's not just the bookcase and his PJs that are odd. There's a blanket on the couch, folded neatly, along with a pillow I keep in the trunk that serves as a coffee table in case a rare guest needs to camp on the sofa.

"What the hell?" I mutter, then jump when the walls seem to reply.

"Ronan."

I spin around, to see Devlin standing behind me. "Ronan?"

"He showed up last night."

"I didn't hear him knock."

"That's because he didn't."

I cross my arms over my chest. "You're slipping, Mr. Saint. You sneakily make your girlfriend's condo a fortress, but just any old person can break in?"

Ronan Thorne, of course, is not *any old person*. The guy has mad skills and we both know it. Even so...

"He has your bypass code," Devlin says, and *that* surprises me.

"He what? My key code?" All the units in the building have keypad locks with two codes. One assigned to the security desk and the other set by the tenant. "Why?"

"I gave it to him years ago," Devlin says. "Ronan spends more time in Manhattan than I do, and I wanted him to be able to get to you if you were ever in trouble."

"I—oh." I shake my head, letting my thoughts settle. Not long ago, that revelation would have annoyed me. Today, I'm not surprised at all. On the contrary, I like knowing how much effort he spent to watch and protect me in the time we were apart.

Not that I'm going to say so right away. Instead, I cross to him and give him a half-hearted smack on the chest, which is, I note, deliciously bare. "I wasn't in trouble last night," I say. "Captive, maybe. But not in trouble."

"Captive? I like that." As if in demonstration, his hand closes around my wrist as he pulls me closer, then twists my arm behind me as I melt against him. I'm wearing nothing but the silky robe, and I can feel how hard he is beneath the loose flannel PJs. My pulse immediately kicks up, as if I'm nothing more than a windup toy, and Devlin Saint is the key.

But I'm still curious about why Ronan was here, so I pull away, intending to step back and ask. He doesn't let me. If anything, my struggle has made him harder.

I squirm against him, my breath shallow, and I decide that I don't really care about Ronan at all. "Didn't you get your fill last night?"

"Never," he says. There's a new wildness to his voice. A heat and a hardness I haven't heard before.

"Devlin..."

He yanks me closer, and I gasp as desire thrums through me, spurred by the knife-edge of his passion. "I don't like having things I want pulled out of my grasp. His free hand—the one not holding my arm tight behind my back, slips between my thighs. I'm already wet, my body on fire for him, and I gasp as his fingers thrust inside of me. "I much prefer to take what I want."

He tightens his grip, my shoulder aching from the pressure.

I bite my lip, then force out the words. "What do you want?"

"Can't you tell?"

"Then take it," I say, and, thank God, he does.

We're insatiable, the both of us. Hands and mouths and

fingers. Everything and anything. I'm still sore from yesterday, which had been like a marathon of hard, driving, incredible sex. And yet all I want is more. Devlin, I know, feels the same.

This is more than just the heat that we've always generated when we're together. This is a battle. A war. The world has thrown down the gauntlet against Devlin Saint, and between the two of us we're generating the kind of nuclear reaction inside him that will wipe those bastards away. Maybe not off the earth, but at least out of his mind.

We're fucking for strength, to fight and to forget. But at the end of the day, it doesn't even matter. I can't remember a moment when I didn't want Devlin, and as he grips my hair—as his kisses draw blood—as he fucks me hard against the wall until I am held up only by his arms, a limp rag to be used for his pleasure—I know that I will always, *always*, surrender to his needs no matter how dark.

I need it too, after all.

When we're finally spent, we slide down the wall, then cling to each other on the hard floor. I'd loved the way the flooring looked when I moved in, but now I'm thinking that carpet or a few well-placed rugs would have been smart.

"I love you," he says, brushing a lock of hair away from my eye and hooking it behind my ear.

"Do you think I don't know that?"

He smiles, his sandy brown eyes taking me in. "Maybe I just like saying it."

"Good," I say, letting my eyes roam over that incredible body. "I like hearing it."

After a few minutes, his lazy smile turns into a grin. "You're staring."

"You're very pleasant to look at." Understatement of the year. Really.

"And?"

I scowl. Seriously, the man has the power to read my mind. "I see you better than anyone, you know."

"You do."

I reach out and trail my fingers over his bare skin, tracing the line of his body as he's stretched out on his side. "I see what Packard and that snake Livingston don't."

He makes a show of glancing down toward his cock. "Can't argue with that," he says, and I pretend to be annoyed even as I'm giving a silent hurrah that he has a sense of humor about it.

"I see how strong you are," I continue. "How much you can shoulder. And I see how much you deserve to be recognized. For this," I add, pressing my hand to his heart. "Because you're a good man with a good heart."

I start to take my hand away, but he puts his over mine, trapping me in place. "Thank you," he says, the words softer than a whisper, but they reverberate all through me.

"You should have fought," I say. "That award should be yours."

"No. That would have seemed like a tantrum. But I'll have my say later." The corner of his mouth curves up, the expression a little bit smug. "It's a dance, El, and it's one I've been learning the steps to for years."

"What is?"

"Living life in public."

I frown. "I'm not sure that's a cotillion I'd willingly sign up for."

He cocks his head, studying me. "Wouldn't you?"

I lick my lips, suddenly understanding what he's asking. "All things being equal, no. But you tip the scales, Mr. Saint."

His eyes lock on mine. "Do I? How so?"

"Don't pretend to not understand me. You know damn well I'd walk through hellfire for you. And in case you're

unclear, being in the public eye pretty much qualifies as hell."
I move my shoulder in what could be considered a shrug.
"What can I say? You make even hell feel like heaven to me."

"I like hearing that. Even if it is completely corny."

We both laugh, and it's a nice reprieve before he gets
serious again. "The truth is, I've always known it could come
to this. I'd expected it would be a few more years down the
road, though,"

"Is that why Ronan was here? Looking for leaks?"

Devlin nods, then summarizes their conversation for me.

I frown, taking it all in. "So he's hoping that even though
the leak was from an untraceable gmail, one of the reporters
will have a clue who sent it?"

"Pretty much. He's playing detective for the next few
days. And setting me up with a security detail."

"I think the quest to find the leak is a wild goose chase,
though I hope I'm wrong. I think security is a great idea, and
I'm positive I'm right."

"I agree on all counts. And I'm sorry."

I frown. "For what?"

"The spotlight will shine on you, too. Unless you leave
me. And I won't let you leave me."

"No? Well, then I guess it's a good thing I don't plan on
going." I sigh. "Like I said, you tip the scales, Saint. For me,
you always have.

CHAPTER TEN

I'm grateful to Roger for stocking the kitchen, but not grateful enough to call him back when my phone vibrates with an incoming call while I'm waiting for my coffee to brew after a quick shower with Devlin. Had he called yesterday before the fiasco, I would have answered eagerly. Now, I'm not prepared to deal with the inevitable questions about Devlin's true identity.

He'll assume—rightly—that I've known about The Wolf for awhile. He'll be concerned about me as a friend. He's even savvy enough to worry about my safety in light of the enemies that will undoubtedly start to creep out of the woodwork.

But concern will only be part of the reason for his call. The rest will be work. I was writing a profile on Saint and his foundation, after all. And this little tidbit is about as news-worthy as it gets. Leaving it out shows my bias, and that's not something Roger is going to look kindly toward. His boss, publisher Franklin Coates, is going to be even less happy with me.

So, yeah. I'm dodging the call. Sue me.

I let the call roll to voicemail as I reach for my coffee, and when it does, I notice two other missed calls—Brandy and Lamar.

Both have known the truth about Devlin's father for a while, and both left messages. Brandy's is short and sweet. "Just wanted to give you a virtual hug. Call me if you need to. And hug Devlin for me, too."

Lamar's message is similar, and I smile when he adds that Devlin didn't deserve to get outed that way. He's dating Tracy Wheeler, Devlin's intern, who's fast becoming one of my favorite people, and she got on the line for a second to add that the Council was stupid, and Devlin deserved the award even more because he'd overcome so much.

Their messages lift my spirits, but especially Lamar's. He'd been a late convert to Team Devlin, and the sincerity in his voice is like a warm hug.

As soon as I've brewed two cups, I head back to the bedroom area. I'd slipped out of the shower before Devlin, and now I leave both our mugs on the dresser while I shimmy out of my robe. I'm bent over, pulling a pair of folded jeans from the bottom drawer when I hear Devlin behind me.

"I like the view," he says. "Maybe we should stay in for breakfast."

"We can't. You wore me out. I don't even have the energy to cook." I'm naked, and now I turn around, offering him the rest of the view, and enjoying mine of him in only a towel around his hips. "Besides," I add, "I think you got enough last night."

His brows rise. "Oh, really? Did you?"

"Get my fill of you? Never." I ease closer. "But if we don't stop for breaks, there's never any anticipation for when we start up again."

He laughs. "I should never have told you that was a turn-on."

"Nonsense," I say, brushing a kiss over his lips. "You're supposed to tell me everything. Speaking of which, Brandy and Lamar called. They both think you got screwed. Tracy chimed in, too," I add, relaying the details of their messages to him.

"She's going to be an asset wherever she ends up after college," he says about Tracy, and I wholeheartedly agree.

"Tamra texted," he adds, referring to Tamra Danvers, the foundation's Publicity Director. She was friends with his mother and has been like a guardian angel, watching him for years.

"What's her take on the leak?"

He grimaces, and I hear the heat in his voice when he says. "She's working to spin the story. What else can she do? Whoever leaked that dropped a bomb. Now we're dealing with the shrapnel."

"Devlin..." I say, letting my voice trail off.

He shakes his head. "I'm fine. It's personal, but it's business, too. I'm fine."

I nod. It's the truth. He *is* fine. Pissed, yes. But he's a man who learned to compartmentalize things at a very young age. Who's lived a dual life for about half his life. Maybe "fine" isn't the most accurate word, but it fits. And right now, that's good enough.

I take his hand, adding a flirtatious smile when I say, "You're more than fine in my book. Now get dressed. I'm buying you breakfast."

"Oh, good. For a minute there I thought you were going to cook."

I give him a playful slap, then scurry away before he can return the favor on my rear. I make a show of getting dressed, adding more wriggle than necessary as I tug up the jeans.

As soon as we're both clothed, he tugs me toward him, then kisses me hard. "Thank you," he says.

I tilt my head. "For what?"

"For yesterday. For turning around a very shitty night."

My smile is a little sad as I brush my lips over his. "Mr. Saint, it was my sincere pleasure." I pull back and make a show of looking him up and down. He's in jeans and a gray tee and he looks more or less like a mythical god. "Baseball cap," I say. "You're too good-looking and too recognizable. And I don't think either one of us wants any more press."

"I didn't bring a cap," he says. In response, I rummage in my closet, find a souvenir cap I'd bought when Roger had taken me to a Yankees game, and toss it his way. "Now feed me," I say. "Or I won't have any energy left to continue improving your mood."

"That's all the encouragement I need."

My go-to diner is just around the corner, but it's a gorgeous fall Saturday, and we opt to take our bagels and coffee to-go, then head into the park.

"Surely no one will notice us," I say. "It's not as if all of those publicity hounds at the theater last night are expecting you to go strolling through Morningside Park."

"We'll be safe," he agrees. "We have eyes on us, remember."

I frown. "Do we?" Devlin had told me that Ronan assigned security. "I don't see anyone."

Devlin chuckles. "That's because my people are good at their job."

I smirk. "Fair point."

"And even if we didn't have security, and the publicity hounds are pulling out their cameras..."

"What?" I ask, when he trails off.

He lifts a shoulder as he grins. "Fuck them."

My hands are full, so I resist the urge to high-five him. Instead, I manage a hip bump. "I like the way you think."

"Here," he says, pointing to a bench near a tiny play area for toddlers.

I settle on it, then use the space between us as a tabletop and shift on the bench to face him.

"You always knew this would happen one day, didn't you?" I ask as I unwrap my bagel and schmear.

"Not with any certainty. But I'm also not surprised."

"I suppose the upside is that you're no longer in hiding."

He nods slowly, his eyes narrowing. "But..."

"The *but* is obvious," I say. "Somebody pushed you out into the light. Somebody tipped off the press."

"They did. But who?"

"Well, that's the question of the hour, isn't it? What Ronan's now trying to figure out." We'd avoided all talk of who pulled the trigger on this story last night, but now I'm ready to start mining for answers. He's already started, of course, and from what he said earlier, Ronan is all over the investigation.

"Who could it be other than Blackstone?" About ten years older than Devlin, Joseph Blackstone had also grown up on The Wolf's compound. Now, he's got his own criminal enterprise going, one that he operates out of the Chicago area, and he's managed to evade prosecution because he's a clever bastard. He'd landed on Devlin's radar when an investigation into security breaches at the Devlin Saint Foundation led back to Blackstone's network.

Add to that the little fact that Blackstone and that bitch Anna were both friends and lovers and possibly enemies at various times. It's hard to be certain since she's now dead, something I am extremely happy about. She knew Blackstone from their years together at The Wolf's compound. More recently, she'd apparently enlisted Blackstone's help in her efforts to kill me because, in her eyes, I'd stolen what was supposed to be hers—*Devlin*.

Bottom line? Though we can't yet be certain, everything adds up to Blackstone being very much *not* in the Good Guy column of the checklist.

I wipe cream cheese off the corner of my mouth as I gaze across the park. A mom in jeans is pushing a little boy with bouncy curls on a swing set. Further on, a jogger in red slows on the path as he passes the playscape, then speeds up again.

I take another bite, swallow, then turn my attention back to Devlin. "I assume you have Ronan looking even harder at Blackstone than before?"

"I do," he says. "And this morning he mentioned that word on the street is that Joseph recently took over Harvey White's operation. Apparently it wasn't an amicable takeover."

I'd glanced toward the jogger, but that pulls my full attention back to Devlin. "Should I know who that is?"

"One of my father's former lieutenants. Anna and I knew him well in Nevada. He carved out a niche for himself after dear old Dad was assassinated. And he wasn't happy that so much of my father's empire went to Alejandro. Who, until yesterday, had gone into the wind after being discharged from the military."

"So that means Joseph could be the one who outed you. And White would have had reason to as well. You left and screwed him out of what he believed was his. If he somehow learned the truth..."

Devlin nods. "I don't know how he could have, but as you once mentioned, no secret is completely in the vault. I trust the brass who helped me, but there were others down the ladder who would have had access."

"If they were bribed, might be a good place to start asking questions."

He nods. "Ronan's already got some of the team on that."

I'm not surprised. Devlin and his people are nothing if not thorough.

"My money's still on Blackstone," I tell him. "The timing is too coincidental. And surely Anna told him who you really are."

He nods. "It's a concern, but Christopher swears she didn't."

I scowl at the name. "Assuming she would have told him. For that matter, assuming he's telling the truth."

"You're still concerned about him."

I start to deny it, then shrug. A thriller writer, Christopher Doyle came to Laguna Cortez ostensibly to use the foundation's library to research a new novel with a human trafficking element. All of which is true. It's the part he didn't share that worries me.

"He's dating Brandy," I say, stating the obvious. "And he's Joseph Blackstone's half-brother, and he was Anna's close friend. We know that Blackstone's either causing the leaks in your operation or he's benefitting from them. And, oh yeah, Anna tried to kill me. Several times. On the one hand I hate the idea of guilt by association. On the other..."

I trail off. Because, honestly, it really *is* all guilt by association. And isn't that what the press is doing to Devlin right this very minute?

I gather my thoughts as I watch a couple stroll on a nearby path. A jogger overtakes them, his head turning to stare in our direction. I frown, because I'm pretty sure he's the same jogger in red I noticed a few moments ago. I almost say something to Devlin, but the guy shifts his attention back to the path and continues on.

"Did I lose you?"

"Sorry. Distracted." I draw a breath. "I guess I'm not being fair to Christopher. He's been good to Brandy. Good for her, too. And, yes, I understand why he didn't want to have his name associated with Blackstone. Who would?"

"Agree," Devlin said. "Add to that the fact that the investigation after Anna's death turned up nothing to suggest he was involved. To the contrary, Christopher testified against Joseph, remember?"

I nod. After Anna's death, the investigation had revealed that Christopher had turned snitch against his half-brother on some drug-related charges years before. "I know. I just—"

"You don't want to see Brandy hurt." He puts down his coffee and takes my hand as an energetic Labrador that reminds me of Jake bounds by, chasing a frisbee. "Believe me, I don't either. But Christopher was completely cooperative. Lamar said he passed the polygraph with flying colors."

"I know." I shrug, remembering when Lamar had confirmed that piece of information. "He's just a guy from a bad family who came to the foundation to research a thriller and got sucked into the quagmire. Hell, it could be the plot for his next book."

He shares my smile. "It really could." He finishes his bagel, then tosses the wrapping into the can next to our bench. "How's Brandy doing?"

"She's good. Like you said, he's never been anything but awesome to her. I think she was a little pissed that he didn't tell her he was connected to Joseph Blackstone, but why would he? Blackstone was part of The Wolf's world, and Christopher didn't know that was a world you were part of."

He frowns. "Did she tell him?"

I shake my head. "No. But I guess he knows now. The

whole world does. Including Joseph Blackstone." I suck in a deep breath. "Which means that he's not the only threat."

"No," Devlin agrees. "Just the most identifiable one."

I sigh and crumple the paper my bagel had been wrapped in. "Mr. Saint, you do lead a complicated life."

"Fortunately, I have a very uncomplicated woman at my side."

I almost spit the sip of coffee I'd just taken in an effort not to laugh. "You better not."

"Fair enough. I have a complicated woman who I dearly love. And," he adds, his eyes darkening, "about whom I worry."

"I get that," I say. "Honestly, I worry about both of us. But I still say that maybe this is a positive thing. No more hiding, right?"

He chuckles. "Baby, I was hiding for a reason. And, well, it wasn't even really hiding, was it? I'm not Alex. I'm not Alejandro. I'm Devlin Saint, and he's always been very much in the open."

"Yes," I say softly. "That's true."

"But that's not something my enemies care about. There are men who lost the opportunity to take control of my father's empire when I shut it down. And there are men who were friends of my father who want revenge against the man who killed him."

"Even if they know you used to be Alejandro, they can't know that you're the one who killed The Wolf."

"You know better than that," he says, and he's right. Daniel Lopez was killed, and Alejandro inherited. Then Alejandro disappeared. It's a safe bet that The Wolf's friends always believed that Alejandro killed his father.

But as there was no Alejandro to be found, no one could exact revenge.

Now Alejandro is back as Devlin Saint. And that means the target on his back just got bigger. But by how much, we still don't know.

"What about Ronan and Tamra?" I ask as we walk down a sidewalk on our way back to the apartment. "Or Reggie," I add, referring to Regina Perez, the only other member of Saint's Angel's who I've met so far. I don't know many details about her background, but I know she does undercover work. And as for Ronan, he's as much of a bad ass as Devlin. Both of them were in Special Forces and have the skills to prove it.

I glance at him sideways. "They're all doubling down on their resources, right? Trying to figure out not only who leaked your identity, but also who else might be gunning for you?"

"Way ahead of you," he says, which doesn't surprise me at all. "Everyone on the team is working intelligence. We should have a list of potential threats and sources for the leak within forty-eight hours."

"Good," I say. I crumple the last of my trash and score a few points when I hit a nearby trashcan. "You know, it's possible the list isn't that long. After all, most of the men your father worked with would be pretty old now. They might have retired to some ranch in South America or a villa in Greece. Or they could be in prison. Hell, they might be chugging along just fine in the underworld, and figure the risk isn't worth the reward of going after you."

"I don't disagree," he says. "But we won't know until we know. And if there is a threat, I need to be on top of that."

"Damn right," I say. "Because—"

I bite off the word as he shoves me behind him. Almost

instantaneously, I see the red jogger hurrying forward. Terror spikes through me, and a few yards away a man and a woman seem to magically appear from a nearby doorway.

"Mr. Saint!" the jogger says, breathless, as the man—Charlie, I assume—lifts a hand draped with a light sweater that I'm certain hides a gun. The woman, Grace, is only a few feet away now, having jogged closer behind the threat. I start to move around Devlin, but he holds me back, his arm an impenetrable barrier.

"I'm really sorry to bother you," the man blurts out. Hardly any time has passed, but everything has changed. The tension in the air around us fades. And though Charlie and Grace are clearly still on their guard, this no longer feels like a threat. "I just—I just had to say that I'm sorry. For what they're reporting, I mean."

"I appreciate that," Devlin says, and though I doubt the jogger can tell, I can hear the tension in his voice clearly enough. He's still uncertain, and he's playing it exactly right as Charlie and Grace come even closer.

I ease forward, too, and Devlin takes my hand, and I know he's positioned to leap in front of me if he needs to. He won't need to, though. This guy's no threat, a conclusion that's borne home when he tells Devlin how he'd been living in a shelter that the foundation had partnered with to provide job training. Now he works data entry at an insurance company and has his own apartment.

"They're assholes for trying to make you look bad," the man says. "I just had to say thanks."

"And I'm glad you did," Devlin said, his voice smooth and friendly. "It's wonderful to know the Foundation is making a difference."

They exchange a few more words before the man heads off. I see the tension drain from Devlin's body and the way he nods at Charlie and Grace, acknowledging both them and the fact that the threat—such that it was—is over.

The he turns to me, and all of a sudden, I'm fighting tears. "He was nice," I say, having to speak in order to force back a flood of relieved tears. "I thought—but he was nice."

I draw a breath, calming myself as Devlin pulls me close. "I didn't like that," I say, tilting my head back to look at him. "Being scared. Devlin, you have to be careful. Because honestly, if I lost you again, I don't think I'd survive."

He strokes my hair. "You're strong, baby. You would."

"Maybe," I concede. "But I wouldn't want to."

CHAPTER ELEVEN

Devlin's arm is around me, and I'm laughing as he tries to kiss me in the hall. "Security cameras," I tease. "Do you really want a picture of the owner canoodling with one of his tenants?"

"I don't want any picture that involves canoodling. But with you I would make an exception. Care to canoodle with me once we get inside? For that matter, care to let me film your canoodle?"

My brows rise as I slide the key into the lock. "Mr. Saint, I had no idea that was something that got you going. Maybe we can—"

I bite off my words as I push the door open, then gasp when I see the man standing in the middle of my apartment. Devlin pushes me aside, his gun up and aimed in less than the split-second it takes for reality to slam into place.

"*No*," I shout. "It's okay. It's Roger. It's my editor."

Poor Roger is frozen in place, his hands in the air, his eyes wide. He's let his hair go full-on silver, and he's back to sporting a beard. All in all, he looks a bit like a svelte Santa caught in the act.

"My apologies," Devlin says, holstering his gun. "But do you want to tell me what the fuck you're doing in Ellie's living room?"

"It's okay," I tell Devlin, who knows perfectly well how close I am to Roger. Not romantically, but as friends. "He takes care of the place when I travel. I told you that. He stocked the kitchen for us."

"And yet here we are in town, and he just pops in?"

"I appreciate you looking out for Ellie," Roger says. "But as she's trying to tell you, I'm hardly a threat to her safety."

Devlin's eyes narrow. "But you are a threat, aren't you?"

I look between the two of them. "What are you talking about?"

"Tell her why you're here."

Now I'm really confused, because why on earth would Devlin know anything about Roger and my work? Unless, of course, it involved Devlin.

"*Fuck.*" The curse is barely a whisper, but both men turn to me. "You came here to fire me, didn't you?"

Roger grimaces. "Actually, I came to take you back to the office. Franklin wants to speak with you. In person, he says."

I close my eyes and draw a breath now that I've caught the sweet scent of a reprieve. Franklin's clearly pissed—the man hardly ever comes to the office on the weekend—but I'll willingly endure a lecture. Even a rant. And with luck, I'll only have to power through a few months of shit assignments before my world rights itself again.

"She's one of your best assets," Devlin snaps. "And you're going to cut her off like that?"

To his credit, Roger doesn't cower. He steps toward Devlin, his chin held eye, his eyes never leaving Devlin's face. "I went to the mat for her," he says. "Fire? That was Franklin's plan. I talked him out of it."

Devlin cocks his head, clearly still on edge.

"Devlin." I put my hand gently on his arm. "It's okay."

"Ellie is like a daughter to me," Roger continues, his eyes narrowing behind wire-frame glasses. "I've watched her grow into an excellent reporter, and I know that even excellent reporters make mistakes."

"Mistakes?"

I hear the edge in Devlin's voice and put my hand on his elbow. "It's okay," I repeat. "Really. I'll be back soon, and it's not like I haven't known this conversation is long overdue."

"I'm coming with you."

I shake my head. "No. I'm—"

"Have you forgotten the last twenty-four hours? Do you not understand that anyone wanting to hurt me is going to do it most effectively through you?"

"I have a car waiting," Roger hurries to say. "It's at the building's service entrance."

"I'll be back soon," I tell Devlin, then rise on my toes to kiss him. "And I'll be fine," I whisper. "You can spank me if I'm not."

"I've a mind to do that anyway," he growls, but I hear the tiniest bit of humor underneath.

"You have work to do, too," I remind him. "Lots of calls to make, I'm sure. This way, we're both taking care of business."

"All right," he says. "You win." He shifts his attention from me to Roger. "Even a hair of hers ends up out of place, and I swear I will gut you."

"It's a pleasure meeting you, too, Mr. Saint. I wish it had been under other circumstances, because I have to admit, I like you very much."

We leave on that note. Me biting back a laugh, Devlin fighting a smile I recognize as one of admiration, and Roger looking more than a little shocked by his own boldness.

My good mood fades quickly once we reach the car. For the first time I can remember, silence hangs awkwardly between me and Roger. Whatever lecture I'm about to endure, Franklin is the one who will be giving it. But it's not just work we're avoiding, it's everything.

We pass a classic Mustang convertible, and Roger shifts beside me. I expect him to use that to break the ice, maybe comment on how much he misses Shelby, my now-battered but beloved classic 1965 Shelby Cobra that I used to keep garaged at his house since parking in Manhattan is so freaking expensive.

But the moment passes, and he pulls out his phone as if he'd just gotten a text, though I'm quite certain he hasn't.

It's not until we're in the elevator heading up to the publisher's office that he finally says, "I'm so sorry, Ellie. It's terribly unfair."

It's the first he's spoken directly about Devlin and what happened last night. "I know," I say.

He hesitates, as if expecting me to say more, but I really don't want to talk about it. So silence lingers until we reach Franklin's office.

"Well, there she is," Franklin Coates, the publisher of *The Spall Monthly* says as Roger and I walk into his office, all dark wood and dim lighting. He's a large man, a former football player who comes from old money. He's bald and his usually ruddy cheeks are even more red today as he glowers across the room at me. "Our newest ex-employee."

I stumble as his words hit me, and I glance back at Roger, who looks like he's been bombarded with shrapnel.

"Franklin, what the hell? You said—"

"What?" Franklin fires back. "That I would keep her on as a fact checker? A reporter who doesn't even have a sense of the value of a story? A reporter who, though she'd already been chastised for her close relationship with Devlin Saint didn't scoop the story that he's the long-lost son of one of this country's most notorious criminals?"

He turns his attention to me as Roger stands in shock beside me. "Care to explain that, Ms. Holmes?"

"Not really," I say. "And since I don't work here anymore, I don't think I have to." *Fired.* The son-of-a-bitch had Roger drag me down here just so he could fire me?

"Aren't you even going to say something," I snap, ignoring Franklin. "He played you and you're just standing here—"

"Roger is not involved in this conversation," Franklin says, forcing my attention back to him as he comes around his desk and stalks toward me, his eyes narrowing into slits, like that's going to intimidate me.

I meet him halfway, not intimidated at all. Just pissed.

"You knew," he says. "But you didn't say a word."

Franklin's voice is like ice, and I'm tempted to just walk out. Why not? What's he going to do, fire me again?

"I would appreciate a response, Ms. Holmes."

"You didn't ask me a question. You stated a fact. I didn't say a word about who Devlin's father was. Not to you, not to my readers. It's his personal life. *My* personal life."

"It's news." Franklin practically growls the word.

"It's gossip," I retort, my body hot with fury.

His eyes narrow, and I hold up my hand. "I know," I say. "I'm fired." I turn to Roger, who looks miserable. "I'm sorry if I disappointed you."

"Never," he says.

I swallow, my mouth dry as I look him in the eye. "Yeah, well, I wish I could say the same."

He clears his throat. "Come on. I'll walk you to out."

"I can walk myself."

"It's the right decision," Franklin says as I reach the door.

I pause and turn back. "Maybe so. But my decision was the right one, too." I turn back and exit the office without waiting for a response.

Roger catches up to me at the elevator.

"You should have stood up for me," I say. "You didn't say a single word. Why the hell didn't you say anything?" It's not as if I don't understand why Franklin fired me, I do. But he lied to Roger, my friend. And yet Roger just stood there and took it. "Why?" I repeat.

His body seems to slump. "I'm sixty-two and overextended. I can't afford to lose my job now. It doesn't make me proud, but it's the reality I live under."

I exhale, then nod. I get it; I do. But at the same time, I can't help but think about Devlin who's risked his actual life in Saint's Angels to try and balance the scales of justice. He's stuck his neck out time and time again. That's not something Roger would ever do. Hell, it's not something most people would do. It doesn't make them bad people, but it does make Devlin extraordinary.

I realize I'm actually smiling a little when Roger presses a hand to my shoulder, and I don't shake it off. "You're going to be fine, Ellie."

Once again, I think about Devlin. I'm not a woman who'd be happy living in the shadow of her man, but I also know that he will always be there for me, ready to reach out and help me over any stumbling blocks I might encounter as I figure out my next step. "I know," I tell Roger. "I'm going to be just fine."

We hug, and I promise to stay in touch. I mean it, too. Maybe I should be angrier that he's siding so easily with Franklin, but I'm not. I get why I was fired and why Roger toed the party line.

And at the end of the day, as much as I love my job, I love

Devlin more. Now, I just need to figure out what to do with my slightly tarnished journalism degree.

It's something I'm thinking about as I load my few personal things into a cardboard box. It's Sunday, and so there's only a few people around, a fact for which I'm grateful. I like all my co-workers, but I never really bonded with anyone.

The closest I came to having an actual professional relationship with was with Corbin Dailey, and that was based on mutual dislike.

Even so, I glance over at his desk and realize that I'm feeling a little melancholy. He might have been my arch nemesis, but he'd helped out where it counted. And the truth is he's a damn good reporter.

I head over to his desk, planning to leave a note, when I hear his smooth voice from across the room. "Snooping for a lead? Damn, Holmes, I never thought you'd stoop so low."

I look up, prepared to defend myself, only to see he's grinning. Strangely, I find myself grinning back.

"Let me guess. The revelation that Saint's the son of the world's biggest a-hole drove you from him, and now you're moving back to New York to be a pain in my ass."

"Not exactly."

He comes closer and leans against the desk. He's got white-blonde hair and pale blue eyes that are focused on me like two lasers. After a moment, he clears his throat. "Listen, I really am sorry about what happened. He seems like a good guy. Hell of a thing to get slapped with on his big night."

"Yeah," I say. "It was." I glance around, then peer under his desk before rising up with a shrug.

"What was all that?"

"Just wondering what rabbit hole I fell down. I'm feeling a little like Alice."

He shrugs. "Nah. I just—oh, fuck. Franklin cut you loose, didn't he? The prick."

Tears sting my eyes, and I want to melt into the floor. "Yeah." My voice sounds raw and I hate—*hate*—that it's Corbin who's seeing me like this.

"I'm really sorry," he says, with an unfamiliar gentleness.

I sniffle and reach for a tissue. "It would have been nice if you'd told me years ago that you weren't a complete dick, you know that, right?"

A slow grin spreads across his face. "Yeah, but where's the fun in that?" He nods to my box filled with papers and knick-knacks. "Come on, I'll carry that down for you."

"Thanks," I say, then fall in step beside him.

"So what now?" he asks.

"Now I go back to California. I was already planning to stay out there anyway."

"When are you leaving?"

"Soon. We were planning to stay at least a week, but what with the media explosion we need to get back as soon as I can find a realtor to handle a sublet. But after that, we're out of here."

"Sorry you're not getting your New York vacation with your man."

I pause on the sidewalk outside *The Spall's* building. "Why are you being so nice?"

"Hey, I may be a jerk, but I'm not an asshole. You're a solid reporter, even if you did manage to snag most of the good stories because Roger had a hard-on for you."

"He did not!"

He waves it away. "Oh, please. Why wouldn't he? I'm not blaming the guy. You're hot in that bitchy nerd-girl sort of way."

"I'm starting to feel like we're getting back to normal here.

Not having asshole Corbin around was making me feel off-center."

He chuckles. "Point is, I hate it when talent gets fucked over. And they're fucking you over big time. Ergo, the nice. That and I wanted to ask you about your apartment."

I pause on the sidewalk, my arms crossed. "You are *not* being nice to me because you want a sublet."

He tilts his head as he shrugs. "Might be. Or you might just be seeing a whole new side of me."

I shake my head. "I can't believe you had me going like that," I say as I continue down the sidewalk. "For a moment there, I thought there might be one decent bone in your body."

"Oh, I have *one*," he says, with the kind of leer in his voice that has me rolling my eyes and fighting a laugh. "But I don't think Devlin Saint would like me showing it to you."

"Devlin's not the only one," I mutter.

He scoffs, then stops. "Listen, Holmes, I know we've had our run-ins, but you're a solid reporter. For that, I'll always give you props. Your place is a short walk from work, and mine's forty-five minutes on the subway. So if you're moving on, I'd appreciate a good word with your landlord. Even better if I can take over your lease. You told me once what your rent is. Would've kicked my ass in Phoenix, but in Manhattan, it's a pretty sweet deal."

"I never knew you were from Arizona."

"Never knew I could be civil, either. It's a wild and wacky world out there."

I reach to take the box from him. "That it is."

"So?"

"It's yours." I probably shouldn't give in so quickly, but weirdly Corbin has been the brightest spot on my last day at *The Spall*, and that's something I never would have guessed.

"That means you'll put in a good word?"

"That means I'll introduce you to the owner. And I can pretty much guarantee he'll do as I ask."

I catch his eye and shrug.

It takes him a second, then he barks out a laugh. "You're shitting me. Saint owns your building?"

"One of life's weirder coincidences," I tell him, because I'm sure as hell not telling him the real truth. "Not the only weird thing, come to that."

"What do you mean?"

I frown, thinking of Roger. "Sometimes people you count on let you down." I meet his eyes. "And sometimes other people surprise you."

His brows rise. "Is that a fact?"

I shrug. "Don't make a thing of it. And come on. We can finalize this now."

As advertised, it's not a long walk, and Corbin takes the box back, now in full gentleman mode.

When we get to the apartment, I open the door and gesture for him to follow. Then I stop dead in front of him, the box banging into my back as Corbin stumbles against me.

I barely notice. All I see is Devlin slowly lowering the phone, his expression tight, his eyes lost.

"Devlin?" I hurry to his side, Corbin forgotten. "What's going on?"

"It's Tracy," Devlin says. "She's dead."

CHAPTER TWELVE

B*efore...*
          Alejandro looked at the rounded slab of gray granite through tear-filled eyes. *Aurelia Espinoza.*

That's all it said. Just her name and the years she'd been alive. Twenty-three in total.

She'd been his stepmom since he was nine. He was fourteen now. And she was dead.

Nothing on the stone said that she'd been anyone's daughter. Nothing said she'd been anyone's wife. Nothing said she'd been anyone's mother. Or stepmother, anyway.

The gravestone didn't even say Lopez. His prick of a father wouldn't even give her that. Not in life, not in death. He'd married her. He'd fucked her. He'd used her and beaten her, but since she didn't give him another son, he hadn't claimed her.

In the end, he killed her. Beaten her to death in the kitchen because she'd made his breakfast wrong.

Not that anyone would say that out loud, but everyone knew. The reality was especially hard for Alex to bear. He should have stayed home that morning. He knew his father was in a mood, and he'd wanted to get out of the house. He'd skipped breakfast and gone to the range. He'd fired off five clips before Marta, the housekeeper, came to tell him that his father had sent for him. Aurelia was dead, Marta had told him, her eyes wide and frightened. It was, she'd said, a terrible accident.

Accident.

What a stinking load of crap.

The official word was that she'd fallen and hit her head. But anyone who believed that had shit for brains.

Daniel Lopez had a temper. He was The Wolf, after all. And The Wolf had certain expectations. His woman had to act a certain way. His lieutenants had to act a certain way.

And his son damn sure had to act a certain way.

Alex felt the burn on his cheek where his father had slapped him just that morning. Called him a pussy for wanting to come to Aurelia's grave. And he felt the ache in his ribs where his father had fractured one a few months ago when he'd thrown Alex to the ground and kicked the shit out of him for talking back.

His father had said his shot wasn't good enough, but Alex had hit the painted eye on that fucking target with twelve of the thirteen rounds in his pistol. The target was dead, and he'd told his father so. And earned a beating in the process.

He'd almost fought back. But he'd only been thirteen then, one month shy of his birthday. He was strong for his age, he knew that. But he was still smaller than The Wolf. Even at fourteen, he wasn't quite ready.

But he was getting close. Bigger. Stronger. And his marksmanship was dead on. And he was working to make it even better.

"I'll make it up to you," he told Aurelia now. "Someday, I promise I will."

"Big promise for a little boy."

Alex turned and saw Marco Giatti strolling toward him, his dark black hair slicked back from his forehead. He was grinning. Unlike The Wolf, Marco grinned a lot. And he talked to Alex like a man, even when he called him *boy*. Told him stories about his life on the East Coast. Stories that reminded Alex that there were other places. Other lives.

"I'm not a little boy," Alex said.

"No, you're not. Wish you were. Growing up too fast. But you're still just a *cugine*. One more soldier in the ranks. You ain't the *don* yet, kid."

And he never wanted to be. He didn't say that, though. Not even to Marco. Instead, he just lifted his chin. "I'm almost fifteen."

"And still young enough to be a damn fool."

"Am not." He felt like an idiot as soon as he said the words.

"You think it's going to go well if your father learns you came out here? That you got all boo-hoo weepy for his *goomah?*"

"She wasn't. She was his wife."

"And you're crying for her. Sentimental nonsense. You know he'll think so. You think he won't tell you as much with his fists if he finds you out here?"

Alex shrugged, feeling sulky. Marco was right. "Why are you here?"

"Because I like you, boy-o. And I don't want to see you roughed up because you got on the wrong side of The Wolf's temper."

"You shouldn't stay stuff like that." Fear cut though him. Alex liked Marco. Liked him a lot. He didn't want him gone, disappeared like some of his father's other men.

"Yeah, well if you won't tell on me, I won't tell on you."

Alex shoved his hands in his pockets and nodded. "I won't."

For a moment, they both stood in silence. Then Marco said, "She was a sweet girl who grew up into a kind woman. She deserved better."

Alex tilted his head, studying the older man. Beside him, Marco shrugged. "Just saying the truth in front of you and Aurelia and God. But it stays here, right? Just between us."

"Just between us," Alex said. He drew in a breath. "I meant what I said. I didn't protect her from *him* because I couldn't. But someday, I'll avenge her."

"And I meant what *I* said," Marco retorted. "That's a big promise to make. But I hope it's one you can keep." He nodded at the grave. "Say your goodbyes and get home before someone sees you. And for the record, I wasn't ever here."

"Okay," Alex said. As he watched Marco walk away, he saw someone else standing behind a nearby gravestone. A short, heavyset boy he recognized immediately—Manuel Espinoza. *Manny.* Aurelia's brother.

He waited, expecting Manny to come over, but the boy just turned and walked the opposite direction. Alex frowned, but brushed it off. Manny had always been a strange kid, and he seemed to have gotten stranger after Aurelia's death. Not that Alex saw him much. After Aurelia died, The Wolf had sent Manny away to live with one of his second cousins, a quiet, skinny man named Romeo Duarte who ran "errands" with Joseph Blackstone, an ass-kissing creep who was also one of the up-and-comers in The Wolf's operation.

Manny had cried and cried, but Alex would have given anything to move out of his father's house. Manny didn't have a clue that he'd been blessed with the only good thing that came from Aurelia's death.

With a sigh, he blinked away the tears that threatened as

he once again looked at Aurelia's grave. "Goodbye," he whispered, then added, "I'll keep my promise."

He would never speak of it again, but Alex knew he would always remember that promise. One he'd silently made to all the women in his father's life. His own mother. The wives who would come after Aurelia. The girlfriends, too. Because The Wolf would devour them all.

His father thought there was no price for hurting women and scaring children.

But there was.

And now that Alex was no longer a child, he relished the day when he could teach his father that lesson in person.

CHAPTER THIRTEEN

The present...

Devlin stood in the condo unit's entrance hall, his body numb. It was a crime scene now. No longer Tracy's home. Now it was the place she'd died.

The place where she'd been murdered.

And, dammit, the place where Ellie had been threatened.

He realized his hands were clenched at his sides and forced himself to relax. This wasn't a time for emotion—that could come later. Right now, he needed to assess the situation. To learn what he could.

And to start to plan his next steps.

Centered again, he looked down at the chalk outline in the tiled entryway. Adhesive tags on the wall identified the single bullet's impact. It had gone through her skull, killed her instantly, then lodged in the wall. The ballistics team had retrieved it last night.

They'd also retrieved Tracy's eye. It had been gouged out after she was dead, then placed in a small gift box by the sick fuck who'd killed her.

An eye for an eye.

Now, the entire Laguna Cortez police force was working round the clock to get to the bottom of the murder.

Devlin drew in a breath, then moved toward the living room where Ellie's friend, Detective Lamar Gage, sat tense beside her. A large man who had once been a child star, he tended to carry himself with confidence, filling whatever space he occupied. Not today. Today, he seemed lost inside himself, and his dark skin had gone ashen with grief.

When Devlin and Ellie had arrived less than an hour ago, well after dark, Lamar had been pacing. He'd been on the scene for hours, and he'd still been barking orders, a river of motion churning with manic purpose, as if he'd fall over if he had to stand still. Then he'd seen Ellie, and he'd let the weight of grief bear down on him. He'd collapsed against her. She'd shot Devlin a look filled with infinite pain, then led the detective to the sofa.

"They were getting serious," Tamra Danvers, his longtime friend and the DSF's publicity director, had said, stating what Devlin already knew. Grief lined her face, and the one gray streak in her hair had seemed more pronounced. "He feels helpless."

Devlin had only nodded. What more could he say? He felt helpless, too. More, he felt scared. Not an emotion he liked to cop to, but it was the truth. Because how the hell would he survive if that chalk mark had been outlining El's body?

He wouldn't, and as far as Devlin was concerned, that meant that Lamar Gage was one of the strongest men he knew.

Not that Tracy's murder wasn't hitting Devlin hard, too. It was. Tracy had been one of his, dammit. A member of his staff. An intern who would have undoubtedly been offered a permanent position when she graduated. She'd been a vibrant, caring women and someone had taken her from the world.

Worse, they'd taken her because of him.

Her blood was on his hands as sure as the target he'd painted on Ellie's back. He knew it. And he was damn sure everyone in the room knew it, too.

"This isn't your fault," Tamra said, her soft voice at his side pulling him from his thoughts and memories.

"Isn't it? I'm not so sure."

"Devlin, you—"

He held up a hand. "Does it matter? Even if it's not my fault, it's still my burden."

Her mouth pulled into a tight line as she nodded. "You've borne so much. I don't want this on your shoulders, too."

She placed a hand on one of those shoulders, and he felt his chest tighten with the weight of his grief. He *had* borne too much. So many years of loss and anger and pain. When Ellie had come back into his life, he'd let in a few wispy rays of hope that, finally, the pain would stop.

But it never stopped.

He was the man that destiny had made him. And he would always bear the mark of his father.

Tamra knew that as well as he did. She'd been a friend to his mother. Had come to him when he was still Alejandro. And she'd become an essential cog in the wheels that made up both the foundation and Saint's Angels. She knew his secrets. More important, she understood why he had them.

"They killed her as a message to me."

"I know."

It was all so obvious. So wickedly simple. A package delivered to Tracy's address. She'd probably opened the door to sign for the courier, then noticed that the package had Devlin's name but her address.

She would have lifted her head to tell the courier that she wasn't the proper recipient. Maybe she noticed that he was wearing a full-face, special effects quality latex mask. It hadn't been obvious from the image her doorbell camera caught, not with a cap pulled down low over the courier's eyes. Nothing that would have made her hesitate to open the door and sign for a package.

But she'd probably seen it in that last moment. The fake face and nefarious purpose. Fear would have spiked through her, and according to the forensics team, she'd taken a step back.

That's when he'd lifted the gun that had probably been concealed by his jacket. He'd fired—swift and accurate. And Tracy had gone down, the package tumbling to the floor with her.

It was a simple box, the bottom and top wrapped separately, and the top secured in place only by string.

The police hadn't waited for Devlin to arrive to open it. They'd called in the bomb squad just in case and removed the twine holding the lid in place on the five-by-five box. Devlin and Ellie had been in the air when Lamar had radioed. His voice had been strong, but Devlin heard the pain underneath.

"An eye for an eye," Lamar had said, relaying the words that had been included with the eye itself. *"With interest still owing."*

His voice had caught on a sob, and Devlin had squeezed Ellie's hand, his blood turning to ice.

"That's what it says," Lamar had whispered, as Devlin burned with rage. "That's all it says."

"We'll find who did this," Devlin had promised, letting rage seep through him as he pictured the masked courier calmly gouging out Tracy's eye, opening the empty package, and placing it inside with that damned note. He could hear the steel in his voice when he added, "We'll find him, and we'll make him pay."

"Yeah," Lamar had said. "We will."

Now, as if he had caught the scent of Devlin's memories, Lamar lifted his head, then looked at Devlin over Ellie's shoulder. She turned, too, her eyes red and her face tear-stained. She whispered something to Lamar, then hugged him before she stood up and moved to Devlin's side.

"How's he doing?" Devlin asked.

"He's ripped up," Ellie said. "I am, too."

"I know." He pulled her into his arms and drew strength from the feel of her against him.

"It wasn't your fault," she murmured, her voice soft against his chest.

"I know," he said, because that's what he was supposed to say. What he was supposed to feel. He said it, but that didn't mean he believed it.

She pulled back, her forehead lined with pain, her eyes rimmed in red. "It's not your fault," she repeated, and he couldn't hold back the tiny hint of a smile at how well she knew him.

"Our perp wasn't punishing Lamar," Devlin said. "Not intentionally. This was aimed at me. This fallout is on me."

"If it's on anybody other than Blackstone, it's on Anna. You killed her because she was about to kill me."

He nodded, noting that neither one of them were even considering the possibility that anyone other than Joseph Blackstone had been behind the murder. Of course, he was. He'd been a former lieutenant of The Wolf. And despite their public front of being estranged, Devlin had recently confirmed that Blackstone had also been Anna's friend and sometimes lover. All of which added up to one hell of a motive for going after Devlin.

Most likely, Blackstone hadn't committed the murder personally. For that matter, Devlin would lay odds that he was still at his home base in Chicago—probably doing something very public—for the sole purpose of ensuring he had a solid alibi when the police came calling. But the interest on the debt...

Well, that was a different story.

Devlin knew perfectly well that this murder was payback for Devlin killing Anna. And, in the process, saving Ellie.

That was the key. Tracy had died for no reason other than to get Devlin's attention, and that loss weighed heavy on his shoulders.

As far as Blackstone was concerned, the real blow was yet to come. Ellie's death would be the ultimate payback. The interest owed.

Devlin didn't intend to pay that price. Not now. Not ever.

Ellie's hand on his sleeve pulled him from his thoughts. "It's Brandy," she said, indicating her phone, the screen lit up with a text. "She wants an update. On us and Lamar. And an ETA."

"Right." He pressed his fingertips to his temples, trying to push back the threatening ache. They'd come straight from the airport to Tracy's condo, and poor Brandy, Ellie's best friend and roommate, had been left to wait at home without a clue what was going on in this room. "Shit, she must be out of her mind. Tell her we'll be there soon. All of us."

Ellie's brow furrowed as she glanced toward Lamar.

"All of us," Devlin confirmed. "Whether he wants to or not. He shouldn't be alone tonight."

"Good." She kissed his cheek, and for that one fleeting moment, he felt like a hero. Then it faded, and he just felt impotent.

"I'm going to go talk to the Chief," she continued. "Then we should get out of here and let the team do its job."

He nodded, glancing over to where Chief Randall stood talking with a tall, lanky man who Devlin recognized as the District Attorney. Good. Maybe Ellie would get some useful information. As her former guardian, Randall would speak freely around her. And Devlin was happy to take information any way he could get it.

As he watched Ellie, Lamar rose and came to stand by his side.

"You know that his real target is Ellie." Lamar's voice was rough, the emotion he was holding back acting like sandpaper against his words.

"I know." Devlin closed his eyes and took a breath before continuing. "He killed Tracy to get both our attention. But Ellie is the prize."

"He wants to hurt you," Lamar said. "I'm just collateral damage."

"I know. I'm sorry."

"She's worked that out, too, of course."

"She hasn't said so. But you're right." Ellie was no fool. She'd grown up around cops, worn the uniform herself, and had a degree in criminology. A good percentage of her articles now that she was a reporter dealt with crime and law enforcement. She knew the score as well as either Devlin or Lamar.

"She also knows that he may not go straight for her. Why end the game before you've mined all the pain?"

"Detective..." Devlin let his voice trail off. He knew all this, of course. And Lamar had to know that Devlin understood the score. Talking about it now, in the same hallway that still had the chalk mark from Tracy's body—

"It helps," Lamar said dully, as if he'd heard every one of

Devlin's thoughts. "Thinking out loud. Working the case. Weighing how things might go next."

Devlin hesitated, then said slowly, "You may be right. He might not go for Ellie right away. And damn him for going after anyone but me. I'm the one he wants to hurt."

"It's just a theory. The other side of it is that he doesn't want to get caught. And he has to know that the more he rattles your cage, the more he exposes himself. More likely he *wishes* he could lay a line of dead women at your feet. But in practice, he'll just focus on cutting you deep."

"By getting at me through Ellie. She's the interest still owed."

"Sure. Because you don't hurt if you're dead, right? He won't kill you. He wants to *hurt* you. Killing Ellie will do that." Lamar's voice was flat, his eyes toward the doorway. The chalk. The tag indicating the bullet's entry into the wall. The blood splatter.

"Lamar—"

The detective's eyes cut to him, dark with pain. "What?"

"I—she was a good woman."

"Yeah, she was."

"I didn't know her as well as I should have."

"She admired you," Lamar said. "Loved working at the foundation. She believed in what you do. Don't stop," he added, something in his tone making Devlin's back straighten.

"I wouldn't," he said casually. Surely, *surely*, Lamar didn't know about Saint's Angels. He'd told Ellie that she could discuss anything with Lamar and Brandy, but if she'd revealed a secret as volatile as that, then she would have told Devlin. Wouldn't she?

It wasn't a question he couldn't get an answer to right then, so he stayed silent as the detective continued.

"How sure are you that this is Blackstone?" Lamar asked.

"As sure as I can be, but until there's proof, it's just a theory."

"But can you prove it?"

Devlin tilted his head. "Isn't that what the police are for?"

Lamar's throat moved as he swallowed, and he didn't quite meet Devlin's eyes. "You have resources, Saint. I know you do."

Devlin forced himself not to react, but his body went cold. *He did know.*

"I know your foundation participates in rescues. Works closely with investigators. That kind of thing."

Relief flooded Devlin. "That's true. There's a timing factor to a lot of what we do. Not the kind of thing we want to farm out when even ten minutes can make a huge difference."

"That's what I figured. And maybe you're not supposed to use those resources privately. I don't know. But what I do know is that you *will* use them. Because this is Ellie we're talking about."

Lamar wasn't wrong. And Devlin would use a hell of a lot more than that to find his answers. "Go on."

"I want to know what you know. I want your help. Your resources."

"You'll have them."

"Good. Because Blackstone is mine."

Devlin studied him. "That's not you, Lamar."

To his credit, Lamar didn't pretend to misunderstand. "Maybe it is."

Devlin considered his words. Maybe it was ... and maybe one day Lamar would end up as one of Saint's Angels. God knew he'd be an asset. But if he ever walked that path, it wouldn't be because he'd taken that first step in rage.

"Come back with me and Ellie," he said gently. "I'm sure Brandy wants to see you, and you need to be with friends."

"Saint..."

"We can't bring her back ... but we will make him suffer. I promise you that."

Lamar drew a breath, then shoved his hands in his pants pockets. "Take Ellie home. I need to talk to the team. I'm working this case. Wild horses couldn't drag me off this case."

"I believe you. But you don't need to be working it tonight."

"I'm only going to stay a bit longer."

"Lamar. Ellie's worried." It was a Hail Mary play, but it worked. The detective's shoulders slumped and he nodded.

"I'll be right behind you. I swear."

"You shouldn't be driving."

"I'll have a black and white bring me by."

"Your word?"

He inclined his head. "Less than an hour."

"All right, then," Devlin said, wishing he could erase the man's pain. He and the detective had bumped heads more than once, but they were solid now. Even if they weren't, no one should have to go through this. "Hurry, though. We'll be waiting."

CHAPTER FOURTEEN

"Oh, God." Brandy throws her arms around me the moment we walk in the door. "I can't believe it." She pulls back and wipes her nose as she aims red and puffy eyes at Devlin. "I'm so sorry. Tracy was awesome and fun and—and I can't believe this is real."

"I know," Devlin says, pulling her into a hug. "Me either." He pushes her back gently, and I watch as he studies her face. "Are you okay?"

She nods, then runs her fingers through her shoulder-length blond hair, looking as lost as I feel. "I don't know."

I frown, as I glance around. "Where's Christopher? You said he was with you." I'd felt horrible leaving Brandy alone, but she'd assured me that Christopher had been with her since they learned of the murder, and they'd been holding each other together. "Did he take Jake for a walk?" I look around for the ancient and lovable Labrador mix who usually greets me with a wagging tail and crotch sniffing.

"Jake's in his crate. I was about to let him out when you pulled up. And Christopher was here when you called, really. He's been great. But he left a few minutes ago."

I frown. "Why?"

Her cheeks flush. "He said he had to take care of some stuff."

I narrow my eyes because she's not telling us everything. "And?"

Her shoulders sag as she looks from me to Devlin. "It's just—you know. I think he still feels awkward. I mean, he and Anna were pretty good friends, and then she turns out to be a psycho. And add to that his half-brother and those security leaks ... I mean, you made him nervous before. Now he'll probably be a basket case."

Devlin's bisected brow rises. "I made him nervous?"

Brandy tilts her head. "Duh. You're you. You make everyone nervous."

I'm not sure whether to laugh or cry, but I appreciate that there's room today for even a tiny bit of humor and teasing.

Brandy catches my eye and we share a smile.

Then Devlin ushers us toward the living room, and I know that Brandy's smile is about to fade. "Listen, Brandy," he says as we all sit. "I'm afraid he's going to feel more awkward soon. Joseph Blackstone is our primary suspect."

Her hand goes to her mouth and she shakes her head. "Wait—what?" She looks to me, and I reach out for her hand. She clutches mine, so tight it's painful, but I bite the inside of my cheek and bear it. "You're saying this wasn't random?"

"I'm afraid so," Devlin says.

"But—but I don't understand."

I gently extricate my hand. "Let me get you some green tea, okay? Devlin can fill you in on everything."

She nods and I move to the adjacent kitchen area. I need to do something if I'm going to survive hearing the whole thing all over again, and I put on water to boil for tea and coffee as I listen to Devlin fill her in on all the horrible, gory details.

We end, of course, back where we started, with Joseph Blackstone as the primary suspect. Only now she knows that I'm in the crosshairs, too.

"No," she says, shaking her head. "No, this can't be happening." She scrubs her hands over her face. "I mean, it *is* happening. I get that. But going after you?" she says to me, "that's sick."

"That's how my father trained him," Devlin says, his voice flat.

"But it's vile. He shouldn't be going after anyone at all, but if it's revenge for Anna he's looking for, then it's not Ellie he should be going after. Ellie didn't do anything. It should be—"

She cuts her words off fast.

"Me," Devlin says. "This is all happening because of me."

"No, wait. No." The words tumble from Brandy. "I didn't mean it like that. I wasn't saying—"

"It's okay." He's in a chair opposite hers, and he moves to perch on the table in front of her, then takes her hands. "I understand. And honestly, you're not wrong."

"But—"

"Brandy," he says firmly. "It's okay."

Her eyes cut to me, and I nod. Slowly, she exhales. In his crate near the pantry, Jake whimpers. I open the door, and he licks my hand, then goes to Brandy and curls up on the sofa beside her, as if he knows she needs him.

"This is so fucked up," she says as Jake rests his head on her thigh and she strokes his fur. She's got that right, but hearing Brandy curse drives the truth home even more.

"It is," Devlin agrees. "On so many levels." He drags his fingers through his hair, looking so miserable I want to race around the kitchen island and wrap my arms around him. "I didn't see it coming." His voice is low and tinged with pain. "I've always believed myself to be a good judge of people. But I never saw Anna's duplicity coming. And now we're picking up the shards of my mistake."

"You trusted her," Brandy says. "She was close to you."

He makes a scoffing sound. "Trust her? Yeah, I did. That was the mistake."

"No," I say, this time coming toward him. "You have to trust people." I kneel in front of him, my hands on his knees, and look at his face, so dark now with misery. "You have to," I repeat. "After all, without trust, we wouldn't be back together."

For a moment, he doesn't react. Then he nods slowly and strokes my hair, his eyes hard on mine.

"It's not your fault," Brandy says softly. "She really did love you. It just all went sideways for her. She was messed up, but that's not on you."

"No," he agrees. "It's not. But it still hurts."

"I get that," she says as I stand. The electric kettle is beeping, and I go back to get her water and the coffees for me and Devlin.

"I should probably call Christopher," Brandy says. "He was a mess about the murder in general, and he probably knows about Joseph by now—he's got his research sources in the LCPD. I hate that he's alone."

"You should tell him to come back," I say, setting down a tray with our drinks before taking a seat on the arm of Devlin's chair.

"Yes," Devlin says. "Let him know that there's no blowback on him. We're not painting him with the same brush as his brother. Believe me, I know what it's like to be judged by the actions of a family member."

"I guess you do," Brandy says. "I'm really sorry about that. I saw the coverage." She makes a face. "Hard to avoid since it's all over social media. And to have that tossed at you on what was supposed to be such an amazing day. It sucks."

"I'll survive," Devlin says. "So will Christopher."

She pulls her feet up and hugs her knees to her chest. "Yeah. I hope so." I'm trying to think what to say, when she continues. "How's Lamar?"

"It's hard," I say as Devlin puts an arm around my shoulder. "But he's hanging in there."

"And he's really coming here? You texted that he's staying the night, too, but where is he?"

"On his way," Devlin says. "He promised."

I grimace, not entirely sure he'll keep that promise. "He lives in Tracy's building," I point out. "Easy enough for him to change his mind and simply go crash in his own unit."

"Then we'll go there," Brandy says firmly. "He shouldn't be alone."

"No, he shouldn't," Devlin said. "But he gave me his word. Let's give him a few more minutes before we call to check on him."

"Will he be allowed to work the case?" Brandy asks. "For that matter, should he?"

"He will," I tell her. "I asked the Chief about that. We both think it'll help him with closure. I hope we're right."

"Good," she says. "And he can stay here as long as he wants. We can put him in your room. Honestly, I'll be glad for the company. Not trying to guilt you, but I miss having you around."

The house is a two-story with three bedrooms, the master taking up the entire upstairs. Brandy has a sweet deal in that she essentially has the place to herself in exchange for minimal rent and basic housekeeping tasks. The owner—who she calls Mr. Big Shot—is away except for a few weeks out of every year, so when I got the Laguna Cortez assignment, I'd bunked in the guest room, and it was almost like we were college roomies again.

Technically, I haven't moved out, but I spend most nights at Devlin's. Eventually, of course, I expect to move in with Devlin. But what with him killing my uncle, running away, and then turning into an entirely different person, we missed out on a lot of basic dating moments. And the truth is, I want that. Meeting for coffee. Going to the movies. Staying over at each other's places.

Silly, maybe, but it's important to me, and I'm lucky enough to be in love with a man who understands that.

"I miss you, too," I say. "And Devlin and I are going to stay here, to." We hadn't talked about it, but Devlin nods. "So Lamar can take the master," I add.

Brandy makes a face. "I've never let anyone use the master. I suppose I could—Big Shot never said not to—but it feels weird. And, honestly, it's fine. If Lamar's here, it's all good. Go on to Devlin's, and you two can bound around naked without worrying about getting caught."

Devlin squeezes my hip. "See? I told you we should be bounding. She never takes advantage of opportunities," he adds to Brandy, making her laugh. "But despite the allure of chasing Ellie naked around the house, we are staying here for the time being. Give Lamar the master suite. You have the run of the place, right? So I can't imagine your boss would mind. And, honestly, I'll feel better having both of you in my sight."

"You're sure?"

He nods. "Absolutely."

"Okay. But you two take upstairs. It's got a king bed, and it just feels more fair."

"And Lamar can have my room," I say. "Done."

"Slumber party," Brandy says with a grin. The humor fades quickly, though, and she draws a deep breath. "God. Poor Lamar." She blinks. "Poor Tracy." A tear escapes, and she grimaces. "Sorry. It just sort of hits me, you know?"

"I know," I say. "Me, too."

"I'm am truly sorry about all of this," Devlin says.

"Sorry? We've already established that it's not your fault. And you two are the ones he's targeting."

"But he started with Tracy," Devlin says gravely. He reaches over and takes her hand. "Not Ellie, who he knew would truly wreck me." He closes his eyes, draws a breath, then goes on. "He might be working his way down a list. It's a long shot—Lamar and I both think he won't run the risk of getting caught by taking his time that way—but I want you to stay diligent."

"I don't know what—" Her eyes dart to me and then back to Devlin. "*Oh.*"

"Like I said, I'm sorry."

"Be diligent about setting the alarm," I say.

"And they're assigning an officer to watch the house."

Her brow furrows. "How worried do I need to be?"

Devlin takes one of her hands. "Not worried. Diligent. Okay?"

"Yeah. Yeah, right." She nods, reassuring herself. "Just precautions."

"We're working on neutralizing the threat," he says, and Brandy snickers.

Devlin and I exchange glances. "Not the reaction I was expecting," Devlin says.

"It's just that I feel better hearing you say that. Sounds very in command and serious."

"In that case, I'll batten down the hatches, too," he promises, making her laugh outright. "Seriously, this is priority. Hopefully, we'll have Blackstone charged and in custody soon. You're not a glaring target, but we'll take the potential seriously. Hopefully, the threat will be short term."

"I get it. I don't like it, but I get it." She bites her lower lip.

"What?" I ask.

"Is it okay if—I mean, if he doesn't feel too awkward—if Christopher stays here with us? The place will be crowded, so maybe not all the time, but—"

"Are you kidding? Of course, that's fine with us." I probably sound too eager, but at the time we'd left for New York, they'd slept together, but everything was still very new. If they're close enough that she wants him her to help her through all this, then I suppose everything is going well on the relationship front. Which, considering all of Brandy's hesitations and issues, is absolutely terrific news.

And, yeah, I'm nosy enough to want to get a better sense of who my best friend is dating. Especially considering who his half-brother is.

I frown, immediately chastising myself for letting my thoughts go that direction. Like Devlin had already pointed out, it was unfair of me to paint him with the same brush as his brother.

"Devlin?" Brandy asks, as if where Christopher sleeps is up to him.

"That's your call," he tells her. "And like I said, the goal is for this investigation to happen fast. Get proof, get Blackstone, get this thing wrapped up." He's outlining what Saint's Angels will do, of course, but Brandy doesn't know that. I assume that she believes he's consulting with the police. Or simply being the powerful local citizen he is and stepping up to the plate. God knows he could buy an army of private investigators.

Whatever Brandy thinks, though, the ultimate goal is to find Blackstone and confirm that he's guilty.

And then, as Devlin said, they'll neutralize the threat.

And, I think, that's another reason for Christopher to stay here. Good relationship or not, it will be weird when his brother is arrested. If nothing else, Brandy will want to be around to console him.

I draw a breath, that word lingering in my mind.

Neutralize.

Such plain language for a not very plain deed.

Even a day or so ago, that might have been something I would take Devlin to task for. Not today. Not when stopping Blackstone's vendetta could save lives, my own included.

I blink, realizing I've been lost in my own thoughts, only to find Devlin's looking at me. "What?" I ask.

I see the smile in his eye and am certain he can read my thoughts. I scowl a little as the smile spreads to his lips. "I love you," he says. "That's all."

Brandy presses a hand over her heart and looks about as melty as I feel. "We're all going to be fine," she says, because Brandy always looks on the sunny side of things. "And I promise I'll be careful. I have a ton of work I can do here, so I'll just mostly stay inside."

"A plan," I say, then jump as the doorbell rings.

Brandy gets up to answer it even as Devlin calls out, "Camera!"

"Right, right." She snatches up her phone, looks at the security feed, and smiles at me. "Lamar."

CHAPTER FIFTEEN

"You're here," Brandy says, throwing her arms around Lamar, as tears roll down her cheeks. "I'm so, so sorry about Tracy,"

Lamar clings to her, holding her tight, as if he's afraid of losing her, too. I hurry over and join them, losing myself in this embrace with my two best friends. Behind us, I hear Jake whine, and Lamar actually laughs.

"It's hard," he says. "It's harder now. In her apartment, at least I could tell myself I was working, block it all away. Here though..."

"I know," Brandy says. "But we all understand, and it's better here than by yourself."

He takes her hand and their fingers twine together. Finally, he looks between the two of us and over my head at Devlin. "Yeah. It's better to be here with you guys. Family, right?"

I meet Brandy's eyes, and look back at Devlin, holding my hand out for him. He joins us. "Yes," he says. "Family," and I know he means it. For Devlin more than anyone, family is who you choose, not what you're born into.

Jake bends his front paws down to the ground and whines a little until Lamar drops to his knees and scratches him, accepting big sloppy dog kisses that make him laugh. It lightens the mood a bit, and I'm grateful to the silly dog.

Brandy steps back, released from the tight knit of our embrace. She looks slightly at loose ends as she glances among us. "Um, so do you want coffee? A drink?"

Lamar shakes his head. "I'm not avoiding you, I promise. But I'm exhausted." He'd stepped inside with a bag, and now he bends to pick it up again. "I brought a few things. If you don't mind, right now I need sleep. And I think I need to be alone."

"Whatever you need," I tell him. "You're taking my room. Devlin and I will go upstairs." Lamar shoots a sideways glance at Brandy. "Look at you becoming a risk-taker. Letting someone else sleep upstairs."

She rolls her eyes, but I know that's exactly what she's thinking.

As Lamar heads toward the room, he pauses, then turns back to look to Devlin. "You meant what you said? You'll tell me? Whatever you learn, right?"

Devlin nods. "Of course. And hopefully there'll be reciprocity?"

Lamar's gaze is hard as he meets Devlin's eyes. "Even if I have to share off-book, I will. I'll cut corners if I have to. I want to nail whoever did this to Tracy."

He doesn't meet my eyes as he turns and goes to the bedroom, but I stand in shock looking after him for a moment. Lamar is the most straight-laced cop I know. Tracy's death has hit him hard, but I'm surprised that he's willing to share investigative information that might otherwise be confidential.

"It matters to him," Devlin says, when I raise my brows in question. And that, I think, is the bottom line.

As Brandy follows him to make sure that he's got clean sheets and towels, I turn to Devlin. "Did you tell him about Saint's Angels?"

"No. But he knows about the foundation, and he knows we have an investigative arm. He made assumptions, and I rolled with it."

That makes sense. Lamar might be willing to cut some corners to take down Tracy's killer, but I don't know that he'd be completely on board with an organization like Saint's Angels. That's not the kind of cop he is.

But at the same time, I'm learning that reality shifts all the time. What you once thought you would never be able to do, becomes easier and easier when people you love are in danger. And after that, it's a slippery slope to helping anyone who's in a dark path. Whether you know them or not, you still want to save them. That's how Devlin's been thinking for years, wanting to push all of the people he could out of his father's dark path, and now making up for lost time for what he could never manage as a child.

When Brandy comes back, we say our goodnights, too.

It's been a hell of a day, and thought I just want to retreat upstairs, I hate leaving her alone.

She shakes her head and swears it's fine. "I'm taking Jake to bed with me," she says. "He usually sleeps in his crate, and he'll think it's an incredible treat. And the truth is, I'm completely wiped out. I've never felt so emotionally empty. Unless Jake keeps me awake, I'm pretty sure I'm going to be asleep within minutes."

"Yeah, I get it." We hug, and I hear her stuttered intake of breath, like the precursors of tears that don't quite come.

We're all feeling broken, I think as we head upstairs. And Devlin most of all.

I'm not sure what I'm expecting, but it's not the rough way that he grabs my arm and pulls me to him, capturing my mouth with his, his hands twined in my hair as he tilts my head back, kissing me with such wild intensity that or teeth clash and I taste blood.

He's breathing hard when he pushes me away. "Dammit, El," he begins. "I shouldn't—"

I grab his collar and pull him close again. "Yes," I say. "You should." My body feels hot and cold all at the same time, and I know he's just flipped a switch inside of me. I'd turned everything inside me off in order to get through the last twenty-four hours. Neither one of has really slept, not even on the plane, and the horror of Tracy's death and the circumstances have been chipping away at both of us. I need release. I need oblivion. I need to feel something other than this numb, painful horror.

I need Devlin. And I know that he needs me, too.

"It's eating at me," he says, backing away from me and running his fingers through his hair. He takes off his glasses and tosses them onto the bedside table, then rubs his hands over his face as if in exhaustion.

And he *is* exhausted. His face is pale, making the scar that cuts down the right side of his face stand out. "I need you," he says. "I need to dial this in."

I nod. I need him, too. More than that, I understand what he's saying. These last few days, the world has been unraveling around us. Around *him*. A man used to being in control. Used to pushing buttons and making things happen behind the scenes. A man used to saving people, not losing them. Control has slipped from his grasp, and more than anything he needs to get it back. He will, I know. Of course, he will. But he needs it now, and the world isn't bending to his will.

But me...

I'll bend, and willingly, too. Because I need it as much as he does. He needs to push the limits of control? Well, I need to push the danger.

I draw a breath and step closer, my heart pounding in my chest, my skin tingling with need. I start to speak, but I don't get the chance. He takes my wrist and pulls me to him, then twists it behind me so that I'm pressed up against him, unable to move.

"I need it hard," he says, his body pressing against mine and his erection underscoring the words. "Tell me to stop now if you want, because once I have you in that bed, I'm not stopping for anything."

"Don't you dare stop," I say, then cry out when he grabs the waistband of the leggings I'm wearing and rips them right down the seam. He tumbles me back onto the bed, then tugs the remnants of the leggings off me. "Over," he says, using his hands to indicate that he wants me on my stomach.

I do as he says, my body flat on the bed. My head is turned, and I can see him in my periphery as he undresses, then joins me on the bed. He straddles my legs, his hands on my back. He brushes my hair away, then kisses the back of my neck as his hands slip between me and the mattress to cup my breasts as his cock teases my ass.

Slowly—so deliciously slowly, he kisses his way down my spine, then urges me onto my knees. I'm nothing but greed and sensation now, and I cry out in surprised delight when he smacks my ass, not once, but twice. And then, when he slips his hand between my legs and eases his fingers inside me, I close my eyes and arch back, desperate for more, for everything.

"Christ, I need you," he whispers, then traces his fingertip from my clit all the way to my ass. I bite my lip as he teases me there, then suck in a gasp when he slips his fingertip past the tight muscle as he eases forward to whisper in my ear, "Do you remember what I said."

I moan, my body firing with need as he reaches over me for the lube we've left on the bedside table.

"My fingers in your pussy, my cock in your ass." The words are raw. Graphic. And a huge fucking turn on.

"Yes," I say, realizing I'm rocking in anticipation. I want this. There's nothing I don't want with Devlin, and tonight, I know we both need it. I need complete surrender. And so does he. He plays with me at first, teasing and touching. His fingers on my clit, his cock hard against my rear. And then, when I'm ready to beg, he thrusts his fingers inside me at the same time that his cock edges inside me, more pressure than pain, but a wonderfully sensual bite all the same.

He plays me both ways in a rhythm that drives me to the edge and back but never quite takes me over. He's relentless, and I'm floating on the edge, not sure how I'm going to survive this pleasure when the release never seems to come.

Then what seems like, hours later—and yet all too soon—I feel his body stiffen, and then I know that I have to go with him. I have to explode in his arms. I have to lose control with him, because that is what this is all about. Us and control and trust and passion.

Passion, I think as my body turns to starbursts, as he cries out my name and fills me, as I collapse onto the mattress, buried beneath the weight of his body, feeling wonderfully used and completely loved.

We stay that way until the world rights itself, then get cleaned up before sliding back into bed, this time beneath the covers. He holds me close, and for the first time since yesterday, our bodies are drained of tension.

I close my eyes, letting sleep come to claim me, but

Devlin's voice in my ear pulls me back, and I blink in confusion as he whispers, "Thank you."

"For what?" I ask.

"For loving me, El," he says. "Just for loving me."

CHAPTER SIXTEEN

I wake at half-past seven to an empty bed and the smell of frying bacon. Since I hadn't thought to grab clothes from the room Lamar's now occupying, I tug on the t-shirt I'd worn yesterday and my underwear, then head downstairs. Everyone in the house has seen me in less, including Lamar, and I don't feel right borrowing the robe that hangs behind Mr. Big Shot's bathroom door.

Devlin's already fully dressed in what he wore yesterday, and his eyes skim over me as I enter the kitchen, sending a tremor of heat up my spine the same way the touch of his fingers had last night.

"You look very casual," he says as Brandy glances my way, then laughs.

"Admit it," she says. "You're just trying to get a rise out of our Mr. Saint."

"A rise?" I flash Devlin a seductive grin. "That's always a good thing."

He clears his throat. "While I understand the concept of *just friends*, do me a favor and cover that very sweet ass before Lamar wakes up and comes out here."

I shake my head. "After the day he had? He's going to sleep until at least noon. Trust me." I wiggle my ass, simply because I'm enjoying the feel of this lighter mood. I know it can't last, but I want to squeeze out all the moments I can. "Unless you have an issue with the outfit?" I add, raising a brow as I look at Devlin.

"For in-home loungewear when other men aren't around, I have no problem. Suggest we go out to lunch like that, and we'll have a chat."

I smirk, then brush a kiss across his cheek before heading behind the counter to pour a cup of coffee and snag a muffin and a piece of bacon from the paper-towel covered plate.

"Hey," Brandy says, swatting my hand as I dance away, almost spilling my coffee.

I take my score of bacon and settle in at the counter next to Devlin. "This is great," I say, holding up a strip of bacon. "Lamar may regret sleeping in after all."

"Oh, he's already gone," Brandy says. "Said he's eager to get to it."

I shoot her a *what the fuck* look, but she just shrugs.

"What?" she protests. "I was having fun listening to you two bicker."

"Banter," Devlin corrects. "We don't bicker."

I take another bite of my bacon. "Sometimes we do," I say. "But only because we can make up after."

"A definite perk," Devlin says.

"You guys are too freaking adorable," Brandy says. "Which remind me—because Christopher is adorable, too—I talked to him last night."

"Oh, good," I say, the relief so palpable I can feel it flow through me. "Did you tell him what we said? Not painting him with his brother's brush and all that?"

She nods, and her smile telegraphs her answer before she

speaks. "He says he really appreciates hearing that, and he'll definitely come over today. But he said he wasn't going to spend the night." Her cheeks flush. "But that's not because of you guys."

"Oh, isn't it?" I trill.

One of her shoulders rises in time with her brightening smile. "He says he knows I don't want to move too fast, and he's afraid if we're sharing a bed we will."

I sigh and press my hand over my heart.

"Interesting," Devlin says, clearly fighting a smile.

"What?" Brandy asks.

"Ellie's reaction." He turns to me. "I didn't realize restraint was so romantic. I'll make a note."

"Don't you dare. And as for you," I say, turning back to Brandy, "Good news all around."

"I think so. And, oh," she adds to Devlin, "he said he was going to the foundation this morning. More research. But he also said he could do some internet research here if I'd rather." She worries her lower lip a bit before continuing. "I know the sources are better at the foundation, but should I ask him to come here? I mean, I'll lock the doors and everything once you two leave, but—"

"If you want him here, ask him here. But I have security on the house already, so you don't need to worry about being here alone."

"Right." She quirks a half-smile in my direction. "I really should have guessed that."

"That's my guy," I say, then kiss his cheek. "But keep the doors locked and the alarm on anyway," I tell her. "Just in case."

"She loves me, but she impugns my resources. It's a sad world. She's right about all that," Devlin adds. "But it's a sad world."

"I'll cheer you up later," I counter, making him laugh.

"Speaking of the foundation," Devlin says, "I scheduled a meeting for nine. Sources to help with the investigation." He glances at me. "Can you get dressed that quick?"

"Oh." It's the first I've heard of it, but since I'm assuming that *sources* means *Saint's Angels*, there is no way I'm missing out. "Absolutely," I assure him, entirely dropping my teasing tone. I point to Brandy. "Save me a muffin for later," I beg, then take my coffee with me to my old room for a quick shower and to change. I debate casual or professional, then settle on nice jeans, a pair of last year's Manolos, and a plain white tank top under a blazer.

Devlin is still in what he wore yesterday, but he still looks completely pulled together as we say goodbye to Brandy and head out into the world.

"Who are we meeting with?" I ask as we pull into the parking lot for the Devlin Saint Foundation. It's a stunning building, with clean lines and lots of glass that looks out on the Pacific. Designed by "starchitect" Jackson Steele, Damien Stark's half-brother, it's in the ultra-contemporary style that helped make Jackson Steele's name. But even so, it fits into the landscape, complementing the beach-side lot on the Pacific Coast Highway in a way that some of the newer restaurants and hotels can't seem to manage.

We arrive in Devlin's Tesla, and I feel a pang of loss for Shelby, my beloved 1965 Shelby Cobra.

"You okay?"

Devlin is still behind the wheel, his attention on me. I shrug in response, and he gives me a gentle smile. "He's good at what he does. Don't write Shelby off yet."

"It's like you know me," I say, melting a little as I feel that connection spark between us. "And I love that you do."

He leans over to kiss me before we get out and head into

the office. The receptionist, Eric, looks up, his smile faltering slightly before he plasters it back on. It's then that I realize this is the first time Devlin's been back on his own turf since the press outed him as The Wolf's son.

"Good morning, Eric," Devlin says. "And don't worry. I promise you won't say something and step in it."

The younger man winces a little. "Sorry, Mr. Saint. I mean, sorry for not knowing what to say. I wasn't sure if you wanted anyone to know."

Now, Devlin's smile is one of amusement. "As it happens, that choice was taken from me. But to be more specific, I have no problem with you knowing the story of my past, so long as you—and everyone here at the DSF—also understands that I had no choice in who fathered me. But I did choose to leave."

"Yes, sir," Eric says. "That must have been—well, that must have been hard."

"It was. But growing an organization like this and bringing in good people like you has made the journey easier. You have a good day, Eric."

"Oh, yes, sir. Thanks, Mr. Saint."

"You handled that well," I say when we're in the elevator.

"I should have said something much earlier. That oversight's on me."

"You haven't been here, and it was the weekend."

"Under the circumstances, the weekend is no excuse. And believe it or not, my team is remarkably adept at video-conferencing. What with being a cutting edge organization."

I roll my eyes as the doors open on the fourth floor. "Fair enough," I say. "Better late than never?"

"That's what I'm thinking. Tamra," he continues, and I realize that Tamra is sitting at the desk outside his office. "Can you schedule in time for me today to address the staff?"

"Of course. And good morning, Ellie. How are you doing?"

"Still a bit unsteady," I admit. "Seeing you at this desk..." I trail off as she nods.

"I know. First Anna, now Tracy. On the whole, this desk doesn't have the best history."

"It's a goddamn tragedy, but it's not a self-fulfilling prophecy," Devlin snaps.

"Of course not," Tamra says quickly. "I didn't mean—"

"No. Of course you didn't." He presses his fingers to his temple, then reaches out for me. I take his hand and squeeze, offering him my strength. "I'm sorry. I didn't—" He draws in a breath. "I didn't realize how on edge I am."

"Understandably," Tamra says. "And you should know that you don't have to worry about being yourself around me."

"I know," he says, "and I love you for it. I am sorry about the desk. Neither of us is superstitious, but why don't we order a new one. Start fresh with our new hire."

"Of course. And I've already called the agency. They'll start screening candidates to fill the position today."

"Thanks, Tamra."

"Of course." She nods to the double doors that lead to his office. "Penn and Claire are already inside," she adds. "Are you ready, or do you need a moment? I can tell them you were held up."

"No, it's fine. Ellie?"

I nod. I don't know either of them, but out here I feel the loss too potently. The times I laughed with Anna. Tracy's wide smile and eagerness to learn everything she could.

"All right then," Tamra says as she leans over to push the button to open the doors to his office. The huge wooden doors swing open automatically, and as always, I feel as if the motion should be accompanied by a rousing classical score.

But it's just doors, and I follow Devlin inside, curious to see who we're meeting.

Penn turns out to be Cory Pennfield and Claire is his wife, who both rise to greet us. Claire is tall and thin with a wide smile, and she pretty much towers over Penn who stands at least six inches shorter, with the stocky build of a wrestler. "So nice to meet you," Clair says, as we take our seats. Penn and Claire on the sofa with me in one of the chairs and Devlin perched on the arm, his hand resting on my shoulder.

"They've both worked with me for, what?" Devlin asks. "Over five years now?"

"Hard to believe we've put up with him so long," Claire says, aiming a grin my direction. "Fortunately, he's easy on the eyes, so that makes the assignments more palatable."

"You'll have to forgive my wife. Her favorite hobby is to flirt with Devlin."

"I keep trying to get a reaction," she says, laughing. "I've never managed." Her smile widens. "Now I see why. He's been waiting for the right woman to come along."

"I had to," Devlin says. "Penn would have beat the shit out of me if I'd fallen prey to your killer smile."

"Hey," I say, feigning indignation.

"Oh, and the little fact that I was in love with someone else." He takes my hand, then raises it to his lips and kisses it.

"All kidding aside," Claire says, "it's wonderful to finally meet you. Devlin's talked a lot about you over the years."

"I—" I turn to him, confused. "You have?"

"Penn's known me as long as Ronan has. Claire a bit less."

"Devlin and Penn served together," she said. "And I met Penn in a rather unconventional way."

"Oh," I say, surprised and pleased to know he'd talked about me back then. I pause, expecting her to elaborate on the story of how they met. She doesn't, though, and so I clear my throat and add, "So, um, Devlin sort of suggested you might have information about Tracy's murder. Or who leaked his identity?" I realize as I speak that I'm not exactly sure what he meant when he said "source" at breakfast.

"Claire and Penn are two of the original members of Saint's Angels, and they run the Midwestern operation. I've asked them to work on the investigation into Blackstone, especially since he's based in Chicago."

"Great," I say. "Have you learned anything so far?"

"We know he was here in Orange County for the past four days," Penn says. "At the moment, he's on a flight back to Illinois."

"And I know that he killed Tracy," Devlin adds. "But I'm not going forward without proof. My girlfriend has standards, after all."

"She does," I agree. "*Do* you have any proof yet?"

"We're making progress," Claire says. "Give us another twelve hours and we'll update."

I look between the three of them, impressed by how quickly the wheels have begun turning.

Devlin draws a breath and looks at each of them in turn. "I want to know where he goes when he lands. Home? His office? A safe house? Somewhere else entirely? I want confirmation he did this—either by his own hand or by an order. And I want eyes on him. His every move. As much intel and as soon as you can get it."

"Not our first rodeo," Claire says.

"Does Blackstone know about Saint's Angels?" I ask.

Devlin shakes his head. "Not as far as we know. Which gives us an advantage."

"And we're pulling in all North and Central America operatives who aren't in the middle of an active mission," Penn adds.

I say nothing, making sure my face doesn't reveal my surprise that this organization I assumed was a small collection of people is actually large enough and organized enough to have operations around the globe. Instead, I ask the question that has been bugging me the most. "Are you looking into his half-brother, Christopher? We don't think he's involved, especially since he testified against Joseph not that long ago. But I'd love additional confirmation."

"We were involved in the investigation after the incident with Anna," Penn says, making the whole thing seem far away and formal. "As of right now, we still have no indication that he was working with his brother. In fact, everything we've learned suggests that turning state's witness firmly sealed an already growing rift between the two. But we're keeping an open mind."

"Good," I say. I don't want him to be dirty, and I truly don't believe he'd hurt Brandy. But she's falling for him hard, and I want to make sure she has the truth.

"Ronan will be back tomorrow," Devlin says.

"He's in New York," I add with an ironic scowl. "Although, considering his stealthiness, I suppose he could be in that closet." I nod toward Devlin's coat closet as the three of them chuckle.

"Ronan told us about his midnight visit," Claire says. "He was sorry he didn't have time to stay and see you. He likes you, you know. Which is actually saying a lot. Ronan doesn't get close easily."

"Oh." I'm not sure what to say to that. When I'd first met him, Ronan had been hot and cold, and I'd even been convinced for a while that it was him who was gunning for me. Now, it's hard to even imagine having those suspicions. Even so, hearing that he'd actually missed seeing me is a surprise. And a pleasant one at that. "I'm looking forward to seeing him again, too," I admit. "I want his take on everything that's happened. He's sharp."

"He is," Penn says. "And we're already scheduled to meet with him in LA tonight. He's been fully briefed."

"And that's why I work with good people," Devlin says to me. "They're always on top of things."

"Looks that way." As always, I'm impressed by Devlin's operation. Just the fact that he runs this mini-universe amazes me, and it's so different from how I used to imagine my Alex as an adult.

At the same time, I can't picture the man I now know as anything but the powerful, commanding leader he is. It's a riddle, but the good kind.

"You're thinking very loud," Devlin says, as Penn and Claire exchange amused looks.

"Just reminiscing about the boy I knew, and how he grew up into the man you are."

"Now there's a conversation to have over drinks," Claire says, to which I eagerly agree. This is a woman I could see being friends with, and I'm already sad that she lives so far away.

"While you two focus on running the team, I'm going to put together a little press conference." He reaches forward to press the button on the intercom before the rest of us even have a chance to react. A moment later, Tamra enters.

"Think you can pull together an invite-only press conference coupled with cocktails and dessert for Thursday night? I know it's short notice, but I think the sooner the better."

I glance at Penn and Claire, both of whom look as clueless as me.

Tamra frowns. "Logistically? That's tight. I can manage. But Devlin, do you think that's wise? If you want to make a statement, you could go to any television station. You hardly have to throw a party."

Penn makes a scoffing noise. "What she means to say is, are you fucking insane?"

"I couldn't have said it better," I add. "Have we not been talking nonstop about the target on your back ever since that press bomb dropped?"

"An extremely limited guest list. Keep it under seventy-five. Reporters we've worked with over the years. Foundation supporters we know personally. Tight security. Metal detectors at the doors. There are things I want to say, and I need a worldwide audience to say them to. I've never given a formal press conference from the foundation without it being in conjunction with an event, even a small one, and I don't intend to let Joseph Blackstone—or whoever—force me into changing that tradition entirely. And I sure as hell don't want it to look like I'm altering my pattern because I'm running scared."

He pauses, then looks at each of us in turn. "I'm not going into hiding," he says. "But at the same time, this is low risk. Controlled. And the reward outweighs the risk."

"Are you sure?" I ask.

"Absolutely."

I nod. "All right. Not that I have a say, but if you're sure, I'm okay with it."

"Thank you," he says. "And you're wrong. They don't have a say," he says, looking at the other three in the room. "You do."

"Thanks a lot," Claire says, easing the moment considerably.

"I'll get on it right away and send you a draft," Tamra assures him. "You'll send me any additional thoughts you have and your edits? And some language for the press release and invitation? Also, your presentation to the staff is set for fifteen minutes from now."

"Perfect. I'll take care of all of that today. Anything that needs tweaking we can handle while I'm in the air tomorrow morning."

"The air?" I mentally play back the conversation, wondering what I missed.

"I have someone to visit tomorrow," he tells. "You and I are heading to Idaho."

CHAPTER SEVENTEEN

I watch as the Idaho countryside passes by the window of our pick-up truck. We'd come in one of Devlin's private charter jets, leaving early this morning, and landing about lunchtime at an emergency strip about three hours from our ultimate destination. Apparently Devlin knows the sheriff, and he authorized the landing and also lent us his personal truck.

Despite curling up in Devlin's arms last night, I didn't sleep well. How could I with so much uncertainty stirring around us? So of course I fell asleep on the six-hour flight, and waking up to the Idaho landscape was a bit surreal. That, and the fact that I still don't know why we're here. Devlin's been so busy talking to team members around the world and fielding calls from concerned contributors to the DSF that I didn't press when Devlin promised to fill me in on the details during the trip. All I know right now is that we're on our way to meet with an old friend.

"Right," Devlin says into his earpiece. He's on a call with the manager of a hotel he owns in London. Or, no. He ended that call. I have no idea who he's talking to now. "Well, I appreciate that. Yes, it makes a hell of a story. Exactly. I'll see you at the board meeting."

He reaches up and taps the single earpiece. The truck doesn't have Bluetooth, and he couldn't hear the calls on speaker. Since there's no one else for miles, driving with a single earpiece in didn't seem particularly risky. Especially not compared to Devlin's daily life.

"You need to stop taking calls," I tell him. "I get that you have business partners who need reassurance that you're not Satan reborn, but you're allowed some me time, too. And by *me time*, I mean *me*. Ellie. Your girlfriend wants a piece of you, too."

"Believe me, I want a piece of her as well. And you're right. That's it for today. Tamra can stack 'em and rack 'em for tomorrow."

"Is it that bad?" Now I feel guilty pulling him away from crisis management.

"Honestly, no. There've been a few who need hand holding, but most are genuinely sympathetic. My biggest challenge is to satisfy their curiosity without losing an entire day to a primer on what life was like growing up with The Wolf."

"I'm sorry." I slide closer, enjoying the benefits of a bench seat, and rest my hand on his thigh. "So tell me about this friend we're visiting."

"His name's Giatti. Marco Giatti. He's old now, and he keeps a low profile, but that means his ear's close to the ground."

"He's a source."

Devlin nods, then glances down at the map on his phone. He makes a sharp turn on an unmarked road.

"You think he knows the situation with Blackstone?"

"I don't know," Devlin says. "Hopefully he knows something." He turns to face me as our borrowed truck bounces over the rutted dirt road. "I brought you because I want you with me, always. But information has consequences. And depending on what I learn today—and what Claire and Penn and the rest of the team learn—it won't go well for Blackstone."

"*Won't go well for him?* Since when did you start dancing around the truth with euphemisms?"

"Fine. As soon as I've confirmed to my satisfaction that Blackstone either killed Tracy himself or hired the flunky who did, I'm going to take the bastard out. Do you like that better?"

"Yes," I say, my heart pounding as I say the words. "Yes, I'm fine with that. The way you phrased it and what it means."

His hands are at ten and two on the steering wheel, and I see his knuckles go white as he tightens his grip, then relaxes it. Slowly, he turns to look at me. Our eyes lock, and right then I think neither one of us would have even noticed if the truck went over a cliff, and we tumbled off into space. It's just the two of us and this huge revelation.

"Does this mean—" He drums his fingers on the steering wheel. "Does that mean you're okay with Saint's Angels now? I know we talked in New York, but I thought you were just rationalizing that we're serving justice. Finding a way in your heart to let you and me be together. But ... well, are you telling me now that you're genuinely okay with all of it?"

"No," I say automatically, but I'm not certain that answer is one hundred percent truthful.

"No," he repeats as I start to slide back to my side of the bench. He reaches out and puts a firm hand on my leg. "Then why?"

"Because it's you, okay? Because you're the one he's really after. And because I know your code. Your boundaries. But most of all, because there isn't a rule I wouldn't break where your safety is involved."

I expect him to call me out for hypocrisy, but all he does is silently take my hand, then quietly ask, "You're sure?"

"I am. I can't cross that line with you. But despite the life I've lived—or, I don't know, maybe because of it—I'm willing to let you go there."

A moment passes, then another. Then the truck hits a huge pothole, and we bounce. I cry out, just a little, and when the truck steadies again, I realize that he's taken my hand. I look down at our twined fingers, then up at his face.

He smiles. Just a tiny smile, but it says everything.

It says, *I love you.*

"Well, I guess you kept your promise." The man in the front porch rocker has sun-weathered skin, gray-white hair, and deep-set eyes so brown they look almost black. He watches as we climb the farmhouse's wooden porch steps, his eyes never leaving Devlin's face. An ashtray sits on the table beside him, a thin stream of smoke rising from a cigar.

"Did I?" Devlin asks, which doesn't give me a clue as to what promise the old man is talking about.

The man grunts, then lifts his chin, hooking it a bit so that he's pointing at me, almost as if his chin is another hand.

"Ellie," Devlin said. "She's with me."

"Seen your picture with him," he says. "You're Elsa Holmes. The Cinderella reporter swept off her feet by the billionaire philanthropist. You've given your competition some pretty nice sound bites."

"Always ready to help a colleague," I say dryly.

The man's mouth splits into a wide grin, showing off a set of blinding-white teeth. "I like her."

"So do I," Devlin says.

There's quiet after that, as if each is unsure what to say. So I figure *what the hell* and try to fill the yawning gorge of silence. "You have an advantage over me," I tell him. "Devlin hasn't told me anything but your name. And that you're an old friend."

His eyes cut to Devlin. "Is that what I am? Heh. Good to know. But then I have to wonder *whose* friend? Devlin, Alex, Alejandro. So hard to keep straight."

I glance sideways at Devlin, the pieces falling together. "You used to work for The Wolf."

"Clever woman."

"Not clever enough to read minds," I counter.

"Sorry," Devlin said. "I assumed you realized that."

"It's okay," I assure him, then turn back to Mr. Giatti. "You said Devlin kept his promise. What promise?"

The old man chuckles. "Alejandro swore he'd avenge his stepmother. I'd say he's come through on that promise. Didn't realize you were still alive after taking care of that. Glad to see you turned out to be a slippery eel instead of a dumbfuck kid with eyes bigger than his stomach." He grins again. "I was always rooting for you. Glad to see you won."

"Won?" Devlin asks. "It's hard to know. She's still dead. So are a lot of women by his hand who deserved a hell of a lot better. Men, too. Good people who just wanted a life out from under The Wolf's thumb."

"And did you come out here to clip me, too?"

I feel the increased pressure of Devlin's hand on my back, but that's his only reaction. "No," he says. The word is calm. Easy. And I realize that I've never witnessed Devlin like this before. He's walking a tricky line, playing it cool like he is. I trust Devlin's instincts, but for all we know, the guy could press a call button and a van full of armed commandoes could swoop in, demanding Devlin return what they lost and he gained when The Wolf died.

It's not a scenario I want to play out, and I study the man's face, looking for any sign that the affection for Devlin I hear in his voice reflects reality.

The man picks up the cigar, then takes a long puff, his eyes never leaving Devlin. He blows out the smoke slowly, then finally speaks. "Then why did you come? Helluva long way from your neck of the woods. And it sure don't look like you're selling Girl Scout Cookies"

Devlin removes his hand from my back, then twines his fingers with mine. "I came to tell you I'm sorry."

"For killing your old man? I'm not someone you need to be apologizing to. Would have done it myself if I'd had the cajones."

"Who says I killed the bastard?"

The corner of Mr. Giatti's mouth curls up. "Well, I guess it ain't you saying it, huh? I'm not wired. You should know me better than that."

"I know you. That's why I wanted to see you. You were one of the good ones. You're still one of the good ones."

"And you're the one that got away," Mr. Giatti says. "Disappeared right off the map. Turned into someone else."

"I'm still me."

The old man looks at Devlin's eyes. "Yeah. Guess you are at that. You don't have to apologize for leaving. Hell, I woulda bloodied your nose if you risked staying even a minute longer just for the sentimental crap. Don't you dare be sorry." He draws a breath, then licks dry, cracked lips. "You want to apologize, you do it for making me shed tears. I thought you were dead, boy."

"Sorry to disappoint." I see the grin twitch at the corner of Devlin's mouth.

"Ah, hell." The older man starts to laugh, but it turns into a phlegmy stutter. "Well, anyway, apology accepted. Now you want to tell me why you're really here?"

"Gossip," Devlin says flatly. "I hear things. And one thing I hear is that you're still paying attention. I want to know how much blowback I'm looking at."

"For being The Wolf's son, come back from the dead like a filthy rich Lazarus? Or for killing Anna Lindstrom?

Devlin grimaces. There'd never been any suggestion in the press coverage that Devlin Saint had done anything that night other than save the life of his girlfriend. Namely, me. But now that everyone knows that the blood of The Wolf flows in those veins, are folks going to try to rewrite history? Maybe suggest that there was something more nefarious going on than unrequited love and Anna's attempt to get rid of the competition.

It's a real possibility, and I listen eagerly for what Giatti has to say.

"Could be either," Mr. Giatti says. "But a lot of folks know Anna wasn't so stable where men were concerned. Never was as a girl, anyway. Can't imagine she changed much after moving off the compound."

"What about her father? Is he going to be sniffing around?"

Devlin and I have talked a lot about Anna since that night, and I know that her father and The Wolf were close. If he's still alive, he might well be inclined to search out and punish Devlin. Probably by killing me.

An eye for eye. As far as I'm concerned, that seems to be the theme of everyone who walks in this world.

Mr. Giatti looks directly at me as he answers Devlin.

"He's not a threat. Cancer got him. He's on his yacht with a nurse and an IV of morphine. You got no trouble from that direction."

"Then what direction should I be looking?"

"That's a hard question, Alejandro, and you damn well know it. You didn't take over Daddy-O's business, but you're living off his money."

"No. I'm not."

"Eh. Maybe. Maybe not. But it's still money they couldn't lay their hands on. But there's the man who killed their boss profiting off patricide, or at least it looks that way. Not a way to win friends. I'd have to say a lot of them would be pissed off."

Mr. Giatti shrugs. "Then again, a lot of them are dead. The ones who went on and tried to build up their own little fiefdoms? They all seem to be getting picked off. Either by in-fighting or hush-hush government operations, or by I don't know what."

He narrows his eyes at Devlin. "Don't suppose you know anything about that."

"I hear gossip. I read the news. But if you're asking what I think you're asking, then the answer is that I run a charitable foundation. I'm not in the business of hunting down criminals."

I force myself not to react, and wonder if Mr. Giatti also noticed the way Devlin sidestepped that question.

"Good news for me then," Mr. Giatti says, his expression as flat as his tone, and both unreadable.

"You really think someone is picking them off?"

"Yes. No. I don't know." He takes a sip from a beer can sitting beside the ashtray. "The ones still working ... well, it's a dangerous gig, isn't it? I've heard rumors about a few hits following some nasty operations. Brutal competition, pissed off law enforcement, man with a grudge. Who the hell knows?"

"It's impossible to tell," Devlin agrees. "You live that life, you piss off people."

"Did you?"

Devlin frowns. "What makes you think that's my life? You know I never wanted it."

"No, you never did. No matter what your daddy wanted, you stayed your own man. Saw that in you even when you were young." His eyes dart to me again before returning too Devlin. "Also saw a fire in you—you'll protect what's yours."

"Without the slightest hesitation," he agrees.

Now, Mr. Giatti turns his full attention on me. "So, Elsa Holmes, what's your agenda?"

I move closer to Devlin as his arm goes around my waist. "I don't have any agenda except Devlin."

Mr. Giatti nods, then shifts in his rocker until he can pull out his wallet. He opens it, takes out a photo, and hands it to Devlin, who steps away long enough to take it, then moves back to my side. It's a picture of a beautiful young woman with hair that looks to be from the seventies. "My Maria. Do you remember her? That picture's from before you were born, but she never looked a day older in her life."

"I remember."

"A good woman. Kept me steady." He reaches for the photo, and Devlin hands it back to him. Mr. Giatti takes it gently, as if it's both precious and fragile. To him, of course, it is.

"It's good to have a compass," he continues. "Your father never did. Thought a woman was nothing but a slash—pardon my French," he adds to me.

"My father was dead wrong about that."

"Yeah, he was." Mr. Giatti turns to look me straight in the eyes. "You make sure our Mr. Saint treats you right."

"He does. He always has."

"Always," he repeats, his mouth curving down into a frown. "You've known him awhile, then?"

I glance sideways at Devlin, but he's no help, so I just shrug and say, "Yeah. You could say that."

His eyes narrow. "Good God," he finally says. "*Holmes.* You're Peter's niece. Must be getting old not to have made that connection before. That man ... well, he thought you were the cat's whiskers."

My chest tightens with the words. My Uncle Peter did so many things wrong, but he took care of me, and he loved me. And it's nice to know that I'm not the only one who saw that. "Thank you," I whisper.

He narrows his eyes and cocks his head toward Devlin. "You two look good together. Like maybe between the two of you, you can find that compass and stay on the path."

"We can," I say. "We will."

Beside me, Devlin's fingers tighten their grip on mine. "And what about my question? You hear anything about anyone making me—making us—a target?"

"You've got at least one enemy for sure, boy. But all in all, I think there are less folks aiming for your head than you might have feared. That's good news," he says with a thin smile. "Gives you better odds. Then again, I never was much of a gambling man."

CHAPTER EIGHTEEN

"Well, he was an interesting guy," I say as we're bouncing our way down the dirt road toward the paved highway to take us to Garfield, Idaho, where we'll stay the night in a motel before getting back in the air tomorrow morning. The crew's already checked in and Marci, Devlin's favorite pilot, texted earlier that she has our keys and we can swing by her room when we get there. She says the motel is nice, but at this point, I don't even care.

"Why on earth is Giatti in Idaho? He sounds like he's from New Jersey, and he lived in Nevada with you."

"Maria," he said. "That little house and the land have been in her family forever. And they always used to say they'd go back one day and live a quiet, easy life. I don't know if he ever had any of that life with her there. I hope he did."

"Me, too," I say. "I like him. And he really likes you."

"He's cranky and brusque, and he was always a bit of an asshole," Devlin says. "But he does. And I like him, too."

"Thanks for bringing me along. It makes me happy to have these peeks into your past. Seeing hints that it wasn't all bad. I've always hated thinking about your childhood. I'm not saying that now I think it was full of hugs and puppies, but at least I know that there were a few rays of sun peeking through the gloom."

"There were," he says, reaching for my hand. "And then I met you and the sun really came out."

"Until the clouds came back," I add, then immediately regret it. It's a nice moment. Why remind him of the drama that surrounded him leaving me, or those years where I hated him so deeply I could feel it down to my toes?

"We got a second chance," I whisper. "Not everyone does."

"We're lucky," he says. "But it's more than that. Luck brought us back together. But we've worked to get here, where we are."

"In the middle of a field in Idaho?"

He taps the brakes, bringing us to a halt on this lonely dirt road. "I'm serious," he says. "There were a hundred reasons we should have stayed apart. Hell, all I had to do was keep my distance and you would have never suspected who Devlin Saint really was. And then once we truly saw each other, it still wasn't a picnic. My secrets. The knapsack of guilt you haul with you everywhere. So many things that could have kept us from truly becoming us."

I almost comment on the guilt, but he's right. I've carried survivor's guilt with me for so long, I don't even notice the weight. Lately, though, the burden has been lighter.

"We fought and we talked and we fought and we made love and then we fought some more. We're together now because we've worked for it. Fought for it. And I'll keep fighting to keep you forever. Only now you're fighting along-side me, both of us against anyone who wants to rip us apart."

My throat is so thick with emotion that I can barely get the words out. "I'll always fight for us," I say.

Our eyes lock. "Baby, I know."

For a moment, he simply looks at me. We stay lost that way, I'm not sure for how long. The truck is filled with emotion, and finally, when it feels as if my heart may burst with the love I feel for this man, he gives me one final smile and turns his attention back to the wheel.

Ronan is at the hotel when we get there. Not literally, although that's what I'd expected when Marci said that Ronan was set up in our room. Instead, he's waiting impatiently in California for Devlin to login to a video call.

"What's up?" Devlin says once we're in the virtual room.

"Couldn't get you on your phone," Ronan says. As usual, he looks like a mythological god. Or maybe a Marvel hero. But today, there's a wild energy about him. Something's happened, and he's eager to tell. "Next time you travel with the goddamn sat phone like you're supposed to."

"What's happened?"

"Blackstone's our man. We have confirmation."

"Our man," Devlin repeats. The words are careful. Measured. As if he's holding in strong emotion. Which, of course, he is. "He's the leak? Or he killed Tracy?"

"Confirmed on Tracy. Confidence is high on the leak."

Devlin leans back in his chair, his hand automatically finding mine, and our fingers twine together.

"We're one hundred percent on this?" Devlin asks.

"We worked fast, but the work is good. We were able to use the image from the doorbell camera to trace the mask. It was a limited edition, and we traced it to the point of purchase. From there, we were able to get security feed from the store to see who bought it. It was one of Blackstone's men."

"Good work. Go on."

"Also, the string on the box. We traced that back to Chicago."

I look between the two men, duly impressed. This has all happened in an incredibly short period of time and it's some damn good forensic work. Then again, Devlin has more money and resources at his disposal than the average police force.

"Keep going," Devlin says.

"The most damning thing is where I should have started in the first place," Ronan says. "Blackstone himself bragged about the hit. We've had an informant in place for a while," he adds, shifting his attention to me, since Devlin would already know that.

"He'd been hanging around the fringes of Blackstone's organization for a while, and we had him move in closer after the security leaks started in Vegas. I had him arrange a meeting with Blackstone about something minor, then see if he could steer the conversation around to the news about Devlin and The Wolf. Our informant managed it beautifully, and Blackstone flat out admitted he made the hit. Sounded positively gleeful."

"This is incredible," I say.

"It is," Devlin agrees. "Although it helps that Joe's a braggart. That man never was one to hold his secrets close to the vest. He likes recognition for what he perceives as his own brilliance. And his ego just nailed him."

"It's a huge victory for us," I say.

"It is," Devlin agrees. "Unless he's playing us. Could be he's not even trying to hide. Maybe he wants us to come after him."

"Well, he's going to get his wish, since that's exactly what we plan to do," Ronan says.

"Where's he located?" I ask.

"Just outside of Chicago," Ronan tells me. "He has a farmhouse there that's been fortified."

"Do we have a way in?"

"We're analyzing that now, but the short answer is yes. We found a few ways to breach that appear to be low risk."

"Good," Devlin says. "We go in tomorrow. I'll have Marci change the flight plan and meet you in Chicago. Can we get the operation in place by then?"

"Not a problem. I've been working on it since I got the news," Ronan says. "But how exactly are you defining *we*?"

"I'm going with you," Devlin says, and I stiffen beside him.

"The hell you are," Ronan says, before I have a chance to voice that exact thought. "It's too personal."

"He's right," I say.

"Dammit," Devlin says, leaning closer to the camera. "It *is* personal. Tracy was killed as a warning to me. And as a threat against Ellie. You really think I'm not going?"

Ronan moves in closer, too, his face filling the frame. If I didn't know better, I'd expect him to leap through the screen. "Yeah," Ronan says. "I really think you're not going."

"Dammit, Ro—"

"*No.*"

Devlin pulls back, his head cocked as he eyes his friend.

"You want me on your team because I don't let you get away with stupid shit," Ronan says. "I've already fucked up once dealing with Blackstone and his fallout. I'm not making another mistake again."

"What the hell are you talking about?"

"I should never have let you be in the house the night it all went down with Anna. Not you, and damn sure not Ellie. Ellie was the target, and you were too emotionally invested. We're lucky it didn't go completely south."

"Ronan—" Devlin begins.

"No. It worked out, but you know we could have blown it. We don't do personal missions for a reason, and that was *your* rule."

"He's right," I say softly. I haven't really been involved in this conversation. I've just been sitting and listening and watching these men do their work. But I'm not going to stay quiet any longer. Joseph Blackstone has it out for the man I love, and I am willing to do anything to ensure that I don't lose him.

"Ronan's right," I say again. "But think about it this way. Blackstone wants you, right? And considering what happened with Anna, he's going to expect you to be coming for him. He's got his eye on you, too, and we know it."

Devlin's turns to face me, and I lift a shoulder in a casual shrug. "So let him watch you."

"What are you talking about?"

On the screen, I see Ronan smile. He's gotten there ahead of Devlin, which is a rare thing.

"You have a press conference planned for the day after tomorrow, right? Have the team go in then."

"And while you're busy with the press, we'll be busy taking out your enemy," Ronan says.

"I want this fucker," Devlin says. He stands up and starts to pace. "I want him so bad I can taste it. He's been a thorn in my side, and he's only digging in deeper."

"And you'll get him," I say. "This team works for you, doesn't it? You started Saint's Angels. Did you expect to go on every single mission?

"You're a leader," Ronan says, his voice through the speaker filling the dingy motel room. "Fucking lead."

"And you're an ass," Devlin says.

Ronan shrugs, his shoulders rising into the frame. "Part of the job description." He glances at me. "But your girlfriend is right. Her plan is solid. We do that, I think we have an even better chance of ending this now."

He looks hard at Devlin as I preen a little. It's the first time I've really felt included and valued by Ronan.

"Well?" Ronan demands.

I watch as Devlin takes a breath, then releases it. He wants to be there, I get that. This is personal. I get that too. But I see the decision in his eyes before he speaks, and it's the right one. "Okay," he says. "I guess I'm staying behind."

He ends the call right after.

"I need you tonight, El. Hell, I need you every night, but I especially want you now. This night."

I nod. I understand what he's not saying, what he may not even understand himself. Not in the moment, anyway.

He's just surrendered control of this mission to his best friend. It doesn't weaken him, but it's not a place that Devlin Saint is used to being. He needs that sense of being in control, of being the man in charge. Of being the one who makes things happen. Tonight, I know, I will receive all of the essential benefits of that need.

I rise on my toes and put my arms around him and brush my lips over his. "You know, I'm always yours. Whenever, however. You don't have to ask. You can just take. Because that's what we are to each other."

I see heat and love when he looks back into my eyes. "Yes," he says. "That's what we are."

CHAPTER NINETEEN

I hear Christopher's voice the moment we walk through the front door of Brandy's house. He's laughing with her from somewhere in the kitchen, and I catch Devlin's eyes before we head that direction. It's just the two of them, and I assume Lamar got called back to work. Christopher looks up from where he's pouring wine, and I see that some of it dribbles over the glass and onto the stone countertop. He fumbles, puts the bottle down, and wipes up the mess. About thirty, Christopher has a lean face, golden hair, and an easy smile that right now looks a little shaky.

He picks up the glass and takes a long sip of wine.

"It's good to see you," Devlin says. "I'm sorry if it's been awkward for you, but we all understand you can't choose your relatives."

"Thanks for that," Christopher says, and I can hear the relief in his voice that Devlin jumped in and addressed the elephant in the room. "So, um, Brandy says you were out of town. How was your trip? Was it to do with Tracy's murder?"

"Foundation work," Devlin says, taking my hand. "Crisis management following the leak."

I give his hand a squeeze that I hope he interprets as understanding. We trust Christopher, sure. But he's not in the loop. And that is fine by me. Right now, all I really want is a change of subject. Because there's nothing more awkward than knowing your boyfriend is about to have someone killed, and that someone is the half-brother of the guy standing three feet away from you. Estranged half-brother, true, but it still feels surreal.

"I think we should put in a really bad movie and just chill," I say. "We all could use a break from reality. And I'm thinking that wine would be a good idea too. What do you say? Do you guys want to hang out and watch a flick?"

"Does it have to be a bad movie?" Christopher asks.

Brandy and I look at each other, then burst out laughing. One of our favorite things to do together is watch bad movies.

"No," she says, taking his hand. "We can watch whatever you want."

"Let's just not make it a spy movie or a thriller, okay?"

"I second that," Devlin says.

"Deal," Brandy and I say together.

We end up on the couch watching *The Hangover* and laughing our asses off. I snuggle against Devlin, enjoying the comfort of his arm around me. It feels safe, and as this silly comedy plays out on the TV I can't help but note the dichotomy between that fiction and the reality of our life right now.

I know I should be scared, but somehow I'm not. That's one of the things I love the most about Devlin. Just being around him makes me feel safe. Like nothing in the world could go wrong.

Except I'm a person who should know better.

For most of my life, everything did go wrong. I lost my mother, my father, my uncle. Hell, I even lost Devlin. Though he was Alex back then. Of all the people in the world, I should know never to let down my guard. With Devlin I have. And I can't help but fear that somehow that's going to come back to bite me.

After the movie, Devlin and I head upstairs to give Brandy and Christopher their space. Since Devlin let about a million calls roll to voicemail during the movie, he's at the desk, doing crisis management triage.

I'm on the bed, listening to music and scrolling through my own less-urgent emails, when my phone buzzes in my hand and Corbin's name pops up on the screen.

"You take over my lease and suddenly we're besties?"

"Nah," he says. "I just figured you missed me by now."

"Nope," I say, and we both laugh.

He clears his throat. "Listen, I'm actually calling to say I'm really sorry about what happened to Devlin's intern. I've been following the story and it's brutal. Are you okay?"

"Me? It's hard. I really liked Tracy and we were becoming good friends. It's sweet of you to ask." And surreal, considering it's Corbin, but I don't say that much.

"I'm not an idiot, Ellie. I'm sorry about your friend, but I meant, are *you* okay? I mean, Devlin's got to be worried you're the target, right?"

"I guess you really aren't an idiot," I say, after acknowledging that he's right.

"Well, stay safe. I mean, I guess Devlin's all over that, but watch your back."

"I will." I clear my throat. "So, well, thanks."

"You're welcome." An awkward silence hangs between

them, and I wonder at the irony of this strange budding friendship.

"Yeah, right. And I wanted to know if I should have a mover haul your stuff to you by truck, or if there's anything you need faster. I was going to offer to bring a few things to the press conference tomorrow, but it turns out I can't come. Minor emergency here. But I'll still write something up based on the wire reports."

"Oh." I hadn't even realized Devlin had put him on the list. "By truck is fine, thanks. And sorry I won't see you tomorrow. Everything okay?"

"My girlfriend got hit with appendicitis last night. Emergency surgery. I'm calling from the hospital. She's fine, but I'm not going to leave her now."

"No," I say, giving Corbin more points in the Not An Asshole column. "You shouldn't. But, um, thanks for writing it up. The more his speech circulates, the more impact we'll have."

"Got an exclusive for me?"

"Other than that you're not the complete jerk I thought you were? Not really."

"I'll make that the headline," he says, and we share a laugh. "Listen," he continues, "I've been thinking about your situation."

"My situation?"

"Yeah, you know. Jobless and sitting on one of the biggest stories of the decade. Honestly, Franklin was an idiot to let you go, and I think he realizes it. Or he will after this press conference."

"No argument from me."

"So write it. The truth about Saint. Do a juicy piece that shows him the way you know him."

"Freelance for *The Spall*? Not in a million. Not even if

they were willing to pay me triple my salary and give me the cover."

"No, not that. But there's no denying that the story is huge. People will want to read about how the son of The Wolf managed to reinvent himself into a philanthropist. What are you doing about that?"

"What do you mean what am I doing?"

"You're in the perfect position to create the best PR the man's ever had. Write a series of articles and freelance them to *The LA Times* or *Fortune* Magazine, I don't know. Hell, write a proposal and get a book deal. You can spin this, Ellie. And considering the press conference he's holding tomorrow, I bet Devlin would agree that it's a brilliant idea."

"Is that what you'd do if you were in my position?"

"Hell, yes. And you know damn well I might be an asshole, but I'm a good reporter. My instincts on this are dead on. You love him, right?"

"I really do."

"Well, if I was in love and had the chance to do something to help my girl out, I'd do everything in my power."

"You are," I say softly. "You're at the hospital for her."

"Oh. Yeah. I guess I am."

I smile. The man I used to think was the biggest asshole in the world, actually has a sentimental side. "It's a smart idea," I tell him. "And to a certain extent it's already in the works. I started the profile of the foundation for the magazine, and I have a lot of notes on Devlin. And I know where the bodies are buried," I say, more as private joke to myself than for him to understand.

To my surprise, Corbin laughs. "I bet you do."

"I'll talk to Devlin about it. It's a good idea, and thank you. Even if he doesn't want to do it, I appreciate you mentioning it. You're right that it could give him some good PR, and that could be exactly what he needs. Exactly what the foundation needs, too, because we don't know what the fallout will be with regard to donations in the future in light of him and his newfound notoriety. And honestly, even if there's not a smidge of fallout, it would still be worthwhile. He's done amazing things, and it's a story that deserves to be told."

"That's what I'm saying."

"I get it. And Corbin?"

"Yeah?"

"You're still an asshole, but I think you're okay."

CHAPTER TWENTY

B *efore...*
 Alex stared at Anna, certain he'd heard her wrong. "Peter? He really wants me to take out Peter?"

Anna nodded, looking almost as shell shocked as he felt. "Are you really surprised? You must have known that Peter was skimming."

"I didn't. He must keep another set of books." That was a lie. He hated himself for lying to Anna, one of his best friends, but if word got back to his father that Alex had been aware of Peter's disloyalty, it wouldn't go well for him. Better than it would go for Peter, true, but it still wouldn't be good.

He winced at his own gallows humor, but the truth was he knew that he was stuck. He was the weapon, and Peter was the target, and there wasn't a damn thing he could do to change that.

Frustrated, he dragged his fingers through his hair, not believing that this was happening. Wishing that he could just run. Escape. But even if that was an option, where the hell could he go that his father wouldn't find him? "Peter's my friend," he finally said, knowing he sounded petulant.

"Why the hell would the Wolf care about that?"

Alex said nothing. Anna cocked her head.

"Come on, Alex, you know the way it works. You're his heir. Of course, you're the one he ordered to do it. He doesn't care that you've become close to Peter. Hell, that's even more of a commitment. That's the point."

"I know. I know." Of course he knew. He knew his bastard father better than anybody. "When?"

"As soon as you can make it happen."

"I still can't believe this. It doesn't make sense. There's no one else in this territory. He's let other men slide when they're running an area, at least until he gets someone new in place." He grimaced. "Granted, not often, and those other men usually lost a few fingers, but he's done it. And this is Peter, his friend."

Which, of course, answered his own question. The betrayal of a friend or relative hit harder than anything.

In front of him, Anna shrugged. "He's shifting things around right now. Bringing in new people, getting rid of old ones. Hell, he's even gotten Manny working on tech for him now. There's all sorts of things on the internet that Manny knows how to access. They call it the dark web or something, and I guess your father thinks that it's a good place to hide. His money, at least, and details about his operation. I don't know. I just know that he's changing things up, and that he told me to bring the message to you. You have to do it, otherwise you and I will both get screwed."

Alex nodded. She was right. He just didn't want to do it. Hell, he'd stall forever if he could. "I can't believe he's got Manny working for him." He was marking time now, trying to put off the inevitable. "He shouldn't have even been at the complex. Aurelia didn't want him to stay."

"Since when does what a woman wants matter? And Aurelia's dead, remember?"

He heard the vitriol in her voice and tilted his head. "Is Joseph still bothering you?" He saw the blush rise on her cheeks, but she shook her head. "No. Not anymore. He stays away."

He didn't believe her. "You're not still hanging around him, are you? He's too old for you, and he hurts you."

"I'm not hanging around him," she snapped. "And stop changing the subject."

He scowled. She was right. He was stalling.

"You have to leave as soon as it's done, you know."

"I know," he said.

"It'll be too dangerous to stay. You're going to have to just go without saying goodbye. I know you like her, but you need to just run. Very far and very fast."

"I said, I know." He snapped the words out, then regretted it when she flinched.

"I can go with you if you want," she offered, almost in a whisper.

"No. I'll do it alone."

She studied him, then nodded. "Okay. I'll meet you at the safe house in Costa Mesa. And then we can go back to Nevada together."

"All right."

He drew in a breath as the future spread out in front of him, dark and dangerous.

He'd do the hit because he had no choice. He knew perfectly well that if he didn't do what his father asked, then The Wolf would punish him.

Not by hurting him—not physically anyway—but by taking away something that mattered to him. And although Alex had never told The Wolf about Ellie, he knew well damn well that Daniel Lopez made it his business to know everything.

Of course he knew. And if Alex didn't follow his commands, she would be dead within the week.

Fuck.

And that was why Alex Lopez found a spot about two hundred yards away where he could settle in until he could take the shot. He had his duffle bag beside him. He had his rifle and his ammo, but he'd only need one bullet. The Wolf had made sure of that.

He waited, the sun hot on his neck, the traffic moving below him. He waited until he saw the target—not Peter, *the target*—and he tracked him in the sight until the man paused, standing still just long enough for Alex to do his job.

He thought of his father.

He thought of El.

He pulled the trigger.

And as he watched Peter fall from the single hole in his head, he hated himself. And the only thing that made it bearable was his certainty that even though Alex was about to be gone from Ellie's life forever, at least he'd saved her life by taking Peter's.

CHAPTER TWENTY-ONE

The present...
Considering I barely have the skillset to throw together coffee and donuts at my apartment, I have no idea how Tamra managed to pull off a reception with cocktails and dessert in less than seventy-two hours. Granted, the guest list is limited, and Tamra has people working under her to help, but I am still duly impressed.

Because the event is taking place with such short notice, the interior hasn't been done up to the nines like it had been at the gala I'd attended almost immediately after learning that Devlin Saint was in fact Alex Leto.

That night, I'd been on edge, still teetering from the revelation and angry at Devlin for leaving me all those years ago.

Tonight, I'm on his arm, and the only anger I'm feeling is toward the prick who leaked his true identity, forcing the necessity of this reception in the first place.

"She did an incredible job," I tell Devlin.

"She always does," he says, clearly understanding that I'm referring to Tamra.

"I hate why it's necessary," I say, "but I can't deny that an excuse for a new dress and shoes is always welcome."

"That's my motto," Devlin says, making me almost choke on the sip of wine I'd just taken.

In a bit of retail therapy, Brandy and I had gone shopping earlier this afternoon, accompanied by Reggie and her mad skills, just to be safe. Now I'm in a calf-length black dress with a fitted bodice and flirty skirt, paired with red Bruno Magli heels.

Reggie's in a shimmery pink dress that seems to flow over her body and practical flats. "Just in case," she'd said in the store, frowning at the heels she'd wanted to buy. I see her on the far side of the room now, talking with two other members of Saint's Angels, whose names I don't recall. There are five here total, pulled off operations in California and Arizona to come offer protection during the press conference. Ronan, of course, is conspicuously absent. He's leading the team that's breaching Joseph Blackstone's home today, and I'm on pins and needles waiting for the outcome.

Devlin must be, too, but he's not showing it.

Brandy, of course doesn't know any of that is going on, but even so, she's been edgy all evening. She'd come decked out in a backless red dress that Christopher had noticed when they were window shopping one day. She'd accessorized with a darling cocktail bag of her own design, something she'd been working up recently to add to the *BB Bags* inventory.

I don't see either of them, though, and I'm hoping Brandy found him and they're off in a corner together. He'd texted her this morning to say that something came up with his editor and he'd meet her here. But as of a half hour ago, he still hadn't shown up, and the last time I saw Brandy, she'd looked both irritated and worried.

All the other guests, however, seem to be enjoying the

drinks and desserts offered from the stations and the waiters circulating among the crowd. In addition to familiar faces from various news bureaus, I see local businessmen, and community leaders such as Chief Randall. Lamar is here, and it breaks my heart to see the pain on his face when he glances around this room filled with couples. I've checked on him several times, though, and each time he tells me that he's fine. That it hurts, but that he'll get through it. I know that's true, I just wish I could help.

I draw a breath, forcing my thoughts away from Lamar's loss. I look around the room again, taking it in with a neutral eye and decide that it really is perfect. "I wasn't sure at first," I tell Devlin. "About not having tables, I mean. But it works." The room has only a few cocktail style tables scattered around, primarily to aid reporters who might actually still be taking notes with pen and paper.

"I think so, too," he says. "Tamra's thinking was that a seated speech suggests something intense and weighty, whereas cocktails are among friends."

"And while your content is definitely intense, you want everyone to see you as you. Not as some billionaire big shot."

"Not exactly how I'd have put it, but yes."

The wall of glass that looks out over the ocean has been pushed aside, allowing for people to mingle on the stone patio. We head that way now, and Devlin doesn't have to tell me why. The patio overlooks the tidal pools—*our* tidal pools. And he'll want that in his mind before he talks, a reminder about why he's going public tonight. So that hopefully the enemies of his past will back down, making the life he has now a safer one. For him, for me, and for everyone he cares about.

"I think this is going very well," Tamra says as she comes over to greet Devlin and me. "Of course I'm not surprised. We may not be advertising it as such, but everyone realizes that this is the first event since the Humanitarian Award was pulled. They want to know what you have to say for yourself."

Devlin smirks. "Don't worry. I have plenty to say for myself."

Tamra laughs. "Well, I would've liked to have had a preview of your speech, but I for one will be in the audience with bated breath."

She presses her hand to his shoulder in a maternal gesture, and I realize again how long they've known each other, and how much she's seen Devlin overcome. Of everyone who knows him, she's probably the least worried about the revelation that he's The Wolf's son negatively impacting him. After all, she's seen him survive almost everything.

"About that," I say when she leaves to work the room some more.

"About what?" Devlin asks.

"Having something to say. I want to start releasing a series of articles about you. A follow-up to the talk you're giving tonight, breaking down your background and what you're doing with the foundation. I was thinking we could release them on the foundation's website."

"El, baby, I'm not sure I—"

"We need to control the narrative," I say. "I was talking with Corbin about it, and he—"

Devlin starts to laugh.

"What? It's a good idea. You're going to stand up tonight and announce that you're a good guy, but you're still going to be battling everyone who wants it to be otherwise, because villains make better stories. One per week. It's the smart thing," I tell him. "Ask Tamra. She'll agree with me."

"Have you raised it with her yet?"

"No, but I know I'm right."

"To be honest, I think you are, too."

"Yeah?"

"But I pay her for publicity and PR because that's not what I do. We'll talk with her after we see how tonight's speech is received, okay?"

I grin. "Absolutely. And we'll be sure to tell her that the articles will be leading up to a book, either published by a major publisher or the foundation itself if we can't find one. But you *know* we'll be able to find one." I rise up onto my toes and kiss him. "Especially if we add me to the narrative. Sex sells, you know."

"That we dated, yes. Any more detailed than that, and I'm going to axe the project."

"Agree. But maybe I'll write those pages just for you..." I trail off, a sensual lilt in my voice.

He laughs. "Careful. I have to go stand in front of everyone in a minute, and there's no podium in front of me."

I'm fishing for a lurid reply when Lamar joins us. "I don't know how you do it, Saint. You don't look the slightest bit nervous."

"I've given a lot of talks, though never this focused on me. Thankfully, Ellie is distracting me."

I bat my eyes innocently. "Any time..."

They chat for a bit before Tamra pulls Devlin away, then announces that he'll be addressing the room in just a few minutes. Lamar leaves me to go find the Chief, and I glance around the room looking for Brandy. I finally find her on the far side of the room talking with Eric. I join them, and we make polite conversation until Eric wanders off to circulate, making sure he greets the various VIPs who are attending.

Brandy turns to me, but I don't know what she intends to say, because the lights dim, and a single light focuses on the staircase where Devlin stands, about halfway up. He looks calm and in charge, not the least bit nervous.

Then the entire room falls into silence as Devlin's eyes sweep the room, lingering on mine before he looks out over the crowd.

"Ladies and gentlemen," he says. "Tonight, I'd like to tell you a story."

CHAPTER TWENTY-TWO

Devlin pressed his hands to the rail as he looked out over the crowd, at the faces looking up at him, all filled with curiosity. He hated the circumstances that had brought him to this moment, but he had to admit that he felt a bit of relief, too. Keeping secrets was exhausting work, and so long as he could manage the fall-out, he was glad to have one less thing to juggle.

"First of all," he began, "I want to thank you for coming tonight on such short notice. I realize there's a curiosity factor involved, and I promise I haven't pulled a bait and switch. You're not here simply to learn that I recently bought real estate for a children's hospital in Riverside. Though, of course, I hope you cover that story as well."

He paused, appreciating the low rumble of laughter. He knew damn well that many of the reporters and foundation supporters felt conflicted. On the one hand, they wanted to hear the truth behind the sensational story about Devlin Saint's parentage. On the other, they genuinely admired his work, and hated that they were participating at all in something that Devlin hadn't released to the public himself.

"I'm here tonight not to talk about the foundation—not directly, anyway. I'm here for one very simple reason. Me."

He paused a moment, his gaze finding Ellie and her supportive smile. "I'm here to paint you a picture of a Devlin Saint you haven't met before. Except, of course, you have. My past shaped who I am now. Who I've been for all the time my foundation has been in existence."

So far, the crowd looked rapt, and he made eye contact with a few as he continued to speak. "Because of what this foundation does, maybe some of you assumed that my childhood was not sunshine and roses. Or perhaps you assumed I simply had money and wanted to either do good or find a tax shelter."

As he'd hoped, a smattering of chuckles drifted up from the audience.

"But what I really hope is that you weren't thinking about me at all, but about the people this foundation has helped. We've rescued those who've been abused. We've helped train and educate those who needed a hand up. We've worked with law enforcement to shut down the drug rings that enslave the innocent, and we've helped rescue hundreds of victims across the globe who became caught in a deadly web of human trafficking."

He leaned forward, his hands on the rail. "That is what you should be focusing on. What you had been focusing on. You helped tell the stories of the good work we do here. You helped spread a message of hope to those who had lost a loved one or who themselves needed help.

"But then one story—one prurient fact shifted that focus. Suddenly it wasn't about the good that the foundation has done and will do in the future. Instead it became about my father. A man who is exactly the type of horrific human being this foundation was created to fight."

He closed his eyes and drew in a breath, not caring if he showed a hint of weakness. Because the truth was, he *was* weak where his relationship to his father was concerned. He'd fought and suffered to leave that man behind, but you could never really escape your past. That was a lesson Devlin had learned the hard way.

He tamped the anger down to continue his speech, seeking out familiar faces in the audience as he said, "There was never a time that Daniel Lopez—my father—wasn't a vicious, violent bastard. And now that man—that cruel excuse for a human being—is stealing the spotlight from those who deserve it. Now, a man who never felt love and who ruled with fear and intimidation is reaching out from the grave to weaken the very organization that I built to be a stronghold against men like him."

His voice had taken on a hard edge, reflecting the hatred that he was allowing to bubble to the surface.

It took some effort, but he managed to dial it back, wanting to keep this conference professional. He'd show emotion, yes. But there was a limit to how much he was willing to expose of himself to anyone other than El.

He drew a breath. "This isn't a conversation I ever wanted to have, but it's one we must, because Daniel Lopez—the Wolf—has no place in these halls. So I will tell you a story. Once, and only once. And then this foundation will return its focus to our mission of battling the disease of human trafficking and other similar crimes and providing help, education, and training to those who need it.

He paused, looking out on the crowd. Finding El in the audience, the pride in her eyes bolstering him as he paused before continuing to sing the praises of his foundation and the good, work they did, raising up those who needed help and supporting law enforcement as best they could.

The irony wasn't lost on him. The twisted reality that—because of an order he gave—a team was in Chicago right now preparing to kill a man. A man who deserved it, yes. But it was still Devlin who had signed that death warrant.

Some in this room might call him a hypocrite, but he himself had no doubts. Neither did Tamra or Reggie or Ronan or any of the other Saint's Angels in that room. Most important, he knew that El was behind him. That she supported not only who he was, but what he did. And that she understood the deeper story. The one he wouldn't tell the crowd tonight, but that informed everything he'd ever done, including leaving her all those years ago.

He squared his shoulders and began again. "Once upon a time, a young woman ran away from her exceedingly wealthy parents. She met a man. An exotic man. A man with power and charisma who took her off the street and brought her to his home. She married this man, got pregnant, and had a boy. And somewhere in there she learned the truth about her husband. That he wasn't a good man. That he hurt people, and not only considered it a business model, but that he actually took pleasure in it."

He swallowed, then continued. "She got up the courage to run, taking the child with her. That child, of course, was me. Daniel Lopez is a relentless man, and he had soon found her. He killed her. He killed her parents, and he took me. I was very young, but he made me a wealthy man, as I inherited my grandparents' fortune. And try though he might, The Wolf never got those funds. That money—built over generations through hard work and legitimate investments, is the only money I touch personally."

He let his eyes skim the room. "Did I inherit The Wolf's fortune when he died? I did. I also made it my mission to disappear, and for years I was successful in hiding. I knew

The Wolf's lieutenants and enemies would begrudge me that ill-earned fortune, and so I resolved to change my identity. As you know, I became Devlin Saint. And during that time I was in hiding, someone killed my father. I could have become Alejandro Lopez again, but I wanted no part of that life, and no connection to that man. What I wanted was to erase the past. But that, of course, wasn't possible.

"So I did the next best thing. I founded this organization."

Slowly, he cast his gaze over the entire room. "As for the money I inherited from my father—money I consider to be tainted—I have used it solely for this foundation, to make good from the bad. To support those who need help. To fund programs and services to help the lives of people that my father and men like him hurt and took advantage of. My father used and abused people, then threw them out like garbage. Now, the money that he was so proud of earning is being used to undo as much of the damage he caused as possible."

He found Ellie, and held her gaze as he continued. "I would not be the man that I am were it not for my father. It is his sins and the sins of men like him I am trying to stop and remediate. I am not my father, and I damn sure do not admire that man. Under no circumstances would I use what I inherited from him for myself. The idea makes me sick. But I will gladly funnel it into programs that help destroy what he built by any and all means at my disposal."

His eyes were locked on Ellie, and he saw her wipe away a tear. She knew all the ways—the secret ways he did his work, the ways he could never announce publicly—and yet the pride on her face shone bright, and that was the best validation of his life he could hope for.

He drew in a breath, feeling renewed as he said, "I have a goal. To make the world a better place. A safer place. I am not my father. I know it. One day, I hope the world understands it.

"I won't deny that it was a painful shock to have the Humanitarian of the Year award pulled from me at the eleventh hour. But not because I now have an empty space on my mantel. No, my pain comes from the unpleasant realization that the world judges me—judges all of us—on things other than our own actions. On where we were born. On the color of our skin. On the type of job we hold. And, of course, on who our parents were.

"One of the goals of the DSF has always been to fight injustice and to help the victims of active criminal activities. Today, I am announcing the creation of the Value Within program to help individuals rise above the circumstances of their birth by helping to remediate poverty and improve education. This program will work directly with business of all sizes, both with regard to training and the continuing education of their workforce, but in recruiting them to join our mission."

He continued, laying out the skeletal details of the new program before straightening his shoulders and sweeping his gaze over the room.

"In sum, I would like to thank the Council for giving me a new purpose. An award would only sit on my mantel. But pulling the award—well, that has led to the creation of another program that has the potential to help millions. And about that, I cannot be sorry.

"I appreciate your time," he added with a nod to the room. "We have information packets and a press release about the Value Within program available. And, of course, more drinks and dessert. Thank you."

The room began to buzz, and the spotlight on Devlin

clicked off. He forced himself not to draw in a breath, not to show any weakness at all.

But he did look for El, and the light he saw in her eyes eased any lingering doubts.

Then she was heading toward him, weaving through the crowd with her attention focused entirely on him. He started toward her, then hesitated as his phone buzzed in his pocket. He pulled it out and saw the simple message from Ronan —*Done*.

Blackstone was dead.

Relief slammed through Devlin, so potent it almost sent him tumbling down the stairs. Then Ellie was standing in front of him, telling him he was amazing and asking what was wrong, and the answer was nothing—right then nothing was wrong.

He took her hand and pulled her to him. "I love you," he said. "I need you."

He was wired, he knew that. From the speech. From the message. From the weight of the secret he'd been keeping being finally released. He needed her—damn social obligations, he'd make the rounds in a few minutes. Right then, all he wanted was El.

He drew her up the stairs to the second floor, then into the elevator so they could get to his office quicker.

"Devlin, what are you—" But he silenced her with a hard, bruising kiss that had her moaning and then melting against him, so that she was just as eager as he was when the elevator opened in front of his office.

They were through the doors and at his desk in what felt like seconds, and he lifted her onto his desk, pushing her legs apart as she struggled to pull down his fly. He hesitated only a second to look into her eyes. To see more than hear her whispered, "Yes, oh, God, yes," before he clutched her hips and tugged her closer, then lost himself inside her.

Christ, she felt good. He looked at her face, drinking her in. "Open your eyes," he said, then just about lost it when she did, and he was overwhelmed with the love and passion he saw reflected there.

"Harder," she whispered. "Devlin, I need it, too."

He bent over her, pushing her back onto the desk and pulling her knees up. His cock was inside her, his hands on her breasts, and his mouth claiming hers with a kiss as wild as fucking.

He was close—so damn close. And he knew her body well enough to know that she was, too.

"That's it, baby," he murmured against her mouth. "Come for—"

The door burst open.

"Saint, dammit, we have to—*oh, shit.*"

CHAPTER TWENTY-THREE

"Jesus Christ," I say, struggling to adjust my clothes as Devlin does the same. Not that Lamar hasn't seen me in my underwear. But as far as I know, he's never seen me having sex. And I don't think that we need to expand our friendship into that dimension. "Don't you knock?"

Devlin scowls at Lamar, who's repeating "Sorry, sorry," his words coming out on top of ours. "But—"

"You can't just—" I begin. Then the words die on my tongue as Brandy steps out from behind Lamar, mascara-tinted tears staining her cheeks. "Oh, no." I grapple for Devlin's hand, then squeeze. "What happened?"

Lamar's expression is tight as he gestures to the seating area in Devlin's office.

"I'm really sorry," Lamar says. "I wasn't thinking. I just wanted to get to both of you."

"It's fine," Devlin says dismissively, though my cheeks are still burning with embarrassment. "I should have thought to lock it. What's going on?"

Devlin settles into a chair across from the sofa where

Lamar and Brandy are now seated. I perch on the armrest, letting Devlin's hand at my back steady me.

Lamar looks at both of us, his expression completely miserable as he holds Brandy's hand. Brandy is silent, but tears still track dark lines down her face. Fear cuts through my gut, replacing what earlier had been irritation.

"Lamar, you're scaring me. What's going on?"

"Christopher," Brandy whispers, her voice raw and rough and very audible.

I look to Lamar. "Oh, God. Is he hurt? What happened?"

Brandy chokes back a sob as she tries—and fails—to answer.

"I'm so sorry, Sherlock," he says gently, as if the nickname will soften a blow. "But he was driving the SUV. The one that almost killed you."

I gape at Lamar, then turn to Devlin. I'm completely shell-shocked, unable to believe it. We'd vetted him. Hell, we were with him last night, laughing on the couch, and everything had seemed perfectly normal. There was nothing —nothing—to suggest he was keeping such a huge secret. And yet now that I'm looking at Devlin's face, I realize that this isn't a surprise.

Quickly, I look back at Lamar, but I see nothing on his face to indicate that he knows that Devlin is one step ahead of him. And that, of course, means that Devlin wants Lamar to believe that he's just as surprised as I am.

"This is crazy," I say, which pretty much sums up all of my emotions. "Are you sure?"

"Tell us what happened. What's your source? Is Christopher in custody?" Devlin steadies me so I don't slide off the chair as he stands up. Then he heads to the bar. "I need a drink. Anyone else?"

"I'm on duty." Lamar says, as Brandy shakes her head. I get up and go sit by her, and she reaches out for my hand.

"Well, I'll take one," I say. "Scotch. Straight up."

Devlin brings the drinks back and nods at Lamar. "Well?"

"A few minutes ago, someone called the station asking where they could send evidence in Ellie's hit and run. The sergeant gave him the email for the department, and a few minutes later a message came in. No text, no explanation. Just a photograph. Three photographs actually showing multiple angles, and all of Christopher in the car."

He looks at our faces in turn as if to make sure that we're paying attention. I can't speak for Devlin or Brandy, but as for me, I'm completely rapt. "Could it have been Photoshopped?"

"Theoretically, but I doubt it." He grimaces. "The sergeant forwarded it to me since I was working the case, and he knows that you and I are friends. He remembered what happened when you were almost run down."

"So you're digging into one of the foundation's lovely desserts when you get a text with three images."

"That's pretty much it."

"And he got the call from the sergeant when we were talking," Brandy says. She's wiped her cheeks with a tissue and some of her color is coming back. "Christopher was supposed to meet me here to listen to Devlin, but he didn't show. I'd been calling and texting, but nothing. I was telling Lamar how worried I was getting."

"Once Brandy told me he'd stood her up, I had a black-and-white go to his AirBnB. No one had been dispatched yet, since they didn't have a positive ID until I saw the photos, and even then there was no way for LCPD to know where he was staying. Not easily. We got lucky, since I was with Brandy."

"He wasn't there," Devlin guesses.

"No, he wasn't. Nothing was. His laptop's gone. Suitcases

gone. The refrigerator was still stocked, but other than food, the place had been cleared of any sign of him. Mostly, anyway."

"Mostly?"

"There was a note," Brandy says. "For me."

"He left you a note?" Devlin looks between her and Lamar. "What did it say?"

Lamar passes over his phone. "That's a picture the officer on duty sent me."

"NYCnewsFairy@gmail.com plus something that looks like a password."

"That's the email that distributed the leak," I say. "Was that a password? Did you log in?"

"We did," Lamar says, taking back his phone. "As far as we can tell, that's the only thing that email account was ever used for."

Brandy looks from me to Devlin. "That means he was the leak, doesn't it?"

I nod, feeling miserable for my friend. "Yeah," I say. "It does."

"Why tell me?"

"I don't know," I say. "But I think it's because he genuinely cared about you. He knows he has to run, but he wants to help you and your friends."

"Who cares what he wants?" she snaps. "God, I wish I'd never met him."

"I know." I put my arm around her and look helplessly toward Devlin. I want to console her, but there are things to do and more questions to ask. And I know damn well that Devlin is itching to get them out of his office so he can contact Ronan and the other angels who are downstairs mingling this very minute.

"Thank you for letting us know," Devlin says, his attention on Lamar as he starts to rise. "I assume you're heading for the scene?"

"Actually, there's more."

Devlin's brows rise and he settles back, then nods for Lamar to continue.

"As I was talking with the officer onsite at Christopher's AirBnB, I got an email. This one wasn't from the station. This one came from Joseph Blackstone's email address."

I look at Devlin, confused. Especially because by the time Devlin was making his speech, the team should have taken out Joseph Blackstone. Devlin's face is still completely unreadable, so I turn back to Lamar for answers. "You're saying Joseph Blackstone sent you an email?"

"Or someone pretending to be him. But this one didn't have the pictures. It was text."

"What does it say?" Devlin asks.

Lamar taps his phone again, then passes it to Devlin. I'm curious enough that I leave Brandy's side to look over Devlin's shoulder. It's an email chain, and in it, Joseph Blackstone is messaging with his half-brother Christopher about the preparations for Anna's revenge. Including a very specific mention of the plan to have Christopher run me over in the SUV in order to distract Devlin.

I look over Devlin's head to Lamar. "There was nothing in any of Anna's belongings or on any of her devices that suggested that this was happening. That Christopher had anything to do with it. Is it fake or did she not know?"

"Good question," Lamar says.

Devlin passes the phone back to Lamar. "It sounds to me like either Christopher really did drive that SUV, or someone very much wants us to think he did."

"Joseph Blackstone?"

Devlin nods. "Quite possibly."

I almost screw up and blurt out that Blackstone's dead. At least, I assume the team's taken him out by now. Fortunately, I realize that Devlin's playing it cool around Lamar and hold my tongue as Lamar frowns, then tugs on his chin, a sure sign he's thinking. "He wants you focused on who tried to run Ellie down as opposed to who decided to tell the world about your father."

"A solid theory," Devlin tells Lamar. "If it's true, it means that Blackstone's running scared."

"Hang on," I say. "I want to see something." I move to Lamar's side and take the phone from him. This time I scroll through the email chain to the bottom. "There are other names on the first one," I say. I recognize some from things Devlin has told me. M. Espinoza, R. Duarte, and several others. "They got taken off as the chain became about the attack on me. But they must be Blackstone's people."

"We're working on tracking them down," Lamar says, which doesn't surprise me at all. My Watson is good at his job, after all.

"Can you forward all of that information to me?" Devlin asks, looking up from scrolling on his phone, presumably skimming texts from Ronan.

"Already done," Lamar says. "Reciprocity, remember?"

"Of course," Devlin says with a nod.

"Listen, obviously this is hot. I'm heading to the precinct." He looks between the two of us. "Watch your backs. He's not in his penthouse in the city. He might be at one of his other residences, and Chicago PD is going to check on that. But he could be heading here, too."

Lamar's focus shifts to me. "Stay with Devlin, Sherlock. You, too, Brandy. Stay safe. If Blackstone sent this email to

turn the attention on Christopher, it might be that something's about to go down with Blackstone that's new. I want
you all covered. You should get back to the house."

"I'll take care of it," Devlin says. He extends his hand to
Lamar, and to my relief, Lamar takes it easily. I'd been a little
worried that he blames Devlin for Tracy's death, even if
subconsciously, and that easy handshake goes a long way
toward alleviating that concern.

As soon as he's out of the room, I want to ask all sorts of
questions of Devlin, but I can't because Brandy is there and
she doesn't know it all. We could pull her into the secret, but
after the blow she's had today, I really don't think it's the time
to lay anything else on her.

Devlin must be thinking the same thing, because a
moment later, there's a quick tap on his door and Reggie
enters without waiting for an invite.

I realize then that Devlin had texted her. "Could you stick
with Ms. Bradshaw while she says her goodbyes, then take her
home and stay with her? She's had some bad news and I don't
want her alone."

"Of course," Reggie says.

"Reggie does some freelance security work for the foundation," Devlin tells Brandy, which is more or less accurate.
"She'll stay with you until Ellie and I can make the rounds,
say our farewells, and leave the party without any questions
being raised."

I almost point out that our escape for a quickie has taken
longer than we'd intended. So there are already probably
speculations and questions galore.

I say nothing, though. Just hug Brandy and promise we'll
be there soon.

As soon as she and Reggie are out the door, I toss back
the rest of the Scotch. "I know we need to go mingle, but tell

me the rest of it first. Blackstone didn't send that email, did he?"

"Oh, he sent it," Devlin says. "But only the one time. And only to Christopher as an order."

"Lamar's news wasn't a surprise to you, was it? That was the text you got downstairs, wasn't it?"

He nods. "Penn and Claire have a team in Chicago, remember? Ronan's there, too, along with Charlie and Grace and several you haven't met yet."

"I figured. I was wondering why Reggie was here, actually, instead of with them."

"She drew the short straw," Devlin says, and I laugh.

"Fair enough. But I'm still confused. Was the mission a success? Is Joseph Blackstone dead?"

"Yes."

It's a short, to-the-point answer, and relief floods through me. "So tell me the rest of it. How did Lamar get that email?"

"While the team was on-site, they went through as much of his electronics and paperwork as they could."

"They found those photos of Christopher."

He nods. "It breaks my heart for Brandy, but there's really no doubt that Christopher drove the SUV. There were more images and other email chains on the computer—a lot more— but Ronan only forwarded a few. The rest are being analyzed."

"He might have been coerced," I say.

"True. Possibly even likely. They weren't Photoshopped or staged, but someone got in place ahead of time and took the photographs. You'll note the use of the special lens so that Christopher is identifiable through the window despite the tinting."

"Good God," I say. "That probably means that Blackstone got his brother to do that, then had the balls to save the evidence so that he could use it against him later if he ever needed to."

"Exactly."

I drag my fingers through my hair, ruining my careful styling. "We know that Christopher testified against Joseph. The two didn't like each other. My money's on coercion."

"Well, there's more."

I grimace, but nod for him to continue.

"There was some evidence that Christopher was trying to get back in good with his brother. There was even some suggestion that his testifying on the drug charges was planned. Part of a longer con so that Christopher could be working with Joseph, and yet anybody watching would have reason to believe that he would never do such a thing because the two were estranged."

"That's absolutely nefarious." Again, Brandy fills my thoughts. "Was he working a long con on Brandy?"

Devlin's expression is utterly sad. "I don't know. I hate the thought of her getting hurt, but I don't think there's any other possible outcome. He either truly loved her, in which case it doesn't matter, because he's on the run now, or he was scamming her all along to get close to either you or me or possibly her business. We may never know. Either way, she gets hurt."

"This is so fucked up. And what about reciprocity? You didn't tell Lamar a thing."

He frowns. "I know. But it's one thing to tell him information. It's another thing to tell him information that was obtained illegally. I'll filter it down to him as I can, though."

I nod, wishing Lamar could just know everything right now, but I understand why he can't.

"You should go home with Reggie and Brandy. I just texted that you're on your way down. They're still in the lobby talking with Tamra."

"Devlin—"

"I'll be along soon. Brandy needs you, not Reggie."

Since he's right about that, I don't argue. "You'll really come soon? Or are you going back to your place?" Since Blackstone's dead, he might want to be in his own place tonight.

"I'll see you later," he says firmly. "The good news is that Blackstone and several on his team are dead. The survivors aren't going to come after us. I know those men, they're useless without a leader. They're paid soldiers going to the highest bidder. They'll find a new boss and move on. But I don't want you to be alone tonight, either. So I'll come by later. We'll make sure Brandy's okay, and Lamar, too, if he stays another night. I hope he does. We could all use another night in front of the television, I think."

I move into his arms and hold him tight. "I love you," I say again.

And one of the reasons I love him is that he thinks about my friends, as well as about me.

"I just can't believe it," Brandy says as I hand her a cup of green tea. I brought a muffin too, one of the chocolate chip ones she had baked yesterday, and I set it on the coffee table in front of her. "I mean, I can't wrap my head around it. It's all so surreal. Christopher. My Christopher, and he actually tried to kill you?"

I sit on the edge of the coffee table, leaning forward with my elbows on my knees so that I can see her face as we talk. Her eyes are swollen from tears, and we're both still in the dresses that we had worn to the press conference and cocktails. Her nose is running, and she uses the back of her hand to wipe under it.

She sniffs, then looks at me, her smile rueful as she reaches for a napkin. "I'm a mess. Reggie must think I'm totally lame."

"She does not," I tell her. "You've been through hell." She's not there to say so herself, as she's in my room so that she can make some calls. I think it's also so that Brandy and I feel free to talk. I appreciate it. I like Reggie fine, but neither Brandy nor I know her well.

"Maybe he was only trying to scare me," I say, bringing my Pollyanna side back around to the original conversation. "It worked, but that may have been all it was."

"Well, since he's disappeared, I guess we'll never know." I hear the vitriol in her voice. She trusted this man. He was the first guy she'd ever gotten truly serious about.

She'd believed that they had a future. That he was the patient, caring guy she'd been looking for all this time. A man who understood her issues. Not like her father, who shunned her after she'd been raped. And not like the only other man she'd ever gone to bed with, a jerk who hadn't listened to her fears and hesitations, but who'd just used her for a fuck.

And God knows he wasn't like Walt. The man who'd drugged and raped her, and set the stage for Brandy's issues with men. His ugly face had popped up recently at our favorite bar, and Devlin had beat the shit out of him, raising Devlin to the level of hero as far as Brandy was concerned.

"You have nothing to regret," I tell her. "Nothing on you, anyway. The man you dated—the man you maybe were falling in love with—looked like a prince as far as you were concerned. Sometimes people get fucked up. And it sounds like Anna and Joseph fucked with Christopher's head big time."

"You'd think I would have seen that, though, wouldn't you?" She shrugs. "How could I fall for a guy who was so easily manipulated by his brother and that bitch?"

"Do not put this on yourself," I say firmly. "This isn't any more your fault than it was when Walt did that to you."

She nods and hugs herself. "I know. I really do know. I'm just having a pity party."

I flash her a smile. "Well, you're an amazing hostess, so I guess any party you throw will be a good one."

As I hoped, she laughs. And because we're both overly sad, overly tired, and overly stressed, that one little burst of laughter turns into a full-on fit of giggles, then snorts, then tears, until I'm on the couch beside her and we're hugging each other and cursing all relationships across the board.

"I can't even look at you and be jealous," she says. "I mean I'm jealous of where you are now with Devlin, but you had to go through hell to get there."

"I know. We did."

"But you're together now, and all your issues have just gone away. I mean, I know you had to work to get through them, but at least their gone." She shrugs. "I guess I'm a little jealous, after all."

"Well, you're right that it was a long time coming." But she's also right that Devlin and I are a team now. I may not ever be Saint's Angels biggest cheerleader, but I'd be a hypocrite to say it shouldn't exist, not when I'm cheering Joseph Blackstone's demise this very moment.

"The truth is, every relationship has problems. Although I'll grant you this one is a lot more complicated than most."

The corner of her mouth curls up, but I don't get a full-on laugh. I probably don't deserve it.

"Do you think I should have seen a sign?"

"No. I already told you. I really believe that he loves you. I think this is just one of those star-crossed relationships where everything else in his life works against you. What would you do if he came back?"

Her eyes widen. "Oh, God, do you think he will? He tried to kill you. Surely he's gone, right?"

"Probably," I say, and honestly, I hope so. I don't think he'd try to hurt Brandy, and now that Joseph's dead, he's probably not interested in hurting me. But unless he's behind bars, I don't want to see him again.

Brandy's shaking her head. "Wow. If he came back. That's—that's just a no. I mean, unless he could somehow prove that he wasn't driving that car, then we are absolutely done. I can't think of any explanation that I could get behind, not even that he was coerced by his brother." She looks at me and meets my eyes. "I need a guy with more integrity than that. And honestly, I need trust. How would I ever trust him again?"

"I get that," I say. "And I don't think you had any reason to see anything weird." I bite my lower lip. "But I think maybe I did."

Brandy nods. "That time you walked in on him and Anna, and they were supposedly plotting a book and talking about a character hitting someone with a truck." She grimaces. "I guess truth is stranger than fiction."

I roll my eyes.

"So Anna wanted you gone so that she could have Devlin, and Christopher was helping her?"

"I think it was more that Joseph was using Anna to get information about the DSF. She was behind those security breaches—feeding him information. And Christopher was trying to get back in tight with his brother."

"Why?"

"I don't know," I admit. "But Devlin and I talked about it

some. He thinks that Christopher legitimately started writing thrillers set in the kind of world that they all grew up in. But because some of his bad guys turned into good guys, he started to get an urge to meet his brother again. Then they started hanging out together more and more. I'm guessing he was a little awed. Maybe he wanted to make up for testifying against his brother. Or maybe that was some sort of long con to make it seem like the brothers were estranged."

Her mouth twists. "Devious. But possible, I guess."

"The bottom line is he did a shitty thing. Maybe a lot of shitty things. But I still believe that what he felt for you was real." I hesitate, then add, "Were you in love with him?"

She sips her tea, an obvious ploy to avoid answering right away. "I don't know. But it still hurts. Would it hurt even if it's not love?"

I reach over and take her hand. "Yeah," I say. "It would."

She hasn't touched her muffin, so I lean over to reach for it, but I'm stopped when I hear the code key being pressed to disarm the system. I turn and lean sideways so that I can see into the entrance hall. The second I see that it's Devlin, it's like a weight's been lifted, and only then do I realize that I was worried he might be wrong about Blackstone's team. They may be more than happy to take revenge instead of scattering to the wind.

He comes into the room and takes my hand, but his attention is on Brandy. "Are you hanging in there?"

"By a thread," she says. "But I'll get better."

"Yes," he says firmly. "You will." He looks between the two of us. "Do either of you need anything? I need to go make a quick phone call."

I shake my head. "No, go right ahead." He kisses my forehead and gives Brandy's shoulder a squeeze before he heads upstairs to our temporary bedroom.

As if my thoughts have conjured him, my phone rings, and Lamar's face appears on the screen. I answer the call. "Hey, we were just talking about you."

"Is Devlin there?"

"Yeah. You need me to go get him?"

"No. I'll be there soon. I need to talk to him right now."

CHAPTER TWENTY-FOUR

Devlin was finishing up a call with Penn when he heard the beep beep beep of the keypad lock. That noise was followed immediately by the sound of the door opening, and that simultaneous with Lamar calling out, "Where is he? Where the hell is Devlin?"

"Penn? I'm going to have to call you back."

"Is everything okay?" his friend asked.

"Fine. But there's something I need to handle."

"Roger that. Talk soon."

As soon as Penn ended the call, Devlin shifted his attention to the conversation downstairs. He couldn't make out words, but he assumed that Ellie was telling Lamar where Devlin was. His suspicion was confirmed a moment later when her voice called out to him, "Devlin, Lamar needs to talk to you. Do you want to come down?"

"No." The louder voice was from Lamar himself. "I'm coming up." It was a statement, not a question, and Devlin didn't bother to answer. He was currently in the study area, working at the desk. He turned over the papers on which he'd been writing notes and stood as Lamar stepped from the stairs to the landing. "What's on your mind, Detective?"

"You didn't do it personally," Lamar said, circling Devlin as he spoke. "I know that. But somehow, you *did* do it."

Devlin had never before noticed what a large man Lamar was. Usually Lamar's size seemed a bit diminished simply because of his congenial personality, as if he intentionally made himself smaller so as to not intimidate. Now, the opposite was happening. He was a big man. A strong man, with arms and hands that could crush a lesser man.

Devlin didn't have his size, but he had strength. He'd worked on it for years, and he knew the extent of his skill. Looking at Lamar, though, he wondered which one of them would come out ahead in the fight. Devlin with all of his skills and the trickery he'd learned over the years, or Lamar with pure, cold rage.

Because one thing was certain, Lamar was pissed.

"I think you'd better sit down, Detective."

"Dammit, Saint, I told you if you ever hurt her..."

"What in hell are you talking about? Hurt who?"

"Ellie. What do you think I'm talking about?"

"Ellie?" Devlin's head was spinning. "How have I hurt Ellie?"

"She thinks you're one of the good guys. She thinks you're what we used to believe Christopher was. A good man smeared by his father's name. Or in Christopher's case, his brother's. But Good Christopher turned out to be a facade. And you're one hell of a long way from a saint, aren't you? And Ellie has no idea what she's gotten into."

Devlin felt his chest tighten, not with the need to lash out against this man, but with a bitter aching need to tell him the truth. The whole truth. Like Ellie, he would probably resist.

Like Ellie, he would probably end up understanding.

But he couldn't lay it all out. Not now. Maybe not ever. But he couldn't completely bullshit the detective, either. Or, he could. He just didn't want to. So instead he drew a breath and said, "I don't have any secrets from Ellie. She knows exactly what she's gotten into with me."

Lamar's eyes narrowed. "Is that a fact?"

Devlin gestured toward the chair opposite the desk. "Sit down."

To his surprise, Lamar sat.

"I'm not kicking you out. Give me points for that. And you know damn well I love Ellie, so give me points for that too. Agreed?"

The detective's brow furrowed. "Agreed."

Devlin exhaled, then pulled out his chair and sat across from Lamar. "Something's happened, and you obviously think I'm involved. Will you lay it out for me in small, simple sentences? Because believe me when I say I don't know what the fuck you're talking about."

It was clear from Lamar's face that he didn't believe him, but that was okay. So long as he didn't argue—so long as he told Devlin what he knew or thought he knew—then everything could probably be worked out.

"Well?" Devlin pressed.

"I know you didn't do it. You were in front of a room full of people singing the praises of your foundation and explaining the circumstances of your life when it happened. What I want to know is did you hire somebody?"

"To do what? Something that happened during my speech, obviously, but I need more information."

"Joseph Blackstone is dead. Killed in his extremely well-protected home by a single shot to the head fired from a sniper's rifle as he crossed in front of his bedroom window. There was a raid, too. His electronic equipment was breached. Most of his lieutenants scattered, but some were killed as well.

Devlin leaned back, his face completely blank. "Well. I hadn't heard." It was an easy lie. The truth was he hadn't asked the specifics of how Blackstone was killed. He just took his team's word that it had been taken care of.

"Did you hire someone?" Lamar repeated.

"No." That was the literal truth. He hadn't *hired* anyone for the job. "Why would you think that?"

"The timing. The convenience. Joseph Blackstone was a thorn in your side, and now he's gone."

"Well, I won't say that I'll mourn him," Devlin said. "You're right. The man was a problem. He was stealing secrets from my operation and managing to interfere with a number of rescue missions. Innocent people died because of that man. And a lot of assholes who should have been shut down by now are still in existence. We'll get them, eventually, but the people that his actions got killed aren't ever coming back."

Lamar leaned forward. "I get that you have money. I get that you have power. And I even believe that you want to help the world and the people who got the short end of the stick. People who can't help themselves and are being tortured and tormented. You have a big stick. There's no doubt about it. But hiring killers is not the way to wield it."

"I already said that I didn't hire anyone. But from a purely hypothetical point of view, I'm not sure I agree with you."

Lamar tilted his head to the side but said nothing, and Devlin took that as an invitation to continue.

"What should the wealthy do if not protect?" he asked. "Shouldn't we give back to the community? If you have the resources to make the world a better place shouldn't you do that?"

"Killing isn't the way to do it," Lamar said.

"Sometimes, maybe it is. Do you really want to condemn whoever killed Joseph Blackstone? He's the reason Tracy is dead. Doesn't she deserve to be vindicated?"

Lamar shook his head, his hands clenched tight on his knees. "That isn't the way it works. I swore an oath —"

"And you are not the one who killed him. You didn't break your oath, Detective. But deep down, aren't you glad that he's dead?"

"You're damn right I'm glad. But I can be glad that a monster is dead, and still know that rules were shattered."

"We live in a world filled with shades of gray, Detective. And someone has to stand on the line between good and bad."

"Yes," Lamar said. "Someone does. That someone is me and people like me, people who have sworn to protect and to serve. Not people who slink around behind the scenes, outside of the proper channels. Anarchy isn't the answer. And neither is net value. Your bank account doesn't give you carte blanche to make decisions for the rest of the world."

"We're still speaking hypothetically? I agree with you. Net value is not the test. But you have to admit that it damn sure helps with implementation. At least," he added, meeting Lamar's eyes, "I imagine that it would."

Lamar sighed, his shoulders sagging. "I would have given anything, anything to have been the one who pulled the trigger and took that son of a bitch out."

Devlin leaned back. That was not what he'd expected Lamar to say. "I understand. Believe me, I do."

"Reciprocity, Saint. I'm pretty sure you fucked me over. I'm pretty sure you've stayed quiet about a whole lot of things."

Devlin stayed perfectly still, studying the man's face before asking, "Would you have pulled the trigger, Detective?

If you'd been the one with that sniper's rifle, would you have done the deed?"

For a moment, Lamar said nothing. Then he shook his head. "Not in a million years would I have done that. Because that's not the way things are supposed to work. But," he added, his breath catching in his throat, "I wish to hell I could be that man."

Devlin stayed quiet, not sure what to say and hoping Lamar didn't regret his words tomorrow. He was speaking from anger and grief, Devlin knew. But he was speaking the truth as well, and he might not be comfortable knowing Devlin had seen even that brief moment of vulnerability.

After a moment, Lamar sighed, breaking the silence. "I like you. And Ellie loves you. And I love Ellie. She's one of the best friends I've ever had."

"I know."

"So don't put me in an awkward position, okay Saint?"

"All right," Devlin said. "I'll do my very best."

CHAPTER TWENTY-FIVE

"So what was that about?" I ask Lamar as he comes down the stairs. I look past him expecting to see Devlin, but there's no sign that he's following in Lamar's footsteps. I shift my attention back to Lamar and wait for him to answer.

"It was nothing. A misunderstanding. I'm just on edge."

I move to his side and put my arms around him. "I'm so sorry about Tracy. Are you sure you should be working the case? It's got to be driving you crazy, not being able to let it go for even a moment."

He squeezes me tight, then pulls back shaking his head. "No. But it's sweet of you to think about me. I just ... I needed answers. And, well, it looks like we got answers."

"Joseph Blackstone," I confirm. "I can't believe it all happened so quickly."

"Did you know that Blackstone is dead?"

"Dead?" I repeat, which is the kind of answer that isn't an answer. And means I don't have to lie to my friend.

"Killed by a sniper's rifle."

I reach out and brush his arm. "Don't feel guilt for being glad about that," I tell him. "He's the man that killed Tracy."

"I don't feel bad," he says. "And I'm glad he's dead." He meets my eyes. "But Jesus, Holmes, I'm actually angry that I'm not the one who took the bastard down."

"I get it," I say, "and you don't have a thing to feel guilty about. You should go put on PJ's. Another movie tonight, right?"

He shakes his head. "Not in the mood. I think I'm going to go back to my place."

I frown. "Are you sure it's safe?"

He lifts a shoulder. "How can we ever be sure? But if you're thinking about Christopher, I don't think he'll retaliate. He left the note for Brandy, didn't he? That felt like a confession and an apology."

"Maybe." I hug myself. "But he drove that SUV."

"I know. But I can take care of myself. And Saint's here with you two. And when do we say it's enough? For all we know he's gone for good."

"I get it."

"It's more than that," Lamar says. "I want to be home. And I want to stop by the florist and pick up some roses on the way."

"For Tracy?"

"To leave them outside her door."

I nod. "I think that's a sweet idea." I look around, noticing that Brandy has disappeared, probably giving us space to talk about the case. "You should go say goodbye to Brandy." He nods, and as he goes to her room, I head into my old bedroom to gather his things for him.

As much as I like the master bedroom, I have a feeling that Mr. Big Shot would prefer we not continue to stay in it. Tonight, Devlin and I will move back to my bedroom. Depending on how Brandy's doing, tomorrow we might even move back to Devlin's house. Lamar's right. There will always be threats. At some point, you have to slide back into your life.

Lamar comes back in as I'm zipping his duffle. "I kept your dirty clothes. I thought I'd wash them for you."

He smiles, "Thanks, Sherlock."

"Are you sure you're okay?"

"I will be. I just need a little time. I don't know if I was in love with her, but I miss her."

"I get it."

"Is it strange that I'm almost disappointed that this case was wrapped so quickly?" His voice is heavy with guilt.

I move to him and take his hands, shaking my head. "No. Oh, Lamar, no. You need closure. You were working it out through this case. Considering you figured out who killed her and then someone else shut him down so quickly, of course you're feeling a little lost. Your head must be spinning."

I frown as I study his face. "Are you positive you don't want to stay another night? I'm not sure I want you to be alone."

He shakes his head. "No. I'm fine. I'm going to go home, do the flowers, have a glass of Scotch, and sleep for a year."

"All right, then. I love you, Watson," I say.

"Love you back, Sherlock." He kisses my forehead and heads out, pausing in the doorway to my bedroom. "By the way, Brandy was just talking with her mother. She told her that she and Christopher broke up. That was probably the best spin to give Mrs. Bradshaw don't you think?"

I nod, but I feel bad for Brandy. She needs girl talk, and I'm really the only one there for her. Her mom's not a bad choice, but she doesn't understand, and her dad has been distant for years.

I follow Lamar to the door, then see him out and reset the

lock. Once again, I look at the stairs to see if Devlin is coming down, but I see no sign of him. I frown, wondering what it was that they talked about. Lamar seemed on edge, but not upset. But I don't know how that translates for Devlin. I start to head that direction, but then decide I want to check on Brandy.

I pop by her room and tap lightly on the door. I think I hear her say come in, so I push it open, only to see that all I've heard is the low mumble of voices on her television. I tiptoe across the room and shut it off. Then I go back to my friend. She's asleep, curled up in a ball on top of her covers. I take the folded blanket and pull it over her, gratified when she smiles in her sleep. I'll talk to her in the morning. Right now, what she needs most is rest. It really has been a hell of a few days, the kind that feel like it's been a year.

I still don't see Devlin when I leave her room, and now I'm out of excuses. I head up the stairs wondering what kind of mood I'm going to find him in. When I reach the landing, I see him, and my heart melts.

He's sitting straight on the sofa that's in the lounge area. His body is tense, but he's bent over with his elbows on his knees and his head in his hands. He tilts his head up, and I meet his eyes. I see pain there, and grief, and it could be from so many causes that I don't even know where to begin.

All I can do is go to him. I fall to my knees in front of him and put my hands on his. "Hey," I say.

He doesn't say a word, instead he just strokes my cheek then pulls me to him. He kisses me tenderly, and pulls me into his lap. We stay like that for a while, kissing and touching, but not saying a word.

Then he cradles me in his arms as he stands, and carries me to the bed. I start to speak, but he presses a fingertip to my lips. Slowly, he undresses me, and then I watch as he does the same. All the while, we watch each other, the heat that is always between us building.

We make love in silence, not the wild, punishing sex that I know he sometimes need. Hell, that we both sometimes need. No, this is gentle and sweet and so full of love and tenderness my heart aches. And the only time I speak is when my orgasm finally overtakes me and I arch up, crying out his name as my entire body sings with sweetness and love.

It's not until later, when we are sated and spooned together that he whispers, "What are you thinking?"

"That I'm not sure how I'm supposed to feel right now."

His body shakes with laughter "I'm not entirely sure how I should take that."

I roll over so that I'm facing him, my own laughter bubbling inside me. "Not because of that. About everything. I spent my entire life around law enforcement, and yet I don't have a sense of whether or not we're done. Are we done?"

"Done?"

"Are we safe now?" I ask, repeating what I'd asked Lamar.

He shifts so that he can slide up the bed, the sheet falling down around his hips as he leans up against the headboard. "Safe is a relative term." He looks at me. "Christopher is still out there."

"I know. I just had this conversation with Lamar. He's not concerned."

"He might be right."

I nod, then sit up myself holding the sheet over my bare breasts even though it's ridiculous to have any sort of modesty with this man. He's seen more of me than anybody. Still, right now I feel better not feeling exposed. "But Joseph Blackstone is dead. And so is Anna. They were the biggest threats. And I think your speech at the luncheon made it clear to anyone who might be after you for your father's money, that those funds don't exist for you anymore. It's all tied into the foundation."

I draw a breath. "My point is that it feels like we're back on an even keel. There's pain that we need to get over, and there's grief that we need to experience. We need to let time heal, but I don't think there's anyone coming after us now. Is there?"

He shakes his head. "It's always bad to talk in absolutes, but all the intelligence that I and my team can put together suggests that we're in the clear now. Except, of course, that Christopher remains a question mark. Probably not a threat, but we don't know for sure."

"I think he was manipulated. I think he was weak. I think he wanted a relationship with a brother he would have been better off to ignore. But he's a good man. I know he is. I've seen him around Brandy too much. He has a good heart."

"That doesn't mean we cross him off the list," Devlin says. "You should know that as well as I do."

I pull my knees up to my chest and hug them close. "I know. I do. But I don't like being that person."

"I can be that person for both of us. The one who's extra cautious. You know I'll always protect you. Maybe that's part of the job."

I offer him a smile, and I know he means it, but at the same moment I wonder if I'm losing my edge. I grew up dreaming of a career in law enforcement. To get the bad guys and put them away. I switched to trying to seek justice with a pen and paper, and I think I've done good along the way. But the whole thing is exhausting. I'm tired of looking for bad guys around corners. I have love back in my life now, and I want to revel in it. And maybe, just maybe, the world is about to let us do that.

"You're thinking too loud," Devlin says, reaching out to stroke my hair.

I shrug. "It's one of my bigger flaws."

He feigns shock. "You? Flaws?"

I take my pillow and smack him, grateful that he's lightening the moment. He grabs the pillow and since I don't let go of it he manages to pull me toward him. I laugh, then shift so that I'm settled on his lap, naked now that the sheet has fallen off me and all there is is a thin sheet between us. I can feel his arousal again and I shake my head. "Oh no. We've already had that part of the evening's entertainment."

"What if I want an encore?"

"I could be talked into it."

"Good," he says, twirling a strand of my hair around his finger. He meets my eyes, and the love I see reflected back at me makes me feel like the luckiest woman on earth and the most humbled, because what did I ever do to deserve a man like this?

"I do think he really loves her," Devlin says softly. It takes me a minute to realize that he's talking about Christopher and Brandy.

"I think so too," I say.

"The documents that the team found in Blackstone's house suggest that he was pressured. So you're probably right. He's probably not a threat to us."

"I don't like that he hurt her," I say. "I don't like thinking that he's bad or that he did bad things. But now that he's gone I really do think all of this is over. His relationship with Brandy, and all the threats to us and the people close to us." I draw a breath. "Do you understand what I'm saying?"

"You don't want us to go after him."

"I don't. I think he was a victim of circumstance. I think he was a victim of his own lack of backbone. But I think he really loved Brandy. And I think if you find him and either aim the police toward him or even do your own kind of justice, all that's going to do for Brandy is make it last even longer than it would have. She's in mourning now, much like Lamar is. But Tracy can't come back. Christopher could. We could bring him back, and that would be like bringing a ghost back into her life. I don't want her to be haunted."

"The man almost killed you. He took an SUV and almost ran you down."

I nod slowly. "I'm not discounting that. But there are other factors. Brandy's my very best friend. I don't want this whole thing to linger for her any longer than it has to. It's a tragedy, and I want her to get past it. God knows it's not the first tragedy she's had to endure. But she won't move on if you keep investigating and it keeps getting tossed in her face or if he ends up dragged back."

I study his face, trying to read whether or not he agrees with me, but Devlin can be the most unreadable man on the planet when he wants to, and right now, it appears that he's trying very hard.

"Devlin, what are you thinking?"

He leans back, his expression tense. "I do want Christopher to pay," he says, making my heart sink. "I want him to pay for what he did to you, for the way he helped Anna keep her secrets and enact her plans. For all the things he's done for Joseph Blackstone over the years. Selfishly, I think what I want him to pay for the most is the fact that he made me feel a kinship toward him. The fact that we were both tainted with the sins of our family. I don't deserve that label, and I didn't think he did either. But he does."

"And that hurts. He played you."

Devlin chuckles. "Well, I wouldn't put it quite that way, but yes, he played me."

"I'm sorry. He did, and it's a terrible thing. But I stand by my own decision. If it were up to me, I would let him walk."

He crosses his arms over his chest and studies me, the corners of his mouth turning down. He's silent for so long that I start to get edgy.

"What?"

"This man committed crimes, you know that right?"

"Yes, but —"

Devlin shakes his finger. "No, no, no buts. He committed crimes, and you're saying that we should let him go. That the justice system shouldn't do its job."

I'm not entirely sure where he's going with this, but I have an inkling. And so I bite my lower lip and wait for him to answer for me.

He does. "How is that different from what Saint's Angels does?"

"Because I'm not suggesting you kill him."

"But you *are* making that decision. You're taking that step. You're saying hold back. What we do is simply the reverse."

I don't want to argue with him about this, especially because I'm tired enough that my mind can't come up with a good counter-argument, which frustrates me. So instead I just snap, "Look, are you going to go after him or not?"

He laughs, and I know he understands why I'm frustrated. "No. I want to. The man's pissed me off in a million ways, not the least of which is hurting Brandy and making me feel like a fool. But I won't go after him because you don't want me to. And the thing I want most of all is for you and your friends to be happy."

Pleasure soaks through me and I smile. "Oh. Well, okay then." I lean forward my hands on his chest as I give him a soft kiss. Then I pull back, another question dancing on my lips, one I'm not sure I should ask, but once again Devlin knows me well.

"What is it?"

I shrug. "It's just—It's just that I don't like him not knowing. Or Brandy." I don't have to explain that the him I'm referring to is Lamar, and the subject I'm referring to is Saint's Angels.

"I know you don't, but I'm not yet to that point where we should let them know. I think that really is too dangerous."

"I thought you were concerned with me keeping secrets from my friends."

"I suppose if you were part of it, things might be different. But you're not. You're a bystander and a watcher. Hell, you're my talisman for what's good and solid and centered."

"I don't think I—"

"I do. And that's not the point. But I don't think that it's fair to the others on the team that your emotions about your friends should come into play under those circumstances."

It's a fair argument, and one I hadn't thought of.

He tilts my chin up with his fingertip. "If I were in the CIA, would you feel strange about not being able to tell your friends what I do?"

"No, I suppose not. But you're not in the CIA."

"Are you sure?" He winks, and I laugh, and even though I am sure, I have to actually concede that no, I really don't know.

"So I'm supposed to just pretend like you're an undercover operative, and I'm the poor woman left behind who doesn't know what you're up to when you go on your secret missions?"

"I think we can play that game for a while." He flips me over making me squeal. "Right now," he says, "I think we both need to be undercover."

He slides down my body and pulls the sheet up over both of us. And then he kisses me, long and deep and with enough passion that I forget all of my fears, all of my wishes, all of my problems, and all of my secrets. Right now, I'm nothing but desire, and once again, I let Devlin take me away on a wave of sweet forgetfulness, lost in the pleasure of skin against skin.

CHAPTER TWENTY-SIX

Late the next morning I watch as Devlin packs the suitcase he's been living out of since we left for New York what seems like a millennium ago. After going straight to Tracy's murder scene, we'd come here to be with Brandy, then almost immediately headed off to Idaho.

It's been a whirlwind, and now that Blackstone's out of the picture, Devlin's ready to get back to his own place. And me...

Well, I'm feeling at loose ends.

"Come home with me," Devlin says.

"I want to be with you," I tell him. "You know that. But I don't want to leave Brandy alone right now. She's fragile."

"Is she scared Christopher might come back?"

I shake my head. "No. We all agree the odds are low, and she knows you have security watching the house. But she's been through hell and she's my best friend."

"I get it," he says. "And I'll miss being here. But I miss my house, too. And my closet."

I laugh. I can't argue with that.

"Well, you should know that Jake's going to be a wreck if

the house empties out. He's been in doggie heaven with everyone here. Another reason for me to stay."

He comes and sits beside me on the bed. "You're a good friend. To both of them."

"You really don't mind?"

"Are you breaking up with me?"

I cock my head and give him *that* look.

"Am I going to have to resort to cold showers?"

"Definitely not."

"Then I think it's just fine. Truly. But you still have to come with me to my place today. I have something for you."

I perk up. "Really. For me? What is it?"

"If I told you, it wouldn't be surprise, would it?"

It's silly to be so happy over something so small, especially when I don't even know what the surprise it, but it's been a stressful few days, and the thought that Devlin has gotten something for me in the midst of chaos makes me undeniably happy. "Thank you."

He laughs. "You haven't even seen what it is yet."

I lean forward and kiss him. "It doesn't matter. You thought of it. You were thinking of me. It will be amazing."

He cups the back of my head and kisses me again, this time using his tongue to urge my mouth open. The kiss deepens, and I start to lose myself in it, to crave more. Then he pushes me away with a devilish grin. "That's something to look forward to."

"Jerk." But I'm smiling as I say it.

We play twenty questions on the way to his house. I don't manage to guess what it is, though I have learned that it is bigger than a breadbox, it's not alive, and it's something I want. Beyond that, I'm clueless.

We're in his Tesla, and he pauses before the turn onto his

street. "I want you to close your eyes, and I'll tell you when you can open them."

I do what he says with complete obedience. I feel the car move, and as we go down the street, I notice when he turns into the driveway. The car stops, and it's only then that he says, "Okay. Open your eyes." I do, then turn to him with a frown. All I see is his garage door.

"Unfair. You got me all riled up about nothing."

"Oh ye of little faith." He takes the clicker for the garage door and taps the button. It starts to scroll up and, to my delight, Devlin taps a button on the radio and Beethoven's *Ode to Joy* starts to play, making me laugh.

The sound catches in my throat though when I see what's being revealed. My Shelby, looking as brand new and shiny as the day that Uncle Peter presented her to me. I sit in shock for a moment then turn to look at Devlin. "She's fixed. You fixed her?"

Devlin knows better than anyone how much Shelby means to me. She's part of our history, and I realize as I'm looking at her in the garage that I'm crying. I turn back to him, a tear-stained mess. "You're amazing."

"I told you I was going to fix her. Did you think I was joking?"

"I didn't think it would be this fast."

"Well, she's part of the family. We had to make sure she had the best, most expeditious care possible."

I don't know what to say, so I just gaze in wonder at my beautiful car. Then I turn and gaze in wonder at the man I love, almost unable to believe that with the life I've had, I managed to get so lucky.

He takes my hand and squeezes it, and I'm sure he's reading my thoughts.

"Come on. Let's take her out for a spin."

I'm so giddy at the idea that I actually clap my hands. He parks the Tesla in one side of the two-car garage, and while he runs inside the house to grab something, I slide behind Shelby's wheel and sigh, then bend over and kiss her steering wheel. I brush my hand over her dashboard, then I get out of the car because I just have to walk all the way around her. She's in perfect condition. Her blue paint sparkling. Her tires brand new. Her headlights shining.

The moment he returns, I throw my arms around Devlin again. "You are amazing. You are getting as much sex as you want tonight, just so you know."

He laughs, then pulls me close. "If I'd known that would be your reaction, I would've had her fixed even sooner."

"Just don't go crashing her so you can fix her again. I'll tell you a secret. You can pretty much always get sex anytime you want. But don't let it go to your head."

"Believe me. I'm very glad to hear that."

I get behind the wheel again, and this time I fire her engine. She practically purrs, and I know she's as happy to see me as I am to see her.

"Where to?" I ask.

"Just drive," Devlin says. "Maybe see how she handles on the curves, then end up at the tidal pools."

I glance at him. "I like that idea."

She handles as well as she always has, and I take the roads at what most people would consider an unreasonably fast speed, but to me it's freedom and glory. I love the control, the responsiveness. It's a thrill. A rush. Hell, it's a little like sex, and I glance over at Devlin, my smile so broad my cheeks ache.

I calm it down once we hit the Pacific Coast Highway, then turn left so that I can continue back south to Laguna Cortez's official border. The Devlin Saint Foundation isn't that far away, and as soon as I've passed Pacific Avenue, I pull into the parking lot.

I'm breathing hard and feel incredible. I know my hair is a mess since I didn't put on the ball cap that's usually in my glove box, but I don't care. "That was the best present ever." I'm so happy, I'm probably glowing.

"I thought you took those curves a little bit slower than I expected."

I shrug. The truth is I did. A tiny bit. Maybe. I take his hand and squeeze "I guess I'm not as reckless as I used to be."

He nods, and I know he understands what I mean. I've come too close to losing him before. I won't lose him again.

We get out of the car and start walking toward the foundation, but we don't go inside. He mentions that before we leave to go back home, he needs to pop in and get a box that he's had Tamra put together for him with certain papers that he needs to review.

But right now this is only about us. The tidal pools are behind the foundation, and that's where we head. They're the site of our first kiss, and we both always seem drawn back to them, almost like a magnet.

As we walk hand-in-hand, it strikes me that I'm feeling light and free for the first time in days. "I love feeling like this," I tell him. "But at the same time I can't help but think of Lamar and Brandy. They both lost somebody, and I know it's going to be a long time before they feel as light as I do right now."

"Don't," he says. "Don't feel guilty that you're doing okay. You have to take your pleasure where you can find it, and they would tell you the same. It's not as if you haven't earned it. You've had your share of hell. More than your share. We both have. And while I mourn for what they've lost, too, right now what I feel most is the joy of being with you."

I nod slowly, soaking up his words. "You're right. And I know that Lamar and Brandy would feel the same way, too." I squeeze his hand in silent acknowledgement as we reach the pools. I'm about to say more, but he presses a finger to my lips, shushing me, and then to my complete shock, he drops to one knee. My hand flies to my mouth, because this can't be happening. Except it is.

It really is.

"El, you know you're the love of my life. You know all my secrets now, and you haven't run. At this point, even if you did, I would go chasing after you. I want you forever. And I want you publicly. I want you to belong to me. You may be mine right now, but I want the world to know it. I want it to be official. So what I'm saying, my darling El, is that I want you to marry me. Will you do me the honor of being my wife?"

My knees turn to rubber and I fall to the sand beside him. My heart is pounding. My mind is spinning. I want this man —I want him forever.

And I know with absolute certainty what my answer has to be.

"I don't have an engagement ring he says, but I know you kept your mother's. I thought you might like that one, so I thought we could get it resized."

"I—that's a beautiful thought."

I swallow and blink back tears, then I draw a breath and meet his eyes. "I love you, Devlin. I love you more than I ever imagined I was capable of loving anyone. And it's a miracle that we're back together."

His head tilts just slightly. "I hear a *but* coming."

"Dammit, it's surprising me as much as it is you. It's only —" I stumble, trying to explain what's in my heart. "It's just that I love this, too. And I'm not ready for it to end."

"This?" He shakes his head slowly, and I twirl my hand, as if that's a form of coherent conversation.

Since he clearly still doesn't get it, I try again. "The way we were before all hell broke loose. Me at Brandy's, you at your place. A few sleepovers to keep things interesting. Dinner dates. Cocktails." I shrug. "Normal stuff."

"Are you saying we aren't normal?"

I bite back a laugh as I take his hands. "I'm saying I want to pretend to be. At least a little. We never got that, and I like it. Besides, if I move in with you, I lose out on my house. And I'm looking forward to fixing it up and moving in." My childhood home had gone on the rental market after my father was killed, with the income going into a trust for me until I was twenty-one. Since then, I've kept it rented and applied the income to my Manhattan rent.

Now, though, my tenant is in the process of moving out. I want to go in, update the place, and live there for awhile, surrounded by the thrill of owning real estate and the nostalgia of being in my childhood home.

"I want you to help me replace the countertops and varnish the floors. Then I want us to christen all the rooms in the house. I want you to come over on a whim, to sweep me into the bedroom or just to leave flowers on the doorstep. I want you to call me late at night and we can watch a show together, like in *When Harry Met Sally.*"

That makes him grin, and he reaches out, brushing the pad of his thumb over my cheek. "You want the romance."

"I have romance," I tell him. "I want the storybook. I want what we never got when we were young. I think we deserve it." I pause, trying to read his reaction, but he's got his corporate face on, and I can't be sure of what's in his head. "Are you mad?"

"Mad?" Now I can see what he's thinking—he's incredulous. "Mad? Not at all. I'm—I'm not sure. I think I'm strangely flattered."

"Really? You really understand?"

"I do. And even if I didn't, I'd accept that's what you want."

I didn't think it was possible to be happier than I'd been when that garage door rose, but I am. "You're really okay with it?"

He taps his lower lip, making a show of thinking. "You said there were dates?"

"Lots of dates," I assure him.

"And sleepovers?"

"I can't guarantee much sleeping," I tease, "but in theory, yes."

"Then yes. I am really okay with this."

"Yeah?" My voice is soft, almost shy, and I don't know why.

He holds my gaze for a moment, then cups the back of my head. "All I want is you, baby. Don't you know that?"

"Then we're even. Because you're all I want, too. And my fancy wedding dress with the season's designer shoes. I just don't want that last part right now."

"Except for the shoes," Devlin says.

I laugh. "It's like you know me."

I don't even realize that we've stood and started walking again until we're already a ways down the beach. We're talking about nothing and everything. About life, about our past, about our memories, about how wonderful it is that despite all the torment that we suffered in our tumultuous relationship that we were able to end up at this point. A solid couple. Together.

I never wanted anything when I was young other than to be Alex Leto's girl, and now that he's Devlin Saint, he's still all

I want. One day, he'll put a ring on my finger. And I'm holding tight to that future, excited by the adventures we'll have as we move toward it.

It's not until we reach the north edge of town where the cliffs start to rise from the sand that I realize where we are. We're standing right in front of Uncle Peter's house. It's one of the few houses in Laguna Cortez that's on the beach side of the highway. It's a stunning contemporary with lots of glass and beautiful views.

"Some of my best memories are here," I say. "And you're in all of them."

"And some of your worst memories, too," he says.

I nod. "You leaving. That's my worst memory of all." I sigh deeply "But you're back. And you're mine. So I guess it all worked out all right." I shoot him a cocky grin and he laughs.

"I love you."

"You better."

"I really want to be home with you right now," he says.

I flash him a wicked grin. "Well, maybe we should hurry back."

"I like that idea. We have to stop in and pick up those files, but as soon as the box is in my hands, we can take Shelby home."

Our return walk is much faster than our leisurely walk to Peter's house. We're back at the foundation in record time, and on the way Devlin texts Tamra to make sure that she's already left the file box at reception. I check my phone at the same time, and see that I missed a call from Brandy. I consider calling her back, but Devlin frowns and says we should hurry.

"What's going on?"

"I don't know," he says. "But Tamra's not answering her text, and that's not like her."

I frown, too. He's right; it's not like her at all. Anyone else, and I'd say give it a few minutes. But Tamra always responds to Devlin within seconds.

We hurry, the glow fading as worry sets in. I tell myself we're being silly, but the moment we step from the covered patio into the lobby, I know we were right to be concerned.

Tamra is hovering by Eric at the reception desk, her expression murderous. Brandy is beside her, her eyes red and swollen.

"What the hell?" I ask, rushing toward her.

"He did it," Brandy says. "That wormy little prick went and did it."

I look over my shoulder to Devlin, but he looks as confused as I feel. Before we can ask, Tamra speaks. "William Tarkington—Walt," she says, her eyes locked on Devlin's. "He's suing you for assault."

CHAPTER TWENTY-SEVEN

Cold fury cut through Devlin, and if Eric hadn't been sitting right there, he probably would have smashed one of the glass coffee tables. But Eric was an employee, whereas the others were family.

So instead, he very calmly asked that they move the conversation to his office, then headed that way, barely feeling the supportive grip of Ellie's hand in his as he marched across the lobby to the elevator, wishing he could justify even fifteen minutes with a speed bag to work off some of the rage that was curling through him.

"I knew we should have done more damage control," Tamra said, the moment his office doors closed behind them. "You're not a man who needs to be getting into bar fights."

"He had it coming," Devlin said. "I told you as much at the time."

"And nothing else." She sighed, then steepled her fingers under her chin as she gathered her thoughts. He'd never realized how much of a stand-in for a mother Tamra had become, but now he felt an unpleasant twisting in his gut for disappointing her, even though he would do it all over again if he had to.

He drew a breath, forcing himself not to look at Brandy.

Tamra narrowed her eyes at him. "You never did tell me what that was about, Devlin. I can't do my job unless I know the facts. Neither can Arnold," she added, referring to the attorney he kept on retainer. "And his lawyer? Think about what a field day he's going to have pointing out that The Wolf's son is wandering the streets of Laguna Cortez beating people up. And for what? What did this vile little man do at that restaurant that bothered you so, so much?"

"It doesn't matter," Devlin said, as Ellie squeezed his hand. She was standing beside him, giving him strength. And, he noticed, also not looking at Brandy.

Tamra was looking, though. "What happened at that dinner, Brandy?" She frowned. "For that matter, why are you here? How did you even know? I only found out because Arnold accepted service. How did you know?"

"I—" She squirmed as if she was sitting on coals. "Lamar heard about it. And he told me. Because I was there, you know. At the dinner."

"Exactly," Tamra said. "What happened at that dinner?"

Brandy looked up, her eyes meeting his, and Devlin shook his head. He did not want her telling the truth. Not this way, where she felt trapped again, with no choices.

"Brandy?" Tamra pressed.

"It was because of Ellie," Devlin said before Brandy could respond. "He said some particularly vile things about her sleeping with me."

"And you lost your temper?" He heard the incredulity in her voice. He had a temper, that much was true. But they all knew that he had remarkable control, too.

"I did," he said. "It was about Ellie, after all." Tamra would believe that. And the lie only had to hold for a while. Long enough for him to offer the kind of settlement that would make Walt go away, all tied up with a nice, ironclad confidentiality agreement.

Tamra's shoulders slumped. "I'm surprised at you." She shook it off. "Well, we'll deal with it. I suppose that's part of my job. And whatever he said to you, Ellie, I'm sorry. It must have been horrible."

"Oh. Yeah. You know how—"

"*He raped me.*"

The words seemed to hang in the air. Even Brandy, who had spoken, looked confused as to where they'd come from.

"Brandy," he said softly, and the words seemed to bring her back to life.

"No." She drew a breath. "No, you're not telling Tamra some bullshit story because of me. He drugged me and he raped me when I was in high school. He got me pregnant. That's why Devlin did it."

Tamra met Devlin's eyes, and he nodded, confirming the truth.

"I see," Tamra said. "Thank you for telling me. Let me think about how we can proceed without having to share your secret with the world." She took a step toward Brandy, then met the younger woman's eyes. "Are you okay now? Would you like me to find someone professional for you to talk to about this?"

"I don't know." Brandy's gaze darted to Ellie. "I'll think about it. Mostly, I just appreciate you asking. You can keep Devlin from getting dragged through the mud? Really?"

"I'll do my very best. In fact, I think we should—"

The vibration of his phone caught Devlin's attention, and he tuned out the conversation between the women so that he could check his phone, just in case it was Arnold calling to talk about the lawsuit.

It wasn't Arnold. It was worse. Because that apparently was the way this day was going. It started off wonderful, and it was slowly spiraling down into hell.

Beside him, Ellie drew in a sharp gasp, and he realized that she'd been reading over his shoulder.

He met her eyes. She looked as angry and frustrated as he felt.

In front of them, Tamra's gaze darted between both of them. "What? Is it bad news? Is it about Walt?"

"I don't know," Devlin said, working to keep his voice level. "All it says is *You're going to lose everything, Saint. I'm going to make sure it happens.*"

Tamra's brow furrowed, and he saw the anger flare in her eyes. She kept it together though, always the consummate professional. "Who's it from?"

"I don't know. Just a phone number. I'll try to find out, but I have a feeling we'll have about as much luck with that as we have with the earlier texts that Ellie was getting."

"Anna was sending me those," Ellie said. "At least that's what we've been assuming, especially since they stopped once she died. And that's a big thing to point out. She's dead, so I don't think she's sending this text. And so is Joseph Blackstone. I suppose a lieutenant could have sent it, but considering the timing, shouldn't we be considering Walt?"

"I'll agree as to the timing," Devlin said. "But it seems ballsier than I'd expect from that little bastard."

"There's someone else," Brandy said, her wide eyes darting between Devlin and Ellie. "It could have been Christopher. I know everyone thinks he hated his brother, but what if he didn't? Or what if it's just about family?"

Her words were like a punch in the gut, because he knew

how much that suggestion was costing Brandy. Ellie released his hand, then went over and sat on the arm of Brandy's chair.

"She's right," Ellie said. "He's our prime suspect now, isn't he?" Devlin saw the pain on her face. That horrible feeling of not being able to protect the people you love. A pain he knew only too well, and he wished he could have shielded Ellie and Brandy from it forever.

But he couldn't. So all he said was, "Yes. He tops the list."

"Christopher and Walt," Brandy said. "It's like I'm cursed."

"I'm so sorry," Ellie said. "Why don't we go? Tamra and Devlin don't need us. Let's go home and eat so many chocolate chip muffins we're too bloated to remember any of this."

She met Devlin's eyes, and he saw the grief mixed with loss. The horror of what Brandy was going through. And the loss of their perfect day, which had become tarnished by the intrusion of reality.

"That's a good idea," Devlin said. "I'll be along soon. You're right that Tamra and I have a few things to go over."

"It's okay," Brandy said. "I'm fine to go by myself." She glanced up at Ellie. "I do want to talk and then veg, but right now, I just want to be alone in my head. Maybe lock myself in the sewing room and clear my thoughts." She grimaced. Her nose wrinkling. "Is that okay?"

"I—well, sure. But are you okay to drive?"

"Totally. It's not far. And I'm upset, but I'm not incapable."

"Sorry." Ellie pulled her into a hug. "I just want—I just want to make it better."

"I know you do. I wish you could."

"Yeah…"

"See you at home." She turned to Devlin. "No keeping

Ellie at your place tonight. I'm calling best friend privilege and keeping her home."

"No worries there. In fact, I'll join you at Big Shot Mansion tonight."

As he'd hoped, she grinned. "Well, in that case, I really will make muffins."

As Ellie walked Brandy to her car, he and Tamra went over some thoughts on how to spin the Walt litigation. By the time they finished, Ellie had rejoined them.

"We can go soon, too," he said as he composed a new text. "I just want to pull Lamar in on the Walt side of things."

"A detective?" Tamra asked. "It'll be Lamar's job to investigate you."

"I trust Lamar to do the right thing and to investigate the shit out of this case," Devlin said. "The police deserve to have all the facts as well."

Tamra frowned, but ultimately nodded.

"Honestly," Ellie began, "We're not going to know anything until we find out something about the text or they send another one. There are too many possibilities. The timing may suggest Walt, but it also suggests Christopher or one of Blackstone's lieutenants."

"That's true," he agreed. "Except for the fact that I wasn't on that mission. And Blackstone didn't know about Saint's Angels. That much seems pretty clear from the documents that the team found in his home. Which means his men wouldn't have reason to believe that I was behind the assault."

"Devlin," Ellie said, "don't be naive. Of course they would. He'd been harassing you. He'd been pulling your strings with regard to the security breaches for months. Saint's Angels went in, sure, but nobody there would know their affiliation. Only that someone finally bested Joseph Blackstone.

And anybody paying attention would assume—quite rightly—that it was you who pulled the trigger."

CHAPTER TWENTY-EIGHT

B*efore...*
"I understand, General." Alex stood at attention in front of the gray-haired man. His title was General, but Alex knew that he wasn't serving. Not anymore. Maybe not ever. He was one of those commanders who looked like he served in the military, but actually served in secret. In the kind of organization that hid in the shadows. The kind that movies made up, thinking they were fiction, but they really weren't.

"You understand the ramifications?" the general asked. Alex nodded. Right then, the government was offering him the deal of a lifetime. Something he had fantasized about, that he was certain he could never pull off entirely on his own. "Absolutely. I think I've made clear that this is a mission I am more than eager to take on."

For a moment, the general stayed at his desk. Then he pushed back and stood. He came around the desk and put his hand on Alex's shoulder. "You're a good soldier. We won't be losing you forever. But some people will. You can live with that?"

"Yes sir." Alex answered with hesitation, but even as he

spoke, he knew it was a lie. The general had come to him with a scheme for accomplishing something he had always wanted to take care of, and Alex would be eternally grateful. He would willingly accept the help, and in payment, he would carry out the missions, committing three years of his life in exchange for the help he needed. But some of the parameters weren't acceptable. That, however, was something he intended to keep to himself. He'd learned a lot of things over the course of his life, and one of them was how to keep a secret, and how to choose confidantes who would keep that secret too.

So all he said now was, "I'm ready, sir."

"Tomorrow then. 0800. Report to Mr. Johnson." He stuck out his hand for Alex to shake, the action startling him, since it was such an un-military like gesture. Alex resisted the urge to salute, and instead took the other man's hand firmly in his.

"We understand that this is something you want, but we also acknowledge that you're making a big sacrifice. We thank you. Your country thanks you."

Alex nodded. "Thank you, sir."

"Have you decided on what your name will be?"

"Saint," Alex said. "My new name will be Devlin Saint."

"So you're really going through with it?"

"Do you think I shouldn't?" Alex asked, looking at his friend Ronan, the only one with whom he'd shared the secret. So far, anyway.

"No. I'm completely on board," Ronan said. "It just feels like something out of the Bourne books."

Alex laughed. Ronan wasn't wrong.

"You're clear on the parameters?"

Ronan cocked his head and looked down his nose at Alex. "What do you think?"

Alex laughed. Ronan was the most capable man he knew. And he was glad he would have him on his team when this was all over. He hadn't decided who else would ultimately join him. He was going to talk to Tamra for sure. That would be a little dicey. She wasn't in the military, so she couldn't be an active part of the team he was putting together. But he thought she was a good choice as a coordinator. Someone who could help him with both sides of the world he wanted to build. The secret side and the public side. A public side that would try to solve the world's problems with philanthropy and education. A secret side with a similar goal, but much different methods.

"And you're okay with doing this?" Ronan asked. "The price they want you to pay."

"I am. Hell, it's been a fantasy of mine my entire life." Ronan knew the story of Alex's life. Who his father was, how he escaped to the military by telling The Wolf that he was joining up to gain respectability as well as skills. So that he could hide better in plain sight and further his father's business. That, of course, was a lot of bullshit.

"I can go with you."

"No. I know you could, but I have to do this alone."

Ronan nodded slowly. "Then I'll see you when you get back."

"Not me."

Ronan laughs. "Well, I suppose that is true. Good luck, man."

Ronan's wish of good luck stuck with him as he left the base on the East Coast and traveled west to Nevada. He went in secret, using routes that he'd planned years ago, winding his way into the compound undetected, as only someone who had grown up there could possibly know how to do. He got himself situated, hiding near the practice range where his father went every morning. His post was a quarter of a mile away, and he laid in the dirt, his rifle at the ready for more than half an hour until the man finally appeared.

Daniel Lopez, AKA The Wolf. He had his pistol in his hand, his shoulders thrown back, his chest out. He walked with a pride he didn't deserve, his step heavy.

If he carried the weight of any of the thousands of people whose deaths he has caused, Alex didn't see it. Finally, his father was in position standing on the range, his gun lifted towards the target.

Alex never gave him time to shoot. He'd already aimed his own rifle, and he gently pulled the trigger. He'd made allowances for the wind, for the distance, and the shot was clean. Right through his father's eye, the kind of shot that would have made his father proud.

The report rang out across the compound. He hadn't used a silencer. He hadn't wanted to.

Now, he packed up his gear and moved out quickly, once again using the knowledge he had gained from living in this hell to get him out without anyone seeing him. Once he was clear of the compound, he took the car that had been left for him and drove to the pre-arranged safe house. He stayed there for a week, before receiving his instructions.

He followed them to the next safe house, then a week after that to the next. Finally he ended up in the last safe house that also acted as a medical facility. He was there two months. But it was worth the time, and it was worth the pain because when he walked out after what felt like an eternity it wasn't Alejandro Lopez who was leaving that place.

It was Devlin Saint, and he was walking into a whole new life.

CHAPTER TWENTY-NINE

he present...

I let Devlin drive Shelby because I want to call Brandy as soon as we get in the car. She answers on the first ring, and I blurt, "How are you doing?"

"Good." The word is hard, and I hear no sound of tears, so I'm grateful for that. "Fury is making it easier to deal," she says, as if answering my unspoken question.

"I'm glad to hear it." I grimace. "Not the fury part, but the—"

"—the part where I'm not completely breaking down into a sobbing little ball and whimpering in the corner until you get back?"

I laugh. "Okay, maybe not that dramatic, but that's the basic idea. You're really okay?"

"Yeah. I think so. I'm just—I'm just so damn angry. I don't think I've ever been this angry in all my life."

"It's because Walt's horrible, and he's trying to suggest that it's Devlin who's the one who's a terrible person."

"That's it. Yes. That's it exactly. He's a total creep, and

he's latching onto the fact that Devlin's getting all this crap thrown on him. And he's more than happy to catch me in the middle of it just so he can try to, I don't know, get his name in the news or something. Does he think I won't fight this? Does he think I won't tell what he did?"

I don't answer that. Of course he thinks that she won't say anything. It's been years, and she said nothing. What else would he think? He doesn't know that she was prepared to speak out tonight to protect Devlin, something I love her even more for. But I'm glad it didn't go that way. Devlin is steel, but Brandy's softer. And the truth is, I don't want fate to temper her.

"Please tell me you two are on your way over here. I thought I wanted to be alone, but it turns out I want company in my fury."

"We are," I assure her. "We're going to pop by Devlin's first, because he needs to pick something up. But then we'll be there. Is that okay? Do you need us to come sooner? You're sure you're okay?" I sound like a machine gun firing questions at her, and I try to ramp it back, but I'm angry, and I'm scared for her.

"No, no. It's fine. I'm fine. Truly. I'm just pissed, and I want my friends."

"Okay. Good. Stay pissed, and we'll join you in that as soon as we get there."

"No worries about that. I have a feeling I'm going to be pissed for at least twenty-four hours. Then it might settle down into a slow burn, but I kind of doubt it."

Despite everything I laugh. "Alarm set?"

"Yes, yes. You don't have to worry. And Jake's right here beside me."

"I'm not entirely sure that that's going to reassure me that you're safe," I say. "Jake might be the sweetest dog in the world, and I'm pretty sure that he would just lick a bad guy to death."

She makes a snorting sound. "Jake says to tell you that he's insulted by your lack of trust."

I laugh. "Well, give him a kiss for me." Honestly, it's only partly true anyway. He really is a sweet dog, but I also know that he wouldn't hesitate to protect Brandy.

I end the call about the time we reach Devlin's street. He forgoes pulling into the driveway and simply parks Shelby on the street in front of his house. He hops out and pauses long enough to look back at me. "Do you want to come? I'll only be a minute."

"I'm happy to if you want me, but I'm also happy to just sit here in my restored beauty and bask in the awesomeness of Shelby."

He laughs. "Bask all you want. Like I said, I'll only be a minute."

I watch as he circles the car then moves down the sidewalk to the front door. He really does have the most amazing ass, and it is particularly nice in the jeans he's been wearing today.

I sigh, enjoying the view of what is mine. I watch as he reaches the door and punches in the code. I can even hear the little beeps from where we are. Then I hear him curse. He turns around and trots back towards me. He's midway to the car when he says, "By the way I was going to ask you if —"

And that's when the world explodes.

Devlin is thrown forward by a fiery ball of flame and debris, and my throat is suddenly raw. I realize I'm screaming, scrambling to get out of the car, pushing Shelby's door open as I burst forward, grabbing Devlin's arms and pulling him toward me. His shirt is singed and we fight it off of him. I knock him to the grass and roll him over, amazed that he's gotten away mostly unscathed.

He clings to me, both of us breathing hard as we shove back on the unmarred grass and watch what's left of his house go up in a massive fireball.

***

My ears are ringing, and it looks like an all-out war on the street. Devlin's saying something but I can't hear him, and his weight on top of me is crushing. I'm breathing hard and I look out at the surreal landscape. The world seems to be burning.

There's a roaring in my head, and it takes me a moment to realize it's sirens approaching.

"Baby? Baby, are you okay?"

I blink, trying to process the words. They sound like sand in my ears, thick and heavy.

"*El.* Ellie, baby." Devlin shifts so that he's no longer on top of me. I draw a breath, then immediately start coughing. He pulls me up, then holds me as he pats my back as I try to get my body under control. When I stop hacking, I push back, needing to see his face. It's ash-covered, but it's him, and I almost burst into tears at the realization of what I'd almost lost. "Oh, God," I say. "Devlin, oh, God, Devlin."

"It's okay. I'm fine, baby. I'm fine. Are you hurt?"

For a moment, I don't understand. "Me? *Me?*"

The horror plays through my mind again, like a movie in a perpetual loop. "Are *you* okay? Are you hurt? Did you break anything? God, that explosion actually threw you into the yard."

My words are tumbling out on top of each other. "Did you

know? Did you sense that something was wrong? What happened? Why aren't you in that house? Thank God you weren't in that house."

He doesn't answer. He just pulls me close again, and I cling to him, my whole body shaking. I could have lost him. I almost did lose him right in that moment. I start to sob, and at the same time I hate myself for losing it like this, but I can't bear the thought of not having Devlin beside me anymore, and I can't quite wrap my head around how close I came to almost losing him.

He holds me, his face pressed against my hair. I can hear his breathing, his soft murmurs of *we're okay, we're okay.* I hold the words close, because right now, they're the only thing that matters. *We're okay.* The house is gone, but he's alive. By some miracle, Devlin's alive.

I start to shake. "You almost—Devlin, if you hadn't turned back to—"

"I know, I know." He holds me tighter, rocking me, and I cling to him, certain I will never let him go again.

"We almost lost each other."

"We didn't. You're here. I'm here. We're safe."

"But—"

"*No.*" The word is fierce, as if he can hold back tragedy by sheer will. But I know he can't. Like my parents—like Peter—I almost lost him. A few inches in the wrong direction, and I would have lost him.

"We're fine," he says, though his voice is shaky. "El, look at me. I'm still here. I'm not your mom or your dad. We beat her," he says. "We beat the bitch."

A choking laugh escapes me, the sound startling me. "That bitch Fate," I say, then wipe my damp cheeks. "We did, didn't we?"

"We did."

"You can't control the world," I say, my eyes drawn back to what was once his home.

"No." He takes my chin and makes me look at him. "But I'll damn well try."

I nod, then cling to him again. We're bathed in flashing lights, and soon a fireman puts a blanket around both of us and gently leads us aside. We sit at the end of the fire truck, and an EMT looks over both of us, saying that we're both in fine shape, though Devlin has a few bumps and bruises on his arms and knees.

It's such a dry assessment for something so surreal. He doesn't even say a word about the damage to my soul.

"Dear God, you two are lucky." I look up, relief flooding my body when I see that it's Lamar. Immediately, I burst into tears. I cling to Devlin even as I stand up, then throw one arm around Lamar, who hugs me so tight I'm afraid he's going to break a rib, but I don't care. I don't even try to wriggle loose.

"What happened?" he asks, murmuring in my ear. "What happened?"

I shake my head and pull away blinking through tears until I can see both him and Devlin more clearly. I'm still holding onto Devlin, and I sink down beside him on the little ledge at the back of the truck. I glance over and see that Shelby is safe, a few bits of burning wood have landed close to her, but nothing scraped her. I'm weirdly grateful. In the grand scheme of things if she were all I had lost, I could live with it, but I'm so grateful that I didn't lose anything. Or anybody.

I realize that Devlin and Lamar are both looking at me. I nod, forcing myself to get my shit together. "I'm okay," I reassure them. "Really. I'm okay." I take Devlin's hands. "Are you?"

His jaw tightens, and he nods. One short quick beat. "If you'd gone into that house with me, we'd both be dead," he says. "I came back to the car to ask you something. If you'd been with me, you would have been standing beside me and I would have asked you at the door. We would have been right there when the bomb went off."

I ride out another wave of nausea and look up to meet Devlin's eyes. "What were you going to ask me?" I say stupidly.

He actually laughs, and I join in. "I don't even remember. Oh, wait. I was going to ask you if you wanted me to bring one of my bottles of Scotch back to your place." He glances at the house. "I guess that's a moot point now."

I giggle, high pitched and strange. It's the shock, I know, but I still want to cringe.

"Are your father's enemies behind this?" Lamar asks, and I'm so grateful to him for trying to keep this business-like. I need to get removed from the emotions, from the horror. I need to think like the cop I used to be and the reporter I still am.

"I don't think so," Devlin says. "I spoke with someone from the old days not too long ago, and the intel from him is that there aren't that many people left who are active in the business who would have a grudge against me. On top of that, if they were paying attention to my speech, they would know that I'm not benefiting personally from my father's assets. Maybe they would be upset about them being used for charitable purposes, but I don't think so. Believe it or not most of them are perfectly fine with helping out women and children. They just want to make sure that they were getting their share of the profit."

He shrugs. "Bottom line, I honestly don't think they care enough about me. If the money were in my bank account, maybe it would be different. If some of my father's colleagues were still actively in the business, I'm sure it would be different. As it is now, they're low on my list."

I already know this of course, but for the first time it strikes me what a change this is. Early on one of the reasons that Devlin had stayed so far away from me was fear of retribution by the men his father moved with.

"If not them, then who?" Lamar asks.

"Someone close to Joseph," I say. We've already been over some of this with Tamra, though the circumstances were significantly less dire.

"Christopher," Devlin's voice is cold and hard and level. I turn to look at him.

"You really think—"

"He had the code," he interrupts me. "Christopher is the one who gave my keypad code to Anna. *We* gave him the code."

I feel sick all over again. "You're right. That was part of the sting."

"And I didn't change it. Fuck me, I can't believe I didn't change it. I was in the wrong headspace after everything that went down. I let that personal assault get to me and I missed that detail. I didn't change my goddamn code back."

I reach for his hand. "It wasn't your fault."

He looks at me, his eyes suggesting that I'm wrong. That it was.

"You didn't get a notification on your phone that someone was on your porch? Messing with your lock?"

"No," Devlin says. "I didn't." He looks irritated at not having realized that earlier. He takes off his glasses—one lens is cracked—and rubs the bridge of his nose. "So someone with tech skills. Possibly Christopher, assuming he's been keeping them hidden. Or he had help."

"It may not have been him," Lamar says. "A man like you has other enemies."

He says it, but it's clear that Christopher is the best bet. Considering all his secrets, I wouldn't be surprised to learn he's tech savvy. Plus, he disappeared with such convenient timing. That coupled with his relationship with Blackstone and Anna make him very much at the top of the list in big bold letters. None of us would be hesitating, either, if it weren't for the fact that his guilt will cause more pain to Brandy, who we all three love.

The chime from my phone startles us all, and I look down, not surprised when I see that it's her. I look up and meet both their eyes, seeing their realization that it's her as well. "Should I take it?"

"Answer," Lamar says. "This must be all over the news. She's probably worried sick."

I almost kick myself. Of course it's all over the news. This is Devlin Saint's house, and this is the world of social media. I answer before it rings a third time.

"Oh my God, oh my God. Are you okay?" The words spill out before I even have a chance to say hello. "The news is saying that Devlin's house exploded —"

"Brandy, we're fine! Brandy!" She doesn't answer, and I'm starting to get really worried. Then her voice comes back on the line. "Oh, fuck."

Now I really am worried. I know she's scared, but Brandy's not a curser. "What? What is it? Are you okay?"

"I just got a text. It's from Christopher. He says that he didn't do it. That he's sorry about everything. But he wants me to know that he didn't do this."

I look up and see Devlin's brow furrowed in curiosity. Clearly he can't parse out what I'm saying from one side of the conversation. "Christopher texted you?" I say, both so

Devlin and Lamar can hear, but also so that I'm absolutely sure I'm understanding this.

"Yes, yes!"

"And he says that he didn't do this. Just out of the blue like that?"

"Yes."

"Do you believe him?" I don't actually mean the question for Brandy. It's Devlin's opinion I want. But she answers in my ear.

"I don't know. I don't know what to think."

"Brandy. I have to go. The police are here. Lamar's here too. He's going to get a black and white to take me and Devlin to you. We'll be there soon. Okay? I don't think you're in any danger but keep the door locked and the alarm set. Promise?"

She promises, and as soon as I hang up the phone, I look between Devlin and Lamar. "Well? What do you guys believe?"

"About Christopher?" Devlin says. "I don't know either. To be honest right now I don't even care. The only thing that I have in my mind is keeping you safe."

"I'm doing what you said," Lamar says. He signals for a uniformed officer to come over then gives them Brandy's address. "No argument. Go to her place, stay there, don't leave until I get there. I'll be there as soon as I can, and I'll update you both."

He looks at both of us hard, his expression determined. "Promise me that you'll stay there. Promise me you won't do anything stupid."

I squeeze Devlin's hand, then nod. "We promise. We're staying and waiting for you. Bring us back some news, okay?"

Lamar nods, and Devlin reaches out to shake his hand. "Thank you," he says.

Lamar frowns. "For what?"

"I don't know. For caring. For being a friend. For just being there."

CHAPTER THIRTY

We do as Lamar says and go to Brandy's. Devlin immediately starts pacing the house, the energy seeming to come off him in waves as he searches for answers. I want answers too, but right now I can't help him get them. I'm still too numb, as the realization that I could have lost Devlin in the blink of an eye keeps hitting me over and over and over again.

It weighs on me—terrifies me. And I'm not a woman used to being so damn scared.

Which is why I push down my own fears to focus on Brandy. I, at least, have lived my entire life with the knowledge that people can be taken from you in an instant. But these last few days have slammed my best friend hard. She's had glimpses into the dark underbelly of the world that I'd hoped she'd never have. She'd gone through hell with Walt all those years ago, and I always believed that filled her quota.

I should have known better. After all, who knows better than me how much of a bitch the universe can be.

"I just can't believe it," she says, curled up on the couch

with Jake. "Not Walt—I wouldn't put anything past him, although I can't believe he'd be smart enough or ballsy enough to plant a bomb."

"You're thinking Christopher, right? I get it," I say. "I like him, too."

"I trusted him," she says. "Am I the most naive person on the planet?"

"Oh, sweetie, no. Of course not. I trusted him, too. Do you think Devlin or I would have ever let you alone with him if we hadn't once we knew about Joseph?"

"We had all these talks. I shared so much with him." She hugs herself. "If he did this, then he's a freaking psychopath. Or sociopath. Or, hell, both. I can't ever keep that straight. He's not a good person." She sniffles, then chokes back tears. "I thought he was a good person."

"It's not your fault," I say, taking the hand that isn't stroking Jake.

"I know. But that doesn't help. And—well, I know he could do it. A bomb, I mean. I read his first book. There was a bomb in it, and he did all sorts of research. It said so in the back. He would know how."

"That's why we're looking into him," Devlin says from behind us, making us both jump. "Because it's possible, and we want to be smart. But Ellie is right—it's not your fault."

She nods, but doesn't look any more convinced than she did when I told her the same thing.

"It would help if we knew where he was. Did he ever say anything that might give you a clue?"

She shakes her head. "But he left that note for me, so we know he caused the leak. But this is so much more serious. Why would he have put a spotlight on himself like that? It doesn't make sense."

"No, it doesn't," Devlin agrees. "But like you said, he has the knowledge, probably even more than we know because of his connection to Joseph. It's possible that when he essentially confessed to being behind the leak, he didn't expect to be put in this position."

It takes me a moment to figure out what he means. "You're saying someone ordered him."

Devlin nods. "Or his relationship with Joseph was on better terms than we believed. Grief and anger can drive a man to do foolish things."

"Like blow up the house of the man who killed your brother," Brandy says. "Even if you know you'll be at the top of the suspect list."

"I'm sorry," Devlin says. "But yes."

Her throat moves as she swallows. "I wish I could, but I can't think of any place he might be."

"Don't worry about it. We have resources, and it might not be him." He presses a hand to Brandy's shoulder, then offers to bring her a cup of cocoa.

"I'm fine," she says.

"Well, I'm getting one, so let me know if you change your mind."

She nods, and he heads toward the kitchen. I get up and follow him, not ready to be done with this conversation. "Surely it's not Walt," I say, cornering him at the pantry. "So if it turns out Christopher's text was telling the truth, then what does that mean? Somebody new on the radar?"

Devlin sighs, looking completely exhausted. "At this point, I'm not taking anything on faith. But, you're right. I don't think it's Walt. His claim sounds like opportunism to force me to settle in light of the bad press surrounding the revelation about my father. What happened to my house, on the other hand, is payback."

"Agree," I say as I loop my arms around him. "But by who? Tied to Blackstone, most likely, but he's dead. So what are you going to do?"

"Do you really want to know the answer to that question?"

I frown. What I know is that he's going to go back upstairs and get on the phone with Ronan and Reggie and Penn and Claire and Charlie and Grace and all of the other Saint's Angels that I haven't yet met. They're going to make a plan for finding out everything they can, using whatever methods they can, including the kind of methods that law enforcement doesn't have access to. Not legally anyway.

As for Walt, though he's not saying so, I'm certain the team will be poking around there, too. Devlin may believe Walt had nothing to do with this, but he won't completely write it off until he's sure. He'll poke around in that cretin's life again, utilizing the kind of tools that constitutes cutting corners in the world of police procedure and judicial conduct.

I want to say that I disapprove. That he can't do that. That he needs to let the process be the process, and trust that the authorities will find the answers. I want to say it, but I can't, because I'm not sure I believe that anymore. So instead I just hold him close. "I'm going to stay with Brandy down here. You do what you have to do, okay?"

His brows rise just slightly, and I'm certain he understands everything that I've left unsaid. Then he nods, kisses my forehead, and turns and goes toward my room.

"Devlin," I call, fighting the urge to join him, to listen in on his meetings and think about whatever information they've come across, to see if I find something in the bits of gossip and information and evidence that perhaps they don't see. But when he stops turns and looks back at me, all I can think to say is, "Let me know if you find anything."

A hint of a smile touches his lips, and I know he understands. "Of course I will," he says. And then he's gone.

CHAPTER THIRTY-ONE

I wake on the couch in the morning with a blanket over me feeling groggy and disoriented. I push myself up, my head pounding. I stumble into the kitchen to start coffee, only to find that Brandy is already there, sipping on something cold and green.

"Hey. Is Devlin up?"

"Not sure. He came in last night and covered you up right before I went to bed."

"He should have woken me up."

She laughs. "Believe me, he tried. He thought about carrying you to bed, but we decided to just leave you."

"Wow. I remember none of that."

"You were exhausted. You'd had a hell of a day."

True enough. I pour myself a cup of coffee and am about to go poke my head in at Devlin, when Brandy blurts out, "How long would it take a statement to go public these days?"

I squint at her, trying to make sense of the words. "What do you mean?"

"Like if I wanted to say something about what Walt is putting Devlin through, how soon could it be printed in an actual publication, so that people see it? I mean, not just on a Twitter feed."

"Honestly, something like that on your own social media would probably go viral pretty quickly once people notice it. But if you want it to have the cast of legitimacy by being published in some sort of official news media, I'd say it depended on the media. Whether or not they're the type of place that posts things regularly, or whether they wait until an official publication date." I study her. "Brandy, what are you thinking?"

"It just pisses me off. All of it, I mean. The house most of all, of course, but there's nothing I can do about that. But this all started when Devlin's reputation was attacked in New York, right?"

I nod, trying to follow her train of thought.

"Well, I can't do anything about that, either. I mean, Devlin's a great guy, and I know it. But it's not like I can say that his father isn't his father."

"Sweetie, I know you're upset about everything. But I am not following you here."

"Don't you get it? He's being maligned by Walt."

"I know. But he's filed assault charges, and Devlin *did* assault him. What can we possibly do about it at this point?"

"I'm going public. Just like I said I might do before."

"Devlin told you not to. That he could take care of himself. And he can. His house getting bombed has nothing to do with you staying silent."

"I know that. But I need to do something. And Devlin told me not to do it for him. But this isn't about Devlin. Not really. It's about me, and what I stand for. I can't let people think that Devlin is that way, when I know he isn't. And you know what else? I'm tired of not standing up for myself where men are concerned. I turned a blind eye to whatever or whoever Christopher is —"

"Wait, wait. So now you really think Christopher is involved in all of this?"

"I think he has to be. So what if he sent that stupid text saying he didn't bomb the house? At the end of the day, me thinks the man doth protest too much, right?"

She takes a sip of her veggie grossness, and continues on. "But the point isn't even whether he's innocent or not. The point is that he says so, and I just blithely go along. He's wrapped up in this somehow, even if he's the most innocent guy on the planet. And all I'm doing is sitting here being swept along in the tide."

Her words pour out on top of each other. "And it's not just Christopher. It's Walt, too. It's the fact that I chickened out and never said anything. How many more women has he done that to? And now he's sitting here accusing Devlin? It's ridiculous. I have power here. Power that I could use to help Devlin. Power that I could use to help myself. To finally, maybe, grow a little bit of a backbone."

She shakes her head, then lifts her hands as if she said too much and doesn't know where to go next.

"I get it," I say softly. "I really get it."

"Will you help me?"

"Yeah. Let me just go run it by—"

"No. This isn't Devlin's decision. This is me. I'm doing this for me. This is something I need to do. Devlin's already told me that he has no problem with me saying whatever I need to say. And I need to say this. Please, just help me get it out there. He's got enough on his mind without worrying about whether or not I'm making the right decision."

I think about that, and she's right. This is Brandy's decision, and Devlin will worry. He'll be afraid about how being in the spotlight will affect her, too, but she's been living in silence for a long time, and I can tell that it's eating away at her.

"All right. I'll help you get the word out. Unfortunately, I can't just publish the column for you, since I'm now unemployed. But we'll see if we can find another magazine that can get it online pretty quickly."

"It would be nice if it had the circulation of *The Spall*," she says.

"Yeah. I'm thinking. I've got to know somebody. One of my colleagues who'd be willing to do this for me at their magazine as a favor. Someone who —"

I cut myself off, realizing I have the perfect person in my back pocket.

Ten minutes later, Brandy's sitting at the kitchen island in front of her laptop on a recorded video call with Corbin. He's asked her if he can use snippets from the video as part of the article. "That will make it go more viral," he says.

I frown, because she looks more than a little nervous.

"Don't do it if you're not comfortable," I say. Because it's a video call, I know he can hear me, even if I'm just outside of the screen.

"But it should be your own decision," Corbin adds. "Not that I don't appreciate Ellie's input," he adds, and I can hear a little bit of a smirk in his voice.

I roll my eyes, but of course he can't see me.

Brandy laughs. I've told her about the detente between Corbin and me, and I think she's amused to see us together.

"So you just want me to talk and tell my story and you'll pick out the good parts to put out there on Twitter or wherever?"

"Yes. If you'd like to approve them first, you can."

"No. I don't want to see myself on video. I wouldn't want

you to post anything if I did." She shoots a quick glance at me before saying, "I trust you."

Corbin laughs. "Considering Ellie's sitting in the room next to you, that means a lot. From both of you."

"Okay," Brandy says. "Should I just start talking?"

"Go for it." Corbin says.

Brandy shoots me a look that is a cross between terror and excitement. I nod in encouragement and make a go-ahead motion with my hand. She bites her lower lip, takes a deep breath, looks at the camera on her phone, then bursts into giggles. "Sorry. Sorry. This is all very weird."

"Take your time," Corbin says, more gently than I thought he was capable of. "I can edit this. And I promise I won't make you look stupid."

"You better not," I put in. "I know where you live now."

He chuckles, but our banter seems to have loosened Brandy up, and she takes a deep breath before beginning.

"I've been quiet for years now," she says "But I know Devlin Saint personally, and in light of the allegations that William Tarkington has made against him, I can't stay quiet any longer. The bottom line is that Devlin is an amazing man. But William—or Walt, as he goes by—isn't."

She takes a deep breath, her eyes catching mine. I mouth that she's doing great, and she continues.

"Walt is the reason I'm speaking out," she says. "His actions have pushed me. Angered me. I listened to the allegations that he's made against Devlin Saint, and fury cut through me. Because I know both these men. More than that, I know why this alleged assault took place. Devlin was standing up for me. He was standing up for me because I hadn't stood up for myself, even though I should have."

She silently holds her hand out below camera view, and I take it, offering my strength. "I should have stood up. Fought back," she continues. "All those years ago when I was young, and more recently when I saw Walt again. When I was in high school, Walt was in college. We met at a party. He drugged me, and he raped me. He got me pregnant, and somewhere out there is a little girl who's in a good and loving home because I gave her up for adoption."

She closes her eyes and takes a deep breath, and I can't help but think it's the perfect video shot.

"But I did one smart thing. I asked the adoptive parents if I could keep a sample of her DNA. They knew how I become pregnant in the first place, and they were kind enough to agree. It's been kept all these years at a facility my doctor recommended. I know that when that DNA is analyzed, it will prove what I am saying. That William Tarkington is a dangerous man. He's a man who thinks he can take whatever he wants, and if the world isn't giving him what he wants, he will bend the facts around to make them fit in his favor. That's what he did to me. That's what he's doing to Devlin."

She smirks. "Devlin Saint hurt him? Poor baby."

She leans forward, and I think she's really getting into a groove now.

"Devlin Saint hurt him in that alley because Devlin was vindicating me. Because Devlin is a good man who knows the story that I've just told you, a story that I've kept hidden away all these years. A story I should have come out with a long time ago, because I believe in my heart that Walt did not do this only to me. If I'd had the courage to say something earlier, maybe he would've been caught. Maybe he would be in jail. Maybe he would never have been in that bar in the first place and Devlin would not have had to stand up and protect me."

She leans back, and Corbin signals for her to keep going as I mouth that she's doing great. She takes a deep breath, bites her lip, then continues.

"I don't know the ramifications of what I'm saying from a legal perspective. I don't know if it makes Devlin innocent of the charge of assault. I'm not a lawyer. I don't know. And while I don't want Devlin to be in trouble with the law, that's not why I'm saying this. I'm saying this because I have to. Because Devlin Saint is a good man, who's had a lot of crap thrown at him recently that he doesn't deserve. And because Walt is a bad man, and he deserves whatever dark looks people give him after they hear what I've just said. I hope it changes everything for him. I hope he finally realizes that he can't get away with things by trying to shift reality whether through lies or through drugs. That's all. Thank you."

She waits a beat, then shrugs, the confidence she seemed to project while recording the video fading away as she looks at me with the same expression she had when we were a little girls in elementary school.

I move over and pull her into a hug. "You did amazing," I say, and Corbin seconds the statement.

"That was really great, Brandy," he says. "Seriously, it was terrific. And if you wanted it to go viral, I think you did the right thing. I think this will definitely do that for you. And if anybody still looks at Devlin like he's an asshole or at Walt like he's a hero for calling out Saint, then they're idiots."

Brandy sniffles and wipes the back of her hand under her nose. "Thank you."

"I have to say one more thing, though, before I write up this article and post this video."

Brandy's brow furrows, and I'm curious as well. "What?"

"Are you sure?"

"Why are you asking me that now?"

"Because what you said was really good. Not only did you say it well and heartfelt and reference actual evidence that you have, which will get everybody interested, but it also involves Devlin Saint. We all know it's going to go viral. A few days ago I wouldn't have said this to you. You'd given me permission, and I would have just posted it. But my perspective has changed a little recently. I saw my colleagues shouting out questions to Devlin about who his father is. And I probably would have too. It was news, right?"

Brandy and I lock eyes and we both nod.

"Yeah, well here's the thing. I've met him. And I listened to his speech the other night. And that revelation kind of fucked him over. It was news, and they had every right to ask him in public. But I just wonder if maybe they shouldn't have. So I'm trying to think a little bit more before I publish. Is this what you really want?"

I'm in complete shock. I'd shifted my perspective on Corbin, true, but I never expected this. There are actual tears in my eyes as I think about what he's willing to give up. One hell of an article and the spotlight that goes with it. And he's doing it because of friendship and respect. Who would have thought?

Brandy's mind has not wandered the way mine has. And she doesn't seem sentimental at all. Instead, she nods fiercely as she looks directly at the camera. "Thank you for asking. But yes. I want you to publish."

Corbin's expression changes into one of absolute glee. "Well, all right. That's all I wanted to know. Brandy, honey, you may have just made my career. Thank you."

I laugh. It's good to see a hint of the old Corbin. I feel like the Earth is moving on its axis again.

"So are we done?" I ask.

He nods. "I'll send you a text before it goes live so you're prepared. I can write this fast and get it up in a couple of hours. That's cool, right? You want it as soon as possible."

"Absolutely," Brandy says. "Walt's apparently pursuing

this thing hard. I keep seeing that his name is trending on all sorts of social media."

"Got it. I'll write it up, put the graphics together, and we'll run with it. I'll keep you posted. And thanks again for this exclusive. Hey, Ellie, where are you?"

I lean over again so that he can see my face.

"Thanks," he says.

"You're welcome. Do us proud. We wouldn't want to have to evict you."

He snorts. "I'm hanging up now. I've got work to do." And then, true to his word, he does.

Brandy closes the app and shuts her laptop, then she turns to me. "Oh my God," she says.

I give her a hug. "You did exactly the right thing. I'm so proud of you."

"Proud of what?" The question comes from behind us, and we both jump, breaking apart guiltily as we turn to see Devlin.

I meet Brandy's eyes and she looks back at me before turning to Devlin. "Just getting over Christopher, you know."

"Uh-huh." He crosses his arms over his chest. "Want to try again?" Brandy shakes her head. "No. It's all good. But I'm feeling a little drained. You can ask Ellie, or you can wait. It's not like it's a secret. It can't be anymore."

She looks between the two of us. "I'm going to go lie down." I nod as she leaves the room, then I move into Devlin's arms.

"Are you going to tell me what that was about?"

I lean against him, shaking my head as I do. "No. She's right that you'll know soon enough. Let's just say that I'm really, really proud of my best friend."

CHAPTER THIRTY-TWO

When the news finally broke around three in the afternoon, and Brandy's interview went live, Devlin had been working at the computer. All of a sudden, he couldn't get anything done because of the notifications that kept flashing across his screen.

At first he just dismissed them, but then he read them. Soon he tracked down the actual video and watched it. He was sucked in, pleased by the support for both him and Brandy, and as proud as any man could be of the way she handled the situation.

He'd been working in Ellie's bedroom, but he left and found Brandy in the den she'd converted into a studio for her handbag business. "You didn't have to do that."

"I know." She grinned at him, looking both proud of herself and mischievous.

"I'm glad you did, though. I once told you not to do it until you were sure, and I could tell in that interview that you were. What you said .... it means a lot. And I think it'll matter."

"I hope so. That's why I did it."

He smiled. "I've already gotten a lot of support from people who say they're on my side. So thank you."

She came to him, and he gave her a hug.

"I'm really glad you're in my life again," she said. "Mostly I'm glad you're back in Ellie's. You two are so good together."

"I'm not going to argue with you about that." He nodded toward the sewing machine. "I'll leave you to that. You need anything? Water? Tea?"

"I'm good. But thanks."

He gave her a thumbs-up, then went to make a coffee for himself. He hoped Lamar would swing by, as he'd like to know if her video had resulted in any calls to the station, but the detective hadn't checked in with Ellie today, and Devlin could only assume he was deep in the midst of the bombing investigation.

It was barely past lunch, but it already felt as if Brandy's video had capped off a long, hard day. He took his coffee and headed to the back porch, assuming he'd find Ellie writing.

Instead, she was asleep on the lounge chair.

He wasn't surprised. They'd been through the wringer, after all.

Now, Devlin felt ragged and spent, and was tempted to join her in a nap. His day so far had been full of computer screens and video conferences with various members of Saint's Angels going over theories and suspects. He'd delegated tasks to everyone, and they'd been reporting in throughout the morning with tiny details, none of which seemed to lead them any closer to finding the bomber. It was probably related to Blackstone—probably retribution for taking the sonofabitch out—but they had no way of knowing for sure.

The one thing that they had going for them was that the box that the team had taken from Blackstone's house—and that Tamra had given him after the walk on the beach—hadn't been in his hands when he had gone to the front door. If it had, it would have burned, as he would have undoubtedly set it by the door when he'd walked back to talk to Ellie. They would have lost all that intel.

Instead, it had been in Shelby's trunk, and he'd spent much of the day poring over the information, hoping for some clue to pop out at him. Instead, the only things that pinged were a few familiar names from his years on the compound. Boys he'd played with who'd grown into men who followed his father's code.

He'd recognized at least a dozen names, and a dozen more that seemed familiar. Men like Franklin Dewitt whose father had handled The Wolf's books for years. Romeo Duarte, who'd been so tight with Joseph. Manuel Espinoza, Aurelia's little brother. Carlos Garcia, who'd been a huge bully as a kid, then grown into an even bigger one. He'd worked security for The Wolf at sixteen, the youngest to ever do that, but the kid had mad skills and the kind of chip on his shoulder that The Wolf considered loyalty. On and on the list went, so many names. So many memories. So many goddamn possibilities.

And no way to know if any of them had arranged the bomb. No way to even know if he was barking up the right tree. Not until they tracked one of the men down and brought them in for interrogation.

One of them knew something—they had to.

And if they didn't? Well, then Devlin and the team went back to square one. Until then, he was staying optimistic.

Since Blackstone's base was in Chicago, Penn and Claire were at the frontline of the operation. So far, though, they hadn't reported in with any good news, and Devlin feared this would be a long operation rather than the quick jump to a resolution that he'd hoped.

In addition to coordinating with the team, he'd been dealing with calls from the insurance company about the fire, from the press about the explosion and the revelation about his father, and more calls from foundation backers either offering support or seeking further reassurance even after his press conference. Not to mention calls about Brandy's story and Devlin's supposed heroism in taking Walt down a peg.

Tamra, thank goodness, was handling everything at the foundation, but Devlin knew he needed to be there. One more day, and then he would go in. He needed to make sure everything was safe here first. Lamar had arranged for the police to watch the house, but he wanted more of his own team here, and he'd recalled several from stagnant operations to come to Laguna Cortez until things calmed down.

Of course, the thing he wanted most of all was to simply curl up next to El and sleep. As a rule, he wasn't one for escaping reality, but right then he was bone tired, and he knew he wasn't thinking clearly. There'd been too much thrown at him all at once. Too much shit to go through, too many questions that remained to be answered.

Hell, maybe he needed a nap. Maybe that would clear his head. Maybe—

The sharp ring of his phone pulled him out of his thoughts. It was Lamar, and Devlin answered the call with a quick, "Hang on."

His phone had also indicated that Ronan had pulled up, and he texted his friend the new alarm code, which they had started to change every two hours, so that he could enter the house.

"OK," he said to Lamar. "Sorry about that. Go ahead."

"We got some good news after Brandy's video," Lamar said. Devlin knew that the detective hadn't been pleased to learn that Brandy had done that without letting him know.

But he'd said he understood why, and he only wished that he'd known so he could have been around to support her when the thing went live.

"What's going on?" Devlin asked.

"Walt says that someone offered him cash to file the assault charge."

Devlin sat up straighter. "Who?"

"He doesn't know. Said it was anonymous. He also said that he agrees it was stupid to take cash under those circumstances, but he stands by his complaint. You did beat the shit out of him."

"Under the circumstances, I'm not terribly worried about a conviction. Are you putting him in front of mug shots to identify the payor?"

"Yes, but nothing so far."

"Well, that's too bad. Keep me posted, okay?" Devlin was about to end the call, when Lamar continued.

"That's not all of it. I want to get you and Brandy down here to the station first thing in the morning. Apparently Walt wants a sit-down. Are you up for that?"

"It's a civil case. What's he doing pulling in the police?"

"His attorney's been on us to press charges. He must want to address that, too. Honestly, I'm happy to be in the loop. Makes it easier for me to look after Brandy."

"Well, I don't know what he expects will happen, but I'm game." If nothing else, he wanted to look in the bastard's eyes. And let Walt look into his. "When?"

"I'll book a conference room for nine tomorrow morning."

Devlin hesitated.

"Come on, man. This is a good thing."

"No. I'm not hesitating because of that. I just hate putting Brandy through this again so quickly. But you're right. I'll go talk to her. Or have you already called her?"

"No. I can if you want."

"It's fine," Devlin said. "I'll let her know, and unless she balks, we'll see you tomorrow."

Brandy leaned forward and rubbed her hand lovingly over the dashboard as they turned out of the neighborhood, the morning sun shining down on them. "I'm so glad you got Shelby restored," she said. "I missed her."

"So did I," Devlin said, not mentioning that he missed his Tesla as well. The fact that it had been destroyed in the bombing was the reason they'd borrowed Shelby, promising Ellie they'd be extra careful with her restored baby.

"They did an incredible job fixing her up," Devlin continued. "I know how much Shelby means to Ellie."

Brandy shifted in her seat. "It means so much that you understand that. More important, that you understand why Shelby is so important to her." She hesitated, then added, "You're good for her, you know. To be honest, I wasn't completely sure before."

He turned and looked at her more directly as he paused at a yield sign. "You mean when she came to town, and I was doing my best to push her away?"

Brandy laughed. "Yeah well, you failed miserably in that regard."

Devlin grinned. "Deep down, I wasn't even trying."

"I get that. But that's not what I meant. I meant when we were kids. I mean, I liked you a lot. Heck, I liked you from that first day when you offered to go get us pizza for movie night. But then you guys got involved, and I was the only one who knew, and I had to keep it a secret, and that scared me."

She sighed, her shoulders rising and falling. "I just—I

guess I was afraid that you were an older guy who was going to hurt her, even though you seemed so good together. It felt like it couldn't last. And then you went away, and I pretty much hated you."

"For that, I hated myself."

"It seemed like you guys were star-crossed, you know. And I always got the feeling you were a little bit haunted." She shrugged. "I guess the truth is you were."

"Yeah," Devlin said with a hint of a laugh. "Secrets clung to me like ghosts back then."

"But not anymore? I don't mean with me. I don't care if there are secrets with me or Lamar or any of that. But it still worries me a little. That you might go away again."

"No," he said with as much force and conviction as any statement he'd ever made in his life. "I don't keep secrets from Ellie anymore. And I will swear to you what I've sworn to her. I'm never going to leave her."

Brandy studied him for a minute, then nodded, looking pleased, "Well, okay then."

"I asked her to marry me." He hadn't intended to tell her that, but the words rushed out of him. He immediately regretted them. Wasn't that Ellie's purview to tell her best friend? He wasn't sure. All he knew was that in the context of this conversation, it was important to him that Brandy knew. Not only because he'd come to love her like a sister, but because he wanted to reassure her that he would never again hurt El.

Brandy gaped at him. "You're engaged? Oh my God, I'm going to kill her. She didn't say a word."

"Yeah, well, I think I spoke out of turn. And, no. We're not engaged. The truth is she said no."

"No way."

He laughed. "Believe me, I was as surprised as you are. But her reason is good."

Brandy made a harrumphing sound and crossed her arms over her chest. "Yeah?"

"She wants to date. She wants to not have all of that sneaking around that you found so disturbing when we were kids. She wants something open, with more time in public together than we've had so far. And I get that. I even support it. So long as at the end of the day, she's wearing a ring on her finger."

"I like that," Brandy said. "Thank you for telling me. And I'm excited for both of you. It's like you're engaged to be engaged."

He chuckled and they shared a quick grin, then drove silently for the next few blocks. There was a wreck up ahead, so he shifted to a different route, going the back way to the precinct.

"So why are we doing this?" Brandy asked, and Devlin didn't have to ask what she meant.

"Lamar seems to think it will help. He thinks that Walt might even drop the charges after this."

"Do you believe that?"

"To avoid the publicity that you could throw on him? Yeah. I think we have a good shot."

"But...?"

He chuckled. "You're beginning to know me too well," he said. "The but is that he's a wild card, and I don't know what —"

"Oh!"

Devlin glanced over and saw that she was looking at her phone. "What is it?"

"It's from Ellie. She says there's an emergency. That we

need to go back right away. Shit, can you turn the car around? I just texted that we're on our way."

He already was, turning into the parking lot of a strip mall that was in the midst of renovations. He made a circle, avoiding the few cars and workmen's vans that dotted the lot. He was aiming Shelby's nose back at the street when those same cars gunned it, racing forward to surround Shelby.

Men in black wearing masks jumped out, guns aimed at them.

Two fired, taking out the tires. Four others aimed the guns directly at them.

Beside him, Brandy whimpered, and he reached for her hand, hoping to ease her fear even though he knew it wouldn't help at all.

"Out of the car," one of the men said. "You're coming with us."

CHAPTER THIRTY-THREE

B*efore…*

Devlin stood in the lobby of the magnificent concrete, steel, and glass office building of the Devlin Saint Foundation. He'd spent hours with architect Jackson Steele discussing Devlin's vision of the foundation and the image he wanted to project to the world.

Now, he turned slowly in a circle, taking in the incredible floating staircase, the welcoming reception area, and the incredible wall of glass that could be pushed aside to open onto a stunning outdoor patio with a view of the Pacific. "It's perfect," he said to the man standing beside him. "It's everything I imagined and more."

Jackson Steele grinned. "I thought it would be," he said, not a man for false modesty. "There's a sense of acceptance here. But the materials are hard and harsh, not warm like wood."

"Reflecting what the people we've helped have been through."

"Exactly," Jackson said. "No one will notice consciously,

but somewhere inside themselves, they'll understand that this building matches your mission."

Devlin nodded, in full agreement. He could see how the world-renowned architect—or "starchitect"—had built his reputation so quickly. "I'm glad you accepted the commission," Devlin said. "I don't think I could have asked for a better face for the public."

"You're going to do incredible work here at the Devlin Saint Foundation. I had to do justice to the mission of the DSF."

That was true, Devlin thought. The whole purpose of the DSF was to remediate the damage caused by his father and men like him. To help women and children. To assist those who needed rehabilitation or job training after being imprisoned or forced against their will to work in sweatshops and drug manufacturing and other equally vile arenas.

He wanted to assist and educate. To offer counseling and adoption services if needed. To do whatever he could to try to make the world right again for the people who has been caught in the spider web cast by vile men like his father. He wanted to make those people strong again, so they could shake off the label of victim and become the people they were meant to be in the first place.

The fact that Jackson understood that, even a little bit, affected Devlin more than he'd expected. The man had talent and vision and believed in his project. And that feedback and support was worth the world.

At the same time, he couldn't help but wonder what Jackson Steele would say if he knew about Devlin's less-than-public endeavor. An organization—really more of a loose collective—that his friend Ronan had dubbed Saint's Angels.

The Angels had no affiliation with the DSF, but as far as Devlin was concerned, it was an equally important entity.

Whereas the foundation provided help in a very public manner, the Angels' mission was more private—to prevent men like his father from creating victims in the first place, or to exact retribution when they did.

It was a mission he'd fantasized about since he'd been a child on the compound. A mission he'd worked toward from the moment he'd left Laguna Cortez all those years ago.

Saint's Angels was the reason Alex Lopez had disappeared, and Devlin Saint had been born. He'd been a ghost in those between years, and a lethal one, taking out the type of people the Angels now pursued. He'd honed his skills with government support, albeit with full deniability, and he'd earned his freedom from the military by putting those skills to work.

Even with the Angels and the Foundation, he knew he could only make a dent in the pain and corruption in the world, but every life he saved or helped rebuild made it worth it. He'd paid a huge price to have this, not the smallest part of which was walking away from Ellie.

It was worth it, he told himself. Even though she could never be his, the life he'd now built would be enough.

It had to be.

CHAPTER THIRTY-FOUR

he present...
Devlin took his hands off the wheel and slowly raised them into the air. He glanced sideways and nodded, silently telling Brandy to do the same. She'd gone pale, completely white, and terror seemed to come off her in waves.

He wanted to tell her they'd get through this. That it would be okay, but he said nothing. For one, he didn't know if his captors had itchy trigger fingers. For another, he was afraid to make a promise that he might not be able to keep.

He knew that they'd been followed by one of the cops assigned to watch the house. For a moment, he let himself hope that the cop had seen the attack and radioed in before casually driving on. But then he heard one of the thugs talking to the other. *The pig died at the corner*, and Devlin's hope that their situation had been reported faded to nothing.

"Out of the car, you fucking bastard." The voice was unfamiliar. Rough. And though Devlin tried to match it to a voice in his memory, he couldn't. It didn't matter. He knew that this man must be tied to Joseph Blackstone. He knew why they'd been carjacked, and he was kicking himself for underestimating Blackstone's men. Without a leader, he'd truly thought they would scatter.

Now, here he was, surrounded by the very species of men that he'd dedicated his life to fighting. And Brandy was the kind of woman he'd spent his entire life trying to protect. And yet here they were, facing death because of the choices he made.

"Come on, bitch," said another one, yanking open the passenger side, and grabbing Brandy's upper arm. She fumbled to undo the seatbelt, and he screamed at her, telling her to keep her hands up.

"She's trying to get out, you son of a bitch," Devlin said. "Can't you see she's strapped in?"

The gunman at his side lashed out, smacking Devlin across the forehead with the side of his gun. "Shut your mouth."

Devlin's head rang, and he saw flashes of light from the impact. He wanted to punch the fucker. He wanted to lash out and smash him in the face. One on one, he knew that he could take him. But there were no good odds in this circumstance, and if he did start a fight—even if he had the slightest chance of winning—he knew damn well that Brandy's presence reduced his odds.

At the end of the day, one of them would be dead, and he couldn't live with himself if it was her.

Bottom line, he wasn't a stupid man; he wouldn't fight. And he wouldn't let her fight either. "Do what they say," he told her, glaring at the man and daring him to hit him again. "Just do exactly what he says."

The man beside him said nothing. Just gestured with the gun for both of them to get out of the car.

"Hands behind your backs," a third man said. Brandy's eyes met Devlin's over Shelby, and the terror he saw there made his gut twist.

"It'll be okay," he said, and he hoped desperately it wasn't a lie.

"The hell you say," one of the men said.

The two standing closest to each of them used cable ties to bind their hands behind them. Devlin had one more chance to meet Brandy's terrified eyes before the men pulled bags over their heads, loosely tied around their necks. There were no eyeholes. He was in the dark, just a bit of light sneaking in from the bottom.

Then someone took him by the elbow and shoved him forward. He heard the gunning of an engine, then the sound of brakes. He was told to step up, then shoved roughly inside. Another set of hands grabbed him and settled him on a bench, and he assumed they were in one of the vans he'd seen in the parking lot.

"Sit down," his captor said. "And shut up."

He did as he was told, and from the shuffle of movement he could hear through the sack, he was certain that Brandy was complying as well. Good. The situation was fucked, but the more cooperative she was, the longer she would last, and the better their odds.

Who was he fooling? Their odds were shit. No one would know for a while that they'd even been taken, much less the destination. He hoped that there were security cameras around the strip mall that would help the police and his own team identify the van and then track it.

He knew that ultimately, once they realized that Brandy and Devlin had disappeared, Ellie and Lamar would be able to find Shelby. He'd had a tracking device put in her after the accident, and the app was on El's phone. That would be the first thing she'd do.

But that was cold comfort, since Devlin and Brandy

would be gone. Their only hope was that his friends found the van in time and were able to follow it. And that, he knew, was a damn thin hope.

The thought wrecked him.

The memory of that morning swept over him, along with the fear that the quick brush of a kiss across Ellie's lips would be their last kiss. *No.* He couldn't let himself think like that. He had to stay clear, and he had to keep her at the forefront of his mind.

He and Brandy would come through this somehow. No other outcome was acceptable.

Across the van, he heard Brandy breathing. He wanted to console her, but was afraid that if he did, they'd both get punished.

Instead, he concentrated on Ellie. On visualizing being back in her arms. Of getting out of this. He had skills, after all. Training. But this wasn't a movie, and he could hardly fight off a half-dozen men with guns. Especially not with Brandy in the crossfire.

Instead, he focused on gathering intel. He paid attention to the turns, to the texture of the road. To when they switched from the van to a regular car.

He could tell when the pavement shifted, when the car accelerated, when they were on a highway, and when they merged with another.

Inland, he thought. They were heading inland, and he tried to count so that he could estimate how far they'd traveled. It might do no good at all, but it was information, and right then, information was the only asset he could acquire.

The other benefit of concentrating on the road was that it kept his mind off the nagging fear that Ellie was in danger, too. For all he knew, there'd been a second raid at the house, and she'd been taken as well.

He didn't know. He *couldn't* know.

And no matter what they did to him once they reached their destination, Devlin knew that horrible gap of information would be the worst punishment of all.

CHAPTER THIRTY-FIVE

"**D**ammit, Lamar, I don't know!"

I'm sorry to yell at my friend, but I am completely freaking out. "All I know is that I got this bizarre text from Brandy telling me not to worry, and that they were on their way back home."

As soon as the text had landed on my phone, I'd called Ronan, only to get his voicemail. I'd called Lamar right after, not feeling the least bit guilty about trying Ronan first. Devlin and Brandy are in trouble, and Ronan isn't fettered by rules.

I want his help desperately, but I'm also so grateful to have Lamar on my side.

"Deep breaths." His voice is calm and level, but I know him well enough to know that he's worried, too. "I'm on my way. Tell me where I'm meeting you."

"That abandoned strip shopping center at the intersection of Hancock and Grace Street." I'm in Brandy's car, and I have my phone on speaker since I'm not tied into her system. I'm so thankful that Devlin installed a tracker on Shelby, but at the same time I'm terrified as to what I'll find when I get to the shopping center, and whatever mojo I had as a cop has completely fizzled away in this crisis. I'm numb and I'm scared. But I force myself to think. To talk. "I'm about a mile away."

"I'll be be right behind you. Stay on the phone with me, and if there is anything at all going down, you drive on past. Do you understand me?"

I swallow, not certain I'll have the strength to keep driving, but understanding why I have to. "Yes. Anything. Just hurry."

I let silence linger on the line, too terrified to talk, but I'm reassured by Lamar's presence on the other side of the phone line. I know I'm not overreacting— there's absolutely no reason in the world for Brandy to send me the text that she did—but I'm desperately hoping that it's just a horrible, terrifying mix-up.

What's going on? Don't worry? We're on our way back to you.

On the one hand, Brandy's text clearly suggested an emergency, but it sounded like I was the one who had called out for help. Except I hadn't. So what the hell was Brandy talking about?

All I know for sure is that they were in Shelby, that I have the ability to track Shelby, and that Shelby is now parked less than a block away. I'm driving like a banshee, putting Brandy's little Ford to the test as I race the final distance into the lot, then screech to a halt beside Shelby.

"Ellie?" Lamar's voice sounds thin over the speaker.

I hear the catch in my voice as I say, "They're gone."

I throw the door open and launch myself toward Shelby. I don't touch anything, but I peer into the cab, as if maybe they're hiding on the floorboards. But they're just gone. No sign, no clue.

"Don't touch anything." Lamar's voice drifts from the

open door of the Ford, and I return to grab my phone, then hold onto it as if it can keep me sane.

"Lamar..." I hear the fear and hate myself for it. I want to be stronger, but I'm not, and it is taking all of my strength not to collapse onto the asphalt.

"Don't touch anything," Lamar says again.

"I know. I didn't. They need to dust for prints."

"I'm one block over, and I've got a team responding. Not just prints. The car could be rigged."

"Oh, God..."

"I'm sorry to be so blunt, but I don't want you to get hurt."

I nod my head. I understand; I do. And I try to dig deep into my training, to my heritage, but none of it's coming through. Something has happened to the man I love and my best friend in the world, and I am having one hell of a time thinking straight.

As he promised, Lamar is right on my heels. He slams his car to a stop beside me then lurches out of the car. "Help is on its way," he says, though the sirens in the distance already tell me as much. "Now let's go over everything again."

I run him through the whole thing once more—how I got the text, the text not making any sense, and me realizing that something had to be wrong. "And now here's the car and no Devlin or Brandy. So obviously I'm right."

Beside me, Lamar nods his head. "Yeah, I think you are."

I press my fist hard against my lips, as if that strange and uncomfortable pressure will keep the tears at bay. It doesn't work, and the next thing I know I'm in Lamar's arms as he tries to console me.

But I'm not consoled. I won't be—I can't be—until I find Devlin and Brandy. But I do manage to get the tears under control, and I pull back from Lamar, my cheeks wet and my heart racing. I'm helpless, and I hate it.

As he's been holding me, other cops have arrived, and the team is scouring the area for vagrants who may be living inside the abandoned buildings and might have seen something. Apparently the owner lost his financing and the space has become a haven for the homeless. "There are security cameras," Lamar tells me. "Benton's talking with the bank. Hopefully they kept the feed on after the foreclosure."

I nod, reassured by the activity, but it isn't enough. It isn't nearly enough.

I turn again to Lamar, wanting to beg for a next step, but he's already looking at me, his forehead creased. "What?" I demand.

"I already told Devlin this, so you might know. But Walt fessed up to being paid a hundred large to file the lawsuit."

"So he's in on this?" I hear my voice rise with incredulity. Walt's an ass, but none of us really saw him for the bombing. He's a whiner, not a fighter. And I can't imagine him pulling off a kidnapping.

Lamar shakes his head. "I don't think so. He says he swears it was anonymous. Someone came to him and told him that he should file the suit, and if he did that the guy's boss would pay him. He filed, they paid, and he said that was the end of it."

"Do you believe him?" I do, but I want Lamar's take on it, too, especially since my judgment is impaired right now.

"I do," Lamar says. "He's an asshole, yes, but he's not a stupid asshole."

"Agree. He realized that he'd stepped in it, and told you everything he knew."

"Right," Lamar says. "We would have found that eventually, but him bringing it up on his own is a mark in his favor."

As much as I despise the man, I can't disagree.

I start to pace, my mind churning. "They're still watching

him," I say. "I mean, maybe not this second, but they have been. This isn't about getting Walt to sue Devlin, it's about manipulation. I bet they even suggested that Walt ask for this meeting. He did, didn't he?"

Lamar frowns. "Yeah. It was his idea."

"They needed a way to grab Devlin when he was alone and feeling safe. Like on the way to the police station."

"They couldn't have foreseen that Brandy would go public. But they weren't going to pass up their chance just because Brandy was in the car."

"Oh, God," I say, hating that she'd been pulled into all of this, and knowing she must be terrified.

Assuming she's still alive.

I choke a bit at the thought, then try desperately to pull myself back together.

"We got video!" A cop I don't know waves to Lamar from across the parking lot, his words helping me get centered. Lamar and I race that direction, but as soon as I see the image, I want to throw up—Devlin and Brandy, hands bound and faces covered, being shoved into the back of a white panel van.

But they're alive. At least at that moment, they were both very much alive.

"Start checking traffic footage," Lamar orders. "Let's trace these fuckers."

"Lamar," I begin, then stop when my phone chimes. I'd programmed a specific tone for Ronan after I left the messages and now I stiffen with anticipation. "I—let me take this. It's Ronan. I should tell him what's happened."

Lamar knows that Ronan and Devlin are close. That, however, is all he knows.

He nods, signaling to another officer, then hurries away as I check my phone.

It's not a call, it's a text.

I'll be there in five. Make your excuses. You're coming with me.

My breath catches, and I look at Lamar. Ronan must have some intel—although how he even knows about the abduction is a mystery. But I can't tell Lamar about Saint's Angels.

Instead, I decide I'll tell Lamar that Ronan came at my request, and now we're leaving together so that I'm not alone while Lamar works.

It's a story he doesn't even question, as he's too intent on his conversation with the tech guy pulling the video feed.

"Shouldn't we wait?" I ask Ronan when he pulls up. He never asked where I was, and I realize that Devlin must have put a tracker on Brandy's car. Or my phone. I'll ask about that later. At the moment, I'm just glad he did.

"No. They dumped the van at Fashion Island. The cops will realize soon enough. After that, it's a dead end."

"Fashion Island?" That's an outdoor mall in Newport Beach. "How did you even know that Devlin's in trouble?"

"His watch," Ronan says. "It has a tracker. He triggered the SOS."

I exhale, relief mixing with hope. "You found him? Ronan how—"

"Ellie, no." I hear the regret in his voice. "We found the watch." His voice is hard. "Charlie and Grace are still there working the evidence. Apparently their abductors had them change into jump suits. We found their clothes and the watch in the Dumpster. Nice watch, too. Tempting for a criminal, but they dumped it. Our perps are being careful."

"And Brandy's clothes? She's really with them?" I hate that she is, but at least that means she's alive. For now.

He sucks in air, and his hands tighten on the steering

wheel. "That woman does not deserve this. She's been through too damn much."

"She'll be okay," I say, but I hear the shake in my voice.

"She's stronger than she looks," Ronan says, glancing sideways at me. "I heard her interview. She'll get through this."

I nod, appreciating that he's trying to console and soothe, but I know the score. I might be one variety of victim in this scenario, but I've been on the other side, too. And I know that strength doesn't always matter, and that the real truth is that I might never see either Brandy or Devlin again.

I absolutely hate feeling helpless but that's how I feel for the next hour, during which time I'm wanting things to happen that are already in motion, but no results have come in yet.

The Saint's Angels who are in town, like Charlie and Grace and a few others I'd seen at the reception are in the field. Ronan is coordinating from the kitchen. And Reggie— who I hadn't realized was a whiz on a computer—is working remotely from the Seaside Inn, hacking into the traffic camera system.

Me? I'm feeling useless as I pace the kitchen.

"Excellent," Ronan says. "Run with that." He taps his earpiece to mute the call, then tells me that Reggie found an image of a Toyota leaving Fashion Island, and the angle was just enough that it caught a glimpse of the backseat. "Passenger with a bag over their head. Doesn't get much more certain than that."

"Right," I say. "What about more cameras? Can we figure out the route?"

"We're working on it. And we're coordinating with the police, too," he says, making me look up in surprise. "Really?"

"Whatever it takes. And everyone on the team is a legitimately licensed investigator. Reggie called the license plate in and an APB went out. Anyone sees it, we'll hear about it. And in the meantime, we're searching ourselves."

Thirty minutes later there's a knock on the door. I check the security app, then frown when I see it's Reggie.

"Why are you here?" I demand. "You're supposed to be watching the traffic cameras."

She's pale and looks tired, her straight brown hair pulled back from her head in a ponytail. She pinches the bridge of her nose as she looks between Ronan and me. "We've hit a dead-end," she says. "Ellie, I'm so sorry. We'll pick him up again, but right now we're completely blind."

My whole body goes icy-cold. "What are you talking about?"

"We were tracking the Toyota. We managed to find it on some traffic cams. They were heading east on Interstate 10."

"Okay, okay. What happened?"

"We lost it, but we figured we'd pick it up again. We usually do, and we've got a lot of resources across the state. The trouble is, we found the car."

"What do you mean you found the car?"

She looks at Ronan. "Abandoned," she says. "In an area where we can't find any cameras to tell us what happened next. We assume that Devlin and Brandy were transferred to another vehicle, but we don't know what it looks like and we don't know where it went."

"Oh my God," I hear myself saying. "No, no, no."

I feel the pressure of Ronan's hand on my shoulder and his calm voice saying, "We'll find them again." That's all he says, but it makes me feel slightly better, though I don't know why. We don't have a single goddamn lead.

"Where is the car exactly?" I ask. "And who found it?"

"Local police found the car," Reggie says gently. "It's in Riverside, and our best guess is that they're taking them up into the mountains. But it's just a guess."

"Shit," Ronan says. "Cameras are limited up there, and with all the abandoned buildings and homes closed for the off-season, this is going to be a challenge. I'm sorry, Ellie," he says, "but I can't sugarcoat this for you."

I shake my head. "No. I wouldn't want you to. I just..." My voice trails off, and Reggie reaches out and puts a hand against my back. The pressure is nice. It steadies me. But it's not enough. "So what's our next step?"

"We'll keep looking, obviously. We'll get maps of the area and see if there's anything that looks isolated enough that it might appeal to whoever abducted them, then we'll send a team in to check each place one by one. But it's a lot of space. Honestly, our best hope may be to wait until they contact us."

"Do you think they will?"

"I hope so," Ronan says. "But if this is about revenge..."

I don't need to hear the rest. I know what it means. Devlin and Brandy are in terrible trouble, and we're completely at a loss as to how to save them.

My phone is vibrating, and I look down, desperately hoping that it will be from Devlin, but knowing that it won't be. I yank it out of my back pocket and pull it out. Then gasp as I read the message on my lock screen.

They die at dawn.

I don't even realize that my knees have gone weak until Ronan reaches out to steady me. He takes the phone, reads the message, then bites out a foul curse.

"It's already almost noon," I say, hating the way my voice is catching, my throat already clogged with tears. "How the hell are we going to find them?"

My question is hanging in the air, when there's a

pounding at the door. I look at Ronan and Reggie, but it's clear they're not expecting another team member. Ronan still has my phone, and he opens the security app, then mutters, "Motherfucker."

"What?" I demand. "Who is it?"

He pulls his gun as he walks closer to the door, and Reggie does the same. I'm not armed at the moment, though I realize I should be even though I'm safe in Brandy's house.

I step back letting them take the lead. Ronan rips open the door, and I gasp. Because standing right there is Christopher Doyle.

CHAPTER THIRTY-SIX

He was with her again.
Devlin didn't know how, he didn't know why, all he knew was that Ellie was in his arms again, and he finally felt whole. She said nothing, just looked at him, her eyes staring deep into his.

It was a moment he didn't want to lose, this sense of her, this feel of her, as if she surrounded him. As if she was protecting him, blanketing him, but from what, he couldn't remember. He only knew that there'd been something wrong. But now ... well, now everything was right again.

He reached for her, frowning when she seemed to fade away into so much mist, only to return when he pulled back his hand.

"El?" She only smiled, then reached up and pressed her hands on either side of his face. It was an odd touch, like being kissed by electricity. And when he looked at her face again, it seemed as though her eyes were on fire.

Her lips parted and she spoke two words — *"Wake up."*

He frowned.

"Wake up."

Once again he shook his head. He didn't understand. He wasn't asleep. He was with Ellie. He was where he wanted to be, and—

"Devlin, Devlin, please, please wake up!"

It was as if he'd been ripped from heaven. His head was pounding, and he was on the verge of throwing up. Everything around him was gray. Nothing made sense.

He was standing against a post, his hands tied together behind him, trapping him. He struggled, but he couldn't budge the bindings.

"Devlin?"

Brandy. He drew in a breath as reality slammed back against him. Slowly, the room came into focus. His head throbbed, and he remembered something hard and fast slamming against him as their captors tugged them out of the van before moving them into the backseat of a car.

Their captors had only taken the bags off once they were not only in this room, but tied to poles. And then, once Devlin was out of the bag, they'd lashed out against his head again.

"Devlin?"

He could hear the urgency in Brandy's voice, but he was moving—thinking—so slowly.

"Devlin, are you okay?"

"Yeah. Yeah, just groggy."

"I thought they were going to kill you. I mean, I really thought you were dead."

He could hear the terror—and the tears—in her voice.

"I'm not dead yet," he said, and was gratified when she hiccupped out a tiny laugh. "Have they been in the room since they tied us here? Have you seen any faces? Do you know where we are?"

"No. But we drove a long way."

"And into elevation," he said, as his memories began to

return. The way his ears popped, the angle of the car, the strain of the engine. They'd gone north, then east, and his best guess was that they'd gone out Interstate 10, then probably up toward Big Bear.

That, however, was only a guess.

"How long have I been out?"

"I think a couple of hours. I was so scared that they'd actually killed you. Then you started talking. You called out for Ellie." He heard the choking sound as she said her friend's name. "Devlin, are we ever going to get back?"

"Of course we will." What else could he say? She deserved the truth, but he didn't want her to have the fear that went along with it. At least not yet. At least not until he could fully assess the situation and decide if maybe—just maybe—they had a shot at a positive outcome.

"We need information. We need to know their endgame. That means we need time. Can you stay calm? Can you trust me?"

"Stay calm? I don't know. Trust you? Absolutely. Although to be honest, Devlin, even though you're a really amazing guy, I'm not sure what you can do standing in a cellar with your arms tied behind you." There was humor in her voice, but also a frenetic note. She was freaked, and doing whatever she could to stay calm.

So far, she was doing a solid job of it.

As for his current predicament, she wasn't wrong. "It feels like they took off the cable ties and tied my wrists with rope. Do you know if that's true? Did you see them tie me up?"

"Yes. They took us out of the car and hit you again before they carried you inside and dumped you on the floor. I didn't know what they were going to do with me, but then they brought me in here right after you. They pushed me against the pole and then they took out some rope. White. Nylon, I think. And they put my arms behind me and tied my wrists together."

"Did they hurt you?"

"No." She paused. "My whole body's going numb, and I'm really hungry, but I'm okay. They tied my ankles to the pole, too. But they didn't do that to you. I'm not sure why."

He wasn't sure either, but he had a feeling he would find out. "Did you happen to see what kind of knot they tied?"

"No idea. I'm sorry."

"It's okay." He didn't know why he was asking these questions. His wrists were bound too tight for him to get any sort of purchase on the ropes with his fingers, anyway.

But depending on the knot, if he wiggled enough, perhaps he could loosen it. He doubted it—surely whoever tied him up knew what they were doing—but he never took competence for granted. Perhaps his captor didn't know a thing about knots.

"I'm so sorry. I'm no help at all, and now you're —"

"Hush," he said gently. "You're doing great. Just breathe, Brandy. Just breathe."

"Such excellent advice from the great Devlin Saint."

The words echoed in the room, and though Devlin twisted, he couldn't locate the speaker.

There was something about the voice that was familiar, though, and he was certain that when the speaker stepped in front of him, he'd know him. A ghost from the past. A revenant of a former life.

He listened, the footsteps approaching from the rear. He heard Brandy's shuttered breathing, and wished that he could take her hand. Then the man moved into his line of sight. A stocky man a few years younger than Devlin, but more worn around the edge. His deep-set eyes seemed too large for his small mouth, and his dark hair framed a puffy, babyish face.

He saw it then—the reflection of the child's face on the countenance of the adult. A man he hadn't seen in over a decade. Manuel Espinoza. *Manny.*

Aurelia's little brother.

"Manny? Is that really you?"

"*Well, well.* I think I'm flattered." He had a low voice, deep and resonant. A radio voice. And one that didn't match the face of the man speaking. "The great Devlin Saint knows who I am. Who would have believed it?"

"Why are you doing this?"

Manny blinked at him, slow and deliberate so that he looked like an owl. "Goodness, *Devlin.* I thought it would be obvious. So that you'll lose everything."

Devlin shook his head, not comprehending. "Do you want money? I'll give you money. I have no problems there. Let her go, and we'll talk this out."

Manny took two steps toward him, got right in Devlin's face, then reached out and punched him hard in the gut. All of the air left Devlin's lungs, and he flinched, pulling his knees up in reflex.

Then Manny punched him again, and Devlin knew why his ankles hadn't been tied like Brandy's. Manny wanted the illusion of a fight.

He wanted Devlin to kick out, furiously lashing out at Manny. But Devlin wasn't going to do that. There was no profit in kicking a tormentor who had you tied up. Not unless you had a plan for winning.

And the horrible truth was that Devlin didn't have a plan at all. He was helpless in a way he hadn't been for years. Helpless and responsible for Brandy, and that reality weighed heavy on him.

He needed a plan, but to formulate one, he needed to know Manny's endgame.

"Nothing to say, *Saint*. Fucking bullshit, that is. You're just a wolf in saint's clothing, you fucking prick."

Devlin made a point of not reacting. Instead, he met Manny's gaze dead on. "You tied me up so that you could call me names and punch me? What's the matter, Manny? Never got out of first grade?"

"Don't you—"

"You should have just called me out. Met me in the ring. We could have had a fair fight."

"Fuck you," Manny said, then punched him in the gut again.

Devlin gasped, lights flashing behind his eyes, but he kept his eyes on Manny and managed an edge to his voice when he said, "Then again, you always were a little cheater, weren't you? All those computer games you played? Aurelia told me how you would reprogram them so that you could win. She was proud you had computer skills. I thought you were a sore loser."

"Cheat? Me? That's a laugh riot coming from you. Because cheating's all about setting the stage, isn't it? And you set the stage on a worldwide scale. Remade yourself, broke the rules. Kicked the game in the balls and just started over."

He took a step closer his head tilted back so he could sneer into Devlin's eyes. "So you tell me, *Saint*? Who's the bigger rule breaker, Manny Espinoza or Alejandro Lopez?"

Devlin said nothing.

"Well?"

Devlin held his tongue. Manny took another step forward, staying just out of range should Devlin decide to lash out and kick him. He reached a hand down and flipped two fingers. Immediately a man dressed all in black scurried to his side. Presumably one of the men from the car. He had a gun, and he aimed it at Devlin's knee. "Move a muscle, you lose the knee. Do you understand me?"

Devlin kept his voice level. "I do."

"You want to know why I'm doing this?" Manny's voice was soft, but hard. "Because I want to watch you lose everything. Every goddamn thing. I want to watch you lose your reputation, your house, your woman, your friend."

He tossed a sideways toward Brandy. "She wasn't part of our original plan. Pity I got the wrong girl, but I'm sure her death will haunt you as well." He turned and faced Brandy. "Sorry, sugar. Wrong place, wrong time, wrong friends."

Brandy's throat moved, but she didn't otherwise react, and in that moment, he was not only proud of her, he understood how she'd managed to cope so well after the rape, and how she'd found the strength to go public. Brandy Bradshaw was a hell of a lot stronger than anyone had realized.

Not that he could tell her any of that. Hell, he couldn't even look at her, not without risking their lives. He needed to keep his attention on Manny. He needed to figure out how to deal with this boy he'd once known, who'd grown into a vengeful monster.

"Aren't you even going to tell me why?"

"Why? What kind of an idiot are you? You took everything from me. I lost my sister because of you. She used to have so much fun with you in the evenings. I had to go to bed. I had to go away. But little Alex Lopez got to be wherever he wanted to be. You took Joseph, too, don't you even think of denying it. And the worst of all? You took The Wolf."

"Who says it was me?"

Manny just laughed. "Do you really think I'm stupid?" He stared at Devlin. "Admit it. Admit that you killed him."

And even though Devlin knew that he was playing with fire—that he was taunting a goddamn snake—for once he wanted to tell the truth. He wanted the people who had admired The Wolf to know that he was the one who had taken that bastard out.

He looked in Manny's eyes and said slowly and clearly, "Yes. I killed him."

He thought that Manny would fly off the handle with the admission. He thought that he might order the man with the gun to shoot him. He thought he might at least punch Devlin in the gut again.

Devlin was braced for all of that, but he wasn't ready when Manny started to laugh.

"He always told you to watch your back," Manny said when the peals of laughter had died. "He always told you that the enemy you had to fear was the one you didn't see coming. Didn't he? Didn't he?"

Devlin just nodded.

"Well you didn't learn your lesson very well, did you? Because you never saw me coming, did you?"

"No, Manny, I never saw you coming. I guess I expected too much. I thought you would have the heart your sister did. I thought you would be good. Too bad I was wrong."

"Good? *Good*? I was fucking incredible. And after you left, your father was mine. He liked me. He trusted me. He used me for all his computer work. I was fucking *vital* to him. And you just took him away, like *that*," he added, with a snap of his fingers. "Now we'll see how you like it. But don't worry. I'll let you watch when I kill your pretty little Elsa. And just so you know, I'm not bluffing."

Icy terror slashed through Devlin. Had Manny already abducted Ellie? Was she somewhere in this building right now? Was Manny really intending to bring her here and kill her while Devlin watched?

No. Fucking. Way.

Devlin clung to those words letting them fuel his fury. No. Fucking. Way.

"Everything," Manny continued, "Including your life. Everything you've built will tumble to the ground. You think your precious foundation will survive after they learn you killed her?"

"Her?"

"Your little bitch of a girlfriend, who else? It will look like a lover's quarrel, and they'll have all the DNA they need. Thank you for that in advance. And don't worry too much about it hurting. We'll be sure and get the skin scrapings and blood after you're already dead." He shrugged. "Or maybe not. Might as well make it fun."

Manny chuckled. "And I almost forgot. After she's gone, all those nasty texts you sent her will come to light. The ones where you talked about hurting her. Called her a little cunt who needed to watch herself or you'd make her pay."

"I never—"

"Everyone will learn what kind of man you are. They'll see that you killed her, not me. You killed her because you could."

Across the room, Brandy sucked in a breath. Devlin didn't dare look toward her. He kept his eyes on Manny. "You sick son-of-a-bitch."

The words hung in the air as Devlin fought to keep his breathing steady. To stay calm and not let fury overtake him. He had to think. He couldn't react out of passion, he had to be smart. He had to be careful and precise. Ellie's life depended on it.

Bottom line, he had to get out of there. Ellie needed him.

But there wasn't a thing he could do.

He was fucking trapped, and the wolves were circling.

CHAPTER THIRTY-SEVEN

"Christopher?"

I stare at the man on the doorstep, fear spiking through me, because there is no way that this is a coincidence. "Where is she? Where are Devlin and Brandy?"

I step forward, not even sure what it is that I intend to do, but suddenly I'm pulled backward by a strong hand tugging at my T-shirt. In one quick move, Ronan shoves me behind him, and has the muzzle of a gun up underneath Christopher's chin.

Christopher stands perfectly still, his chin tilted up, and I can see his Adam's apple bobbing in his throat. His pulse beating against the taut skin. He says nothing, and considering the tension in Ronan, I think that's for the best. Not that I care if Ronan blows him away, but I'm really not in the mood to clean blood off the front porch.

"One wrong move, and you are a dead man," Ronan says. Slowly, he pulls the gun back, letting Christopher lower his chin. "Inside," he orders, then kicks the door shut behind Christopher.

"Now talk," I demand. "Where the hell are Devlin and Brandy?"

"I, I came here to help. I didn't help take them. I didn't have anything to do with it. I promise."

"Why the hell should we believe you?" I ask. "You tried to run me down with an SUV, you son of a bitch."

"I didn't want to do that. Joseph he said I had to. Please, please you have to believe me. I went out of my way not to hit you. He wasn't happy. He really wasn't happy with me after that."

I look at Ronan who meets my eyes, his as cold as ice. I have no idea what he's thinking. As for me, all I'm thinking about is Devlin and Brandy.

"Do you know where Devlin and Brandy are being held?" The question is from Reggie, who's moved to my side, her expression fierce. "Because otherwise, you're no fucking use to us at all."

I hold my breath, waiting for Christopher to answer, then jump when someone pounds on the door, and I hear Lamar's voice. "Dammit, Ellie, let me in."

I meet Ronan's eyes, trying to read his thoughts, but his expression is entirely flat. I think that he must be damn good in an interrogation, then nod for him to open the door.

Lamar bursts in, then stops short when he sees Christopher. He looks from Christopher to Ronan and then to me.

"Well," he says. "I guess I made the right call."

I frown. "What do you mean.?"

"Officially we don't have shit. I'm coming with you."

"Lamar..." I'm shaking my head. "We're not—I mean, oh, hell."

"She means we're not intending to play by the rules," Ronan says flatly.

"But you intend to get them back."

"Absolutely," Ronan says.

Lamar glares at Christopher. "And you have a lead."

"Looks that way," I say.

"Then I'm in."

I swallow. "Are you sure? The consequences."

"It's Brandy," he says, then takes my hand. "And it's Devlin."

I nod, blinking back tears.

Ronan, apparently satisfied, returns his attention to Christopher. "Answer the fucking question. Do you know where they're being held?"

"I do, at least I think so. That's why I'm here. I'm supposed to bring supplies up. But, Manny has Brandy, and—"

"Manny?"

"One of the kids who was on the compound with Devlin," Ronan says. "One of Joseph's lieutenants."

Christopher nods. "I know what he's capable of. I thought—"

"What?" I demand.

He looks down at the ground. "All I want to do is help. Please," he says, his voice cracking. "They have Brandy."

I hear the pain in his voice and try not to let it affect me. "You tried to kill me," I say again, this time clutching Lamar's hand.

"Because of Joseph. He's—he was—my family. The only family I ever really had. So when he wanted my help, I agreed. I like Devlin, and I should never have gone along with it. But you didn't know Joseph."

"That's all ancient history. Tell me why the fuck I should trust you now." Because, dammit, as much as I'd like to think that Christopher is our answer, I know that it's way more likely that he's the bait to a much bigger trap.

He looks between me and Lamar, and I see Reggie and Ronan exchanging glances.

"I love her," Christopher says, his eyes on me. "I love Brandy. I understand why you might not believe me," he says, as Ronan makes a raw scoffing noise, "but I never meant to hurt anybody."

"You goddamn son-of-a-bitch," Ronan growls.

Christopher cringes and hurries on. "I came to the DSF because Joseph wanted me there. Because Anna had told him who Devlin really is. I used my books as cover, and all I was supposed to be doing was gathering intel on Devlin. Where he went, who was important to him. Anything that Joseph might be able to use against him."

He draws a shaky breath. "And, yes, when Joseph thought that the best way to get to Devlin would be to take you out, I had a hand in that. I regret it. I do. And I know you don't believe me, and I don't even care. But you have to believe me about Brandy. I love her. He wasn't supposed to take her. She wasn't supposed to be with Devlin today."

Ronan looks at me, and I don't know what to do. I want to hate this man, and I do. But part of me feels sorry for him, too.

He's a naive man who got caught up with a powerful brother, a man who had power for all the wrong reasons. Now he's dead and Christopher is lost. And whether he loves Brandy or not, he was never the man she believed him to be.

But none of that matters. All that really matters is whether or not I believe that he loves her. Because if he does, then he might really be here to help us. And that means that we might actually have a chance.

More than that, it means that Christopher is probably our *only* chance. Because if he knows where Devlin and Brandy are, or even if he just says he does, that's a risk that I'm willing to take.

"Put the gun down," I tell Ronan. The Nordic god towers over me, a look of incredulity on his face. "The hell you say. You aren't running this operation."

"The hell I'm not. My best friend. My boyfriend. The man I love with all of my heart. They're the ones who are at risk here. Not me, not you, not Lamar, not Reggie. *Them.* And I will do anything in my power, including selling my soul to the devil if that's what it takes to get them back."

"You listen to him, and you really might be selling your soul to the devil. Don't you see? If this is retribution for what Devlin did, then the best plan is to get you there and kill you in front of Devlin. Make him watch. Killing him? No big deal. Devlin's been trained for a hell of a lot more than that. But watching you die? That's about the only form of torture I can think of that would break him."

I hadn't thought of it that way, and without thinking I glance toward Reggie. She nods. "He's right."

I feel cold all the way down to my bones. "I can't just stand still because I might be at risk," I say.

"You won't be at risk," Christopher says. "Or you would if they knew you were there. But I'm not going to be the one who tells them. I swear to you. I swear to you on Brandy's life."

I can hear the passion and the heat in his voice. I think of all the times I've seen him and Brandy together. I think of the way this man has laughed in my living room.

And then I make my decision. "If it's the wrong call, then it's on my shoulders. But we're going to trust him. And I need you two to follow my lead."

To her credit, Reggie nods, just one quick inclination of her head as evidence that she's agreed to my terms. Lamar does the same. Ronan is not so amenable. Instead of answering me, he looks to Christopher. "What exactly do you have to offer?"

"I know where they are. I'm supposed to meet them there with supplies. Years ago, Joseph bought this place. I mean like it's been at least ten years. It was this cabin up close to Big Bear right at a pass. An old pass, one of those Indian trails. It was a cabin at first, like a century ago. And then later it was used by trappers. And then during the WPA era it was used as office space while they tried to build a road. But it never got finished. So it was only a half-built little road out there with that secluded cabin just sort of cut into the mountains."

"Keep going. They're at the cabin?"

"He built a house over it, but yeah. The cabin's at the base of it. There was some mining there at some point, and then it was a place where settlers traded with the Native Americans. It's got a lot of history. It's actually pretty cool. I thought about writing a book about it, but—"

"Christopher." My voice is harsh and sharp. I don't give a fuck what kind of book he wants to write. I want to know where Devlin and Brandy are.

"Sorry, sorry." He wipes his hands on his jeans. "Yeah, so, that's where they'll be. It's had so many layers built upon layers that there's this stone basement. He'll have them in there."

"And what's he proposing to do with them?"

Christopher shrugs. "Kill them. But he wants Ellie first. That's why he sent me. I told you. He wants Devlin to hurt before he dies."

"You're supposed to take me to Manny."

"Yeah. With the supplies."

"It's a trap," Lamar says. "It has to be a trap."

"I promise you it's not," Christopher says. "Please. Please, I have to make sure Brandy's safe. She'll be the first he kills. He'll do it to punish Devlin, so he feels weak. And so that he'll know what's coming when they bring Ellie in. I don't think she has much time. If you don't trust me that's okay, but please at least believe me."

Ronan looks at Reggie, and she understands the silent message. She leans against the wall, pulls out a gun and aims it casually at him. "Why don't we just wait here while those three go have a little chat?"

CHAPTER THIRTY-EIGHT

"We're screwed, aren't we?" Brandy whispered, and the terror that Devlin heard in her voice tortured him more than anything Manny had done.

"I'm not counting us out yet," he said, also whispering. They were alone now, but he imagined people were listening at the doors. Not that their conversation meant anything. It's not as if they had a plan for escape.

"But..."

He closed his eyes and drew in a breath, acknowledging the reality of their situation.

"But, yes, we're not in a good position. I'm sorry, Brandy."

"For telling me the truth? It's not like I couldn't figure it out on my own."

"For not realizing this was a trap in the first place. For not having the foresight to suggest we go in separate cars or have Lamar send a cruiser by to take us to the station. You're here because you were with me." It was like living with his father all over again. He made a friend, got close to a trainer, and eventually they'd die. It was as if his father could sniff out even the tiniest bud of joy, and made it his mission to pulverize it under the heel of his snakeskin boots.

"This is not your fault, Devlin. And we're not dead yet." Her voice was strong, but there was no denying the tremors.

"*Not dead yet. Not dead* yet?" Manny's voice rang through the cavernous room. "You want to explain to me how *yet* fits into this equation? Because yet is bearing down on you pretty damn fast."

He turned, signaling to someone in the shadows. "Get the girl. Bring her over here."

"*No!*" The plea was ripped from Devlin. "Leave her alone. She doesn't have anything to do with this."

"She's important to you. She's the bitch you're fucking's best friend. And since the bitch isn't here, this one will do."

Devlin writhed, kicking out with all his strength, though it didn't do a damn bit of good.

He watched as they gagged Brandy, then untied her. His heart twisted as they dragged her in front of him, then used a pulley to hang her upside down from the ceiling. And then—oh, Christ—they actually nicked her neck. Not a lot, but enough that the blood would drain out slowly, but not clotting because the gravity would keep it flowing.

He saw her tears and her terror. He wanted to cry out that he'd save her, but what the fuck could he do? Everything he'd worked for, everything he'd built, and there wasn't a goddamn thing he could do to save this poor, innocent woman.

Manny came closer, then shoved the gun under his chin. "Kick me, and I fire. Close your eyes, and I fire. You're going to watch her die, Saint. And if you follow the rules, then maybe I'll kill you once she's dead and spare you watching your precious Ellie die, too." He cocked the gun. "Then again, I probably won't."

"I will fucking kill you," Devlin growled. "I swear to God, somehow, you are mine."

"Um, no," Manny said. "I really don't think so. And honestly, the game's already getting old." He faked a yawn. "*Bo*-ring. I think I'll let you die knowing she's going to follow, and you were too fucking impotent to do a thing about it."

He took a step back, then looked Devlin up and down before coming back and placing the gun once again. "You're no Saint, Alejandro. But if you believe in that bullshit, it's time to say your prayers. Because the next sound you hear is going to be the blast of my gun."

CHAPTER THIRTY-NINE

I twist my mother's engagement ring on my finger as I stand beside Ronan's Land Rover. We're on a hill overlooking the cabin, and Lamar and the team of Saint's Angels are prepping as I pace, frustrated and scared.

"I want to go in with you," I tell Ronan when he comes back after leading Christopher to where Reggie and the others are studying his crudely drawn map. "I can't just wait out here."

"You can, and you will."

"Dammit, Ro—"

"No. You listen to me. You are not trained for this. You were a beat cop for what? Five minutes? You can shoot, but you aren't trained. And once we get Devlin free, do you really want him distracted by trying to protect you? Because my goal is to get him out of there as quickly and safely as possible. Him and Brandy. He needs to be sharp. Do you think he can be sharp if he thinks you're in danger?"

"Ronan..." This time my voice is weighed down with unshed tears.

His shoulders drop, and for the first time, I see this man

look vulnerable. "He loves you Ellie. You're his weakness. He doesn't need a weakness right now. Trust me to bring him back to you."

I swallow. "What if you can't?"

"Then we can both hate me."

I blink back tears and nod. "So I'm just supposed to wait?"

He shakes his head. "No. You're armed. And you're here watching this area. And Christopher will be with you. I trust him—and yet I don't. It still might be a trap, and he might be giving an Oscar winning performance. So he's not going in, and if he does anything off, you take the little bastard out."

I nod, then check my Glock, making sure I have a full magazine and one in the chamber.

I sigh and lean against the Land Rover. Below, I see a clump of trees and rocks among which, Christopher has assured us, is the camouflaged rear exit to the stone cellar. And it's through there that the team will bring Devlin and Brandy.

If I'm not going in, I intend to stay right here, not moving a muscle from this site.

Christopher comes over, his hands cable-tied behind his back. "So now we wait," he says.

I lean against the front of the Land Rover. "Yeah," I say, forcing myself to stay calm, "we wait."

Fifteen minutes later, I'm not calm anymore. I'm starting to get frantic. The team's out of sight, having infiltrated the house and, presumably, made it down to that stone basement. But I can see nothing. And I can hear nothing.

Christopher is pacing in front of me, and I spit out a curse, yelling at him to stop. "You're driving me crazy," I tell him. "They should be out by now, right? Why aren't they out by now?"

"I don't know. I'm sorry."

I turn from him, returning my attention to those rocks and trees.

I hear his footsteps behind me, then spin around, suddenly afraid he's about to send me tumbling down the cliffside.

But I don't see an attack. I see remorse. Tears fill his eyes. "I really do love her," he says. "They have to save her. They have to."

I nod, tears pricking at my own eyes. Without thinking about it, I start to reach for him, wanting to cling to someone else who shares my grief. But I freeze at the last moment, noticing his face. At first, I'm confused. Then I realize that he's looking over my shoulder.

I spin around, then gasp as I look down into the valley. I see a form, then another. The whole team emerging from the copse.

I see a flash of blonde and hear Christopher's soft, joyous gasp. And then—

Well, then I'm gasping myself. Because Ronan's carrying Brandy and Devlin's beside them. He stops and looks up, and our eyes meet, and right then I think I'm the happiest I have ever been.

I want to cry out to him, but I know it's not safe yet. Instead, I spin around, wanting to share the joy with Christopher—but I cry out in fear, instead.

Because there's a dark haired, baby-faced man standing there—and he has a gun aimed right at my chest.

"You fucking little bitch," he says. And then, as the world ceases to make sense, he fires.

CHAPTER FORTY

arlier...
     It's time to say your prayers. Because the next sound you hear is going to be the blast of my gun.

The vile words rang in Devlin's head, and he heard the truth of them. He almost kicked out, wanting at least to inflict as much pain as possible.

But he fought the urge, because he knew damn well that all that would happen to him is that he'd have his head blown off. But Brandy...

Well, Brandy would be tortured.

Now—oh, God, now—she wasn't feeling pain. Fear, yes. Discomfort, sure. But not pain.

If Devlin fought back, though, he knew that Manny would cut her down and torture her. Flay her. Rape her. Burn her.

And he'd make Devlin watch.

Manny might not have said as much, But Devlin knew. He knew, because that's what his father would have done.

And so he held back. Because without backup, there was no point in fighting back.

Manny stepped in closer, the muzzle moving to Devlin's temple. "You think you're so damn smart. But you won't be after I splatter your brains against the wall. *Now*," he said, then laughed when—goddammit all—Devlin flinched.

"You're a fucking pussy," he cackled. He actually *cackled*. "The great Devlin Saint's a goddamn fucking pussy. Oh, man, if only your father could—"

Kablam!

For a split second, Devlin thought Manny had fired. Then he realized the truth—and he lifted his knees and thrust out hard. Manny had already turned away, the gun moving with him, and Devlin shifted his head as he kicked, and was gratified when the fucker went down, the gun flying from his hand.

Manny leaped back to his feet, then scurried into a darkened corner as the team burst into the room. Nearby, in connecting rooms and above, Devlin heard the battle play out. In this room, Devlin saw Ronan burst inside, followed by Lamar.

"Brandy!" Devlin called. "She's injured."

Ronan raced toward her as Lamar spun around, landing a rock solid kick in the chest of one of the thugs who had helped tie Devlin down.

Then Lamar was racing across the cavernous room toward Devlin and cutting him free.

"Ellie?"

"Outside," he said. "She's fine."

"How did you find us?"

"Christopher," Lamar said. "The little prick came through."

From across the room, he could hear the team's calls of *clear!* echoing through the house. Lamar's radio sputtered, and Devlin listened as he got an update from Reggie. The house was clear, Manny's men dead or captured.

But Manny himself was gone.

"This building is ancient. He's got a thieves hole somewhere," Devlin said. A tunnel that would see him clear of the property or a hiding place where he could stay until they cleared out. They'd find him, though. Devlin knew his team wouldn't stop until they did.

"Brandy?" he asked as Ronan stood.

"Woozy. She's lost a lot of blood, and we'll get her checked out, but I bandaged the wound and she's going to be fine. Come on, now," Ronan said to her, his voice more gentle than Devlin had ever heard. "Put your arms around my neck."

"I'm okay," Brandy said. "Just feel lightheaded."

"I've got you."

"Thank you for coming," she said, her eyelids sagging. "I really, really didn't want to die."

"No," Ronan said. "That would have been bad." He shot Devlin and Lamar a look that spoke volumes. Joy that they'd been rescued. Sadness at what they'd endured, especially Brandy.

"Let's go," Devlin said. "The rest of the team can finish the sweep."

Ronan led the way to a stone corridor, a few shafts of light cutting into the dark from holes in a rickety wooden door. Lamar pushed it open, and Ronan went first, cradling Brandy. Devlin fell in step behind them, and Lamar followed, checking their perimeter as they moved into the open.

And then Devlin looked up and to the left, and he stopped dead in his tracks.

Ellie.

She met his eyes, and for that singular moment, all was right in the world. Then she turned around, and, to Devlin's horror, he saw Manny on that same hilltop. And then, *oh God,* Manny raising a gun.

A blur of motion and then the sharp report of the weapon.

Devlin thought his heart would explode, then reality set in.

Ellie was still alive.

That blur he'd seen was Christopher—he'd taken the bullet meant for Ellie.

But Ellie was still up there, and so was Manny, and oh, Christ, the bastard had rushed forward and grabbed Ellie, and now he—

"*Here!*"

Devlin turned to find Lamar tossing him a gun. It wasn't his piece. He didn't know its accuracy.

But there wasn't another choice and there wasn't any time.

There was only one way out, and all Devlin could do was pray that when the dust settled, Ellie would be back in his arms.

CHAPTER FORTY-ONE

I'm shaking.

Damn me, Christopher's fallen at my feet, and I'm actually shaking and I hate myself for it. But I'm terrified. Really and truly terrified. Not of dying—that hasn't scared me for a long, long time. But of not seeing Devlin again. Of losing this chance—having it ripped away from us—especially when he's so damn close.

"You fucking little bitch," the attacker snarls. "So you're the sweet little cunt he's taken a fancy to."

I react from reflex, intending to run, but he lunges and grabs me, then yanks me to him. I stumble over Christopher, and my captor makes a show of sniffing my hair, then licks my cheek. "Smell good. Taste good. I see why he likes you. I'm sure he's going to miss you."

He starts to lift his gun and terror slashes through me again because I know damn well I only have seconds to live. Fear and loss and Devlin—Oh, God, Devlin.

Crack!

I feel the wet blood. The tissue. The sharp bits of bone.

I sway, disoriented. Confused.

But still alive.

Alive?

I reach up to feel my head. There's slime in my hair and on my skin, but my head's intact. Slowly, I look down. And then, damn me, I vomit all over the corpse of the baby-faced man who'd held me hostage.

There's a hole in his eye, and the back of his skull has been ripped away. A hollow point bullet.

How?

My mind isn't functioning, and I sink to my knees

It's only then as I'm sitting there between two corpses that I realize what happened. I crawl to the edge of the cliff and look down into the valley. I'm searching for Devlin, but he's not there.

He's not there?

I start to climb up on my knees, and then I freeze. I hear limbs snapping and feet pounding, and I start to shrink away, searching for a hiding place, only to see the foliage shoved aside and Devlin burst into my line of sight.

"*Ellie.* Baby, baby, are you okay?"

He's on his knees and I cling to him, crying now. Sobbing, actually, as the events of the day wash over me. I could have lost him. Hell, I could have lost myself. And yet here we are, alive. Blissfully alive.

"Brandy?"

He nods. "With Ronan. She'll be fine. She lost some blood. He's making her sip juice."

I nod, trying to process that, but I can't. All I can keep in my head is that they're safe.

"Come on," he says, helping me to my feet. "I'll take you to her."

He leads me toward one of the other SUVs. "You killed

him. The one holding me. You shot him from all the way in the valley."

"Manny," he says flatly. "And I'm sorry."

I blink, confused.

"It was risky. Downright foolish. I could have killed you if I'd been off—if the sight had been off—but I didn't know what else to do, and I had—"

"You saved me," I say firmly. "He would have killed me. We both know that."

I'm starting to calm a bit, and I pull him to a stop, his hands in mine. "Is it really over now?"

"Yeah. It's really over." He glances down, then lifts my hand, his finger going to the diamond solitaire on my left hand.

"Something you want to tell me?"

I choke back a laugh. "A talisman," I say. "You couldn't die on me if we were engaged. You'd never do that to me."

He chuckles, and I think it's the sweetest sound on earth. "Never," he agrees. "But what happened to just dating for a while?"

I blink and smile, a teary mess. "I need you, Devlin. I need to claim you. I need it here," I say, pressing my hand to my heart.

"Me, too," he says softly.

"So maybe we can do the dating thing while we're engaged."

"Whatever you want, El. So long as you're mine."

"Always," I say.

And then, with the entire team watching, I melt into the circle of his arms and lose myself in a long, slow kiss with the man I love.

EPILOGUE

The sun hovers over the horizon, making the Pacific glow. I'm on the edge of the patio at the foundation, gazing out toward the tidal pools and the vibrant ocean beyond.

"You look beautiful," Devlin says, coming up beside me and taking my hand. "Like you're bathed in fire."

I tilt my head and look at him. The curve of his jaw, the battle scar on his face. "And you look like a warrior. But I guess you are."

"I'll always fight for you."

"I know," I say, leaning close as he puts his arm around me. Behind us, I hear the clink of glasses and conversation. It's a party, after all, but I don't feel guilty having Devlin to myself for these few minutes.

All too short, I think when I hear the click of heels approaching. But I smile when I look over my shoulder and see Tamra, the other guests at the small party mingling behind her. "You're here!"

"I'm so sorry I'm late," she says, taking each of our hands. "And congratulations. When's the big day?"

"Spring," I say. "March."

"And you're excited?"

"Of course." I smile up at Devlin. "We both are."

He chuckles. "I'm not sure how happy I am to be even more in the spotlight, but I'm definitely happy for Ellie. And for the additional publicity for the foundation."

I roll my eyes. Tonight's party is a gathering of friends to celebrate my upcoming book, *Saints and Sinners,* which is already in production, and so far the advance reviews, preorders, and general buzz are excellent. People are pretty much lining up to read about The Wolf's son turned philanthropist, not to mention the juicier bits like our lifelong romance and the kidnapping. We've even had calls from producers like Michael Holt, a very big deal in LA. Mostly though, I'm just excited to raise awareness for the foundation and all the good that Devlin does.

As we speak, Brandy and Lamar come over and join us. I expect Ronan as well, but he's still by the fire pit, ostensibly talking with Reggie, a few of the other Angels, and Corbin, to whom I dedicated the book. After all, he'd suggested it.

Even though Ronan doesn't join us, I see the way his eyes cut this direction. Or, rather, in the direction of Brandy.

I almost ask her if there's something going on between them, but she seems entirely oblivious.

"Have you told Tamra the rest of it?" she asks, and I can see that she's practically buzzing with the strain of keeping my secret.

Devlin chuckles, then lightly smacks my ass. "Someone broke our pact."

"Brandy gets a pass," I say. "Roommate rules."

"Well, it *is* Brandy," he says, and they share a smile. They've always gotten along, but since the horror in Big Bear, their friendship has really solidified, as has mine with Ronan. I glance his way again—wondering if he's still looking toward Brandy—but he's completely focused on Reggie. I frown. Maybe it was all my imagination?

"Ahem," Tamra says. "The rest of it? What exactly am I missing out on?"

"Also missing out," Lamar says, raising his hand in a way that make me chuckle. "I'd like my disapproval to be noted."

I glance at Devlin, wondering if he wants to bring Ronan over to hear the news before we announce it officially next week. It's clear he doesn't, and I narrow my eyes, realizing that of course he's already told Ronan, just like I told Brandy.

He meets my eyes, then bends and whispers, soft enough that only I can hear him. "We'll punish each other later," he says, making me choke back a burst of laughter.

When I can talk again, I take Devlin's hand. "We have a date," I say. "The Saturday after the book releases we're getting married. Brandy's my maid of honor, of course. But I was hoping you'd give me away?" I take Lamar's hand.

"Ellie, are you kidding? Of course, I will."

I smile at him, tearing up a bit, which is silly because I'm just not that sentimental. Then again, maybe I am.

I look to Tamra next, but it's Devlin who speaks. "You've been as close to me as any mother could," he says. "And it would be a great honor if you'd stand with us when we say our vows."

"Oh." I see the tears in her eyes, and then she nods. "Of course I will," she says, looking between the two of us. "We're family."

I don't realize I'm crying until I feel the tears running down my cheeks.

"Ellie?" Brandy says.

I squeeze Devlin's hand and flash a teary smile at my friends—my family. "I'm okay, I say. I'm just happy."

It's more than that, though, and as I meet Devlin's eyes, I know he understands. Once upon a time, I lost everything in this town. But now, with Devlin and the people I love, I have the world again.

Don't miss Brandy and Ronan in Sinner's Game!

WANTED: AN EXCERPT

I hope you enjoy the first three chapters of J. Kenner's wickedly sensual romance, Wanted.

One

I know exactly when my life shifted. That precise instant when his eyes met mine and I no longer saw the bland look of familiarity, but danger and fire, lust and hunger.

Perhaps I should have turned away. Perhaps I should have run.

I didn't. I wanted him. More, I needed him. The man, and the fire that he ignited inside of me.

And in his eyes, I saw that he needed me, too.

That was the moment that everything changed. Me, most of all.

But whether it changed for good or for ill ... well, that remains to be seen.

Even dead, my Uncle Jahn knew how to throw one hell of a party.

His Chicago lakeside penthouse was bursting at the seams with an eclectic collection of mourners, most of whom had imbibed so much wine from the famous Howard Jahn cellar that whatever melancholy they'd brought with them had been sweetly erased, and now this wake or reception or whatever the hell you wanted to call it wasn't the least bit somber. Politicians mingled with financiers mingled with artists and academics, and everyone was smiling and laughing and toasting the deceased.

At his request, there'd been no formal funeral. Just this gathering of friends and family, food and drink, music and mirth. Jahn—he hated the name Howard—had lived a vibrant life, and that was never more obvious than now in his death.

I missed him so damn much, but I hadn't cried. Hadn't screamed and ranted. Hadn't done anything, really, except move through the days and nights lost in a haze of emotions, my mind numb. My body anesthetized.

I sighed and fingered the charm on my silver bracelet. He'd presented me with the tiny motorcycle just over a month ago, and the gift had made me smile. I hadn't talked about wanting to ride a motorcycle since before I turned sixteen. And it had been years since I'd ridden behind a boy, my arms tight around his waist and my hair blowing in the wind.

But Uncle Jahn knew me better than anyone. He saw past the princess to the girl hidden inside. A girl who'd built up walls out of necessity, but still desperately wanted to break free. Who longed to slip on a pair of well-worn jeans, grab a battered leather jacket, and go a little wild.

Sometimes, she even did. And sometimes it didn't end right at all.

I tightened my grip on the charm as the memory of Jahn

holding my hand—of him promising to keep my secrets—
swept over me, finally bringing tears to my eyes. He should be
beside me, dammit, and the swell of laughter and conversation
that filled the room was making me a little sick.

Despite the fact that I knew Jahn wanted it that way, it
was all I could do not to smack all the people who'd hugged
me and murmured softly that he was in a better place and
wasn't it wonderful that he'd lived such a full life. That was
such bullshit—he hadn't even turned sixty yet. Vibrant men in
their fifties shouldn't drop dead from aneurysms, and there
weren't enough pithy Hallmark quotes in the universe to
make me think otherwise.

Antsy, I shifted my weight from foot to foot. There was a
bar set up on the other side of the room, and I'd positioned
myself as far away as physically possible because right then I
wanted the burn of tequila. Wanted to let go, to explode
through the numbness that clung to me like a cocoon. To run.
To *feel*.

But that wasn't going to happen. No alcohol was passing
these lips tonight. I was Jahn's niece, after all, and that made
me some kind of hostess-by-default, which meant I was stuck
in the penthouse. Four thousand square feet, but I swear I
could feel the art-covered walls pressing in around me.

I wanted to race up the spiral staircase to the rooftop
patio, then leap over the balcony into the darkening sky. I
wanted to take flight over Lake Michigan and the whole
world. I wanted to break things and scream and rant and curse
this damned universe that took away a good man.

Shit. I sucked in a breath and looked down at the exquisite
ancient-looking notebook inside the glass and chrome display
case I'd been leaning against. The leather-bound book was an
exceptionally well-done copy of a recently discovered Da Vinci
notebook. Dubbed the Creature Notebook, it had sixteen

pages of animal studies and was open to the center, revealing a stunning sketch the young master had drawn—his study for the famous, but never located, dragon shield. Jahn had attempted to acquire the notebook, and I remember just how angry he'd been when he'd lost out to Victor Neely, another Chicago businessman with a private collection that rivaled my uncle's.

At the time, I'd just started at Northwestern with a major in poli sci and a minor in art history. I'm not particularly talented, but I've sketched my whole life, and I've been fascinated with art—and in particular with Leonardo da Vinci—since my parents took me to my first museum at the age of three.

I thought the Creature Notebook was beyond cool, and I'd been irritated on Jahn's behalf when he not only lost out on it, but when the press had poured salt in the wound by prattling on about Neely's amazing new acquisition.

About a year later, Jahn showed me the facsimile, bright and shiny in the custom-made display case. As a general rule, my uncle never owned a copy. If he couldn't have the original —be it a Rembrandt or a Rauschenberg or a Da Vinci—he simply moved on. When I'd asked why he'd made an exception for the Creature Notebook, he shrugged and told me that the images were at least as interesting as the provenance. "Besides, anyone who can successfully copy a Da Vinci has created a masterpiece himself."

Despite the fact that it wasn't authentic, the notebook was my favorite of Jahn's many manuscripts and artifacts, and now, standing with my hands pressed to the glass, I felt as if he was, in some small way, beside me.

I drew in a breath, knowing I had to get my act together, if for no other reason than the more wrecked I looked, the more guests would try to cheer me. Not that I looked particularly wrecked. When you grow up as Angelina Hayden Raine, with a United States senator for a father and a mother who served on the board of over a dozen international nonprofit organizations, you learn the difference between a public and a private face very early on. Especially when you have your own secrets to keep.

"This is so goddamn fucked up it makes me want to scream."

I felt a whisper of a smile touch my lips and turned around to find myself looking into Kat's bloodshot eyes.

"Oh, hell, Angie," she said. "He shouldn't be dead."

"He'd be pissed if he knew you'd been crying," I said, blinking away the last of my own tears.

"Fuck that."

I almost laughed. Katrina Laron had a talent for cutting straight through the bullshit.

I'm not sure which one of us leaned in first, but we caught each other in a bone-crushing hug. With a sniffle, I finally pulled away. Perverse, maybe, but just knowing that someone else was acknowledging the utter horror of the situation made me feel infinitesimally better.

"Every time I turn a corner, I feel like I'm going to see him," I said. "I almost wish I'd stayed in my old place."

I'd moved in four months ago when Uncle Jahn's aneurysm was discovered. I'd taken time off from work—easy when you work for your uncle. For two weeks I'd played nurse after he came home from the hospital, and when he'd been given the all-clear by the doctors—yeah, like *that* was a good call—I'd accepted his invitation to move in permanently. Why not? The tiny apartment I'd shared with my lifelong friend Flynn wasn't exactly the lap of luxury. And although I loved Flynn, he wasn't the easiest person to cohabitate with. He knew me too well, and it always made me uneasy when people saw what I wanted to keep hidden.

Now, though, I craved both the cocoon-like comfort of my tiny room and Flynn's steady presence. As much as I loved the condo, without my uncle, it was cold and hollow, and just being in it made me feel brittle. As if at any moment I would shatter into a million pieces.

Kat's eyes were warm and understanding. "I know. But he loved having you here. God knows why," she added with a quirky grin. "You're nothing but trouble."

I rolled my eyes. At twenty-seven, Katrina Laron was only four years older than me, but that didn't stop her from pulling the older-and-wiser card whenever she got the chance. The fact that we'd become friends under decidedly dodgy circumstances probably played a role, too.

She'd been working at one of the coffee shops in Evanston where I used to mainline caffeine during my first year at Northwestern. We'd chatted a couple of times in an "extra cream please, it's been a bitch of a day" kind of way, but we were hardly on a first-name basis.

All that changed when we bumped into each other on a day when extra cream wasn't going to cut it for me—not by a long shot. It was in the Michigan Avenue Neiman Marcus and I'd been surfing on adrenaline, using it to soothe the rough edges of a particularly crappy day. Specifically, I'd just succumbed to my personal demons and surreptitiously dropped a pair of fifteen-dollar clearance earrings into my purse. But, apparently, not as surreptitiously as I'd thought.

"Well, aren't you the stumbling amateur?" she'd whispered, as she steered me toward women's shoes. "With a shit technique like that, it's a wonder you haven't been arrested yet."

"Arrested!" I squeaked, as if that word would carry all the

way to Washington and to my father's all-hearing ears. The *fear* of getting caught might be part of the excitement. *Actually* getting caught wasn't a good thing at all. "No, I didn't—I mean—"

She cut off my protests with a casual flip of her hand. "All I'm saying is be smart. If you're going to take a risk, at least make it worth the trouble. Those earrings? Really not the bomb."

"It's not about the earrings," I'd snapped, then immediately cringed. The words had been a knee-jerk response, but they were also true. It *wasn't* about the earrings. It was about my dad, and the grad school lectures and the career-planning talks, and the never-spoken certainty that no matter what I did, my sister would have done it better.

It was about the oppressive, overwhelming weight of my life and my future that was bearing down on me, harder and harder until I was certain that if I didn't do something to break out a little I'd spontaneously combust.

Kat had glanced at my purse as if she could see through the soft Coach leather to the contraband inside. Then she slowly lifted her eyes back to my face. The silence hung between us for a full minute. Then she nodded. "Don't worry. I get it." She cocked her head toward the exit. "Come on."

Relief flooded through me, and my limbs that had frozen in both fear and mortification began to thaw. She steered me to her car, a cherry-red Mustang that she drove at more or less the speed of light. She careened down Michigan Avenue, maneuvered her way onto Lake Shore Drive, and came so close to the other cars as she zipped in and out of traffic that I'm surprised her convertible didn't lose a layer of paint. In other words, it was freaking awesome. The top was down, the wind was whipping my hair into my face and mouth, and all I could do was tilt my head back and laugh.

Kat risked our lives long enough to shoot me one sideways glance. "Yeah," she said. "We're going to get along just fine."

From that moment on, I'd adored Kat. Now, with Jahn's death sending my universe reeling, I realized that I not only loved her—I relied on her.

"I'm really glad you're here," I said.

"Where else would I be?" She scanned the room. "Are your mom and dad around somewhere?"

"They can't make it. They're stuck overseas." The familiar numbness settled over me again as I remembered my mother's hysterical sobs and the deep well of sorrow that had filled my father's voice when he'd learned about his half-brother. "I hated calling them," I whispered. "It felt like Gracie all over again."

"I'm so sorry." Kat had never met my sister, but she'd heard the story. The public version, anyway, and I knew her sympathy was real.

I managed a wavering smile. "I know. That means a lot to me."

"The whole thing sucks," Kat said. "It's so unfair. Your uncle was too damn cool to die."

"I guess the universe doesn't give a shit about coolness."

"The universe can be a raving bitch sometimes," Kat said. She exhaled loudly. "Want me to crash here tonight so you won't be alone? We could stay up late getting so wasted that there's no way in hell either one of us will dream."

"Thanks, but I think I'll be okay."

She eyed me uncertainly. She was one of the few people I'd confided in about my nightmares, and while I appreciated the sympathy, sometimes I wished I'd kept my mouth shut.

"Really," I said earnestly. "Kevin's here."

"Oh, yeah? And how's that going? Engaged yet?"

"Not quite," I said wryly. I supposed we were dating since

I'd slept with him twice, but so far I'd dodged the let's-be-exclusive conversation. I wasn't sure why I was so reticent. The sex wasn't mind-blowing, but it did the job. And I did genuinely like the guy. But I'd spent the last few months holding him at arm's length, telling him I needed to keep my attention on Jahn's surgery, then his recovery.

Obviously, I hadn't planned on his sudden death.

How horrible was it of me to think that now Jahn was gone, I had no more excuses to hand Kevin?

Beside me, Kat craned her neck and scoped out the crowd. "So where is he?"

"He had to go take a call. Technically, he's working today."

"What are you going to do now?" Kat asked.

"About Kevin?" Honestly, I was hoping to avoid doing anything on that front for the foreseeable future.

"About your job," she countered. "About the roof over your head. About your life. Have you thought about what you're going to do?"

"Oh." My shoulders sagged. "No. Not really." My job in the PR department of Jahn's company might pay my bills, but it was hardly my life's ambition, and Kat was one of the few people to whom I'd confessed that deep, dark secret. Right then, however, that wasn't a conversation I wanted to have. Fortunately, something across the room had caught Kat's attention, effectively erasing my lack of direction and purpose from her mind.

She stood slightly straighter and the corners of her mouth tilted a bit, almost hinting at a smile. Curious, I turned to look in that direction, but saw nothing but suits and dresses and a sea of black. "What is it? Kevin?" I asked, praying he wasn't heading our direction.

"Cole August," she said. "At least I thought I saw him."

"Oh." I licked my lips. My mouth had gone suddenly dry. "Is Evan with him?" I forced my voice to sound casual, but my pulse was racing. If Cole was around, it was always a good bet that Evan was, too.

Then I remembered what day it was and my pulse slowed as disappointment weighed down on me. "Isn't tonight the ribbon-cutting for the hospital wing Evan funded?"

Kat didn't even spare me a glance, her eyes still searching the crowd. "Not sure." She shot me a quick look. "Yeah, it was. You invited me before, you know, all of this happened."

I blinked back the sudden prick of tears. "Evan's going to hate missing this. Jahn was like a dad to him."

Beside me, Kat took a quick step backward, startling me. "What is it?"

She dragged her gaze away from the crowd, then frowned at me. "I ... Oh, shit. I have to go make a call. I'll be right back, okay?"

"Um, okay." Who the hell did she need to call right now? That wasn't a question I pondered for long, though, because I'd caught a glimpse of Cole. And right beside him—looking like he owned the world and everything in it—was Evan.

Immediately, my chest tightened and a current of electricity zinged across my skin. Technically, I saw him first, but it was my body's reaction that caught my attention. Only after I felt him did I truly see him.

And what a sight he was.

Whereas Cole might be sex on wheels, Evan Black was the slow burn of sin and seduction—and tonight he was in rare form. He must have come straight from the hospital, because he was still in a tux, and although he was clearly overdressed, he appeared perfectly at ease. Whether in a tux or jeans, where Evan was concerned, it was the man that mattered, not the garment.

He had the kind of chiseled good looks that would have gotten him plucked from obscurity in the Golden Age of Hollywood, and the kind of confidence and bearing that would have made him a box-office draw. A small scar intersected his left brow, giving the angel's face a hint of the devil.

He both came from money and had made his own fortune, and it showed in the way he held himself, the way he looked around a room, managing to take control of it with nothing more than a glance.

His eyes were as gray as a wolf's and his hair was the color of cherrywood, a deep brown that hinted at golds and reds when the light hit it just right. He wore it long in the back so that it brushed his collar, and the natural waves gave it the quality of a mane—which only enhanced the impression that there was a wildness clinging to the man.

Wild or not, I wanted to get close. I wanted to thrust my fingers into his hair and feel the locks on my skin. I imagined his hair was soft, but that's the only part of him that was. Everything else was edged with steel, the hard planes of his face and body hinting at a dangerous core beneath that beauty.

I didn't know whether the danger was real or an illusion. And right then, I didn't care.

I wanted the touch, the thrill.

That desperate need to fly I'd been feeling all night? So help me, I wanted to fly right into Evan's arms.

I needed the rush. I craved the thrill.

I wanted the man.

And it was just too damn bad that he didn't want me, too.

Two

I'd known Evan Black for almost eight years, and yet I didn't really know the man at all.

I'd just turned sixteen when I first saw him during the sweltering heat of a summer that marked so many firsts in my life. The first summer I spent entirely in Chicago. The first summer away from my parents. The first time I fucked a guy. Because that's what it was. Not a sweet teenage romance. It was release, pure and simple. Release and escape and oblivion.

And damned if I hadn't needed oblivion, because that was also the first summer without my sister, who was back in California, six feet beneath the sun-soaked earth.

I'd been lost after her death. My parents—wracked with their own grief—had tried to pull me close, to help and soothe me. But I wriggled away, too burdened with loss to cleave to them the way I wanted. Too heavy with guilt to believe I had any right to their help or affection.

It was Jahn who'd rescued me from that small corner of hell. He'd appeared at the front door of our La Jolla house the first Friday of summer break, and immediately steered my mother into the dark-paneled office that was forbidden to me. When they'd emerged twenty minutes later there were fresh tears in my mother's eyes, but she'd managed a cheery smile for me. "Go pack your carry-on," she'd said. "You're going to Chicago with Uncle Jahn."

I'd taken three tank tops, my swimsuit, a dress, a pair of jeans, and the shorts I'd worn on the plane. I'd expected to stay a weekend. Instead, I'd stayed the entire summer.

At the time, Jahn was living primarily in his waterfront house in Kenilworth, a jaw-droppingly affluent Chicago suburb. For two solid weeks, I'd done nothing but sit under the gazebo and stare out at Lake Michigan. Not my usual M.O.—during past visits, I'd taken out the Jet Ski or skateboarded in the street or taken off on a borrowed bike down Sheridan Road with Flynn, the boy I would later fuck who lived two doors down and had as much of a wild streak as I did. When I was twelve, I'd even rigged a zip line from the attic bedroom all the way to the far side of the pool, and I'd eagerly tested it out, much to the consternation of my mother who had screamed and cursed once she saw me whipping through the air to land, cannonball style, in the water.

Grace had squealed at me from her chaise lounge throne, accusing me of ruining her hardback copy of *Pride and Prejudice.* My mother had ordered me to spend the rest of the day in my room. And Uncle Jahn had remained completely silent, but as I passed him, I thought I saw the twinkle of amusement in his eyes, along with something that might have been respect.

I saw none of that the summer of my sixteenth year. Instead, all I saw was worry.

"We all miss her," he said to me one afternoon. "But you can't mourn forever. She wouldn't want you to. Take the bike. Go into the village. Go to the park. Drag Flynn to a movie." He cupped my chin and tilted my face up to look at him. "I lost one niece, Lina. Not two."

"Angie," I corrected, making up my mind right then and there to kick Lina soundly to the curb. Lina was the girl I used to be. The one who'd always felt larger than life, and who'd needed to feel the rush of the world around her all the time. Who'd been too alive to be calm or careful. Who'd been a damn stupid fool who smoked cigarettes behind the school and snuck out to dance clubs. A little idiot who made out with boys because she wanted the thrill, and who rode on the back of their motorcycles for the exact same reason. Lina was the girl who'd almost been suspended from high school just one week into her freshman year.

And Lina was the reason that my sister was dead.

I'd lived in Lina's skin all my life, but I didn't want to be that girl anymore.

"Angie," I repeated, firmly cementing the first brick of the wall I was building around myself. Then I'd stood up and gone inside.

Uncle Jahn hadn't bothered me for the rest of that day or the next, though I knew he was worried and confused. When Saturday morning came, he told me that he was having some students from the graduate-level finance seminar he taught as an adjunct over for burgers by the pool, and I was welcome to join them. My call.

I'm not sure what compelled me to emerge from the dark cave of my room that afternoon, all I know is that I came down in my ratty cutoffs with Uncle Jahn's ancient Rolling Stones T-shirt over my bikini top. I thought I'd stay for an hour. Have a burger. Remind myself not to sneak a beer, because that was the kind of thing Lina would do, not Angie.

But when I actually got down to the pool deck, all thoughts of beer and burgers evaporated, replaced by pure, decadent, desperate lust. And not the teenage-crush kind, either. No, I saw Evan Black shirtless and in swim trunks that clung in a way that made my sixteen-year-old hormones light up. His wet hair was swept back from his face, and he was brandishing a metal spatula as he stood by the grill, laughing with two other guys, who I later learned were his best friends, Cole August and Tyler Sharp.

All three seemed younger than the other four students who also populated the lush backyard. I later learned that I was right. The others were in their last year of grad school, whereas Evan was still an undergrad who'd been given special dispensation to take the class. And Tyler and Cole weren't even enrolled at Northwestern. Tyler was a freshman at Loyola. Cole was a year older than Tyler, and had just come back from some sort of art internship in Rome. They'd come with Evan who, along with the others, made up the whole of that summer's seminar class in finance.

Together, Cole, Tyler, and Evan were a smorgasbord of hotness that even my reasonably inexperienced eyes were more than capable of appreciating. But Evan was the only one that I wanted to take a bite out of.

I heard my uncle call my name, and the three of them turned to look in my direction. I stopped breathing as Evan's gaze swept toward me, his expression never changing as he looked me over and then, oh-so casually, went back to flipping burgers.

I'm not sure what sort of movie I'd had running subliminally in my head. Something wild and romantic, I guess, because the moment he turned away, I felt a hot wave of disappointment wash over me. And that, of course, was immediately replaced by mortification. *Could he tell what I was thinking? Was he going to think of me now as Jahn's gawkish niece? The one with the schoolgirl crush?*

Holy crap, the idea was horrifying.

"Hey, Angie," Jahn called, his words jerking my posture straight as effectively as a string pulling a marionette. "You joining us for burgers?"

"I—" My words had stuck in my throat, and I knew I couldn't stay there. I needed space. Hell, I needed air. "I—I think I'm coming down with something." I blurted the words, then turned and ran back into the house, certain that my burning cheeks were a fire hazard.

I tried to concentrate on television. On a book. On screwing around on the Internet. But nothing held my attention. My mind was too full of Evan, and in the end I went to bed early. Not because I was truly sick, but because I wanted the pleasure of the dark. The thrill of sliding my hand down my belly and under the band of my underwear, then touching myself with my eyes closed as I imagined that it was Evan's fingers upon me. His fingers, his tongue, every decadent inch of him.

It was a bedtime fantasy that became a personal favorite, and one I repeated many nights over the next few years. Fortunately, I didn't repeat the squealing and running like a twit every time Evan came around. Fortunate because Jahn took a fatherly liking to them, and those three guys became a fixture at the house. And since I wasn't inclined to spend my summer hiding inside, I began to venture out. By August, I thought of Tyler and Cole like big brothers. As for Evan—no way would I ever feel brotherly toward him, but at least I could carry on a conversation without imagining his lips on mine.

Jahn called them the Three Dog Knights, because the Three Musketeers wasn't original enough for guys as unique as them. "Besides," he'd joked one evening as he hooked an arm around my shoulder and grinned at the guys, "this way I have my knights and my princess."

Evan focused those hypnotic gray eyes on me, obviously considering the comment. "Is that what you are?"

I froze, stunned by the question. Grace had always been the princess to my jester. But now that she was dead, I'd slipped on the mantle even though it was an awkward, uncomfortable fit.

He was watching me—his gaze holding steady on my face as I floundered for a reply, and for a moment I thought that he saw the girl beneath the facade and the family name. I thought that he saw *me*.

Then he smiled, all casual and false, and the spell was broken. "It's just that in the stories, the princess is always dragonbait."

I had no idea how I was supposed to respond to that, and my discomfort made my temper flare—and then explode when Tyler and Cole both guffawed and Evan shot them a cocky *I've won this round* grin.

"Don't worry about me," I said coldly. "I won't ever be dragonbait."

"No?" He looked me up and down, and it took every ounce of my self-control to stand still as his eyes raked over me. "I guess we'll see," he finally said, and then without another word, he turned around and walked away.

I watched him leave, feeling itchy and unsatisfied. I wanted something—something big and wild. Something like the sizzle and pop that Evan's slow, heated gaze had made bubble up inside me.

Something? Oh, please. How much bullshit was that? I knew exactly what I wanted—or more accurately, I knew *who* I wanted. And he'd just flat-out left, as uninterested in me as I was enraptured by him.

As I bit back a frown, I saw my uncle watching me with an odd expression, and for the first time I feared that he knew my secret: I had more than an innocent schoolgirl crush on Evan Black. And somehow, someway, I was going to do something about it.

———

I released a long-suffering sigh, my eyes still fixed on the almost-magical image of Evan in his tux. I didn't know if I was charmingly optimistic or sadly pathetic. All I knew was that despite the years that had passed—and despite the lack of any interest on his part whatsoever—my fascination with Evan Black never waned.

For just a moment, I allowed myself the luxury of a

fantasy. His finger crooked under my chin. The slight pressure as he lifted my face to look into his eyes. His touch would be gentle but firm. His scent masculine and heady. "Angie," he'd say. "Why the hell haven't we done this before?"

I'd open my mouth to answer, but he'd cut me off with a kiss, hot and open and so desperately demanding that I would melt against him, our bodies fusing from the electricity zinging through me, all of it focused between my thighs, making me squirm. Making me *need*.

"And there she is."

I flinched, yanked from my reverie by the caramel masculine tones. I turned to smile at the two-hundred-plus pounds of perfectly proportioned male that made up Cole August. At first glance, he was intimidating as shit, despite being empirically gorgeous. All muscle and power and hard edges, with the kind of air that warned away anyone who might want to fuck with him. He'd been born and raised on Chicago's rather scary South Side, and the rawness of his heritage still clung to him despite the tailored suit and other trappings of success.

His mixed-race background had blessed him with creamy dark skin that boasted a golden undertone, and his eyes flashed a deep ebony. It was in those eyes that you really saw the man. Massive and intense and just a bit menacing. But also fiercely loyal.

He held out his arms and I went willingly into them. "How are you holding up there, Dragonbait?"

"Not great." I sighed, his scent reminding me of Uncle Jahn, a musky male scent that probably came in a bottle but seemed to me to be part and parcel of those men I adored. "I'm glad you're here. I thought you were out of town."

"We came back, of course." By *we*, I knew he meant himself and Tyler Sharp. "We had to be here for Jahn," Cole added. He pressed a chaste kiss to my forehead. "And for you."

"Is Tyler hiding in the crowd somewhere?" I didn't mention that I'd already honed in on Evan.

"He was right behind me. But he was snagged by a limber blond thing who looked like she wanted to wrap herself around him."

I had to laugh. Even at a funeral, Tyler was a girl-magnet.

Cole grinned. "Yeah, well, don't hold it against her. I got the feeling she's been self-medicating her grief for hours."

"I know how she feels."

He looked hard at me, the humor all but erased from his face. "You need anything, you ask."

I nodded, but stayed silent. The only thing I needed was to let myself go a little wild. To shake off the weight of my grief, cut loose, and get lost in an adrenaline haze. It would work—I knew damn well that was the best way to take the edge off the pain and loss I was feeling. But no matter what, I wasn't going to go there.

Beside me, Cole called out a greeting to Tyler. I inched away from Cole and watched as the third of Jahn's knights approached. Where Cole was burly, Tyler was lean and athletic. He had the kind of good looks that could sneak up on a person, and the kind of charm that could make people do whatever Tyler wanted, and be absolutely certain it was their own idea all along.

He reached out for my hand and gave it a squeeze. "Tell us what you need."

"Nothing," I lied. "Just you two." I lifted a shoulder. "Really. It's better just having you guys here."

"Where's Evan?" Tyler asked, and though the question was directed at Cole, I turned to look, too. But Evan had disappeared.

"Well, shit. He was right beside me a minute ago." Cole glanced around. "Should be easy enough to spot. He's still in that damn monkey suit."

"He didn't want to take the time to go change." Tyler's attention turned to me. "You've seen him, though, right?"

"I—no," I responded. "I mean, I've seen him across the room, but I haven't talked to him. Not yet."

"Yeah?" Tyler's mouth curved down in a frown. "He texted me as he was leaving the dedication. Said he was coming straight here to make sure you were okay."

"He did?" A lazy little ripple of pleasure crept up my back.

"Yeah, he—wait. There he is. *Evan*." His voice carried across the room, and several heads turned toward us. I, however, saw only his face. His eyes. And I swear they were looking at me with the kind of wicked heat I'd fantasized about.

I gasped, that sweet ripple of pleasure now moving to decidedly more interesting parts of my body. I glanced down at the floor, telling myself to get a grip. When I looked up, Evan was moving toward us in response to Tyler's insistent gesture. This time, however, I saw nothing in his eyes, leaving me to wonder if the ripples of heat existed only in my imagination.

He came toward us with long, confident strides. The crowd shifted automatically as he walked, as if it was as natural to clear a path for this man as it was to defer to royalty.

When he reached us, he didn't look at me. Not even a glance. Instead his attention was focused entirely on Tyler and Cole. His manner was brusque, his tone all business. "Everything okay in California?"

"We'll talk later," Tyler said, "but it's all good, man."

"Good," Evan said. He shifted his weight, as if he was about to drift away from our group.

"I hear all those movie stars are raving about your burritos," I blurted. I didn't know about all the various business ventures that the three had their hands in, but I'd paid attention when they'd bought the California-based fast-food chain that I used to frequent during high school. The place had been in violation of so many health codes it's a wonder I survived my teenage years without succumbing to hepatitis, but the guys managed to not only clean the place up but actually expand it into a half dozen other states.

Not that I gave a flip about burritos or California—I just wanted the warmth of Evan's eyes on me. Hell, I would have settled for the quick flash of a smile—I mean, both Cole and Tyler managed as much. But it wasn't their reaction I craved—it was Evan's. And all I got there was the chill of his indifference.

It made no sense. My secret lust notwithstanding, I'd known Evan my entire adult life, and the conversation had always flowed easily. After all, I'd had a lot of practice at hiding my secrets.

I told myself that he had business on his mind, but I didn't really believe it. His silence felt like a slight. Like he was intentionally avoiding looking at me. And, frankly, on this of all days, that kind of ticked me off.

I was so intent on being irritated with Evan, that I didn't realize Kevin had approached until he stepped up next to me and tugged me firmly into his embrace.

"Hey." I flashed a quick smile, hoping I didn't look disappointed to see him.

"Hey, yourself."

I leaned in to receive his sweet kiss. And, damn me all to

hell, all I could think as my lips brushed this man's was whether or not Evan was watching.

I pulled away and forced myself to focus entirely on the man I'd just kissed. "Everything okay? Do you have to go in?"

"No crises," he said. "Truth, justice, and the American way can continue on without me."

He gently kissed my temple, and as I glanced between him and Evan, I had to wonder why the hell I was stalling. This was an incredibly kind and thoughtful man who had made it perfectly clear that he wanted to move past casual dating into a more serious relationship, and yet I was still caught up in lingering teenage fantasies? Honestly, did men get more upstanding and eligible than FBI agents? And considering my father had introduced us, he already had the parental seal of approval.

Purposefully, I moved closer, hooking my arms around his waist, then tilting my head up to look at his face. His wavy blond hair was neatly trimmed and his blue eyes held charm and humor. All in all, he had nice-guy good looks, like the cute quarterback who's not as sexy as the guy in leather with the low-slung car, but still totally hot. "I really appreciate you being here with me."

"I told SAC Burnett that I needed to be here for you today," he said, referring to the special agent in charge to whom he reported. His gaze flicked in turn over Cole and Tyler and Evan. "I'll get back to kicking criminal butt tomorrow."

"Who are you hounding now, Agent Warner?" Evan asked. There was a hint of humor in his voice, but also the tightness of control. Both Tyler and Cole must have heard it, too, because they each cut a sharp glance Evan's way. I had the impression that Cole was going to say something but thought better of it.

"Whoever the evidence points to," Kevin said. "Follow the trail long enough, and you find the asshole at the end."

"Evidence," Evan said, his tone musing. "I thought you boys stopped worrying about evidence years ago. Isn't the method now to fling shit and see what sticks?"

"If you're suggesting that we go to whatever lengths are necessary to gather the evidence that we need," Kevin said smoothly, "then you're absolutely right."

Any pretense of humor in the conversation had now been firmly erased. I winced, remembering too late that the FBI had been all in the trio's face about five years ago. I'd seen the newspaper articles and had asked Jahn about it. He told me not to worry—that a business rival had made some nasty accusations, but that his knights would have their names cleared soon enough. I'd been deep into finals, and so I'd taken my uncle at his word. And, since nothing else popped up in the news, I forgot all about it.

Clearly Evan hadn't forgotten, and the air around us crackled with an uncomfortable, prickly kind of tension.

I cleared my throat, determined to change the subject. "How was the hospital dedication?"

"Inconvenient," Evan snapped. He shoved his hands in his pockets, then drew in a breath, and it didn't take super-human observational skills to see he was making an effort to rein in his temper. "Sorry," he said, his voice now gentle.

He turned slightly, and for the first time since he joined our group, he looked in my direction. "The dedication—hell, the entire wing—means a lot to me and even more to the kids we're going to be helping, but I needed to be here." For the briefest of moments, he looked directly into my eyes and I felt my breath catch in my throat. "He was a good man," Evan said, and the pain I heard in his voice reflected my own. "He'll be missed."

"He will," Kevin said. His voice sounded stiff and stilted, and I had to fight the urge to pull out of his arms, because he didn't get it. How could he? He didn't really know my uncle; he didn't really understand what I'd lost.

I tried to swallow, but my throat was suddenly thick with tears. I clenched my fists, as if mere force of will could keep the grief at bay.

It didn't help. I felt suddenly lost. There was nowhere to turn, nowhere to anchor, and any moment now I knew I would spin out of control.

Damn.

I'd been doing so well—missing Jahn, yes, but not crossing the line into self-pity. I'd been surviving, and the fact that I was coping had made me proud.

I wasn't coping anymore. Evan's coldness had thrown me off my game, and without warning, I'd become antsy and all sorts of fucked up. I wanted to step out of this weird triangle made up of me and Evan and Kevin, but I couldn't seem to move.

All I knew was that Uncle Jahn had always been my way in. He'd always understood me. He'd always been there to rescue me.

But he wasn't there right then—and to my total mortification, the tears began to flow.

"Angie," Evan murmured. "Oh, baby, it's okay."

I have no idea how it happened, but suddenly my face was pressed to Evan's chest and he was holding me and his hand was stroking my back and his voice was soothing me, telling me that I should let it out. That it would be okay. That *I* would be okay.

I clung to him, soaking up the solace that he was offering. His body was hard and firm and strong, and I didn't want to let go. I wanted to draw in his strength and claim it as my very own.

But then my nose started to run, and I pulled back, afraid of mucking up his gazillion-dollar tux. "Thanks," I said, or at least I tried to. I don't think the word actually left my mouth, because when I looked up at him, it wasn't friendly concern that I saw. No, it was heat. It was desire. Vibrant and pure and absolutely unmistakable.

And it was wild enough to burn a hole right through me.

I gasped, and the sound seemed to flip a switch in him. Then—as quickly as it appeared—that fire was gone, and I was left feeling cold and bereft and desperately confused.

"She needs you," Evan said, passing me off to Kevin, who took me into his arms even as a shadow crossed his face.

"Didn't you want to say something to the crowd?" Cole asked, his voice reminding me that he and Tyler were standing just inches away, their penetrating eyes taking in everything.

"I did," Evan said, his expression now bland and his tone businesslike, as if that could erase those last few seconds. But it was too late, and everything had changed. I'd seen it. Seen? Hell, what I'd seen in his face had just about knocked me over.

But he was walking away from me now, and as I watched him go—as I stood there clinging tightly to Kevin's hand—I knew that if I wanted him, I was going to have to go after him.

Because where Evan Black and I were concerned, he would always walk away.

And in a moment of sudden clarity, I goddamn knew the reason why.

Three

I started my freshman year at Northwestern right about

the time that Evan was dropping out, too successful in all of his various ventures to bother with anything as mundane as grad school.

The air seemed scented with lilac that fall, and Jahn had thrown one of his famous parties. Evan was there, of course, flanked as usual by Tyler and Cole. I'd sat with them by the pool, my bare feet dangling in the water as I answered their questions about how I was surviving my first weeks.

The conversation was casual and easy, and I was proud of myself for playing it cool. Or I was until Jahn asked me to go inside with him to pick out a bottle of wine.

"You know that you're like a daughter to me," he said, once we were standing in the bright and airy kitchen, looking out at the pool through the huge bay window.

"Sure," I said happily. Then I caught sight of his face and frowned. "Is something wrong?"

He shook his head, just the tiniest of motions. But the shadow in his eyes suggested something else entirely. "I just hope you know that I would do anything for you. That I'll protect you from anything and anyone."

My chest tightened and I felt the beads of perspiration rise on my lip. "What's going on?" My mind filled with images of knives and threats, of assault and rape. Oh, god, no. Surely—

"*No.*" Jahn's voice was as forceful as his hand clutched around my wrist. "No," he repeated, but this time more gently. "That's not what I'm talking about. Nothing like that."

Slowly, my fear ebbed. "Then what is it?"

"I've seen the way you look at them, Angie."

"Them?" For the briefest of moments, I was genuinely confused. Then I got it—and my cheeks flamed with embarrassment.

"Those boys will always look out for you," he said,

ignoring my discomfiture. "They'll watch over you until the end of time because you're important to me. But it can't ever go further than that. Not with any one of them." His voice had hardened, taking on a commanding and serious tone that I rarely heard from him. "I said I'd protect you," he said. "Even if that means protecting you from yourself."

"I don't know what you—" I began, but he cut me off sharply.

"They're not the men for you," he said firmly. He faced me straight on, his expression deadly serious. "And they know that you're off-limits to them."

I opened my mouth to say something, then shut it again, because what the hell was I supposed to say? This was totally freaking surreal.

My instinct was to deny, deny, deny. But curiosity got the better of me. "What's wrong with them?" I asked.

"Not a goddamn thing."

"Then why are we having this conversation?"

He turned his back to the window and leaned against the granite counter, his arms crossed over his chest. His eyes narrowed, and I felt my posture straightening automatically under his appraising gaze.

He glanced quickly away. "They're too old for you."

I almost spit out my laugh. "Seriously? *That's* the problem? Daddy's thirteen years older than Mom, and no one thought that was a big deal."

When he looked at me, there was something almost wistful in his eyes. "Sarah is special," he said.

"And I'm not?" I was teasing, sure, but I was also serious. "Evan's barely six years older than me, and he's the oldest of all three of them. Come on, Uncle J. What's really going on here?"

Instead of answering, he grabbed a corkscrew from where

it sat on the counter, and went to work on one of the bottles he'd pulled out for the evening. I watched silently, both amused and frustrated, as he poured a glass, took a sip, and then poured another. When he handed the second to me, I had to bite back an insolent smirk. Technically, I was under the drinking age.

When he finally spoke, his voice was low and even and tinged with a hint of regret. "When was the last time you've seen me with my wife?"

The question was so unexpected that I answered right away. "Not for years." I hadn't seen his most recent wife, or any of the parade of previous ones, in ages. I knew they'd all left him, but I'd never known why. And since I'd never gotten close to any of them, I hadn't ever asked.

"Too many secrets will destroy a relationship," he said.

"I don't have any secrets." Except, of course, I did.

Jahn paused, and for a moment I thought he was going to call me on my lie. But then he nodded, almost casually, as if my words were a given. "Maybe not. But he does. His own, and those he holds for others."

He.

That one simple word rattled around in my head, making me a little dizzy. Because I knew what it meant. It meant that we weren't really talking about the trio, but about Evan. About the fact that I wanted him—and that Jahn knew it.

I swallowed, embarrassed but also relieved in a weird way. Jahn *knew* me—possibly better than anyone else ever did or ever would.

But he was wrong about one thing—secrets didn't bother me. How could they when I held so many of my own?

Now, as I stood in the open living room of Jahn's condo and listened to Evan speak to the crowd, it was as if Jahn's ghost had drawn me, Scrooge-like, back to the past, to see that afternoon all over again. I'd been unsure before, believing that, like his best friends, Evan thought of me like a sister.

I no longer believed that.

Jahn's lecture that night hadn't just been about warning me to stay away. He'd been telling me that he'd ordered Evan and Tyler and Cole away, too. And while Cole and Tyler might not find that request to be a burden, I'd seen the heat in Evan's eyes.

He wanted me, dammit.

He wanted me, and he was too goddamned loyal to my uncle to do anything about it.

"Howard Jahn was a man who loved his life."

The deep tones of Evan's voice filled the room, mesmerizing and clear. "In the short time that he was on this earth, he not only lived that life to the fullest, but taught others how to do the same. He changed the lives of so many people, many of whom are standing here tonight. I should know. I'm one of the lucky people that he took under his wing."

I took my eyes off Evan long enough to examine the crowd. They were as enthralled as I was, caught up in both Evan's charisma and the words that he was speaking. I watched him—this man who'd made a fortune for himself at such a young age—and understood in that moment how he'd risen to be one of the most influential men in Chicago. Hell, if he were a tent preacher, he could have swindled millions from that crowd.

The only one who didn't look impressed, in fact, was Kevin. I wasn't sure if he was still stinging from his smackdown with Evan earlier or if he was picking up on my Evanlust vibes. But since the latter was enough of a possibility to make my highly tuned guilt antennae hum, I reached over and took his hand—then felt even more guilty because of my own hypocrisy.

"Howard Jahn taught me a different way of looking at the world. In so many ways, he rescued me, and he never once gave up on me." He had been looking out over the crowd as he spoke, but now his eyes found mine. "We're here today to honor his memory," he continued, with an odd kind of ferocity in his voice. "His memory. His requests. His legacy."

He paused and the air was so thick between us that it took all my strength just to draw a breath. I'm surprised that every eye in the room wasn't turned to us, watching the spectacle of the fire that blazed between us. Because it was there. I felt it—I felt it and I wanted to burn in it.

I have no idea what he said next. He must have continued talking, because before I knew it, people were raising glasses in a toast and wiping damp eyes.

The spell that had captured me dissipated, and I watched, breathless, as Evan melted into the crowd. He shook hands with people and accepted consoling pats on his shoulder. He ruled the room, commanding and calm. A steady presence for the mourners to rely on.

And never did he take his eyes off me.

Then he was coming toward me, his gait firm and even, his expression determined. I was only half-aware of Kevin beside me, his fingers still twined with mine. Right then, Evan Black was my entire world. I wanted to feel his touch again. Wanted him to pull me close. To murmur that he knew what I'd lost when Jahn had died.

I wanted him to brush his lips sweetly over mine in consolation, and then to throw all decorum aside and kiss me so wild and hard that grief and regret withered under the heat of our passion.

And it pissed me off royally that it wasn't going to happen because of a promise he made to a dead man.

I'm not sure what I was trying to prove, but I spun around and folded myself into Kevin's arms.

"What—"

I cut him off with a kiss that started out awkward and weird, but then Kevin must have decided I needed this. That my grief had sent me over the wall and into the land of rampant public displays of affection.

His hand cupped the back of my head as his mouth claimed mine. As far as kissing was concerned, Kevin definitely got an A. Empirically, he was everything a girl should want, and yet I wasn't satisfied. I wasn't even close. There was no heat, no burn. No butterflies in my stomach, no longing for more. On the contrary, all Kevin's kiss did was make me more aware of the void inside me. A hunger—a craving—that I couldn't seem to satisfy no matter how much I wanted to.

Evan, I thought, and was shocked by the desperate longing that went along with those two small syllables. Somehow the tight grip I'd kept on my desire all these years had come loose. It was as if my grief had shoved me over the cliff, and for the first time in forever, I wished I could just erase Evan Black from my mind. I felt out of control. Frenzied and reckless.

And for a girl like me, that's never a good place to be.

When Kevin broke our kiss and pulled away from me, all I wanted to do was pull him back again. To kiss him until we broke through my resolve. Until we created a fire out of friction if nothing else. Because I needed that. I needed to get clear. I needed to lose myself in him until the blazing heat that was Evan Black was reduced to nothing more substantial than a burn across my heart.

But that, I knew, was never going to happen.

Kevin's palm cupped my cheek, his smile gentle. "Sweetheart, you look ripped to pieces."

I nodded. I was. Just not for the reason Kevin thought.

I glanced around the room, searching out Evan. Wanting to know that he'd seen. Wanting him to be as twisted and tied up in knots as I was.

But he wasn't even there.

"Angelina, my dear, the young waitress said I might find you in here. It's so good to see you again, even under such sad circumstances."

The Southern-smooth voice rolled over me, and I grimaced. I'd escaped to the kitchen—which was technically off limits to guests—with the hope of squeezing out just one tiny little moment alone. Apparently, that wasn't going to happen.

Forcing a political-daughter smile onto my face, I turned away from the counter and greeted Edwin Mulberry, a congressman from either Alabama or Mississippi or some other state that most definitely wasn't the Midwest.

"Congressman Mulberry. What a pleasure," I lied. I willed my smile wider. "I didn't realize you knew my uncle."

He had silver hair and an audience-ready smile that I only half-believed was genuine. "Your uncle was an amazing man," he said. "Very well connected. When I spoke to your father yesterday and he told me he couldn't be here, I knew I had to come by."

"I appreciate that," I said. Mulberry was a representative with an eye on the Senate, and though my father was still on his first six-year term, he had forged powerful allies, including several who had started tossing his name around as a potential vice presidential candidate. I didn't need to rely on my poli sci degree to realize that Mulberry was more interested in getting in good with the flavor of the month than he was in paying his respects to my uncle.

"It's been what? Almost five years since I've seen you? I have to say, you've grown into quite the lovely young woman."

"Thank you," I said, managing to keep my smile bright though it had become significantly harder. "It's been almost eight," I added, unable to help myself. I'd seen Mulberry last at my sister's funeral, and the memory of that day bumped up against the one I was currently living in a way that made me feel cold and hollow.

I hugged myself tight, trying to remember all my various bits of social training, but now feeling too lost to make small talk. "Well," I said, and then just let the word hang there, suddenly unable to come up with a single thing to say.

It was Evan who rescued me.

"Congressman Mulberry?" The older man turned to Evan, who stood in the doorway looking as dark and mysterious as still water at midnight. "There's a young woman out there looking for you. She seems very anxious to speak to you."

"Is there?" The congressman perked up, his hand rising to straighten his tie as I bit back a grin.

"Long blond hair, short black dress." He moved into the kitchen to stand near us. "She was heading into the library as I left her."

"Well," Mulberry said. He turned to me. "My dear, it's been a pleasure, but if this young woman is a constituent, I should go see what she has on her mind."

"Of course," I said. "It was lovely seeing you again. Thank you for coming."

As soon as he was out the door, I turned to Evan. "You are a very smooth liar."

"Apparently not as smooth as I thought if you found me out so easily."

"Maybe I just know you too well," I quipped.

He looked at me for a moment, then took a single step closer. My breath hitched and my pulse began to pick up tempo, and when he reached out an arm toward me I stood perfectly still, anticipating a touch that never came—it wasn't me he was reaching for, but a bottle of wine.

Idiot, idiot, idiot. But at least I could breathe easy again.

"Too well?" he said, as he poured a glass of pinot noir and passed it to me. "Does that mean you've figured out all my secrets?"

Our fingers brushed as I took the wine from him, and I shivered from the spark of connection that seemed to shoot through me, all the way from my fingers to the very tips of my toes.

I saw the quick flash of awareness in his eyes and wanted to kick myself. Because it wasn't me that knew his secrets—it was the other way around. And damned if I didn't feel confused and exposed and vulnerable.

"Secrets?" I repeated. I stood up straighter, determined to snatch back some measure of control. "Like the mystery behind why you've barely said two words to me all night? Why you've looked everywhere but at me?"

He tilted his head as if considering my words, then he poured his own glass of wine and took a long, slow sip. "I'm looking at you now."

I swallowed. He damn sure was. His cloudy gray eyes were fixed on my face, and I saw the tension in his body, as if he were fighting the coming violence of a storm.

Against my better judgment, I took a drink of my own wine. Yes, I needed a clear head for tonight, but right then I needed courage more. "You are," I agreed. "What do you see?"

"A beautiful woman," he said, his tone making my heart flutter as much as his words. "A beautiful woman," he continued, "who needs to take a step back and think about what the hell she's doing and why she's doing it."

"Excuse me?" His tone had shifted only slightly, but it was enough to totally erase that flutter. "Excuse me?" I repeated, because he had so completely flummoxed me that I couldn't seem to conjure any other words.

"You've had a hard time of it, Angie," he said. "You deserve to be happy."

I twirled the stem of my wineglass between my fingers as I tried to figure out his angle. Was he about to tell me that he could make me happy? The thought sent a small tingle of anticipation running through me, but I didn't believe it. He was too hot and cold, too confusing. And I wasn't going to figure out what the hell he was thinking unless I flat-out asked.

"What makes you think I'm not happy?"

He lifted one shoulder in a small shrug. "I get why you're dating Warner," he said. "Political father. FBI agent boyfriend. It all fits. It all makes sense. The perfect daughter piece in the picture-perfect puzzle that makes up your life."

I'd gone completely tense, my throat tight, my chest heavy. I felt like a walking target that he'd just skewered with a dead-on bull's-eye.

"Not that it's any of your business, but Kevin's wonderful," I said tightly, determined not to let him see that his barb had hit home.

"No," Evan said. We were still standing next to the counter in the kitchen, completely alone except for the few waiters who wandered in to refill their trays. Now he moved a step closer, and I swore I could feel the thrum of the air molecules buzzing between us. "For someone, maybe. But he's not for you."

"What would you know about it?" I'd intended to sound indignant. I didn't even come close.

"I know enough," he said, closing the distance between us even more. "I know you need a man who's strong enough to anchor you. A man who understands what you need, in bed and out of it." A deliciously sexy smile eased across his mouth. "You need a man who can just look at you and get you hot. And, Angie," he said, "I also know that Kevin Warner isn't that man."

Oh, my. Perspiration beaded on the back of my neck. My breathing was shallow, my pulse fast. I felt hyperaware of my body. Of the tiny hairs standing up on my arms. Of the needful, demanding feeling between my legs. I was wet—I was certain of it. And all I wanted right then was Evan's hands upon me.

It took a massive force of will to manage words, and even more strength to look him in the eyes. "If not Kevin, then who?" I asked, but the question that remained unspoken was "You?"

He reached out and tucked a loose lock of hair behind my ear, the soft brush of his finger against my skin just about melting me. "I guess that's something you'll have to figure out."

Be sure to grab your copy of
***Wanted* by J. Kenner**

ABOUT THE AUTHOR

J. Kenner (aka Julie Kenner) is the *New York Times, USA Today, Publishers Weekly, Wall Street Journal* and #1 International bestselling author of over one hundred novels, novellas and short stories in a variety of genres.

JK has been praised by *Publishers Weekly* as an author with a "flair for dialogue and eccentric characterizations" and by *RT Bookclub* for having "cornered the market on sinfully attractive, dominant antiheroes and the women who swoon for them." A six-time finalist for Romance Writers of America's RITA award, JK took home the first RITA trophy awarded in the category of erotic romance in 2014 for her novel, *Claim Me* (book 2 of her Stark Saga) and another RITA trophy for *Wicked Dirty* in the same category in 2017.

In her previous career as an attorney, JK worked as a lawyer in Southern California and Texas. She currently lives in Central Texas, with her husband, two daughters, and two rather spastic cats.

Stay in touch! Text JKenner to 21000 to subscribe to JK's text alerts.

www.jkenner.com